THE HEARTS AND LIVES OF MEN

BY THE SAME AUTHOR

The Fat Woman's Joke

Down Among the Women

Female Friends

Remember Me

Little Sisters

Praxis

Puffball

Watching Me, Watching You (short stories)

The Life and Loves of a She-Devil

The President's Child

Polaris and Other Stories

The Heart of the Country

PLAYS FOR THE STAGE

Mixed Doubles

Action Replay

I Love My Love

Woodworm

The Hole in the Top of the World

NONFICTION

Letters to Alice on First Reading Jane Austen

Rebecca West

THE HEARTS AND LIVES OF MEN

FAY WELDON

VIKING

VIKING
Viking Penguin, Inc.
40 West 23rd Street,
New York, New York 10010, U.S.A.

Published in 1988

LIBRARY OF CONGRESS CATALOGING IN PUBLICATION DATA
Weldon, Fay.
The hearts and lives of men.
I. Title.
PR6073.E374H4 1988 823'.914 87-40303
ISBN 0-670-82098-9

Printed in the United States of America
Set in Linotron Granjon
Designed by Ann Gold

THE HEARTS AND LIVES OF MEN

BEGINNINGS

Reader, I am going to tell you the story of Clifford, Helen and little Nell. Helen and Clifford wanted everything for Nell and wanted it so much and so badly their daughter was in great danger of ending up with nothing at all, not even life. If you want a great deal for yourself it is only natural to want the same for your children. Alas, the two are not necessarily compatible.

Love at first sight—that old thing! Helen and Clifford looked at one another at a party back in the sixties; something quivered in the air between them, and, for good or bad, Nell began. Spirit made flesh, flesh of their flesh, love of their love—and fortunately, and no thanks to the pair of them, it was, in the end, for good. There! You know already this story is to have a happy ending. But it's Christmastime. Why not?

Back in the sixties! What a time that was! When everyone wanted everything, and thought they could have it, and what's more had a *right* to it. Marriage, and freedom within it. Sex without babies. Revolution without poverty. Careers without selfishness. Art without effort. Knowledge without learning by rote. Dinner, in other words, and no dishes to clean up afterward. "Why don't we do it in the road?" they cried. Why not?

Ah, but they were good days! When the Beatles filled the airwaves and if you looked down you discovered you had a flowered plastic carrier bag in your hand and not a plain brown one, and that the shoes on your feet were suddenly green or pink, and not the brown or black your forebears had been wearing for centuries. When a girl took a pill in the morning to prepare her for whatever safe sexual adventures the day might bring, and a youth lit a cigarette without a thought of cancer, and took a girl to bed without fear of worse. When the cream flowed thick into *boeuf en daube* and no one had heard of a low-fat/low-protein diet, and no one dreamed of showing starving babies on TV, and you could have your cake and eat it too.

Those years when the world lurched out of earnestness and into frivolity were fun indeed for Clifford and Helen, but not, when it came to it, for little Nell. Angels of gravity and resolution need to stand around the newborn's crib, the more so if the latter happens to be draped in brilliant psychedelic satin, not sensible white, washable, ironable cotton. Actually, as it happened, I doubt the angels were around for the asking—they were off in other parts of the world: hovering shocked over Vietnam and Biafra or the Golan Heights—even if Clifford and Helen had remembered to send out the invitations, which they didn't.

People like Clifford and Helen love and create havoc in every decade in every century, in every corner of the globe, and the children of lovers, any place, any time, might just as well be orphans, for all the attention they get.

The sixties! In the first half of the seventh decade of the twentieth century, that's when Nell was born. At the party at Leonardo's at which Clifford first saw Helen across a crowded room, and Nell began, caviar and smoked salmon were served.

Leonardo's, as you may know, is a firm rather like Sotheby's and Christie's. It buys and sells the world's art treasures; it knows what is what and, when it comes to a Rembrandt or a Peter Blake, certainly how much; it can tell the difference between a chair by Chippendale and a chair by a disconcertingly skilled Florentine craftsman pretending he is Chippendale. But Leonardo's, unlike Sotheby's or Christie's, also has its own large exhibition halls, where partly for its own pleasure and profit, and partly for the good of the public, it presents major art shows for which it receives, via the Arts Council, a fair whack of the nation's art subsidy (some say too much, others not enough, but that's the way these things go). If you know London you will know Leonardo's well; that mini–Buckingham Palace of a building which stands on the corner of Grosvenor Square and Elliton

Place. These days it has branches in all the major cities of the world; in the sixties, London Leonardo's stood proud, important and alone, and this particular party was in honor of the opening of the first of its really major shows—an exhibition of the works of Hieronymus Bosch, gathered together from public and private collectors all over the world. The project had cost a terrifying amount and Sir Larry Patt, whose brilliant young assistant Clifford Wexford was, was nervous about its success.

He need not have been. This was the sixties. Try anything new; it worked.

Champagne cocktails were served, bouffant hairstyles worn (though a few beehives still rocked the chandeliers), as were amazingly short skirts; and very frilly shirts and long hair by the more avant-garde of the men. On the walls writhed the tormented figures of the artist's vision—in hell, in copulation, the same thing—and beneath, the great, the famous, the talented and the beautiful rubbed shoulders. Gossip columnists took notes. Art schmart! It was a wonderful party, I can tell you. Taxpayers paid and no one queried the bill. I was there, with my first husband.

Clifford was thirty-five when he met Helen, and he was already one of the great and famous, not to mention talented, beautiful and gossip-worthy. He had, he felt, just about worn out bachelorhood. He was looking for a wife. Or at any rate he felt the time had come in his career to start giving dinner parties and impress influential people. For that a man needs a wife. A butler might be chic but a wife spelled solidity. Yes, he needed a wife. He thought Angie the South African heiress might do. He was, in a desultory fashion, courting the poor girl. He walked into the party—his party, really—with Angie on his arm, and walked out with Helen. No way to behave!

Helen was twenty-two when she met Clifford. Even now, in her mid-forties, she is stunning enough, and still quite capable of causing trouble in the hearts and lives of men. (Though I suppose and hope she has learned the value of abstaining from so doing.) But then! You should have seen her then.

"Who is she?" Clifford asked Angie, looking at Helen across the crowded room. Poor Angie!

Now Helen was far from being the perfect beauty of the sixties—which ran, as you may remember, to the round-faced doll-like, punctuated by smouldering Carmen eyes—but was nevertheless a size ten, five-foot-seven stunner, with a heap of thick brown curly hair, which she saw as mousey and her great misfortune in life and through the succeeding years was to bleach, tint and generally torment, before henna came on the market and solved her problems. Her eyes were bright and intelligent; she looked soft, tender, provocative and *how-dare-you!* all at once. She was her own woman. She didn't try to please any more than Clifford did; she just pleased. She couldn't help it. She never shouted at servants, or snapped at hair-dressers—though at the time I speak of, of course, the opportunity had scarcely arisen. She was poor, and lived humbly, making do.

"That?" said Angie. "No one in particular, I shouldn't think. Whoever she is, she has no dress sense."

Helen was wearing a rather thin, rather plain, rather well-washed cotton dress halfway between pink and white, of a misty, fluid, sunlit fashion five years ahead of its time. Her breasts beneath the gentle fabric seemed bare, small and defenseless. She was long-backed, tapered and waisted, as the song has it, like a swan.

As for Angie, the millionairess! Angie was wearing a stiff gold lamé dress with a big red satin bow on the back, cut absurdly low over practically no bosom at all. She looked like a Christmas cracker with no present inside. Three successive dressmakers had wept over the dress, and all three had lost their jobs, but no amount of sacrifice could make the dress a success.

Poor Angie! Angie loved Clifford. Angie's father owned six gold mines, so she thought Clifford ought to love her in return. But what, when it came to it, did she have to offer except a sharp brain and five million dollars and her thirty-year-old, still-unmarried self? She had a dry little body and a dull skin (a good skin can make the plainest girl attractive but Angie did not have one; some inner light, I fear, was missing), and no mother, and a father who gave her everything she wanted, except affection; all of which made her greedy, and tactless, and petulant. And Angie knew these things about herself, and could do nothing about it. As for Clifford, he knew it would be *practical* to marry Angie, as had quite a number of men before him, and Clifford was a practical man; but he just somehow didn't *want* to marry Angie, and neither had they. Those few who did propose—for there is no rich young woman totally without suitors—Angie despised and rejected. Anyone who can love me, Angie's unconscious worked out, is not worth me loving. She was, as you can tell, in a strictly no-win emotional fix. Now she wanted Clifford, and the more he didn't want her, the more she wanted him.

"Angie," said Clifford, "I need to know *exactly* who she is," and do you know that Angie actually went to find out? She should have slapped Clifford's face, but then none of this story would have happened at all. Angie's acquiescence to Clifford's bad behavior was the little acorn from which the whole eventful oak tree grew. But there, the world is so full of should have's and shouldn't have's, isn't it? If only this, if only that! Where will it all end?

I should perhaps describe Clifford to you. He is still around the London scene; you will see his photograph in *Art World* and *Connoisseur* from time to time, though sadly not as often as before, since age does, in the end, wear out drama and scandal. But the eye, more from the habit of decades than anything else, goes straight to his photograph, and what Clifford has to say about "whither art?" or "whence post-surrealism?" remains interesting though no longer exactly subversive. He is a tall, solid, blunt-nosed man with a strong jaw and a broad face, a frequent smile (ah, but is he smiling with you, or about you?) which lights up eyes as blue as Harold Wilson's (and those eyes are very, very blue: I have seen them face to face: I *know*). Clifford has wide shoulders and narrow hips and thick straight hair so fair in those days it was almost white. He is still, though he must by now be approaching sixty, respectably enough thatched. His enemies (and he still has many) amuse themselves by saying he has a portrait of himself in his attic, which grows balder and fatter day by day. Clifford was, and still is, energetic, lively, entertaining, charming and ruthless. Of course Angie wanted to marry Clifford. Who wouldn't?

Now Clifford Wexford's rise in the world was not so much meteoric—for surely meteors fall, rather than ascend?—but missilic, having all the force and energy of Polaris rising from the sea. Or let's put it another way—Clifford Wexford buzzed around his boss, Sir Larry Patt, like a bee determined to get into the honey-pot. The Bosch exhibition had been Clifford's brainchild. If it succeeded, Clifford would get the credit; if it failed, Leonardo's and Sir Larry Patt would get the blame and carry the financial loss. That's the way Clifford worked, then as now. He understood, as men of Sir Larry's generation did not, the power of PR: that glamour and "the buzz" counted as much, if not more, than intrinsic worth: that money must be spent if money is to be earned—that it doesn't matter how good a painting or a sculpture may be—if nobody *knows* it's good, it might as well be bad. Clifford moved Leonardo's out of the first half of the century into the second and hurled it brutally on its way into the next—he was the key to the success story that was to be Leonardo's over the next twenty-five years, and Sir Larry realized it, on that opening night of the Bosch Exhibition, though he didn't much like it.

Angie made her way back to Clifford through the glittery, gossipy crowd as it downed its public-funded champagne cocktails (sugar lump, orange juice, champagne, brandy) beneath the hell-cursed figures of Bosch's vision, and said, "Her name's Helen. Some frame-maker's daughter."

Angie hoped that would be the end of Helen. Frame-makers were surely the dogsbodies of the art world and hardly worth thinking about. Angie assumed that what would count with Clifford when it came to marriage was not so much a girl's looks as her parentage and wealth. In this she wronged him. Clifford, like anyone else, wanted true love. He was actually trying quite hard to love Angie, but failing. He could not find her affectations and snobberies entertaining. He thought that being her husband would in too many respects be disagreeable. She would shout at the servants and be childishly bitchy about women he chose to admire, and make tedious scenes about this, that and the other.

"By 'some frame-maker,'" said Clifford, "I suppose you mean John Lally? The man's a genius. I commissioned him to hang this whole exhibition." And poor Angie understood that once again she had betrayed her ignorance, and said the wrong thing. Frame-makers were, after all, to be admired and respected. It was part of Angie's trouble in her dealings with Clifford that he was not *consistent*—at least in her terms—in what he admired and what he despised. Success, which Angie accorded only to the rich and/or beautiful and/or famous, Clifford would accord to all kinds of unlikely people—quite poor, even disabled poets, elderly writers with whiskery chins and shaky hands or lady artists in dreadful caftans—the kind of people whom Angie would never in a world of Saturday nights ask to dinner.

"But what's the *point* of them?" she'd ask.

"The future will reckon them," he'd reply, simply, "if not the present." How did he *know?* But he seemed to.

If Angie wanted to please Clifford, she had to think first, speak later. He was death to spontaneity. She knew it; yet she wanted him, for ever and ever, for breakfast, lunch, tea and dinner. That's love! Poor Angie! She wasn't nice, but we can pity her, as we can pity any woman in love with a man who doesn't love her, but is deciding whether or not to marry her, and taking his time about it, and in the meantime making her jump through unkind hoops.

"Well, well," said Clifford. "So she's John Lally's daughter!" and to Angie's upset and astonishment simply left her side and crossed to where Helen stood.

John Lally didn't see, which was just as well. He was sulking over by the wine bar, wild-eyed, wild-haired, his eyes deep-set and suspicious, his mouth made loose and over-mobile by rage and protest, and destined within the next twenty years to be the nation's leading painter, though no one (except Clifford) knew it at the time.

Helen raised her eyes to Clifford's and found him staring at her. The color of his eyes seemed to intensify whenever he was animated, and what tended to animate him was pulling off some amazing deal—acquiring for Leonardo's, say, a Tutankhamen mask or a long-lost panel of Elgin Marble. Now they were very blue indeed.

"How blue his eyes are," Helen thought. "As if they were painted—" and then somehow she just stopped thinking at all. She was frightened. She stood defenseless (or so it would seem) and alone amongst chattering, fashionable people, all rather older than she, who knew exactly what to think, feel and do for the best, as she did not; and perhaps when she looked up into the blue, blue eyes she saw her future and that was what frightened her.

Or perhaps she saw Nell's future. Love at first sight is a real enough thing. It happens, and between the unlikeliest people. My own view is that Clifford and Helen were bit-part players in Nell's drama, not center-stage at all, as they of course (like all of us) believed they were. And I do, as I say, believe Nell came into being in that moment when Helen and Clifford just stood and looked at each other and Helen was scared and Clifford determined and both knew their fate. Which was to love and hate each other, until the end of their days. The later joining of flesh to flesh, however overwhelming an experience, was in its way immaterial. Nell came into existence through love: but the passage from the insubstantial into the substantial must needs take place casually in that dark, half conscious, half unconscious passage we know as sex, and all Helen and Clifford knew of this intended miracle, as they looked at each other, was that the sooner they were in bed and in each other's arms the better. Well, so it is for the luckiest of us.

But of course life is not so simple, even for Clifford, who, being fortunate enough to know very clearly what he wanted, usually got it. There were the gods of *politesse* and convention to placate first.

"I hear you're John Lally's daughter," he said. "Do you know who I am?"

"No," she said. Reader, she did know. Of course she did. She was lying. She had seen Clifford Wexford's photograph in the newspapers often enough. She had watched him on television—the hope of the British Art World, according to some, or a sorry symptom of its end, as others would have it. More, she had grown up with the sound of her father's fulminations against Clifford Wexford, his employer and mentor, echoing through her home. (Some thought John Lally's hatred of Clifford Wexford bordered on the paranoid: others said not, that the emotion, in the circumstances, was perfectly reasonable.) If Helen said "no," it was because Clifford's conceit annoyed her, even while his looks entranced her. She said "no" because, reader, I am afraid that lies came easily to her, when they suited her. She said "no" because she was ceasing to be scared and wanted to cause some *frisson* of emotion between him and her—his irritation, her annoyance—and because she was elated by his interest in her, and elation makes one rash. She did not say "no" out of any loyalty to her father—certainly not.

"I'll tell you all about who I am over dinner," he said. And so great was the impression Helen made upon him that that was exactly what he did, in spite of the fact that he should have dined at the Savoy that evening and with Sir Larry Patt and Rowena his wife, and other important, influential and international guests.

"Dinner!" she said, apparently astonished. "You and me?"

"Unless you want to bypass dinner," Clifford said, smiling with such charm and understanding that the implications were all but lost.

"Dinner would be lovely," said Helen, pretending she had indeed lost them. "Let me just tell my mother."

"Baby!" reproached Clifford.

"I never upset my mother if I can help it," said Helen. "Life is upsetting enough for her as it is."

And so Helen, all innocence—well, almost all innocence—crossed over to her mother Evelyn and addressed her by her Christian name. The Lallys were an artistic and bohemian family.

"Evelyn," she said. "You'll never guess. Clifford Wexford's asked me out to dinner."

"Don't go," said Evelyn, panicky. "Please don't go! Supposing your father finds out!"

"You'll just have to lie," said Helen.

A lot of lying went on in the Lally home at Applecore Cottage in Gloucestershire. It had to. John Lally would fly into terrible tempers over small things, and the small things kept arising. His wife and daughter tried to keep him calm and happy, even if it meant misrepresenting the world and the events thereof.

Evelyn blinked, which she did frequently, as if the world was on the whole too much for her. She was a good-looking woman—how otherwise would she have given birth to Helen?—but the years spent with John Lally had tired and somehow stunned her. Now she blinked because Clifford Wexford was not the fate she had intended for her young daughter, and besides, she knew Clifford was expected to attend a dinner at the Savoy, so what was he doing going out with her daughter? She was all too conscious of the Savoy dinner: John Lally having refused, on three separate occasions, to attend it if Clifford was going too, and had waited till the fourth time of asking to consent to go, leaving his wife no time at all to make the new dress she felt so special an occasion required. Dinner at the Savoy! As it was, she wore the blue ribbed cotton dress she had worn on special occasions over the last twelve years, and had to be content to look washed-out but pretty, and not in the least chic. And how she longed, just for once, to look chic.

Helen took her mother's blink for approval, as had been her custom since her earliest years. The blink meant nothing of the sort, of course. If anything, it was, like a suicide attempt, a plea for help, to be excused from making a decision which would bring down her husband's wrath.

"Clifford's gone to get my coat," Helen said. "I must go."

"Clifford Wexford," said Evelyn, faintly. "Gone to get your coat—"

And so, amazingly, Clifford had. Helen went after him, leaving her mother to face the music of wrath.

Now Angie owned a white mink (what else?)—which earlier in the evening Clifford had gratifyingly admired—and in the cloakroom it hung next to and even touched Helen's thin brown cloth coat. Clifford went straight to the latter, and drew it out by the scruff of its neck.

"This is yours," he said to Helen.

"How did you know?"

"Because you're Cinderella," he observed. "And this is a rag."

"I'll have nothing said against my coat," said Helen, firmly. "I like the fabric, and I like the texture. I prefer faded colors to bright ones. I wash it by hand in very hot water and I dry it in direct sunlight. It is exactly as I want it."

It was a speech Helen was accustomed to making. She made it to her mother at least once a week, because at least once a week Evelyn threatened to throw the coat away. Helen's conviction impressed Clifford. Angie's mink, stiff on its hanger, made from the skins of wretched dead animals, now seemed to him both gruesome and pretentious. And, looking at Helen, now wrapped rather than dressed, and enchanting—and remember this was in the days before the old, the faded, the shabby and generally messy became fashionable—he simply *consented,* and never again made any critical remark about the clothes Helen chose to wear, or not wear.

For Helen knew what she was doing when it came to clothes and it was indeed Clifford's talent, great talent, and I am not being sarcastic, to distinguish between the true and the false, the genuine and the fake, the powerful and the pretentious, and have the grace to acknowledge it. Which was why, though still so young, he was Larry Patt's assistant and would presently fulfill his ambition to be Chairman of Leonardo's. Telling the good from the bad is what the Art World (and we must call it that name for lack of a better) is all about, and a sizable chunk of the world's resources is devoted to just this end. Nations which have no religion make do with Art: the imposition of not just order, but beauty and symmetry, upon chaos . . .

GETTING TO KNOW YOU

Enough. Clifford took Helen to dine at The Garden, a vaguely oriental restaurant fashionable in the sixties, situated just outside the old Covent Garden. Here apricots were served with lamb, pears with veal, and prunes with beef. Clifford, assuming Helen's taste would be unformed, and her tongue sweet, thought she'd like it. She did, just a little.

She ate her lamb and apricots with Clifford's eyes upon her. She had little neat even teeth. He watched her intently.

"How do you like the lamb?" he asked.

His eyes were warm, because he so badly wanted her to give a good answer, and also cold, because he knew that tests must exist, inasmuch as love can so dreadfully destroy judgment, and may prove to be temporary.

"I expect," said Helen kindly, "it tastes really good in Nepal, or wherever the dish belongs."

It was an answer, he felt, that could not be bettered. It showed charity, discrimination and knowedge, all at once.

"Clifford," observed Helen, and she spoke so softly and mildy he had to bend over to hear, and there was a gold chain around her neck, and on it a little locket that rested on the blue whiteness of her skin and entranced him, "this is not an exam. This is you taking me out to dinner, and no one has to impress anyone."

He felt at a loss, and was not sure he liked it.

"I should be at the Savoy with the bigwigs," he said, to let her know what he had sacrificed on her account.

"I don't suppose my father will forgive me for this," she said, to let him know the same of her. "You are not his favorite person. Though of course he can't run my life," she added. She was not, when it came to it, in the least frightened of her father: she got the best of him, as her mother got the worst. His rantings, these days, quite entertained her. Her mother took them seriously, and felt threatened and weakened as her husband fulminated against lying never-had-it-so-good governmental claims, and the folly of a misguided electorate, and the philistinism of the art-buying public, and so forth, and she felt dimly responsible for all of it.

"When you said you didn't know me, you were lying? Why?" Clifford asked, but Helen only laughed. Her pink-to-white dress glowed in the candlelight: she knew it would. At its worst under the harsh gallery lighting: at its best here. That was why she had worn it. Her nipples showed discreetly in an era when nipples *never* showed. She was not ashamed of her body. Why should she be? It was beautiful.

"Don't ever lie to me," he said.

"I won't," she said, but she lied, and knew she did.

They went home presently to his place in Goodge Street: No. 5, Coffee Place. It was a narrow house, squashed between shops, but central, very central. He could walk to work. The rooms were white-painted, the contents plain and functional. Her father's paintings were everywhere on the walls.

"These will be worth a million or more in a few years," he said. "Aren't you proud?"

"Why? Because they'll be worth money one day, or because he is a good painter?" she asked. "And 'proud'? That's the wrong word. As well be proud of the sun or the moon." She was her father's daughter, Clifford decided, and he liked her the more for it. She argued with everything yet diminished nothing. Girls like Angie made themselves special by deriding and despising everything around them. But then, they had to.

He showed her the bedroom, in the attic, beneath the eaves. The bed was a large square on the floor: foam rubber (new at the time). It was covered with a fur quilt. There were more Lallys here too. Scenes of satyrs embracing nymphs, and Medusas young Adonises. "Not my father's happiest period."

Reader, I am sorry to say that that evening Clifford and Helen went to bed together, which in the mid-sixties was not altogether the usual thing to do. Courtship rituals were still observed, and delay considered not just decent but prudent too. If a girl gave in to a man too soon, would he not despise her? It was current wisdom that he would. Now it is true that the going to bed with a man at first sight, as it were, can and often does lead to the rejection of the woman who has given her all and yet been found wanting. It is hurtful and demoralizing. But all that has in fact happened, I do believe, is that the relationship has hurried through from beginning to end in a few hours, and not sauntered along through months or years, and the man, not the woman, is the first to know it.

"I'll call you tomorrow," he says. But he doesn't. Well, it's over, isn't it. But just sometimes, just sometimes the stars are right: the relationship holds, seals, lasts. And that was what happened between Clifford and Helen. It simply did not occur to Helen that Clifford might despise her if she said yes so promptly; it did not occur to Clifford to think worse of her because she did. The moon shone down through the attic windows; the fur quilt was both rough and silky beneath their naked bodies. Reader, that night was twenty-three years ago but neither Clifford nor Helen has ever forgotten it.

CONSEQUENCES

Now. A great stir had been caused at the party by Clifford and Helen's precipitous departure. It was as if the guests sensed the significance of the event, and understood that because of it the train of many lives would be disturbed. True, there were other remarkable encounters that night, to go down in the personal histories of the guests—partners were swapped, love declared, hate expressed, feuds begun and ended, blows exchanged, scandals started, jobs found, careers lost and even a baby conceived in the back of the cloakroom beneath Angie's mink, but the Clifford and Helen thing was the most momentous event of all. It was a very good party. A few are; most aren't. It's as if just sometimes Fate itself gets word there's a party and comes along. But these other events don't concern us now. What does is that at the end of the evening Angie found herself without an escort. Poor Angie!

"Where's Clifford?" young Harry Blast, the TV arts commentator, was rash enough to ask her. I wish I could say he became more tactful with the years, but he didn't.

"He left," said Angie, shortly.

"Who with?"

"A girl."

"Which girl?"

"The one who was wearing some kind of nightdress," said Angie. She thought Harry Blast would surely offer to escort her home, but he didn't.

"Oh, that one," was all Harry said. He had a roundly innocent pink face, a fiendishly large nose, and a new degree from Oxford. "Can't say I blame him." (At which Angie vowed in her heart he wouldn't get far in his career if there was anything she could do about it. In fact, as it happened, she couldn't. Some people are just unstoppable; by virtue, I imagine, of their obtuseness. Only recently Harry Blast—his nose remodeled by cosmetic surgery—hosted a major TV program called "Art World Antics.")

Angie stalked off, and caught and tore her red satin bow on a door handle as she went, quite spoiling her exit. She then ripped off the bow altogether, tearing the fabric as she did so, thus ruining £121 worth of fabric and £33 worth of dressmaking (1965 prices) but what did Angie care? She had a personal allowance of £25,000 a year and that didn't include her capital, stocks, bonds and so forth, not to mention her shares in Leonardo's and her expectations on her father's death. Six gold mines, workers included, just to play with! But what use was all this to Angie when all she wanted was Clifford? She saw her life as a tragedy and wondered who to blame. She bullied a doorman into opening up Sir Larry Patt's prestigious office so that she could call her father in South Africa.

And so it was that even Sam Wellbrook, on the other side of the world, found himself affected by Clifford and Helen's behavior. The sound of his daughter's weeping traveled under the seas and across the continent. (This was before the days of satellite communication; but a tear is a tear, even when distorted by the clumsy devices of outmoded telecommunications.)

"You've ruined my life!" Angie wept. "No one wants me. Nobody loves me. Daddy, what's the matter with me?"

Sam Wellbrook sat under an evening sun in a lush subtropical garden; he was rich, he was powerful, he had women of every race and color to fill his bed. He thought he could be happy if only he didn't have a daughter. Fatherhood can be a terrible thing, even for a millionaire.

"Money can't buy me love," as the Beatles were singing, at the very time we speak of. They were only partly right. Men do seem able to buy it: women not. How unfair the world is!

"It's all your fault," she went on, as he knew she would, before he could tell her what the matter with her was. That she was not loved because she was unlovable, and it was not he who'd made her unlovable; she'd just been born like that.

"So what's new," he mourned, and Toby the black butler renewed his gin and tonic.

"I'll tell you what's new," snapped Angie, pulling herself together fast, as she always could when money was at stake. "Leonardo's is going downhill fast and you and I must take our money out while we still can."

"Who's upset you?"

"This isn't personal. It's just that Sir Larry Patt's an ancient old fool, and Clifford Wexford's a phony who can't tell a Boule from a Braque—"

"A what?"

"Just be quiet, Dad, and leave the art-schmartz bit to me. You're a philistine and a provincial. The point is, they've wasted millions on this show. No one's going to turn up to see a lot of souls frying in hell; Old Masters are out, Moderns are in. If Leonardo's is going to keep going it's got to move into contemporary art, but who around here's got the guts or the judgment?"

"Clifford Wexford," replied Sam Wellbrook. Angie's father had a good intelligence system. He didn't invest his money unwisely.

"You will do as I say," his daughter yelled. "Do you want to ruin yourself?"

She did not worry about the cost of the call. It was Leonardo's phone. She had no intention of paying. And there we will leave Angie for the moment, except to mention the fact that Angie refused to tip the coat-check girl on the grounds that her mink had been hung up badly and marks made on the shoulders. No one else could see the marks but Angie. She wasn't just rich, she meant to stay rich.

Sir Larry Patt was most put out by Clifford's behavior; disconcerted to discover that his assistant was not present at the Savoy to help him wine and dine the VIPs from home and abroad.

"Arrogant young pup," said Sir Larry Patt to Mark Chivers, from the Arts Council. They had been to school together.

"Looks like the write-ups are going to be good," said Chivers, who had shrewd little gray eyes in a wrinkled prune face and a goatee of surprisingly energetic growth, "thanks as much to champagne cocktails as Hieronymus Bosch, so I suppose we have to forgive him. Clifford Wexford knows how to manage the new world. We don't, Larry. We're gentlemen. He's not. We need him."

Larry Patt had the pink, cherubic face of a man who has struggled hard all his life for the public good, which fortunately had coincided with his own.

"I suppose you're right," he sighed. "I wish you weren't."

Lady Rowena Patt was disappointed too. She had looked forward to catching Clifford's blue eyes over dinner, from time to time, with her own demure brown ones. Rowena was fifteen years younger than her husband and had an equally sweet expression, though a far less wrinkled face than he. Rowena had an M.A. in History of Art and wrote books on the changing structure of the Byzantine Dome and while Sir Larry thought she was safely working in the British Museum Library she was as often as not in bed with one of his colleagues. Sir Larry, like so many of his generation, thought that sex only happened at night, and had no fears for afternoons. Life is short, thought Lady Rowena, that dark, tiny, shrewd little thing with the hand-span waist, and Sir Larry sweet, but boring. She was not any more pleased than Angie to see Clifford go off with Helen. Her affair with Clifford was all of five years over, but never mind: no woman in her middle years likes to see a girl in her early twenties make so easy a conquest; it is surely unfair that youth and looks should seem to count more than wit, style, intelligence and experience. Let Clifford escort Angie wherever he wanted. There could be no other motive in his heart but money, thought Rowena—and who is there who does not understand the motivation of money?—but Helen, the frame-maker's daughter! It was too bad. Rowena lifted her brown eyes to the stocky Herr Bouser, who knew more about Hieronymus Bosch than anyone else in the world—except for Clifford Wexford, now treading close on his heels—and said:

"Herr Bouser, I hope you will be sitting next to me at dinner. I so look forward to finding out more about you!" and Herr

Bouser's wife, who overheard, was quite startled and not at all pleased either. I tell you, that was quite a party!

But it was John Lally, Helen's father, who was most upset of all.

"Idiot, why didn't you stop her?" he demanded of his wife. John Lally had a wen on the top of his head where his hair thinned, and he trusted no one. His fingers were short and stubby and he painted delicate and exquisite pictures of determinedly unpopular themes—St. Peter at the gates of Heaven (nobody ever buys St. Peters. Something to do with the jangling keys—the sense of being unexpectedly barred, as if by a head-waiter for turning up in the wrong clothes. Too late to go back and get it right!), wilting flowers, foxes with bleeding geese in their mouths; if there was a subject nobody wanted on their walls, John Lally would paint it. He was, Clifford Wexford knew, one of the best, if for the time being one of the most unsalable, painters in the country. Clifford bought Lallys, very cheaply, for his own collection, and in the meanwhile employed the struggling artist to make frames for such paintings as turned up at Leonardo's frameless, and picked his brains wickedly and for free as to how best to mount exhibitions. (This latter is an art in itself, though seldom recognized.) For this, and other reasons to do with the nature and power of arts administrators in general and art dealers in particular (and who more particular than Clifford Wexford), John Lally loathed and despised, and against his will served, the man who had now wrapped a thin brown coat around his young daughter's white shoulders, and abducted her.

Evelyn was affected, too. Indeed, as ever, she was the one who suffered most. She did not retort, as she should have, "Because our daughter is free, white and over twenty-one" or "Because she fancied him" or even "Why shouldn't she?" No. Over the years she had grown to take John Lally's view of what the world was like, and who within it was good or bad. She was in the habit, in fact—never a good one—of looking at the world through her husband's eyes.

"I'm sorry," was all she said. But then she was in the habit of taking the blame for everything. She even apologized for the weather. "I'm sorry it's raining," she had been heard to say, to guests. This is what living with a genius can do to a woman. Evelyn is dead now. I do not think she lived her life to the full. She should have faced up to John Lally more often. He would have accepted it, and even been the happier for it. If men are like children, as some women say, it is certainly more true in this respect than others—that they are happier when obliged to behave, like the little guests at a birthday party, strictly run. Evelyn should have had more courage. She would have lived longer.

"So you should be sorry," said John Lally, adding, "Bloody girl's only done it to upset me," and he too stomped off into the night, leaving his wife to make any number of embarrassing explanations, and go to the Savoy dinner unescorted. This was, John Lally felt, no more than his wife deserved, for having let him down so badly. He thought if only he had married a different woman, how much happier he would now be. John Lally started a new painting that night, of the Rape not of the Sabine Women, but by the Sabine Women. It was they who were falling upon helpless Roman soldiers. John Lally was not always as silly and unpleasant as this; on the contrary, he just went into what his wife called "moods" and this was one of them. He was upset by what he saw as his daughter's disloyalty. Also, of course, he had been drinking a great deal of champagne. Well, alcohol is always seen as an excuse for bad behavior. I would like to be able to report that Evelyn made a hit that evening with, say, Adam Adam of the *Sunday Times,* but she did not. Her inner eye, as it were, turned so totally upon her husband, her emotions were so consumed by him, that she scarcely registered with the outside world as being a person in her own right at all. It is true that the only cure for one man is another man, but how is that man, in some circumstances, if the first eats up her heart and soul, ever to be found? Evelyn made her own way home. This is the fate of rather dowdy, quiet wives who find themselves alone at functions.

MORNINGS AFTER THE NIGHT BEFORE

When the first morning came for Helen and it was the sun's turn to shine down upon the rumpled bed, not the moon's, and Clifford had to go to work, there seemed little point in her getting out of bed at all, except to make a cup of coffee for them both, and have a bath, and make a phone call or two, because that was so obviously where she would be the following night. In Clifford's bed.

On that first morning, it actually hurt Clifford to leave Helen. He gasped when he got out into the cold clean morning air, and not from the shock to his lungs, as from the awareness that he could no longer touch, feel, incorporate Helen's body. He felt actual pain in his heart, but in such a good cause that he ignored it and went whistling and smiling into the office. Secretaries looked at one another. It did not seem likely that this was Angie's doing. Clifford called Helen the first moment he could.

"How are you doing?" he asked. "What are you doing? Exactly."

"Well," she said. "I'm up and I've washed my dress and hung it in the window to dry and I've fed the cat. I think she may have fleas: the poor little thing's scratching. I'll get her a flea collar, shall I?"

"Do what you want," he said, "it's okay by me," and was astounded to hear himself saying so. But it was true. Helen had somehow ironed out of him, at least for the time being, his capacity for being critical. He trusted his body, his life, his cat to her, after fourteen hours of knowing her. He hoped it would not affect his work. He turned his attention to the newspapers. Leonardo's embryonic PR department—that is to say, Clifford in a few snatched hours a week—had clearly done spectacularly well. The party, the exhibition, took up many column inches of the inside pages.

Any minute now the unprecedented sight (unprecedented because this was the sixties, remember) of long lines forming outside Leonardo's, right down Piccadilly, would occur. The punters (forgive me, the public) would be waiting for admission to Hieronymus Bosch, to see what Clifford had described as that great man's vision of the future. The fact that Bosch's phantasmagoric vision was of his own present, and not the world's future, and Clifford knew it gave him a few qualms, but not many. Better the public found pictures interesting; better the broad, bright, attractive strokes of semi-fantasy, than the boring, painstaking, pointillism of actuality. To bend the truth just a little, for the sake of Art, cannot be bad.

On the first night, reader, Nell was conceived. Or so Helen swears. She says she felt it. It was as if, she said, the sun and moon suddenly united, inside her.

On the second night Clifford and Helen managed to stop embracing for long enough to give each other their life histories. Clifford spoke, as he had never spoken to anyone, of the trauma of his childhood, when he was sent to the country, to be out of the way of Hitler's bombs, and was lost, alone and frightened, while his parents went about the world's business, rather than his. Helen took Clifford on a quick and not quite accurate—being abbreviated—tour of her former loves. He stopped her confessions with kisses, rather quickly.

"Your life starts now," he said. "Nothing that has happened before counts. Only this."

And that, reader, was how Clifford and Helen met, and how Nell was conceived in a great flurry of white-hot and enduring passion. I draw back now from saying *love*—it was too wild an emotion for that, a far too sensitive barometer whose needle swung from Much Rain to Set Fair, and hardly ever stayed nicely vertical on Change, in the middle, as somehow a barometer ought to do—guarding its options. But there again, love is the only word we have. It will have to do.

On the third night there was a great banging on the apartment door; and a kick drove through and splintered the wood, and the lock burst open and there was John Lally hoping to catch his daughter Helen and his mentor and enemy Clifford Wexford, in, as they say, *flagrante delicto.*

Clifford and Helen were, fortunately, innocently asleep when John Lally burst in upon them. They lay exhausted on a rumpled bed, a hairy limb here, a smooth one there, her head on his chest, hardly comfortable to outside eyes; to lovers, real lovers, that is, perfectly comfortable, just not to those who know they'll presently have to get up and steal away before the embarrassing time for breakfast arrives. Real lovers sleep soundly, knowing that when they wake nothing has to end, but will simply continue. The conviction suffuses their sleep: they smile as they slumber. The sound of splintering wood entered their dreams and was converted there, in Helen's case, to the sound of a fluffy chicken emerging from an egg she had in the palm of her hand, and in Clifford's case, to the sound of his skis as he swept masterfully and unerringly down snowy mountain slopes. The sight of his sleeping smiling daughter, his smiling sleeping enemy, who had stolen his last treasure, inflamed John Lally the more. He roared. Clifford frowned in his sleep; chasms yawned beneath him. Helen stirred and woke. The cozy cheeping of the newborn chick had turned into a wail. She sat up. She saw her father and pulled the sheet above her breasts. Bruise marks had yet to develop.

"How did you know I was here?" she asked. It was the question of a born conspirator who feels no guilt but whose plans have gone awry. He did not deign to reply, but I will tell you.

By one of those mischances which dog the fates of lovers, Clifford's departure with Helen from the Bosch party had been the subject of a small item in a gossip column, and this had been taken up by one Harry Stephens, a habitué of the Appletree Pub in Lower Appleby. Now Harry had a cousin in Sotheby's, where Helen had her part-time job, restoring earthenware, and had inquired further, and thus word had got back to deepest Gloucestershire that Helen Lally had vanished into Clifford Wexford's house, and had not emerged since.

"Quite a daughter you've got there!" said Harry Stephens. John Lally was not popular in the neighborhood. Lower Appleby forgave his eccentricity, his debts, his neglected orchard, but not the way he, a foreigner, drank cider in the pub and not shots, and the way he treated his wife. Otherwise the subject of his daughter would not have been brought up, but tactfully ignored. As it was, John Lally finished up his cider, got in his battered Volkswagen—its top speed 25 mph—and made the journey to London through the night, through the dawn, not so much to rescue his daughter but to fix Clifford Wexford once and for all as the villain he was.

"Whore!" cried John Lally now, tugging Helen out of bed, because she was nearest.

"Oh really, Dad," she said, slipping out from under his grasp, on her feet, readjusting her slip, and then to the waking, startled Clifford, "I'm sorry, it's my father." She had caught her mother's habit of apologizing. She was never to lose it. Except that where her mother used the phrase pathetically, in the hope of diverting torrents of abuse, Helen used it as a kind of bored reproach to the fates, with a wry lift of a delicate eyebrow. Clifford sat up, startled.

John Lally looked around the bedroom walls, at the paintings which were the sum of five years or so of his life and work: a rotten fig on a branch, a rainbow distorted by a toad, a line of washing in a cavern's mouth—I know they sound dreadful but, reader, they are not; they hang today in the world's most distinguished galleries, and no one blanches when they pass: the colors are so strong, sharp and layered, it is as if one reality is pasted on top of a whole series of others—and then at his daughter, who was half-laughing, half-crying, embarrassed, excited and angry all at once: and at Clifford's strong, naked body with the fuzz of fair, almost white hair along his bronzed arms and legs (Clifford and Angie had recently gone on vacation to Brazil where they had stayed at an art-collector's palace, a place of marble floors and gold-leafed taps and so on, and Tintorettos on the walls, and hot, hot bleaching sun) and back to the rumpled, heated bed.

It was, no doubt, purity of heart and sheer self-righteousness which gave John Lally the strength of ten. He lifted Clifford Wexford, young puppy or hope of the Art World, depending on how you saw it, by a naked arm and a bare leg, and effortlessly, as if the younger man were a rag doll, raised him on high. Helen shrieked. The doll came to life just in time and with his free leg directed a sharp kick at John Lally's crotch, getting him just where it hurt most. John Lally shrieked in his turn; the cat—who had spent a warm but restless night on the end of the foam rubber bed—finally gave up and stalked off just in time, for Clifford Wexford came tumbling down just where a second ago he had been curled, as John Lally simply let him go. Clifford was no sooner down than up, hooked a young and flexible foot behind John Lally's stiff ankle and tugged it so that his beloved's father fell face down on the floor, hitting his face and making his nose bleed. Clifford, broad-shouldered, sinewy, young, stood proud and naked over his defeated foe. (He was no more ashamed of his body than Helen was. Though just as Helen felt more comfortable clothed in front of her father, no doubt, had his mother been present, Clifford would quickly have pulled on at least his underpants.)

"Your father really is a bore," said Clifford to Helen. John Lally lay face down on the floor, his eyes open and burning into the Kelim rug. It was striped in dull oranges and muted reds; colors and pattern which were later to emerge in one of his most well-known paintings—*The Scourging of St. Ida.* (Painters, like writers, have the knack of putting the most distressing and extreme events to artistic good purpose.) In these days, rugs such as the one then flung so casually over Clifford's polished wood attic floor are rare and cost thousands of pounds at Liberty's. Then they could be bought for a fiver or so at any junk shop. Clifford, of course, with his knowing eye to the future, had already managed to pick up a dozen or so very fine specimens.

John Lally was not sure which was worse: the pain or the

humiliation. As the former decreased, the latter intensified. His eyes watered, his nose bled, his groin ached. His fingers tingled. He had been painting obsessively for twenty-eight years, and so far as he could see to no commercial or practical purpose. Canvases stacked in his studio, his garage. The only person who seemed to understand their merit was Clifford Wexford. Worse, and the artist had to acknowledge it, this blond young puppy of a man, with his meretricious view of the world, his easy way with women, money, society, knew exactly how to foster his talent by an encouraging word here, a moral slap there: a lift of an eyebrow as, on his periodic visits, he leafed through the stacked canvases in the Lally attic, garage, garden shed. "Yes, that's interesting. No, no, good try but didn't quite come off, did it—ah, yes—" and young Wexford would pick out the very ones the painter knew to be his best work and so most expected the world to disdain, and by now hoped it would disdain, the better for him to disdain and despise the world—and took them. And a fiver or so would change hands—just enough to replace paints and brushes, though hardly enough to restock the kitchen cupboard, but that was Evelyn's problem—and they'd be whisked away and a check from Leonardo's would come through the mail slot every now and then, unexpected and unasked for. John Lally was torn, he was in conflict: he raged, he burned, he bled: so many passions, thought John Lally, face down, bleeding and weeping into the Kelim rug, might do me some real physical damage—that is to say, paralyze my painting hand. He calmed himself. He stopped writhing and groaning and lay still.

"Now that you've stopped making a fool of yourself," said Clifford, "you'd better get up and get out before I lose my temper and kick you to death."

John Lally continued to lie still. Clifford stirred his prostrate body with a casual foot.

"Don't," said Helen.

"I'll do what I want," said Clifford. "Look what he's done to my door!" And he drew back his foot as if to deliver a hefty kick. He was angry, and not just because of his splintered wood, or having his privacy thus invaded, or Helen insulted, but because he realized at that moment that he actually envied and was jealous of John Lally, who could paint like an angel. And that to paint like an angel was the only thing in the world Clifford Wexford wanted. And because Clifford couldn't, everything else seemed unimportant—money, ambition, the quest for status—mere substitutes, second best. He wanted to kick John Lally to death and that was the truth of it.

"Please don't," said Helen. "He's a bit mad. He can't help himself."

John Lally looked up at his daughter and decided he didn't like her one bit. She was a patronizing bitch, spoiled by Evelyn, ruined by the world; she was shoddy goods, untalented, spoiled. He clambered to his feet.

"Little bitch," he said, "as if I cared whose bed you were in." He was up just in time. Clifford delivered the kick and missed.

"Do what you want," John Lally said to Helen. "Just don't ever come near me or your mother again."

And that, reader, was how Helen and Clifford met and how Helen gave up her family on Clifford's account.

Helen did not doubt but that presently she and Clifford would marry. They were made for each other. They were two halves of the one whole. They could tell, if only from the way their limbs seemed to fuse together, as if finding at last their natural home. Well, that's how love at first sight takes people. For good or bad, that's that.

LOOKING BACK

Clifford was proud and pleased to have discovered Helen just as she was satisfied and gratified to have found him. He looked back with amazement at his life pre-Helen: the casual sexual encounters, his general don't call-me, I'll call-you amorous behavior (and of course he seldom did, finding his attention and interest not fully engaged), the more decorous but still abortive marital skirmishing with a long list of more-or-less suitable girls, the frequent and ultimately tedious outings with the wrong person to the right restaurants and clubs. How had he put up with it? Why? I am sorry to say that Clifford, looking back, did not consider how many women he had wounded emotionally or socially, or both; he recalled only his own desolation and boredom.

And as for Helen, it was as if until now her life had been lived in shadow. Ah, but now! An unthought-of sun illuminated her days, and sent its warm residual glow through her nights. Her eyes shone; how easily her color came and went: she shook her head and her brown curls tossed about, as if even they were suffused with extra life. Just sometimes, she went to her tiny workshop at Sotheby's, returning always not to her own little flat but to Clifford's home and bed. She was paid by the hour—poorly, but the very casualness of the job suited her. She sang as she worked; her specialty was the piecing together of early earthenware (most restorers prefer the hard sharp edges and colors of ceramics. Helen loved the challenging, tricky, melting, flaky softness of early country jugs and mugs). She forgot friends and suitors; she left her roommate to pay the rent, and answer questions. She could not believe anymore that money mattered, or reputation, or the continuing goodwill of friends. She was in love. They were in love. Clifford was rich. Clifford would protect her. Bother the detail. Bother her father's rage, her mother's distress, her employers' raised eyebrows as they totted up the hours she worked each week, and reckoned again the cost of the workshop space she took up. Clifford was all the family, the friends, she would ever need: he was the roof over her head, the cloth on her back, the sun in her sky.

Well, love can't heal everything, can it. Sometimes I see it just as a kind of ointment, which people apply to their wounded egos. True healing has to come from within: a matter of a patient, slow plodding toward self-understanding, of gritting the teeth and enduring boredom and irritation, and smiling at milkmen and paying the rent, and wiping the children's faces and not showing hurt, or exhaustion, or impatience—but Helen would have none of that, reader. She was young, she was beautiful, the world was her oyster. She knew it. She let love sweep her away and swallow her up—and all she did was raise her pretty white hands to heaven and say, "I can't help it! This thing is greater than me!"

A KNIFE IN THE BACK

Clifford arrived at Leonardo's on the morning of his encounter with John Lally with a bruised fist and in a bad temper.

His first appointment that day was with Harry Blast, the ungallant young TV interviewer who had managed not to escort Angie Wellbrook home on the night of the Bosch party. It was Harry's first interview: it was to be inserted as an end piece to a program called "Monitor." Harry was nervous and vulnerable. Clifford knew it.

The interview was set up in Sir Larry Patt's grand paneled office overlooking the Thames. The BBC's cameras were large and unwieldy. The floor was a network of cables. Sir Larry Patt was as nervous as Harry Blast. Clifford was too warm from Helen's bed and his victory over the poor ruined hulk of an artist to be in the least unsure of himself. It was his first time before the cameras too but no one would ever have known it. It was, in fact, this particular interview which set Clifford on his own particular spot-lit path to art stardom. Clifford Wexford says this—Wex says that—quote the great C.W. and you'd be in business; if you were brave enough to ask him, that is; risk the slow put-down or the fast riposte, you could never be sure which: the quick glance of the bright blue eyes which would sum you up as okay and worth the hearing out, or dismiss you as one of the world's little people. He had the kind of even features that television cameras love—and a clear quick intelligence which cut through cant and pretension, while yet not being free of it himself—on the contrary.

"Well, now," said Harry Blast, the interviewer, bluntly, when the cameras had stopped admiring the Jacobean paneling, County Hall across the river, and the Gainsborough on the wall above the wide Georgian fireplace, and got down to business as he'd clearly prepared his question beforehand. "It has been suggested that perhaps the Arts Council—by which of course we mean the unfortunate taxpayer—has underwritten rather too high a proportion of the cost of the Bosch exhibition, and Leonardo's claimed rather too much of the profit. What do you say to this, Mr. Wexford?"

"You mean *you* are suggesting it," said Clifford. "Why don't you just come out with it? Leonardo's is milking the taxpayer..."

"Well—" said Harry Blast, flustered, his large nose growing pinker and pinker as it did when he was stressed. A good thing color television was yet to come, or his career might never have gotten underway. Stress is part of the media man's life!

"And how are we to judge these things?" asked Clifford. "How are we to quantify, when it comes to matters of art, where profit lies? If Leonardo's brings art to an art-starved public, and governmental bodies have failed to do so, then surely we deserve, if not exactly reward, just a little encouragement? You saw those queues down the street. I hope you bothered to point your cameras. I tell you, the people of this country have been starved of beauty for too long."

And of course it just so happened that Harry Blast had neglected to film the queues. Clifford knew it.

"As to the exact proportion of the Arts Council grant to Leonardo's funding, I think it's a matter of matching funds. Isn't that so, Sir Larry? He's king of finances around here."

And the cameras turned, at Clifford's behest, to Sir Larry Patt, who of course didn't know without looking it up, and mumbled words to this effect instead of proclaiming ignorance loudly and clearly to the world, as he would have been better advised to do. Sir Larry had no television presence at all: his face was too old and the marks of self-indulgence written too large upon it, in the form of sloppy jowls and self-satisfied mouth. He, too, had had an upsetting morning. He had been woken by an early morning call from Madame Bouser in Amsterdam.

"What kind of country is England?" she had demanded. "Are you so lost to civilization that a husband can be seduced under his wife's very nose, and the husband of the woman who does it take no notice at all?"

"Madam," said Sir Larry Patt. "I have no idea what you're talking about." Nor had he. Finding his wife unattractive, it did not occur to him that other men might be attracted to her. Sir Larry belonged to a class and generation which viewed women askance; he had married one as much like a boy as possible (which Clifford had once pointed out to Rowena, making her cry). He was not an unimaginative man—just one made uneasy by emotion, who reserved his rapture for art rather than love; for paintings, rather than sex. And this, in itself, was surely a reason for self-congratulation: coming as he did from a background which prided itself on its philistinism; surely he had shown self-determination enough. He knew he had good reason to be smug. The instrument had gone dead suddenly and fortunately—as if it had been wrested out of Madame Bouser's hand. He was not surprised. She was hysterical. Women so often were. He went into Rowena's bedroom and found her sleeping peacefully, in her flat-chested way, and did not disturb her in case she became the same. He did not feel at his best. The fact became obvious to Harry Blast that Sir Larry belonged to the past. He had to, since Clifford belonged to the future, and television believes in polarities. Good, bad, old, new, left, right, funny, tragic, Patt on the way out, Wexford on the way in. And so the interview was the beginning of Sir Larry Patt's downfall; the top of a long gentle slope down, and Clifford it was who quite willfully, that day, nudged him on to it. Sir Larry didn't even notice. Clifford looked into a future and saw that it contained the possibility of dynasty. To make Helen his Queen he would have to be King. That meant he must rule over Leonardo's, and Leonardo's itself would have to grow and change, become one of those intricate complexes of power of which the modern world was fast becoming composed. He would have to do it by stealth, by playing politics, by behaving as kings and emperors always had: by demanding loyalty, and extracting fealty, allowing no one too close to him, by playing one favorite off against another, by keeping to himself the power of life and death and using it (or hiring and firing, the modern equivalent), by giving unexpected favors, meting out unexpected punishments, by letting his smile mean munificence, his frown hardship. He would become Wexford of Leonardo's. He, the ne'er-do-well, the anxious, striving, restless son of a powerful father, would cease to be an outsider, would cease to be the moon revolving around the sun, but become the sun itself. For Helen's sake he would turn the world inside out.

He sighed and stretched; how powerful he felt! Harry Blast's cameras caught the sigh and the stretch and made the still that made the program, and was every picture-editor's favorite thereafter, whenever they ran a story on wheelings and dealings in the Art World. There was just something about it: some feeling, I daresay, of the Act of Accession—that moment which is supposed to be so important, when the Archbishop actually places the crown upon the new monarch's head—that was caught by Harry Blast's cameras, unawares.

MOTHER AND DAUGHTER

And while Clifford Wexford considered his future, and regularized, professionalized, and indeed sanctified what had so far been only a vague ambition, the girl of his dreams, Helen Lally, sat with her mother and sipped herbal tea at Cranks, the new health-food restaurant in Carnaby Street. Cranks was the prototype of a million others which were, over the next twenty-five years, to spring up all over the world. Whole food and herbal tea = spiritual and physical health. It was a very new notion at the time and Evelyn sipped her comfrey tea with some suspicion. (Comfrey is now not taken internally, for fear it may be carcinogenic, but only used in external application, so her instinct may have been right.)

"It will comfort you, Mother," said Helen, hopefully. Evelyn clearly needed comforting. Her eyes were red-rimmed and puffy. She looked plain, desperate and old: not a good combination. On his return from 5 Coffee Place, John Lally had reaffirmed to his wife that her daughter Helen was no longer welcome in Applecore Cottage, that the only possible explanation for the girl's behavior was that she was no child of his, and had locked himself in the garage. There within, presumably, he now painted furiously. Evelyn set food and drink on the windowsill from time to time; the food would be taken—the window raised quickly then banged shut—but the drink, rather pointedly, left. Homemade wine was stored in the garage, so supposedly this was all he required. Black rage seemed to seep out under the garage door. "It isn't fair," said Evelyn to her daughter, as if *she* were the child and not the mother. "It just isn't fair!"

Nor of course was it. She who had done so much for her husband, dedicated her whole life to him, thus to be treated!

"I try not to let you know how upset I get," she said, "but you're a grown girl now, and I suppose this is life."

"Only if you let it be," said Helen, secure in the knowledge of her newfound love, and that she for one meant to live happily ever after.

"If only you'd been more tactful about it," said her mother, as near a reproach as she had ever uttered. "You have no idea how to manage your father."

"Well," said Helen, "I'm sorry. I suppose it is all my fault. But he keeps shutting himself in. Usually it's the attic, and now it's the garage. I don't know why you get so upset about it. It's nothing unusual. If you didn't get so upset, he might not do it."

She was trying to be serious but only managed, to her mother, to sound frivolous. She couldn't help it. She loved Clifford Wexford. So what if her father angered himself to death and her mother grieved herself to an untimely end; she, Helen, loved Clifford Wexford, and youth, energy, future, common sense, and good cheer were on her side, and that was that.

Evelyn presently composed herself and properly admired the unusual stripped-pine country-style of the restaurant, and agreed with her daughter that things had been going on like this for twenty-five years. She expected they'd go on like this for quite a while. Helen was quite right. There was no need to worry and all she had to do was pull herself together. "Good heavens," said Evelyn, pulling herself together, "you hair *is* looking lovely. So curly!"

And Helen, who could afford to be kind, was, and did not instantly try to smooth her hair around her ears, but shook her head so it fluffed out just as her mother liked it. Helen liked to wear her hair straight, flat, silky and smooth long before such a thing was fashionable. Love seemed to be on Evelyn's side in this respect at least, thickening and curling her daughter's hair.

"I'm in love," Helen said. "I expect that's it."

Evelyn looked at her, puzzled. How had life at Applecore Cottage created such naivete?

"Well," she said, "don't rush into anything just because life at home was so horrible."

"Oh Mum, it was never exactly horrible," protested Helen,

though sometimes it truly had been. Applecore Cottage was quaint and charming, but her father's frequent black moods did indeed float like a noxious gas under doors and through cracks, no matter that he shut himself away, both for his family's sake (to protect them from him) and for his (to protect him from their female philistinism and general treachery) and her mother's eyes had been too often red-rimmed, thus somehow dimming the luster of the copper pans which hung so prettily in the kitchen, throwing back the light from latticed windows; at such times Helen had longed, longed just to get away. Yet at other times they'd been a close family, sharing thought, feeling, aspirations; the two women intensely loyal to John Lally's genius, gladly putting up with hardship and penury on that account, understanding that the painter's temperament was as difficult for him to endure as it was for them. But then Helen had gone—off to Art School, and a mysterious life in London, and Evelyn had to take the full undiluted force, not of her husband's attention, for he gave her little, but of his circling, angry energy, and began to understand that though he would survive, and his paintings too, she, Evelyn, might very well not. She felt far older and more tired than she should. What was more, she understood only too well that if John Lally had to choose between his art and her, he would undoubtedly choose his art. If he loved her, she once told Helen in an uncharacteristic burst of anger, it was as a man with a wooden leg loved that leg. He couldn't do without it, but wished he could.

Now she smiled sweetly at Helen, and patted her daughter's small firm white hand with her large loose one and said, "It's nice of you to say so."

"You always did your best," said Helen, and then, panicky—"Why are you talking as if we're saying good-bye?"

"Because if you're with Clifford Wexford," said Evelyn, "it is, more or less."

"He shouldn't have burst in on us the way he did. I'm sorry Clifford hit him but he was provoked."

"It all goes deeper than that," said Evelyn.

"He'll get over it," said Helen.

"No," said her mother. "You do have to choose." It occurred to Helen then that with Clifford for a lover, what did she want with a father.

"Why don't you just leave home, Mum," she said, "and let Dad get on with his genius on his own? Don't you see it's absurd. Living with a man who locks himself in and has to have his food from a plate left on a garage windowsill."

"But darling," said Evelyn, "he's *painting!*" And Helen knew it was no use, and, in any case, hardly wanted it to be. It's one thing to suggest to your parents that they part—and many do—quite horrific if they actually act upon that suggestion.

"It's probably best," said Evelyn to her own daughter, "if you just stay out of the way for a while," and Helen was more than ever glad she had Clifford, for a feeling of hurt and terror welled up inside her and had to be subdued. It looked for a moment as if her own mother was abandoning her. But of course that was nonsense. They shared a particularly novel whole-wheat-and-honey biscuit, which Evelyn quite liked, and shared the bill, and once outside, smiled and kissed and went their separate ways, Evelyn no longer with a child, Helen no longer with a mother.

PROTECTIVE CUSTODY

"Good Lord," said Clifford, when Helen reported the conversation to him that night, "whatever you do, don't encourage your mother to leave home!"

They were having supper in bed, trying not to get the black sheets sticky with taramosalata, whipped up by Clifford from cod's roe, lemon juice and cream, and cheaper than buying it already made up. Not even love could induce Clifford to abandon his habits of economy—some called it parsimony but why not use the kinder word? Clifford insisted on living well, and also took pleasure in never spending a penny more than he had to in so doing.

"Why not, Clifford?"

Sometimes Clifford confused Helen, just as he confused Angie, but Helen had the quickness and sense to ask for guidance. And unlike Angie, not being stubborn, she was a quick learner. How pretty she looked this evening; enchanting! All thin soft arms and plump naked shoulders, her cream silk slip barely covering a swelling breast—cautiously nibbling, with little, even teeth, the edges of her Bath Oliver biscuit, careful not to spill the taramosalata, made by Clifford perhaps just a fraction too liquid.

"Because your mother is your father's inspiration," said Clifford, "and though that's hard luck on your mother, sacrifices must be made in the cause of art. Art is more important than the individual—even than the painter who created it. Your father would be the first to acknowledge that, monster though he is. Moreover a painter needs his gestalt—the peculiar combination of circumstances which enables him to express his particular vision of the universe. Your father's gestalt, more's the pity, includes Applecore Cottage, your mother, quarrels with neighbors, paranoia about the art world in general and me in particular. It also until now has included you. You've been snatched away. That's shock enough. It's driven him into the garage, and with any luck we'll see a change of style when he emerges. Let's just hope that the new is more salable than the old."

He carefully removed Helen's Bath Oliver, put it to one side and kissed her salty mouth.

"I suppose," said Helen, "you didn't move me in here with you just to make my father's painting easier to sell?" and he laughed, but there was a little pause before he did, as if he himself almost wondered. Truly successful people often act by an instinct which works to their advantage: they don't have to plot, or scheme. They just follow their noses, and life itself bows down before them. Clifford loved Helen. Of course he did. Nevertheless, John Lally's daughter! Part of a gestalt which needed a shock, a shove, a shaking-up—

But they forgot these matters soon enough, and Clifford also forgot to say that Angie Wellbrook's father had called him from Johannesburg during the week.

"I thought I should warn you," boomed the sad, powerful voice. "My daughter's on the warpath."

"What about?" Clifford had been light and cool.

"God knows. She doesn't like the Old Masters. She says the future lies with Moderns. She says Leonardo's is throwing its money away. What did you do? Stand her up? No, don't tell me. I don't want to know. Just remember, although I'm a major shareholder, she acts for me in the U.K. and there's no controlling her. She's a shrewd girl though a pain in the ass."

Clifford thanked him and promised to send him the excellent reviews of the Bosch exhibition and press reports of the unprecedented queues outside it, assured him that his investment was well protected, and that the furtherance and support of contemporary art was becoming increasingly part of Leonardo's provenance—in other words that Angie was out on a precarious limb. Then he called Angie and asked her out to lunch. He forgot to tell Helen about this too. But he left her languid on the bed in such a sensuous swoon he knew well enough she'd be only just recovering when he came back that evening.

Angie and Clifford went to Claridges. Miniskirts were just coming in. Angie turned up wearing a beige trouser-suit in fine, supple suede, and asked to be shown to Clifford's table. She'd spent the morning in the beauty parlor but the hand of the girl who applied her false eyelashes had slipped and one of Angie's eyes was red, so she had to wear dark glasses, the wearing of which other than on ski slopes she knew Clifford despised. It made her cross.

"I'm so sorry," said the Headwaiter, rashly, "but it is not our policy to allow ladies in trousers into the Grand Restaurant."

"Really?" inquired Angie, dangerously, made even crosser.

"If you will allow me to take you to the Luncheon Bar—"

"No," said Angie. "You just take the trousers."

And there and then she undid them, stepped out of them, handed them to the Headwaiter, and went on in, miniskirted, to join Clifford. A pity, Clifford thought, Angie's legs were not better. They quite spoiled the gesture. All the same, he was impressed. So were many of the lunchers. Angie received a round of applause as she sat down.

"I know I'm a bastard," Clifford said, over quails' eggs, "I know I let you down, I know I'm a cad and a bounder, but the fact is, I've fallen in love." And he raised his clear blue eyes to hers, and finding them covered by dark glasses, straightaway removed them.

"One of your eyes is red," he remarked. "Quite horrid!" Somehow the gesture, the touch, the remark, made her believe that in love with someone else he might be, but matters between him and her were not finished. She was right.

"So where does that leave us?" she asked, one hand now covering the erring eye, scraping a little fattening mayonnaise from her egg with the knife in the other. He thought that if anything she was too skinny. In his bed she'd kept herself well covered with the black sheet and with good reason. (Thinness, in those days, was not as fashionable as now. A pattern of ribs beneath the skin was seen as unsightly.) Helen, perfectly at ease in her body, could cheerfully expose any part, in any position. Yet Angie's very reticences had their charm.

"Friends," he said.

"You mean," she said, "you don't want my father taking his millions out of Leonardo's."

"How well you know me," he said, and laughed, looking directly at her with his bright knowledgeable eyes, and this time he moved her shielding hand, and her heart turned over, but what was the use?

"They'll be my millions eventually," said Angie. "And leaving you and me right out of it, I don't like seeing them in Leonardo's. Art's a high-risk business."

"Not anymore," said Clifford Wexford, "not now I'm in charge."

"But Clifford, you're not."

"I will be," said Clifford.

She believed him. A crowd of photographers and reporters now clustered at Claridges' door. Word had gotten around. They wanted a glimpse of Angie's legs or, failing that, of the King of the Waiters discomposed, but the staff barred their way. The general uproar impressed Clifford. Publicity always did.

Angie was not ungratified, either. Well, she thought, Clifford will wear out Helen soon enough. Helen can't command the press, as I can. Helen, the frame-maker's daughter. Just another pretty face! Penniless, powerless, without place in the world except by courtesy of Clifford. He'd soon get bored. Angie decided to forgive Clifford and be content just to hate Helen. Should she say something scathing, unforgettable, about her rival? No. Clifford was too shrewd. He'd see through it. She'd go the other way instead.

"She's a sweet, pretty girl," she said, "and just what you need. Though you'll have to sharpen up her dress sense a little. She really shouldn't go around looking so humble. But I give up. I give in. I'll be yours and Helen's friend. And the crits of the Bosch exhibition were really impressive, Clifford. I may have been wrong. I'll give Dad a call and reassure him."

Clifford stood, moved around to where Angie sat, lifted her dull-complexioned face with its poor eye, and kissed her firmly on her lips. It was her reward. It was not enough, but something. She would claim what she deserved, what she had been promised, when the time was ripe. There was, she supposed, no hurry. She would wait, decades if she had to.

While Angie lunched with Clifford, Evelyn was on the phone to Helen.

"Oh, Mum," said Helen, gratefully. "I thought you'd given up on me!"

"Well, I thought you'd better know just how upset your father is," her mother said. "He's left the garage, and now he's up in the attic, cutting up his old canvases with the garden shears. *Fox Plus Chicken Pieces* is in shreds. He threw a section of *Beached Whale with Vultures* downstairs. He's going to be so upset when he calms down and finds out what he's done. He was on the whale painting for two years, Helen. You remember? All through your A levels."

"I think you should go next door, Mum, and wait till he calms down."

"They're getting so sick of me next door."

"Of course they're not, Mum."

"It is so important for your father not to be upset."

"Mum, don't you see, I am the excuse for his upset, not the reason for his upset."

"No, Helen, I'm afraid I can't see it that way."

At three-fifteen Helen, crying, called Leonardo's and left a message for Clifford to call home. Urgent. But he did not arrive back in the office until five o'clock. How he had been spending his time between two and five, reader, I am not going to divulge in detail. He had not meant such a thing to happen. Let us just say that Angie kept a suite at Claridges for her convenience when shopping on Bond Street—her house in Belgravia seeming to her too far from the heart of things, and her actions too closely observed by the butler and other staff—and that opportunity is, if not all, at least four-fifths of illicit and unexpected sexual congress. And Clifford felt he ought to make amends and, to his credit, was amused and more impressed by the news-hounds at her heels than he ever had been by her father's millions. Besides he was so newly in love with Helen, the emotion had not had time to affect a deep-rooted habit of life—that is to say, of taking his pleasures when and as he usefully found them.

Be all that as it may, come five-thirty, Clifford reacted strongly and instantly not so much to Helen's tears as to her account of her father's behavior. *Fox Plus Chicken Pieces* was a minor and flawed piece but *Beached Whale with Vultures,* though unlikable on account of its subject matter—rotting flesh, stretched in glistening strands across an almost ethereal canvas—was a fine major work and Clifford was not about to have it under attack. His lawyers were at Judge Percibar's within the hour—the eloquent Percibar a lifelong friend of Otto Wexford, Clifford's father—and an injunction issued, restraining John Lally from damaging what turned out to be Leonardo's property, inasmuch as, or so they claimed, the artist benefitted by a retainer from that august institution. And by the next morning, after a police car and a Leonardo's van had turned up at the cottage, seven John Lally canvases had been transferred to Leonardo's vaults, plus the shreds, recovered from the garden, of *Fox Plus Chicken Pieces,* and catalogued thus:

1. *Beached Whale with Vultures*—damaged
2. *Massacre of the Turtles*—in fine condition
3. *St. Peter and Cripple at Heaven's Gate*—scratched
4. *The Feast of Eyes*—stained (coffee?)
5. *Kitten with Hand*—stained (bird droppings?)
6. *Dead Flowerpiece*—in fine condition
7. *Landscape of Bones*—slashed
8. *Fox Plus Chicken Pieces*—remnant

The removal was done while John Lally slept off the effects of shock, overwork, temper and homemade wine. Evelyn tried to wake him as the Leonardo's team tramped up and down the steep narrow stairs to the attic, maneuvering the idle canvases with some difficulty, but there was no waking him. She left a note and went to stay with the neighbors.

Reader, if you know even an amateur painter, or if you daub or dabble yourself, you will understand how any painter worth his salt hates to be parted from his paintings, in just the same way as a mother hates to be parted from her children. This leaves the painter in a terrible fix. If he doesn't sell not only does he not eat, but he paints himself out of house and home. And then there is the enormous simple practical matter of *space:* where are the paintings to be kept? Yet if he does sell, and so makes room, it is like having a chunk of living flesh torn away. And it is so agitating. What kind of home is the work going to? Will it be safe? Was it bought because it was truly appreciated, or merely because it matched the wallpaper? Not, of course that John Lally had many worries on the latter score. There was never any question of a Lally canvas *blending.* He is what is called a gallery painter, fit for display on large bare walls and respectful viewing in public places, where little cries of shock and awe and distaste can be quickly sopped up by the warm, gently circulating, stuffy mausoleum air. (And what kind of fate, raged John Lally, is that for a painting? *Kitten with Hand*—the fingers with claws, the paw with nails—had for a time been hoisted into the air between two pine trees in the garden of Applecore Cottage, the better for the birds of the air to admire it, mere earth-swarming human beings so lacking in the capacity for proper appreciation.) And as for the small private galleries, run as they are by undiscriminating rogues who will take as much as fifty percent commission, these are the shit-holes of the Art World. Go to any opening, and see the phonies and the poseurs gawking and gaping and very publicly writing out their checks. On the whole John Lally preferred to simply give paintings away to friends. Then at least he could control who owned them, on whose wall they hung. Friends? What friends? For as quickly as his occasional charm won them, his paranoia and temper would drive them away. There were few enough around who were qualified to be Lally recipients.

This was why, driven to fever pitch by the impossibility of solving the problem, or so John Lally saw it, he had consented to accept a retainer from Leonardo's. And Leonardo's (that is to say, Clifford Wexford) had done him other favors: taken a few canvases off his hands; had the broken-down garage rebuilt, damp-proofed and air-conditioned so that other paintings could be safely stacked and stored. They had windows built into the attic roof the better to illuminate his work with good natural north light. If John Lally chose to paint in the garage and store in the attic, no great harm would be done. But if John Lally took shears to his canvases, Leonardo's would step in to claim what turned out, thanks to the Wexford small print, to be Leonardo's property.

And John Lally had, in a way, trusted Clifford, even while hating and despising him, because in spite of everything Clifford had some sort of proper response to his work; and John Lally had felt sure that whatever else befell, Clifford would at least never do what some collectors did—put the paintings in a bank vault somewhere for safekeeping. This being to the painter the same as rendering him blind and deaf.

And now Clifford had done exactly this. And not, John Lally was convinced, when he roused himself from his stupor, and found the paintings gone, simply in order to preserve the canvases—they had survived many such a storm before and even as he shredded *Fox Plus Chicken Pieces* he was working out a new improved version in his head—but to be revenged. John Lally the impoverished artist, breaking down, splintering Clifford Wexford's bedroom door, bursting in upon him—no, it was not forgotten, let alone forgiven! No. This was why eight fine paintings were now immured in Leonardo's vault, while Clifford smiled and said lightly, "It's for John Lally's own good" and stretched his white daughter yet again upon the black satanic sheets. It was the artist's punishment.

It was fifteen days before Evelyn dared to creep back into Applecore Cottage and start washing and sweeping again, and three months before life returned to anything resembling normal. John Lally then got on with *The Rape by the Sabine Women* in which he depicted the latter as insatiable harpies. A silly idea, but well-executed: he painted it on the wall of the henhouse, on the ground that it could then hardly end up in Leonardo's vaults. Rather, wind and rain would presently obscure the painting altogether.

LITTLE NELL'S INHERITANCE

For six weeks now little Nell had snuggled tenderly and safely in Helen's womb. She had inherited at least a degree of her maternal grandfather's artistic talent, but not, you will be relieved to hear, his temper or his neuroses; she had all and more of her maternal grandmother's sweetness, but not her tendency to the acute masochism which so often goes with it. She had her father's energy and wit and not his, well, sneakiness. She was all set up to have her mother's looks, but, unlike her mother, she was to feel it below her dignity to lie. All this, of course, was simply the luck of the draw: and not just Nell's luck but ours as well—all of us who were to encounter her in later life. But our Nell had another quality too—her capacity to attract toward her the most untoward, even dangerous events, and the most disagreeable people. Perhaps it was in her stars: a tendency to drama inherited from Clifford's father Otto—his early life, too, was lived in hazard—or perhaps it was, as my own mother would have it, that where you have angels, you have demons too. Evil circles good, as if trying to contain it: good being the powerful, moving, active force, and evil the nagging, restraining one. Well, you must make up your own mind as you read Nell's story. This is a Christmas tale, and Christmas is a time for believing in good, rather than bad: for seeing the former, not the latter, on the winning side.

As for Helen, she suspected that perhaps Nell, or someone, had come into existence, inasmuch as she suffered from a faint dizziness which affected her whenever she stood too suddenly, and because her breasts were so swollen and sore she could scarcely forget they were there—which most women do, most of the time, unless and until they're pregnant. These symptoms, mind you, or so she told herself, might be due to love, and nothing more. The fact was that Helen didn't want to be pregnant. Not yet. There was far too much to be done, seen, explored, thought about in the world which so suddenly and newly included Clifford.

And how could she, Helen, scarcely yet herself properly in the world, bring someone else along into it? And how could Clifford love her if she was pregnant; that is to say sick, swollen, tearful—as her mother had been during her last disastrous pregnancy, only five years back. That baby had miscarried, horribly and bloodily late in the pregnancy, and Helen had been horribly sorry and bloodily relieved when it happened, and confused by her own conflicting emotions. And John Lally had sat and held her mother's hand, with a tenderness she had never seen before, and she had found herself jealous—and planned there and then to leave home after A levels and go to Art College, and Get Out, Get Out—

Well now, what it added up to was that Helen now just wanted to forget the past and love Clifford and prepare for a glittering future and *not* be pregnant. Because Clifford had asked her to marry him. Or had he asked her? Or just somehow said, sometime in the middle of one of their lively, enchanted nights, part sticky, part silky, part velvet-black, part glowing lamplight, "I must tell my parents about all this. They'll want some kind of marriage ceremony, they're like that" and so, casually, the matter had been settled. Since the bride's parents were so clearly incapable of arranging anything, it would be left to the bridegroom's. Besides, the latter's income exceeded the former's by a ratio of a hundred to one, or thereabouts.

"Perhaps we should just be married quietly," Helen said to Otto's wife, Cynthia, when the whens and hows of the wedding were discussed. Clifford had taken her down to the family home in Sussex to introduce her for the first time and say they were to be married—all this on the one day. Impetuous lad! The house was Georgian and stood in twelve acres. Dannemore Court, reader. Its gardens are opened to the public once a year. Perhaps you know it. The place is famous for its azaleas.

"Why a quiet wedding?" asked Cynthia. "There is nothing to be ashamed of. Or is there?" Cynthia was sixty, looked forty and acted thirty. She was small, dark, elegant, vivacious and un-English, for all her tweeds.

"Oh no," said Helen, although she had risen in the night twice to go to the bathroom, and in those days, before the Pill was in common use, the symptoms of pregnancy were all too well-known to every young woman. And being pregnant, and unmarried, was in most circles still something to be ashamed of.

"So let's make all the fuss we possibly can of such an important occasion," said Cynthia, "and as for who pays—phooey! All that etiquette is so stuffy and boring, don't you think?"

That was in the big drawing-room after lunch. Cynthia was arranging spring flowers in a bowl: they were fresh from the garden, and of amazing variety. She seemed to Helen more concerned over their welfare than that of her son.

But later Cynthia did say to Clifford, "Darling, are you sure you know what you're doing? You've never been married before, and she's so young, and it's all so sudden."

"I know what I'm doing," said Clifford, gratified by her concern. It was seldom shown. His mother was always busy, looking after his father's needs, or arranging flowers in vases, or making mysterious phone calls, and dressing up and rushing off. His father would smile fondly after her; what pleased his wife pleased him. There seemed no room for Clifford, either as a child or now he was grown, between them. They made no space for him. They squeezed him out.

"In my experience of men," said Cynthia (and Clifford thought sadly, yes, that's quite considerable) "when a man says he knows what he's doing, it means he doesn't."

"She's John Lally's daughter," said Clifford. "He's one of the greatest painters this country has. If not the greatest."

"Well, I've never heard of him," said Cynthia, on whose walls were a minor Manet and a nice collection of Constable sketches. Otto Wexford was a director of The Distillers' Company; the days of the Wexford poverty were a long time ago.

"You will," said Clifford, "one day. If I have anything to do with it."

"Darling," said Cynthia, "painters are great because they

have a great talent, not because you or Leonardo's make them so. You are not God."

Clifford just raised his eyebrows and said, "No? I mean to run Leonardo's, and in the Art World that makes me God."

"Well," said Cynthia, "I can't help feeling someone like Angie Wellbrook, with a couple of gold mines behind her—"

"Six—" said Clifford.

"—would have been a less, shall we say, surprising choice. Not that your Helen isn't very sweet."

It was agreed they were to be married on Midsummer's Day, in the village church (Norman, plus lych-gate) and have the reception in a big tent on the lawn, for all the world as if the Wexfords were landed gentry.

Which of course they were not. Otto Wexford, builder, had fled with his Jewish wife Cynthia from Denmark to London in 1941, with their young son. By the end of the war—which Cynthia spent in a munitions factory, wearing a headscarf, and Clifford running wild as an evacuee in Somerset—Otto was a Major in the Intelligence Forces and a man with many influential friends. Whether or not he actually left the Secret Service was never made clear to his family but, be that as it may, he had risen briskly through the world of postwar finance and property development, and was now a man of wealth, power and discernment, and kept a Rolls Royce as well as horses in the stables of his Georgian country house, and his wife rode to hounds and had affairs with the neighboring gentry. All the same, they never quite "belonged." Perhaps it was just that their eyes were too bright, they were too lively, they read novels, they said surprising things. Come to tea and you might find the stable-hand sitting in the drawing-room, chatting, as bold as brass. No one refused the wedding invitation, all the same. The Wexfords were liked, though cautiously; young Clifford Wexford was already a name: too flashy for his own good but entertaining, and the champagne would be plentiful, and the food good, though un-English.

"Mother," said Clifford to Cynthia, on the Sunday morning, "what does Father say about my marrying Helen?" For Otto had said very little at all. Clifford waited for approval or disapproval, but none came. Otto was friendly, courteous and concerned, but as if Clifford was the child of close friends, rather than his one and only son.

"Why should he say anything? You're old enough to know your own mind."

"Does he find her attractive?" It was the wrong question. He was not sure why he asked it. Only with his father was Clifford so much at a loss.

"Darling, I am the wrong person to ask," was all she replied, and he felt he had offended her as well. Though she was cheerful and flighty and charming enough all day, heaven knows. Otto went hunting, and Cynthia made a point of staying home, to be nice to Helen.

"This house is like a backdrop for the stage," Clifford complained to Helen on Sunday night. They were not leaving until Monday morning. They had been put in separate bedrooms, but on the same corridor, so naturally, and as was expected, Clifford had made his way to Helen's room.

"It isn't real. It isn't home. It is a cover. You know my father's a spy?"

"So you've told me." But Helen found it hard to believe.

"Well, what do you make of him? Do you find him attractive?"

"He's your father. I don't think of him like that. He's old."

"Very well then. Does he find you attractive?"

"How would I know?"

"Women always know things like that."

"No they don't."

They quarreled about it, and Clifford returned to his own room, without making love to her. He did not, in any case, like his mother's expectation that he would—by putting them in separate rooms, but near. He felt insulted by her, and irritated by Helen.

But early in the morning Helen crept into his room. She was laughing and teasing, unimpressed by his bad moods, as she usually was in the first flush of their relationship—and he forgot he was angry. He thought Helen would make up for what his parents had never given him—a feeling of ease and closeness; of not talking behind his back, conspiring against him. When he and Helen had children he would make sure of a proper space for them, between the pair of them. Meanwhile, close together in their white-sheeted bed, in the master bedroom, Cynthia and Otto talked.

"You should take more interest in him," said Cynthia. "He feels your lack of interest."

"I wish he'd stop fidgeting. He's always fidgeting," said Otto, who moved slowly, serenely and powerfully through life.

"He was born like that," said Cynthia. So he had been, nine months to the day after his parents' meeting, as if protesting the suddenness and strangeness of it all. His mother barely seventeen, wild cast-off daughter of a wealthy banking family; his father, already at twenty running his own small firm of builders. Otto had been up a ladder, replacing glass in a conservatory, and had looked down at Cynthia, looking up, and that had been that. Neither of them had expected the baby, nor the pursuing vengeance of Cynthia's family, snatching contracts from under Otto's nose, condemning them to poverty and a perpetual moving on. Nor would it have altered their behavior had they known. And no one expected the overwhelming vengeance of the German occupation, the deportation and murder of the Jews. Cynthia's family made it to America, Cynthia and Otto went underground, joined the Resistance, Clifford handed from household to household the while, until all three were shipped to England, the better for Otto to function. The habit of secrecy was never lost for either of them; Cynthia's love affairs were all to do with it; Otto knew it and put up with it. They were no insult to him, merely the addict's passion for intrigue. He got his fixes with MI5: but where could she get hers?

"I wish he'd find himself a more solid occupation," said Otto. "A picture dealer! Art is not for profiteering."

"He had a hard childhood," said Cynthia. "He feels the need to survive, and to survive he has to scheme. It is our example; it is what we did, you and I, and he watched us."

"But he is the child of peace," said Otto. "And we were the

children of war. Why is it that the products of peace are always so ignoble?"

"Ignoble!"

"He has no moral concern, no political principle; he is eaten up by self-interest."

"Oh dear," said Cynthia, but she did not argue. "Well," she said, "I hope this one makes him happy. Do you find her attractive?"

"I see what he sees in her," said Otto cautiously. "But she'll lead him a dance."

"She's soft and natural, not like me. She'll make a good mother. I look forward to grandchildren. We may do better with the next generation."

"We've waited long enough," said Otto.

"I just hope he settles down."

"He's too fidgety to settle down," said Otto, serenely, and they both slept.

Helen wept a little when she returned to Clifford's home, Clifford's bed.

"What's the matter?" he asked.

"I just wish my parents were coming to my wedding," she said, "that's all." But in her heart she was glad. Her father would only make some kind of scene; her mother turn up in the old blue ribbed cotton dress, her eyes red-rimmed from the previous night's row. No. Better forget them. If only now she weren't beginning to feel sick in the mornings. There still might well be reasons—the change in routine, the nights of wild lovemaking, the many dinners out—and she so accustomed to frugal student's fare, or the pork, beans and cider-if-you're-lucky routine of the Lally household—but it was beginning to seem unlikely. No quick pregnancy tests in those days, no vacuum abortions on the side. Just, for the former, a toad which got injected with your urine and laid eggs and died forty-eight hours later if you *were* pregnant, and laid eggs and survived if you weren't, and for the latter an illegal operation which you, like the toad, had to be lucky, or very rich, to survive.

But of course the mere fact of worrying could so upset your

cycle you never knew where you were. Oh, reader, what days! But at least then the penalty for untoward sex was a new life and not, as it can be now, a disagreeable and disgraceful death.

Another month and Helen could not disguise from herself the fact that she was in fact and in truth pregnant, and that she didn't want to be, and that she didn't want Clifford to know, let alone his parents, and that to go to doctors (two were required) for a legal abortion would require more lies about how damaging to her health and sanity pregnancy would be than she—so sane and healthy—could sustain, and that she couldn't tell her friends because she couldn't trust them not to gossip, and her father would kill her if he knew and her mother simply commit suicide—around and around the thought flew in Helen's head, and there was no one she could turn to for help and advice, until she thought of Angie.

Now, reader, you may think this is no more than Helen deserved, to turn for help to a woman who bore her nothing but malice, however good—and she was *very* good—at disguising it Angie had so far been: giving little dinners for the handsome young couple, chatting away to Helen on the phone, recommending hairdressers and so on—but I do beg you to feel as forgiving as you can about Helen and this initial rejecting of her newly conceived child, our beloved Nell.

Helen was young and this was her first child. She had no idea, as established mothers have, of what she would be throwing away, losing along with the bathwater. It is easier for the childless woman to contemplate the termination of a pregnancy, than for those who already have children. So, please, continue to bear with Helen. Forgive her. She will learn better with the years, I promise you.

GOING TO ANGIE FOR HELP

Helen rose out of her snowy white bed one morning, holding her pale, smooth stomach, which was in inner turmoil, and telephoned Angie.

"Angie," she said, "please come over. I have to talk to someone."

Angie came over. Angie walked up the stairs and into the bedroom where she had spent four memorable if actually rather unsatisfactory nights with Clifford, in all their eleven months together. Well, not exactly together, but in the promise of—eventually—together, or so she had assumed.

"So, what's the matter?" Angie asked, and noticed, for Helen was feeling too ill to so much as fasten her brown silk nightie properly, that Helen's white, full breasts were fuller than ever, almost too full, and felt for once rather proud of the chic discretion of her own, and quite confident that, if she managed this right, Clifford would eventually be hers.

Helen didn't reply. Helen flung herself back upon the fur bedspread and lay crumpled and disheveled but still beautiful, and wept instead of speaking.

"It can only be one thing," said Angie. "You're pregnant. You don't want to be. And you don't dare tell Clifford."

Helen did not attempt to deny it. Angie was wearing red hot-pants, and Helen did not even have the spirit to marvel at Angie's nerve, considering her legs, in so doing. Presently words formed out of tears.

"I can't have a baby," wept Helen. "Not now. I'm too young. I wouldn't know what to do with one."

"What any sensible person does with babies," said Angie, "is hand them over to nannies."

And this, of course, in the world in which Angie moved, was just what mothers did. But for all that Helen was only twenty-two and (as we have seen) as selfish and irresponsible as any other pretty, willful girl of her age, she at least knew better than Angie in this respect. She knew that the handing over of a baby would be no easy matter. A baby draws love out of its mother, and the necessities occasioned by that love can change the mother's life altogether, making her as desperate, savage and impulsive as any wild animal.

"Please help me, Angie," said Helen. "I can't have the baby. Only I don't know where to go and anyway abortions cost money and I don't have any."

Nor had she, poor girl. Clifford was not the kind of man to put money in a woman's bank account and not ask for proof of where every penny had gone, not even if that woman was his legitimate fiancée. Clifford might eat at the best restaurants, where it was useful to be seen, and might sleep between the finest, most expensive cotton sheets, because he liked to be comfortable, but he kept very careful accounts. So this had to be done without Clifford's knowing. What a fix Helen was in! Just consider the times. Only twenty years ago, and a pregnant girl, unmarried, was very much on her own: no Pregnancy Advice Centers then; no payments from the State, just trouble whichever way she turned. Helen's best friend, Lily, at seventeen, had an apparently successful abortion but after two days had been rushed to the hospital with septicemia. She'd hovered between life and death for some six hours, and Helen sat on one side of the bed and a policeman sat on the other, and he was waiting to charge Lily with procuring an illegal abortion operation. Lily died, and so was spared the punishment. Probably two years behind bars, the policeman said, and no more than she deserved. "Think of the poor baby!" he said. Poor little Lily, was all Helen could think. Now how frightened she found herself: frightened to have the baby, frightened not to.

Angie thought fast. She was wearing fashionable hot-pants but did not (as we know) have the best legs in the world. They were pudgy around the knees, and gnarled about the ankles; and as for her face, well, the thick makeup the times required was unkind and the hot South African sun had toughened her skin, and somehow grayed it, and she had a thick, fleshy nose. Only her eyes were large, green and beautiful. Helen, curled up on the bed, tearful and unhappy, soft, pale, female, tugging at her brown silk nightie (suddenly too small) in the attempt to make it cover her properly, and altogether too beautiful, inspired in Angie a great desire for revenge. It is really not fair that some women should have the luck of looks, and others not. You must agree.

"Darling Helen," said Angie. "Of course I'll help you! I know an address. An excellent clinic. Simply everyone goes there. Very safe, very quiet, very discreet. The de Waldo Clinic. I'll lend you the money. It just has to be done. Clifford wouldn't want you pregnant at his wedding. Everyone would think he'd married you because he had to! And it's going to be a white wedding too, isn't it, and simply everyone looks at waists."

Simply everyone, simply everyone! Enough to frighten anyone.

Angie booked Helen into the de Waldo Clinic that very afternoon. Helen had the misfortune—rather expected by Angie—of being put into the care of a certain Dr. Runcorn, a small, plump, fiftyish doctor with thick glasses through which he stared at Helen's most private parts, while his stubby fingers moved lingeringly (or so it seemed to Helen) over her defenseless breasts and body. What could the poor girl do about it? Nothing. For in handing herself over to the de Waldo Clinic it seemed that Helen had surrendered dignity, privacy and honor; she felt she had no right to brush Dr. Runcorn's hand away. She deserved no better than its tacky assault. Was she not doing away with Clifford's baby without his knowing? Was she not outside the law? Whichever way she looked, there was guilt, and Dr. Runcorn's glinting eyes.

"We don't want to leave the little intruder in there any longer than we have to," said Dr. Runcorn, in his wheezy, nasal voice. "At ten tomorrow we'll set about getting you back to normal! A shame for a girl as pretty as you to waste a single day of her youth."

The little intruder! Well, he wasn't so far off. That's what

Nell felt like, to Helen. But the phrase still made her squirm. She said nothing. She knew well enough that she depended on Dr. Runcorn's goodwill as well as on his greed. No matter how much he charged, his clinic was always full. If he "did you" tomorrow, rather than in four weeks' time, you were, quite simply, in luck. For the first time in her life Helen truly understood necessity, truly suffered, and held her tongue.

"Next time you go to a party," said Dr. Runcorn, "remember me and don't get up to mischief. You've been a very naughty girl. You'll stay in the clinic tonight, so we can keep an eye on you."

And a very terrible night it was. Helen was never to forget it. The thick yellowy carpets, the pale green washbasin, the TV and the radio headphones did nothing to disguise the nature of the place she was in. As well train roses up the abattoir wall! And she had to call Clifford, and tell another lie.

It was six o'clock. Clifford was at Leonardo's, negotiating the purchase of an anonymous painting of the Florentine School with a delegation from the Uffizi Gallery. Clifford had a shrewd notion the painting was a Botticelli; he was banking on it, paying over the odds to obtain it but not too much in case they looked too hard at what they were selling. Just sometimes the Italians, accustomed as they were to a sheer superfluity of cultural richness, did miss something wonderful and extraordinary beneath their very noses. Clifford's blue eyes were bluer than ever. He tossed back the wedge of his thick fair hair so it glinted—he had grown his hair long, as was the fashion then amongst the sophisticated young, and was not thirty-five still young? He wore jeans and a casual shirt. The Italians, portly and in their fifties, displayed their cultural and worldly achievement with formal suits, gold rings and ruby cuff links. But they were at a disadvantage. They were confused. Clifford meant to confuse them. What was this young man, who belonged so much to the present, doing within these solid elderly marble portals? It unbalanced the Italians' judgment. Why was Clifford Wexford of all people foraging back into the past? What did he mean by it? Did he know more than they, or less? Was he offering too much? Were they asking too little? Where were they? Perhaps life was not serious and difficult after all? Perhaps the plums went to the frivolous? The telephone rang. Clifford answered it. The men from the Uffizi clustered together and conferred, recognizing a reprieve when they heard one.

"Darling," said Helen brightly, "I know you hate being disturbed in the office, but I won't be at Coffee Place when you get back tonight. My mum called to say I was allowed home. So I'm going to stay at Applecore Cottage for a couple of nights. She says she might even come to the wedding!"

"Take garlic and a crucifix," said Clifford. "And ward your father off!"

Helen laughed lightly and said, "Don't be such a goose!" and hung up. The men from the Uffizi raised their price a full thousand pounds. Clifford sighed.

The phone rang again. This time it was Angie. Since such considerable millions of her father's money were invested in Leonardo's, the switchboard put through her call. This privilege was accorded only to Helen, Angie, and Clifford's stockbroker; the last played a chancy game of instant decisions and played it very well, but sometimes needed a quick yes or no.

"Clifford," said Angie, "it's me, and I want to have breakfast with you tomorrow."

"Breakfast, Angie! These days," he said, trying to keep the Uffizi mesmerized with his smile, and hoping Angie would get off the line quickly, "I have breakfast with Helen. You know that."

"Tomorrow morning you won't," said Angie, "because she won't be there."

"How do you know that?" He sensed danger. "She's gone to visit her mother. Hasn't she?"

"No she hasn't," said Angie flatly, and would elaborate no further and Clifford agreed to meet the next morning at 8 A.M. for breakfast at Coffee Place. The early hour did not, as he had hoped, discourage her. He'd suggested Claridges but she said he might need to scream and shout a bit so he'd be better off at home. Then she hung up. The men from the Uffizi pushed up the price a further five hundred and would not be deflected and by now Clifford had lost his nerve. He reckoned the two phone calls had cost him fifteen hundred pounds. When the Italians had gone, smiling, Clifford, unsmiling, made a quick phone call to Johnnie, his father's stable-man and chauffeur—a man who'd been with Otto in the war, and still had a double-O rating—and asked him to visit the Lally household and investigate. Johnnie reported back at midnight. Helen was not in the house. There was only a middle-aged woman, crying into her dishwater, and a man in the garage painting what looked like a gigantic wasp stinging a naked girl.

Clifford spent as bad a night as did Helen; one that he was never to forget. Into the great bubbling cauldron of distress we call jealousy goes dollop after dollop of every humiliation we have ever endured, every insecurity suffered, every loss we have known and feared; in goes our sense of doubt, futility; in goes the prescience of decay, death, finality. And floating to the top, like scum on jam, the knowledge that all is lost: in particular the hope that someday, somehow, we can properly love and trust and be properly loved and trusted in our turn. Plop! into Clifford's cauldron went the fear that he had only ever been admired and envied, and never truly liked, not even by his parents. Plop! the knowledge that he would never be the man his father was, that his mother saw him as some kind of curiosity. Plop! the memory of a call-girl who'd laughed at him, depising him more than he despised her, and plop! and plop! again, other occasions he had been impotent, and embarrassed; not to mention school, where he'd been fidgety, weedy, skinny, short when others had been tall—he didn't start growing until he was sixteen—and the hundred daily humiliations of childhood. Poor Clifford; both too tough and too sensitive for his own good! How these ingredients stirred and boiled and moiled into a great solid tarry wedge of distress, sealed by the shuddering conviction that Helen was in someone else's arms as he lay unsleeping in their bed, that Helen's lips were pressed beneath the searching mouth of someone younger, fiercer, kinder, yet more virile—no, Clifford was never to forget that night; nor, I'm afraid, was he ever properly to trust Helen again, so potent was the trouble brewed by Angie.

At eight o'clock the doorbell rang. Unshaven, distracted, drugged by his own imaginings, affected by a woman as he had never thought possible, Clifford opened the door to Angie. "What do you know?" he asked. "Where is she? Where is Helen?"

Still Angie wouldn't tell him. She walked up the stairs and took her clothes off, and lay down upon the bed, rather quickly covering herself with the sheet, and waited.

"For old times' sake," she said. "And for my father's millions. He'll need some consoling about the Botticelli, if it is one. I keep telling you, money is in Modern Art, not in Old Masters."

"It's in both," he said.

Now what Angie said was persuasive. And she was, to Clifford, familiar territory, and he was distracted beyond belief and anyway Angie was *there*. (I think we have to forgive him, yet again.) Clifford joined her on the bed, tried to pretend it was Helen there beneath him, and almost succeeded, and then on top of him, and totally failed. He knew the moment it was over that he regretted it. Men do seem to regret these things even more easily than do women.

"Where is Helen?" he asked, as soon as he was able.

"She's in the de Waldo Clinic," said Angie, "having an abortion. The operation is booked for ten this morning."

It was by that time 8:45. Clifford dressed, in haste.

"But why didn't she tell me?" he asked. "The little fool!"

"Clifford," said Angie, languorously from the bed, "I can only suppose because it isn't your baby."

That slowed him down. Angie knew well enough that if you have just deceived your one true love, as Clifford had just done, you are all the more ready to believe you are yourself deceived.

"You're so trusting, Clifford," added Angie, to Clifford's back, and it was a pity for her that she did, for Clifford caught a glimpse of Angie in the big wall-mirror, gold-mounted and mercury-based, three hundred years old, in which a thousand women must have stared, and it somehow cast back a strange reflection of Angie. As if indeed she was the wickedest woman who had ever looked into it. Angie's eyes glinted with what Clifford suddenly perceived was malice, and he realized, too late to save his honor, but at least in time to save Nell, what Angie was up to. He finished tying his tie.

Clifford said not another word to Angie; he left her lying on the fur rug on the bed, where she had no right to be—it was after all Helen's place—and was at the de Waldo Clinic by 9:15 and it was fortunate there was at least some time to spare, for the reception staff was obstructive and the operation had been brought forward by half an hour. Dr. Runcorn, I have a terrible feeling, could not wait to get his hands on Helen's baby and destroy it from within. Abortion is sometimes necessary, sometimes not, always sad. It is to the woman as war is to the man—a living sacrifice in a cause justified or not justified, as the observer may decide. It is the making of hard decisions—that this one must die that that one can live in honor and decency and comfort. Women have no leaders, of course; a woman's conscience must be her General. There are no stirring songs to make the task of killing easier, no victory marches and medals handed around afterwards, merely a sense of loss. And just as in war there are ghouls, vampires, profiteers and grave-robbers as well as brave and noble men, so there are wicked men, as well as good, in abortion clinics and Dr. Runcorn was an evil man.

Clifford pushed aside a Jamaican nurse and two Scottish orderlies—all three fed up with wages in the public sector and so gone into private health care, or so they told their friends—and since no one would tell him where Helen was, he stalked along the shiny, pale corridors of the Clinic, throwing open doors as he went, doing without help. Startled, unhappy women, sitting up neatly in bed in frilly or fluffy bedjackets, looked up at him in sudden hope, as if perhaps there at last was their savior, their knight in shining armor, he who was to come if all was to be explained, made happy and well. But of course it was not so: he was Helen's, not theirs.

Clifford found Helen on a trolley in the theater annex, white-gowned, head turbaned; a nurse bent over her; Helen was unconscious, ready to go into the theater. Clifford tussled with the nurse for possession of the trolley.

"This woman is to go back to the ward at once," he said, "or by God I'll have the police in!" And he pinched her fingers nastily in the trolley's steering mechanism. The nurse yelled. Helen did not stir. Dr. Runcorn emerged to see what the matter was.

"Caught red-handed!" said Clifford, bitterly, and indeed Dr. Runcorn was. He had just disposed of twins, rather late on in a pregnancy, and a very messy matter it had been. But Dr. Runcorn prided himself on his record for twins—not out of his clinic those frequent cases where one twin has been aborted, the other gone on, unobserved by everyone but a bewildered mother, to full term. No, if there was a twin, Dr. Runcorn would weed it out.

"This young lady is about to have an exploratory examination of her abdomen," he said, "of her own free will. And since you are not married to her, you have no legal rights in the matter."

At this Clifford simply hit him, and quite right too. Just occasionally violence can be seen to be justified. In his life Clifford was to hit three men. The first was Helen's father, who tried to prize him apart from Helen, the second was Dr. Runcorn, who was trying to deprive him of Helen's baby, and the third we have not come to yet, but that was to do with Helen too. This is the effect some women have on some men.

Dr. Runcorn fell to the ground and got up with his nose bloodied. I am sorry to say none of his staff assisted him. He was not liked.

"Very well," he said wearily, "I will call a private ambulance. On your own head be it."

And as the ambulance doors closed he remarked to Clifford, "You're wasting your time on this one. These girls are nothing but sluts. I don't do what I do for money. I do it to spare the babies a hellish future, and to save the human race from genetic pollution."

Dr. Runcorn's puffy face was puffier still from Clifford's blow, and his fingers were like red garden slugs; he seemed, all of a sudden, to want Clifford's approval, as the defeated so often do of the victor, but such was not of course forthcoming. Clifford merely despised Dr. Runcorn the more thoroughly for his hypocrisy, and a little of that despising rubbed off, alas, on Helen, as if—quite leaving aside the purpose of her visit to the de Waldo Clinic—the mere stepping inside so awful and vulgar a place had been enough to taint her, and permanently.

The ambulance men carried the still-unconscious Helen up the stairs of the Goodge Street house, and laid her on the bed, suggested Clifford call a doctor, and departed. (The de Waldo Clinic was later to send a bill, which Clifford declined to pay.) Clifford sat beside Helen, and watched, and waited and thought. He didn't call a doctor. He reckoned she'd be all right. She breathed easily. Anesthesia had passed into sleep. Her forehead was damp, and her pretty hair curled and clung in dark tendrils which framed her face. Fine veins in her white temples showed blue; thick eyelashes fringed pale translucent cheeks; her eyebrows made a delicate yet confident arch. Most faces need animation to make them beautiful: Helen's was flawless even in tranquillity; as near the perfection of a painting as Clifford was ever likely to find. His anger, his outrage, failed. This rare creature was the mother of his child. Clifford knew that Angie's insinuations were absurd, by virtue of the sheer intensity of the feelings that welled up in him when he considered how narrow his baby's escape had been. This had been the first act of rescue. He did not doubt but that there would be others. He could see all too clearly that Helen was capable of deceit and folly, and lack of judgment, and worst of all, lack of taste. His child, brushed so near, so early, to the appalling Dr. Runcorn! And as Helen grew older these qualities would become more apparent. The baby must be protected. "I'll look after you," he said aloud. "Don't worry." Absurdly sentimental! But I think he meant Nell, not Helen.

Clifford should have been at Leonardo's that afternoon. The Hieronymus Bosch Exhibition was to be extended another three months. There was a great deal to be done, if the maximum publicity for the Gallery, the maximum advantage for himself, was to be gained. But still Clifford did not leave Helen's side. He let his fingers stray over her forehead. He had wanted her from the moment he saw her: so that no one else could have her and because she was John Lally's daughter, and because that in the end would open more doors to him than Angie's millions ever would—but he had not known until the torment of the previous night just how much he loved her, and in the loving exposed himself to danger. For what woman was ever faithful? His mother Cynthia had betrayed his father Otto half a dozen times a year, and always had. Why should Helen, why should any woman, be different? But now there was the child—and in that child Clifford focused all emotional aspiration, all trust in human goodness, quite bypassing poor Helen, who had been trying to save Clifford as well as herself.

Helen stirred, and woke, and seeing Clifford, smiled. He smiled back.

"It's all right," he said. "You still have the baby. But why didn't you tell me?"

"I was frightened," she said simply. And then she added, abandoning herself to his care, "You'll just have to look after everything. I don't think I'm fit."

Clifford, conscious of simply everyone and thickening waists, rang his parents and said no church wedding, after all. He'd rather make it the Caxton Hall.

"But that's only a trumped-up registry office," complained Cynthia.

"Everyone who's anyone gets married there," he said. "And this is a modern marriage. God need not be present."

"Or only his substitute here on earth," said Cynthia.

Clifford laughed and did not deny it. And at least he'd said "everyone" and not "simply everyone."

LEAPING INTO THE FUTURE

The wedding between Clifford Wexford and Helen Lally took place on Midsummer's Day, 1965. Helen wore a cream satin dress, trimmed with Belgian lace, and everyone said she should have been a model, she was so exquisite. (In fact Helen was altogether too robust in her early twenties to be anything of the sort. It was only later, when trouble, love and general upset had fined her down that she might have thought of earning, thus, a living.) Clifford and Helen made a spectacular pair; his leonine hair shone, and her brown hair curled, and everyone who was anyone was at the wedding. Everyone, that is to say, except the bride's father, John Lally. The bride's mother, Evelyn, sat at the back wearing the same old blue ribbed dress she had worn at the party where Clifford and Helen first met and fell in love. She had defied her husband to attend the ceremony. It would mean a week of not speaking, possibly more. She did not care.

Simon Harvey, the New York writer, was Clifford's best man. Clifford had known him from way back: had met him in a pub, lent him his first typewriter. Now he had to lend him the fare over, but a friend's a friend, and though Clifford's acquaintances were many, his friends were few. Simon wrote funny novels on homosexual themes, too early for their popularity. (The word "gay" was only just finding its feet; to be homosexual a deathly earnest, whispered matter.) Soon he would be a millionaire, of course.

"What do you think of her?" Clifford asked.

"If you have to marry a woman," Simon said, "she's the best you could do." Nor did he lose the ring, and he made an affectionate speech; it was worth the airfare, which Clifford knew he would never get back.

Helen's Uncle Phil, Evelyn's brother, gave her away. He

was a car salesman; middle-aged, red-faced and noisy, but all the younger men she knew had at one time or other been her lovers, or nearly been, and that seemed even less suitable—even though they would not have told and Clifford would not have known. She wanted her marriage to start without lies. Clifford didn't seem to mind Uncle Phillip, strangely, just said it was useful to have someone in the car trade in the family, and set up a deal at once—a Mercedes for his MG, now he was about to be a married man. And when it came to it Helen was glad her Uncle Phillip was there—the guests being so weighted on the Wexford family and friend side, light on the Lallys'. Helen had friends enough, but like many very pretty girls, felt she got on better with men than women, and suffered a little, feeling women didn't like her.

No one (who was anyone) except Clifford knew that Helen was more than three months pregnant on her wedding day—oh, and Angie of course, but she had not been sent an invitation and had returned to Johannesburg to lick her wounds. (Though Angie meant to have Clifford in the end and no amount of "I will's" and "I do's" to someone else would daunt her permanently.) It was a wonderful day in any number of ways. Sir Larry Patt came up to Clifford at the reception and said:

"Clifford, I give up. You are the new world. I am the old. I am resigning. You are to be managing director of Leonardo's. The Board decided yesterday. You are much too young, and I told them so, but they didn't agree. So now it's up to you, lad."

Clifford's happiness was complete. Never would there be such a day as this again! Helen slipped her little white hand in his and squeezed it, and he did not squeeze hers in return, but said, "How's the baby?" and she said "Hush!" and had no idea at all that he no longer totally accepted her, but judged her, and thought the squeeze childish and vulgar.

Lady Rowena looked boyish in a gray tunic dress, white frilly blouse and cravat, and fluttered her false eyelashes (everyone was wearing them) at one of Cynthia Wexford's cousins from Minneapolis, and made a rapid assignation with him beneath his wife's nose. Cynthia noticed and sighed. She should never have invited the cousins over: she should have stuck to her principles and kept no contact at all with the family which had so insulted and abused her in her youth. Bad enough that these things ran in the blood. Her father had loved her dearly one day, spurned her totally the next. She had been instrumental in getting the family out of Denmark; had risked torture, life itself, to do it: he had thanked her coldly, but not smiled at her. He would not forgive. She tried not to think of him. Clifford looked like her father: had stared at her with childish eyes as blue as his grandfather's. That was the trouble. She hoped he would be happy, that Helen would do for him what she could not, that is to say, love him. But perhaps he hadn't noticed. She's always behaved as if she loved him, or thought she had.

Otto and Cynthia went home in their Rolls Royce. Johnnie drove. He kept a loaded revolver in the glove box, for old times' sake. Cynthia thought Otto was a little subdued.

"What's the matter?" she asked. "I'm sure if anyone can make Clifford happy, Helen can. Mind you, as a baby he was never exactly content. She'll have her work cut out for her."

"All that worries me," said Otto gloomily, "is what he'll do for an encore. Head of Leonardo's at his age! It'll go to his head."

"Too late," said Cynthia. "He already thinks he's God."

Clifford and Helen spent the night in the Ritz, where the double beds are the best and softest and prettiest in London.

"What did your parents give us for a wedding present?" asked Clifford, and Helen wished he hadn't asked. He seemed in an odd mood, both elated and yet somehow restless.

"A toaster," she said.

"You'd think your father would have given us one of his paintings," said Clifford. Since Clifford already had a dozen small Lallys on his walls, bought for a song, and eight major paintings in Leonardo's vaults, where no one could see them, Helen didn't think so at all. But she was twenty-two and a nobody, and Clifford was thirty-five, and very much somebody, so she didn't say so. After the episode of the de Waldo clinic, she had become less able to laugh at him, tease him out of his moods, enchant him. She took him, in fact, too seriously for his own good, let alone hers. She had been in the wrong. She was her mother's daughter as well as her father's and it showed.

She had other things to worry about, besides. She lay in bed and worried about them. Clifford had bought a house in Primrose Hill, in the then-unfashionable North West London, near the Zoo, to be their marital home. He'd sold Coffee Place for £2,500 and bought the Chalcot Square house for £6,000, judging that presently it would be worth a great deal more. (He was quite right. That very house changed hands recently for half a million pounds.) Clifford hadn't put the property into joint ownership. He didn't see why he should. This, after all, was the sixties, and a man's property was a man's property, and a man's wife serviced it, and was supposed to feel grateful for the privilege. Could she run it properly? She was so young. She knew she was untidy. She had given up her work at Sotheby's, and started going to Cordon Bleu cookery lessons, but even so! Clifford had said, and she could see that he was right, that she would need all her time and energy to run the house, and entertain his friends and colleagues, who, as he himself pointed out, were getting grander and greater all the time. Would there be enough time, enough energy, with a baby on the way? And when would she tell people about the baby? It was embarrassing. Nevertheless, she was full of hope, as befitted a girl on her wedding night. She hoped, for example, Clifford's friends, colleagues and clients would not think her to be an inefficient, stupid child. She hoped that Clifford would not, either. She hoped she would be able to cope with a baby: she hoped she would not yearn for her freedom and her friends, or miss her mother and father too much; she hoped in fact she had done the right thing. Yet what choice had she ever had? You met someone, and that was that.

Clifford kissed her, and his mouth was warm and passionate and he embraced her, and his arms were lean and strong. It had been a long day, a wedding day; a hundred hands had been shaken, a hundred good wishes received. If she was anxious it was because she was tired. But how strange, that along with the physical reassurances of love, keeping pace, marking step, like some little brother determined to be taken seriously, anxiety came too, and a fear for the future, the sense that life flowed like waves toward the shore, forever dispersed before they quite arrive; and worse, that the higher the crest, the lower the trough must be, so that even happiness is something to be feared.

In the middle of the night, the pretty gold enameled telephone on the bedside table rang. Helen answered it. Clifford always slept heavily; never for long, but soundly, his blond head heavy against the pillow, his hand tucked against his cheek, like a child. Helen thought, even as she picked up the receiver, quickly, so he was not disturbed, how wonderful to know so private a thing about so remarkable a man. The call came from Angie in Johannesburg. She was asking how the wedding had been, apologizing for her absence.

"But you weren't even *invited,*" Helen longed to say, but didn't. Could Angie speak to Clifford, Angie asked, and congratulate him on being made managing director of Leonardo's? After all, it was her father who had arranged it.

"It's two in the morning, Angie," said Helen, as reproachfully as she dared. "Clifford's asleep."

"And he sleeps so heavily!" said Angie. "I know only too well. Try pinching his bum. That usually works. Ah, the thought of it. Lucky old you!"

"How do you know?" asked Helen.

"The way so many of us know, darling."

"When?" asked Helen, bleakly. "Where?"

"Who, me? Long long in the past, darling, for Clifford. At least a couple of months. Not since your abortive night in the Clinic. That was at Coffee Place. Though before that, of course, many times, many places. But you know all that. Do just wake him. Don't be a jealous little goose. If I'm not jealous, and I'm not, why should you be?"

Helen put the phone down and wept, but quietly and silently, so that Clifford didn't hear, and wake. Then, as a practical gesture, she took the phone off the hook, so Angie couldn't call back. Outrage and distress would get her nowhere; she knew that. She must calm herself as quickly as she could, and somehow start constructing a new vision of herself, and Clifford, and her marriage.

It was remarkable, once the wedding was over, how Helen's waist thickened: two days later and the wedding dress would not fasten; a week, and she could not pull it over her bosom without the seams threatening to give.

"Extraordinary," said Clifford, who kept asking her to try on the dress, as if to take the measure of her pregnancy by eye. "I suppose now you feel you can relax. Well, you can't. There's a lot to be done."

And so indeed there was. The house in Primrose Hill had to be turned from a rooming-house to a dwelling fit for a Wexford, his new burgeoning wife, and to receive the friends he meant to have—and since Clifford was always busy, Helen would have to do it. And so she did. He was solicitous of her pregnancy, but would not allow her to be ill. If she bent retching over the basin in the morning, he would clap his hands briskly and say "Enough!" and by some magic it would be. He required no consultation about paper, paint or furniture, other than the walls should be fit to hang paintings upon, and the furniture be antique, not new, since new had no resale value. He seemed to approve of what she did: or at least he did not say he did not. On weekends he played tennis, and she watched, and admired and clapped. He liked her applause. But then he liked anyone's applause. She understood that.

"You are not very *sportif,*" he complained. She supposed that Angie, perhaps, had been, and others.

On the surface, things went well. Days were sunny and active, the baby kicked; the nights awkward and less wild, but reassuring. Presently acquaintances of Clifford's put in a cautious appearance at the house and, finding his new young wife not as silly as they had feared, stayed around and became friends. Her friends came, looked, drifted away, finding her in some way lost to them. How could they, young, poor, mildly bohemian, without ambition, be at ease with Clifford Wexford who required more than mere humanity as a recommendation? How, when it came to it, could she? She saw she must be more Wexford wife, less daughter of Applecore Cottage. She learned to do without the chatter and closeness of her friends, the agreeable warmth of their concern; when they drifted off she did not tug them back. They were nice people; they would have come, Clifford or not. Reader, the truth was, she was weighty, and heavy, and began to lumber—you know how women will in late pregnancy—and the baby pressed upon the sciatic nerve, but she gritted her teeth, and set her smile to Fair against weariness and complaint, for Clifford's sake. She would be everything to Clifford. He would never look at another woman again. And at the same time she knew it was no use. She had lost him, though how or why she was not sure.

A TIME OF HAPPINESS

Baby Nell was born on Christmas Day, 1965, in the Middlesex Hospital. Now, Christmas is not a good time to have a baby. The nurses drink too much sherry and spend their time singing carols; the young doctors kiss them under the mistletoe; senior surgeons dress up as Father Christmas. Helen gave birth to Nell unattended, in a private ward, where she lay alone. Had she been in the ordinary public ward at least one of the other patients would have been there to help; as it was, her red light glowed in the nurses' station hour after hour and no one noticed. It was not yet the fashion for fathers to be present at the birth of their baby, and Clifford, in any case, would have shuddered at the very possibility. As it was, he and Helen had been asked to a Christmas Eve dinner by the eminent painter David Firkin, who was thinking of moving from the Beaux Arts Gallery to Leonardo's, and Clifford did not wish to forgo the invitation. It seemed important. Helen had her first tentative pain in the taxi on the way to the Firkin studio. She did not, of course, want to be a nuisance.

"I don't suppose it's anything," she said. "Probably only indigestion. Tell you what, you drop me off at the hospital and they'll have a look at me and send me home and I'll come on to David's in a taxi."

Clifford took Helen at her word and dropped her off at the hospital, and went on to the dinner alone. Helen did not follow.

"Even if she was in labor," said David Firkin, "which I doubt, first babies take forever so there's no need to worry. It's an entirely natural process. Now don't be a bore and keep calling the hospital." David Firkin hated children, and was proud of it. Helen was a fine, healthy girl, all the guests said, no need to worry. And no one started counting back on their fingers as to how many months it was since the marriage—or at least, no one that Clifford noticed.

As it was, Helen was indeed a fine, healthy girl, if frightened, and Nell was a fine, healthy baby, and arrived safely, if on her own, at 3:10 A.M. Nell's sun had left Sagittarius and was just into Capricorn, making her both lively and effective; she had the moon in Aquarius rising, which made her kind, charming, generous and good; Venus stood strong in mid-heaven, in its own house, Libra, and that made her full of desires, and capable of giving and receiving love. But Mercury was too close to Mars, and Neptune was in opposition to both, and her sun opposed her moon, and so Nell was to be prone to strange events through her life, and to great misfortunes, alternating with great good fortune. Saturn in conjunction with the sun, and powerful, and also opposed in the twelfth house, suggested that prisons and institutions would loom large in her life: there would be times when she would look out at the world from behind bars. Or that's one way of looking at it all. It will do. How better are we to account for the events that fate, and not our natures, causes?

A nurse, shamefaced, came hurrying in on hearing Nell's first cry, and when the baby, washed and wrapped, was finally placed in Helen's arms, Helen fell in love: not as she had fallen in love with Clifford, all erotic excitement and apprehension mixed, but powerfully, steadily, and permanently. When Clifford was wrested from the after-dinner brandy and crackers (Harrods Xmas Best) and came to her bedside at four in the morning, she showed him the baby, almost fearfully, leaning over the crib, pulling back the blanket from the small face. She still never knew quite what Clifford was going to like, or dislike, approve or condemn. She had become shy of him, almost timorous. She did not know what the matter was. She hoped the arrival of Nell would make things better. She did not, you will notice, think of her own pain, or resent Clifford's abandonment of her at such a time, just of how best to please him. In those first few pregnant months of her marriage, she was, as I say, more like her mother than at any other time of her life.

"A girl!" he said, and for a moment Helen thought he meant to disapprove, but he looked at his daughter and smiled, and said, "Don't frown, sweetheart. Everything's going to be okay," and Helen could have sworn the baby stopped frowning at once and smiled back, although the nurses said that was impossible: babies did not smile for six weeks. (All nurses say this, and all mothers know otherwise.)

He picked the baby up.

"Careful," said Helen, but there was no need. Clifford was accustomed to handling objects of great value. And there and then he felt, to his surprise, and acutely, both the pain and pleasure of fatherhood—the piercing anxious needle in the heart which is the drive to protect, the warm reassuring glow which is the conviction of immortality, the recognition of privilege, the knowledge that it is more than just a child you hold in your arms, but the whole future of the world, as it works through you. More, he felt absurdly grateful to Helen for having the baby, making the feeling possible. For the first time since he had rescued her from the de Waldo Clinic, he kissed her with ungrudging love. He had forgiven her, in fact, and Helen glowed in his forgiveness.

"All be well," she said, shutting her eyes and quoting something she had read, but not quite sure what: "—and all shall be well, and all manner of things shall be well," and Clifford did not even snub her by asking for the source of the quotation. And so it was, very well indeed, for a time.

Until she was nearly a year old, then, Nell lived in the cocoon of happiness created by her parents. Leonardo's flourished under Clifford Wexford's guidance—an interesting Rembrandt was acquired, a few tedious Dutch Masters sold, the putative Botticelli labeled and hung as such, to the Uffizi's astonishment, and in the new contemporary section, the price of a David Firkin (now required to paint no more than two paintings a year, lest he spoil his own market) soared to five figures. Helen lost fifteen pounds and worshipped Clifford and baby Nell in turns. It is even pleasanter—if more difficult—to love, than to be loved. When both happen at once, what higher joy can there be?

A TIDAL WAVE OF TROUBLE

Reader, a marriage that is rapidly put together can rapidly unravel: like a hand-knitted sweater, which if you snip just one strand and pull, and go on pulling, comes to nothing at all. Just a pile of wrinkled junk. Or put it another way: you think you're living in a palace but actually it's just a house of cards. Disturb one card and the whole lot falls and flattens and is nothing. When Nell was ten months old, the Wexford marriage fell in ruins about the poor child's ears—phut, phut, phut—one nasty event falling fast upon another quicker than you can imagine.

This is how it happened.

The Conrans gave a Guy Fawkes Day fireworks party. Remember? Terence, who started Habitat? And Shirley, later of *Superwoman* and *Lace*? Everyone who was anyone was there, and that included the Wexfords.

Helen left Nell behind with the Nanny: she didn't want the child frightened by bangs and crashes. She went ahead of Clifford, who was coming straight from Leonardo's. She wore an embroidered leather coat and boots with many tassels, and looked slim, vulnerable, very pretty and tender, and somehow amazed, and slightly stunned, as young women recently married to active men do tend to look: that is to say, very attractive to other men, making them behave like stags in the rutting season, all locked mighty antlers and "I'll have what's yours, by God and nature that I will!" If she'd worn her old brown coat it mightn't have happened.

Clifford arrived later than Helen expected. She felt sulky. Leonardo's took up too much of his time and attention. Sausages crackled and hot potatoes went splut! in cinders; rockets rippled and fountains of light poured skyward, and cries of amazement and delight drifted on a light wind over Camden Town gardens, along with the bonfire smoke. There was a lot of rum in the hot toddy. If there had been less, none of it might have happened.

Helen looked through a veil of smoke and saw Clifford approaching. She forgave him: she began to smile. But who was that by his side? Angie? Helen's smile faded. Surely not. Angie, last heard of, had been in South Africa. But yes, that's who it was. Fur-coated, fur-hatted, high-leather-booted, miniskirted, showing the bare stretch of stockinged thigh fashionable at the time; Angie, smirking at Helen, even while Angie most affectionately squeezed Clifford's hand. Helen blinked and Angie was gone. Worse still. What was she hiding? What collusion was this? Helen had kept Angie's wedding-night phone call to herself, biting pain and insult back, forgetting it, putting it out of her mind. Or that's what she thought she'd done. If only she had, and not just thought she had, none of it might have happened.

Clifford took Helen's arm, comfortingly uxorious. Helen shook it petulantly free—never what a woman should do to a man of high self-regard. But she'd had four hot toddies, waiting for Clifford, and was less sober than she knew. If only she'd let him hold her arm. But no!

"That was Angie, you came with Angie, you've been with Angie."

"It was, I did, I have," said Clifford coolly.

"I thought she was in South Africa."

"She's over here helping me set up the Contemporary Section. If you took any interest at all in Leonardo's, you'd know."

Unfair! Wasn't Helen going to daily courses in the History of Art, in order to catch up? Wasn't she, at twenty-three, running a house with servants, and entertaining, and looking after a small child as well? Wasn't she neglected by her husband for Leonardo's sake? Helen slapped Clifford's face (if only she hadn't) and Angie stepped out of the bonfire smoke, and smiled again at Helen a little victorious smile, which Clifford didn't see. (No suggesting Angie could have behaved other than how she did. No sirree!)

"You're completely mad," said Clifford to Helen, "insanely jealous," and left the party forthwith with Angie. (Oh, oh, oh!)

Well, he was cross. No man likes to be hit in public, or accused of infidelity, without reason. And there certainly was no recent reason. Angie was biding her time. Her relationship with Clifford had of late indeed been bounded by Leonardo's new Contemporary Section. Clifford had all but forgotten it had ever been anything else, or would he have brought Angie to the party? (If only he hadn't! It is to Clifford's credit that he, like Helen and unlike Angie, was capable of moral choice.)

Clifford took Angie back to her house in Belgravia and went straight home to Primrose Hill and listened to music and waited for Helen to come home. He decided to forgive her.

He waited until morning, and still she did not come. Then she rang to say she was at Applecore Cottage: her mother was ill. She put the phone down fast. Clifford had heard that one before—he sent Johnnie to check. Of course Helen was not at Applecore Cottage. How could she be? Her father still barred her from his door. The very folly of the lie compounded her offense.

And where had Helen been last night? Well, I'll tell you. After Clifford had left the party with Angie on his arm, Helen, many hot toddies later, left it on the arm of a certain Laurence Durrance, scriptwriter, and husband of little Anne-Marie Durrance, neighbor and close friend. (After this particular choice of action, there was no going back. No more if-only's. Flop, flop, flop, flop—down came the house of cards.)

Anne-Marie, four-foot-ten and six stone of *joli-laide* energy, stayed behind to weep and wail and tell *everyone,* very excitedly, that Helen Wexford had left the party with *her* husband Laurence. Not content with that, she wrung a confession out of Laurence the very next morning. (I took her to my office, snivelled Laurence. On the sofa. Very uncomfortable. You know all those books and papers. I was terribly drunk. Someone had spiked the hot toddy. She seemed so upset. *She* seemed so upset! cried Anne-Marie. *Anne-Marie.* Just one of those things. Sorry, sorry, sorry.) And, having heard all that, and before Helen returned from wherever (staying wth a girlfriend, actually, trying to compose herself, so great was her guilt), Anne-Marie went and told Clifford where Helen had been the night before, with many unnecessary and untrue embellishments.

So when Helen did come home, Clifford was unforgiving in the most permanent kind of way. Indeed, Johnnie was just finishing changing the locks. Helen was on the doorstep in the keen November wind: her husband and baby on the other side of a locked door, in the warm.

"Let me in, let me in," cried Helen, but he didn't. Even though Nell set up a sympathetic wail, his heart stayed hardened. An unfaithful wife was no wife of his. She was worse than a stranger to him: she was an enemy.

So Helen had to go to a solicitor, didn't she, and Clifford was already seeing his—he wasted no time. Anne-Marie had barely finished her tale than he was on the phone—and a very powerful and expensive solicitor he was and not only that, Anne-Marie thereupon decided to take the opportunity of divorcing Laurence and citing Helen, and by Christmas not only one but two marriages had been destroyed. And the cocoon of warmth and love in which Nell lived had been unwound, faster than the eye could see let alone the mind comprehend it seemed to Helen, and words of hate, despair and spite filled the air around Nell's infant head, and when she smiled no one returned her smile, and Clifford was divorcing Helen, citing Laurence, and claiming custody of their little daughter.

You may not know about the custom of "citing." In the old days, when the institution of marriage was a stronger and more permanent thing than it is now, it was seen to need outside intervention to push asunder any married couple. A marriage didn't just "irretrievably break up" as a result of internal forces. Someone came along and *did* something, usually sexual. That someone was known as "the third party." Sheets would be inspected for evidence, photographs taken through keyholes by private detectives, and the third party cited by the aggrieved spouse and get his (her) name in the papers. It was all perfectly horrid; and even if neither spouse was sincerely aggrieved, but simply wanted to part, the motions of sheets and keyholes would have to be gone through. Mind you, every cloud has a silver lining; a whole race of girls grew up who would inhabit seaside hotels and provide required evidence, and who earned a good and frequently easy living, sitting up all night drinking cups of coffee and embracing only when the light through the keyhole suddenly went dark.

The only other mildly glittery lining to this particular cloud was that Helen made a kind of peace with her father—any enemy of Clifford was a friend of his, albeit his own daughter (*alleged* daughter: he would not give Evelyn the comfort of ceasing to disown Helen as his flesh and blood)—and was allowed back into the little back bedroom of Applecore Cottage to weep her shame and anguish away, there where the familiar robin sat on the apple-tree branch, just outside her bedroom window, red-breasted, head on one side, clucking and chirruping at her distress, promising her better times to come.

LIES, ALL LIES!

There are some babies whom nobody fights over. If they are plain, or dull, or miserable or mopey, divorced and erring mothers are allowed to keep them and toil for them through the years. But what a charmer Nell was! Everyone wanted her: both parents, both sets of grandparents. Nell had a bright clear skin and a bright clear smile, and hardly ever cried, and if she did was quickly pacified. She was a hard and dedicated worker—and no one has to work harder than babies—when it came to developing her skills: learning to touch, to grasp, to sit, to crawl, to stand, to utter the first few words. She was brave, brilliant and spirited—a prize worth having, rather than a burden just about worth the bother of bearing. And how they fought over her.

"She isn't fit to be a mother," said Clifford to Van Erson, his freckled, ferocious solicitor. "She tried to abort the child. She never wanted it."

"He only wants her to get back at me," wept Helen to Edwin Druse, her gentle hippie adviser. "Please make him stop all this. I love him so much. Just that one stupid time, that silly party, I'd had too much to drink, I was only getting back at him for Angie. I can't bear to lose Nell. I can't. Please help me!"

Edwin Druse put out a gentle hand to soothe his distraught client. He thought she was too young to cope. He thought Clifford was a very negative kind of person indeed. She needed looking after. He thought perhaps he, Edwin Druse, would be the best person to do the looking after. He could convert her to vegetarianism, and she would no longer be prey to such despair. In fact he thought he and she could get on very well indeed if only Clifford and little Nell were out of the way. Edwin Druse was not perhaps the best legal representative Helen could have chosen, in the circumstances. However, there it was.

Add to that the fact that Clifford wanted Nell, and was in the habit of getting what he wanted, and you will see that in the struggle for her custody he had everything on his side. Money, power, clever barristers, outraged virtue—and his parents Otto and Cynthia behind him, to back him up with extra dollops of the same.

"Sweetness alone is not enough," said Cynthia of Helen. "There must be some sense and discretion too."

"A man can put up with many things from a wife," said Otto, "but not being made a fool of in public."

And Helen had nothing, except loveliness, and helplessness and mother-love, and Edwin Druse's conscience, to put in the scales. And it was not enough.

Clifford divorced Helen for adultery, and there was no way she could deny the fact: what is more, Anne-Marie actually stood up there on the stand and testified, as she had done in her own divorce, "and I came home unexpectedly and found my husband Laurence in bed with Helen. Yes, it was the marital bed. Yes, the pair of them were naked." Lies, all lies! Helen did not even try to counter-claim that Clifford had committed adultery with Angie Wellbrook—she did not want to bring him into public calumny, and Edwin Druse did not attempt to persuade her so to do. Helen was all too ready to believe she had lost Clifford through her own fault. Even while she hated him, she loved him: and the same could be said of him, for her. But his pride was hurt. He would not forgive, and she would not hurt him further. And so he came out of the divorce the innocent, and she the guilty party, and it was in all the papers for the space of a whole week. I am sorry to say that Clifford Wexford was never averse to the publicity. He thought it would be good for business and so it was.

Angie's father rang from Johannesburg and boomed down the line, "Glad to see you're rid of that no-good wife of yours. It'll cheer Angie up no end!" Which of course it did. That, and the amazing success of David Firkin's paintings, which now hung on the trendiest walls in the land.

"See," said Angie. "All that Old Master junk is out, out, out."

At the custody proceedings, a month later, Helen was to wish she had fought harder. Clifford brought up various matters to prove her unsuitability as a mother; not just her initial attempt to abort Nell, which she had expected, but her father's insanity—a man who cut up his own paintings with the garden shears could hardly be called sane—which she might have inherited, and Helen's own tendency to gross sexual immorality. Moreover, Helen was practically an alcoholic—had she not attempted to justify her sinning with the co-respondent, Durrance, on the grounds that she'd had too much to drink? No, Nell's mother was vain, feckless, hopeless, criminal. Moreover, Helen had no money; Clifford had. How did she mean to support a child? Had she not given up even her meager part-time job at the drop of a hat? Work? Helen? You're joking!

Whichever way the poor girl turned, Clifford faced her, accusing, and so convincing she almost believed him herself. And what could she say against him? That he wanted Nell only to punish her? That all he would do would be to hand Nell over to the care of a nanny, that he was too busy to be a proper father to the child, that her, Helen's, heart would break if her baby was taken away from her? Edwin Druse was not persuasive. And so Helen was branded in the eyes of the world, a second time, as a drunken trollop, and that was that. Clifford won the custody proceedings.

"Custody, Care and Control," said the Judge. Clifford looked across the courtroom at Helen, and for the first time since the proceedings had begun actually met her eyes.

"Clifford!" she whispered, as a wife might whisper her husband's name on his deathbed, and he heard, in spite of the babel all around, and responded in his heart. Rage and spite subsided, and he wished that somehow he could put the clock back, and he, she and Nell could be together again. He waited for Helen outside the court. He wanted just to talk to her, to touch her. She had been punished enough. But Angie came out before Helen, dressed in the miniest of mini leather skirts, and no one looked at her legs, just at the gold and diamond brooch she wore, worth at least a quarter of a million pounds sterling, and tucked her arm into his, and said, "Well, that's an excellent outcome! You have the baby and you don't have Helen. Laurence wasn't the only one, you know," and Clifford's moment of weakness passed.

What happened to Laurence, you ask? Anne-Marie his wife forgave him—though she never forgave Helen—and they remarried a couple of years later. Some people are just unbearably frivolous. But by her one act of indiscretion Helen had lost husband, home and lover—which happens more often than I care to think—not to mention a child, and a friend, and a reputation too. And when Baby Nell took her first steps her mother was not there to see.

AFTER THE DIVORCE

Poor Clifford! Now, reader, you may be surprised to hear me speak thus sympathetically of Clifford, who has behaved to Helen in a cruel and disagreeable way. She had been silly, it was true, but she was only twenty-three, and Clifford, within a month or so of marriage, had been paying more attention to Leonardo's than to her, and she had been made jealous of Angie, as we know, and Laurence was as dark and mirthful as Clifford was fair and serious, and Laurence tempted her, and she had failed to resist temptation, just once, though it must be faced that the episode on his office couch might well have blossomed into something richer and less sordid, left to its own devices, and without Anne-Marie's furious hammer-blows to the relationship. Many another husband would have forgiven his wife for just such an error, sulked and grieved for a month or so and then forgotten, and just gotten on with life. Not Clifford. Poor Clifford, I say, simply because he could *not* forgive, let alone forget.

Poor Clifford, because even though he hated Helen, he longed for her bright presence around him, and was left with Angie, who wore miniskirts although her legs were bad and unfashionable brooches just because they were worth millions, and whose white mink coat seemed ostentatious rather than warm and becoming. And who, if Clifford tried to exercise the quite reasonable rights of the newly divorced man, and play the field a little—and there was no shortage of intelligent, beautiful and charming women waiting to snap Clifford up—would ring up her father in Johannesburg (never using her own phone) and start persuading him to shift his investment out of the uncertainties of the Art World and into the certainties of The Distillers' Company or Armalite Inc. So, poor Clifford! He was not happy.

And poor Nell, who had to get used to new faces and new ways, for now she lived in a great polished nursery with a nice enough Nanny and a doting grandmother and grandfather to visit her—but where was her mother? Her little lower lip quivered quite a lot, in those early days, but even a baby can be brave and proud; she would make an effort to smile and perform, and who around was there to fully appreciate her loss? The ins and outs of a child's psyche were not so discussed and considered then as now.

"Don't pick her up," Cynthia would say to Nanny, on the rare occasions when Nell cried in the night. "Let her cry herself out. She'll soon lose the habit." That was the way she'd reared Clifford, after all, in the manner of the times; and sure enough, Clifford had learned not to give way to grief or fear, but whether it had done him any good was another matter. Fortunately Nanny had been trained in Dr. Spock, and took no notice.

"Just as soon as I can get it together," Clifford said to his mother, "she'll come to live with me." But of course he was busy. Weeks turned into months.

And still poorer Helen! She lived with her parents in the months following the divorce, and it was not easy. John Lally was gaunter than ever with all-pervasive rage, and I-told-you-so's, and inclined more than ever to blame Helen's mother for everything that had gone wrong, that was going wrong, and was about to go wrong. Evelyn's eyes would be red and puffy every morning and Helen knew that this too was her fault. She could hear him through the wall.

"Why didn't you stop her marrying him, you fool? My granddaughter in the hands of that rogue, that villain, and you practically handed her over? Did you hate your own daughter so much? Hate me? Or was it jealousy, because she's young and starting out and you're old and finished?"

Oddly, while denying that Helen was his daughter, he laid full claim to Nell as his granddaughter. And yet, you know, while his wife and daughter grieved under his roof, John Lally, inspired by sheer spleen, painted three splendid paintings in as many months—one of an overflowing rain barrel in which floated a dead cat, one of a kite stuck in a dead tree, and one of a blocked gutter and assorted debris. All are now in the Metropolitan Museum of Art. John Lally owned them by contract to Leonardo's, but was certainly not going to deliver them. No. Never. He hid them in the Applecore basement and it was lucky damp did not rot them, or rats devour them. Better his own basement, raged John Lally, than Leonardo's vaults, where Clifford Wexford, adding insult to injury, had already put eight of his finest canvases.

Helen wept a little less each day, and after three months was prepared to face the world again. She was allowed to see her child under the terms of access for one afternoon a month, in the presence of a third party. Clifford had designated Angie as that third party, and Helen could not find any real reason to object, and Edwin Druse did not find one for her. (If you are ever involved in a divorce, reader, make sure your solicitor is not in love with you.)

This was how the access afternoon would go. Nell's grandmother Cynthia would bring the child up to Waterloo on the train, where Angie, a daily nanny of her choice (whose face changed frequently) and a chauffeur-driven Rolls would be waiting. The daily nanny would hold Nell, since Angie was nervous of carrying so lively and bouncy an infant. Besides, it might wet. The party would repair to a room at Claridges, where Helen would be waiting—uneasily, for the place no longer suited her. As Clifford's wife she could go anywhere, however grand, with ease. As Clifford's ex-wife, it seemed to her that waiters and doormen sniggered and stared. These feelings in Helen Angie understood very well, which is why she chose Claridges. Besides, she had pleasant memories of the place.

The nanny would hand Nell to Helen, and Nell would smile and croon and chirrup, and show off her few words, as she would to any friendly face. She no longer distinguished her mother from anyone else; it was her grandmother she reached for, in alarm or pain. Helen had to put up with it.

"You *have* grown thin, Helen," Angie said, on the fourth of these access occasions. (Cynthia had looked mysterious and glamorous, and gone shopping, or so she said.) Angie was glad enough to see that Helen's breasts, once so plump and positive, were now diminished. She thought Clifford could hardly be interested anymore in the pathetic, timid creature that Helen had become.

"Clifford always said I was too plump," said Helen. "How is he?"

"Very well," said Angie. "We're dining at Mirabelle's tonight, with the Durrances." Ah, the Durrances! Anne-Marie and Laurence, courting again already, once Clifford and Helen's best friends. Laurence, with whom Helen had sinned, forgiven, because when it came to it, Helen counted for so little. Angie loved to twist knives. But this time she had gone too far. Helen stared at Angie, and her eyes grew luminous with an anger she had never felt in her life before.

"My poor little Nell," she said to her child. "How weak and stupid I've been. I betrayed you!"

She handed the baby to the nanny and crossed to Angie, and slapped her, once, twice, thrice, on the same cheek. Angie shrieked. The nanny ran from the room with Nell, who merely laughed at the bouncing she received.

"You're no friend of mine and never have been," Helen said to Angie. "You'll go to hell for what you've done to Clifford and me."

"You're just a nothing," said Angie spitefully. "A frame-maker's daughter. And Clifford knows it. He's going to marry me."

Angie went straight back to Clifford and told him that Helen had turned violent and persuaded him to take the access arrangements back to court and limit still further the meetings between mother and child. Angie hated the way, after she had seen Helen, that Clifford would ask, apparently casually, how Helen had seemed.

"Very ordinary," Angie would reply. "And eaten up with self-pity. So dreary!" or words to that effect, and Clifford would look at her and say nothing, except smile ever so slightly, and not very pleasantly. It made Angie uneasy. Angie did this time encounter some considerable resistance from Clifford.

"Oh, do just shut up and lay off, Angie," was what he said at first.

She was in fact driven to reporting (and it could be dangerous—Clifford might react unexpectedly) that Helen was having an affair with her solicitor Edwin Druse. It worked. (Helen, of course, was not, but Edwin Druse was claiming otherwise. Some men are like that—sheer fantasy gets the better of them.) To Clifford, who had noticed the singular inefficiency of Druse's handling of Helen's case, Angie's assertions came as a shock but seemed all too believable. It would explain a lot. Back he went to court.

The summons came bouncing through the mail slot of Applecore Cottage.

"I told you so," said John Lally. "I expected it."

"It's because you expect it," said Helen, finding her courage at last, "that this kind of thing keeps happening!" And she accepted at last her mother's offer of £200 (Evelyn's own running-away money, saved with difficulty over the years) and put it down as the first month's deposit on a fifth-floor flat in Earl's Court. No elevator. Who cared? She would get a job. She would get her baby back.

Helen turned up in Edwin Druse's office angry, not tearful. He felt he might be losing her. He embraced her. She broke away. He persisted. He did not quite try to rape her, but it could be interpreted as such. If he was a vegetarian it was perhaps in the hope of quelling an alarmingly aggressive nature, disguised beneath a beard and a "Hey, man" cool manner which, I am sorry to say, didn't work. Red meat cannot be blamed for everything. Helen broke free, and found herself another solicitor.

She marched into the offices of a colleague of Van Erson, Cuthbert Way, whom she and Clifford had once had to dinner (ratatouille, veal with lemon, *tarte aux pommes*), and demanded his assistance. He would have to represent her for free, she said, in the name of natural justice. He was impressed; he laughed with pleasure at her animation. Druse's appalling handling of the Wexford Case had been a cause for much comment up and down Grays Inn. Way was as moved by her sparkling eyes, her cheeks flushed with outrage, as Druse had been by her red-rimmed masochism. He said he would be happy to take deferred payments.

And so when Clifford went back to Court he found himself faced not by Edwin Druse but by Cuthbert Way, angry and adamant, who told the Judge that Helen had her own home now to take the baby to, and claimed that Clifford was indifferent to Nell's welfare and wanted only revenge, and maintained that Angie was of low moral character, as indeed was Clifford—had he not been to a smart party where LSD was taken?—and in general was as unreasonable and unkind about Clifford as Clifford had been about Helen, and it worked, and when they left the court, Nell was in Helen's arms. (The Judge had asked to see the child in chambers, in the presence of both parents. Nell crowed with delight and leaped into her mother's arms. Well, she hardly knew Clifford. Had Nanny been there, she would probably have gone to Nanny, but she wasn't, was she, and judges don't think of things like that.)

"Custody to the father," said the Judge. "Care and Control to the mother."

"I suppose Cuthbert Way is your current lover," Clifford hissed as he and Helen left the chambers. "Moving up the legal ladder, I see. I'll die rather than let you get away with this."

"Die then," she said.

TUG OF LOVE

A tug-of-love baby! That's how little Nell ended up, for a full three years. First this way, then that. First the grand, hygienic nursery in her paternal grandparents' house in Sussex; then the less grand, frankly unhygienic bohemian house of the maternal grandparents for weekends and the fifth-floor flat in Earl's Court during the week; then her father's now bleak but elegant town house in Primrose Hill; then the house in Muswell Hill her mother presently shared with her new husband, Simon Cornbrook.

Let me tell you briefly how Helen met and married Simon Cornbrook; a truly decent man, if a little dull, as truly decent men tend to be. He was very clever indeed, and was in the top of his class at Oxford in PPE (Philosophy, Politics and Economics) and wrote important pieces about faraway places for the new *Sunday Times* Color Supplement. Sometimes, by agreement in high places, he would write lead pieces for *The Times*. (In those days the two newspapers shared premises in Printing House Square.) He was five-foot-seven, with bright agreeable eyes in a round, owly face and though only in his late thirties didn't have much hair, as if the sheer surge of thought within his skull made it difficult for it to keep rooted. He was, in fact, very, very different from Clifford, and that may have been his charm for Helen. That, and his kindness, his openness, his consideration, his income and his dedication to her physical and emotional comfort. She did not love him. She tried, she almost convinced herself that she did but, reader, she didn't. She needed a man to provide for herself and Nell and protect her from Clifford and his new battery of lawyers (he had dismissed Van Erson, for allowing himself to be taken unawares). And as for Simon, he simply loved Helen, but also, I think, somewhere in his heart, assumed she would be grateful and that that would make everything work. Was he not taking on a woman with a lurid past and a ready-made baby? Though he would never have dreamed of saying so! And of course Helen was grateful. How could she not be? She really and truly appreciated her clever, kind new husband who, although a journalist, and therefore exciting, never stayed drinking late at El Vino's, never gave her a moment's cause for jealousy, was an attentive lover, and took her home from parties the minute she said she wanted to go. (At a party with Clifford, though dying of tiredness or boredom, she never so much as hinted she wanted to go home until he made the first move to do so.) And at the parties she went to with Simon, anyway, she found a much more down-to-earth, more agreeable, less nervy and less judgmental collection of people. They were not so smart, but much more fun.

Reader, let me not knock the Cornbrook marriage. It was pretty good, as marriages go. And Helen was lucky to find him—to be freed from the necessity of climbing five flights of Earl's Court stairs with toddler Nell, after a day spent painting furniture in Brush Antiques, in Bond Street, then crossing London to collect Nell from her nursery, and back to Earl's Court, exhausted—oh, the price of mother-love can be very high and marriage seem very convenient, very tempting.

Simon Cornbrook, bachelor, had bought a new house in Muswell Hill. It needed large furniture. He went to Bond Street in search of practical antiques. (Such existed there, in those days.) Bill Brush took him into his back workroom to show him the large dark-green cupboard with the red flowers upon which, it just so happened, Helen was working. She looked up at Simon, from where she crouched, and she had a streak of white paint across her cheek, and that was that, for him, if not totally for her. Helen was like that. She had such power over the hearts and lives of men, and so little over her own heart, her own life!

They were married within a month, and the house in Muswell Hill was put into joint ownership at once, and Evelyn was paid back her £200. Simon, as I say, was generous, thoughtful and considerate.

"Muswell Hill!" Clifford was heard to remark. "Helen in

Muswell Hill! She must be desperate for a husband. That poor devil Cornbrook! Still, a man who sets up house in Muswell Hill deserves no better."

Now Muswell Hill, if you don't know it, reader, is a pretty enough place, leafy and prosperous, on the North slopes of London, with a wonderful view over the city. But it is very much a family place, a PTA place, and a long way out for someone who wants to be in the swing of things. Which of course neither Helen nor Simon wanted to be. And their very not wanting made Clifford uneasy.

So Clifford went back to the courts and claimed that Simon was a dissolute alcoholic, but the plea did not stand. (He was, the court decided, merely a journalist like any other.) And Nell stayed with her mother and smiled at them all, everyone, though at her mother most of all, and very seldom at Angie, who spent quite regular Sunday lunchtimes at Clifford's house, but was rarely asked to stay the night—and when she was, felt it was only to keep her quiet. Which it was. Poor Angie—yes, reader, even Angie deserves pity: it is a terrible thing to love and not be loved in return—was hurt, but bided her time. One day Clifford would realize what was what, and would marry her.

Clifford's access arrangements at the time meant that he had Nell every third weekend. The child would be delivered to his Primrose Hill doorstep on Saturday afternoons, and collected from it on Sunday evenings.

"Strange," said Clifford to Angie, on one of those occasions when he had Nell and Angie stayed the night, "it's only when you're here that Nell wakes and cries." It wasn't true. It was just that when Angie was there he spent less time asleep and so was more likely to hear the poor child cry. She told him so but he didn't believe it.

That night Angie wore for a nightdress a beige Zandra Rhodes ballgown ornamented with the palest gauze butterflies, but it looked rather silly in bed, and did not flatter her complexion one bit. Helen would have gotten away with it, and just looked somehow dreamlike, as Clifford could not help but think. These days he tried not to think of Helen at all, since all pleasant memory of her was instantly superseded by a vision of her in Laurence Durrance's arms, Edwin Druse's or Cuthbert Way's or, worst of all, cavorting in beige satin (or such, for some reason was his vision) with Simon Cornbrook. (In fact, Helen wore one of the latter's shirts in bed, if anything, but Clifford was not to know this.)

"You should hire a nanny," said Angie. "Whose duty it is to wake up in the night for a child. It's ridiculous to suppose a man as busy and important as you can possibly manage Nell without one."

"For one weekend in every three," said Clifford, "it hardly seems worth the expense."

He compromised and an au pair girl was hired through an agency, and as luck would have it (Clifford's luck, anyway) she turned out to be the daughter of an Italian count, with a degree in Art History, long wavy dark hair, and a gentle manner. Angie had no idea what they were up to, but feared the worst, and arranged to have the girl deported. (This could be done easily enough in the sixties—if foreign girls were seen to be disrupting British homes, visas would abruptly be canceled. And Angie, such was her wealth and talent, always had an influential ear around in which to whisper.) But all that's another story, reader; and really, the ins and outs of Clifford's love-life need not concern us too much. Let us just say that, one way and another, he frequently evaded Angie's overseeing eye.

And Simon Cornbrook, too, really only concerns us as the man who held little Nell's right hand on family walks on Hampstead Heath, while Helen held the left.

"One-two-three-whee!" they'd cry, swinging Nell into the air, breathless and excited. Simon it was who delivered and collected Nell from Clifford's doorstep every third weekend. And it was under his kind, quasi-paternal aegis that Nell learned not just to talk, but to run, jump, skip, even, by the age of three, to read and write a word or so. She had a thin, delicate body, large bright blue eyes and her father's thick blond hair—though his was straight and Nell's waved and curled as her mother's did. (How hard it is that it takes two to make one. No wonder arguments arise!) But Nell was happy and content and, if anything, life in the Muswell Hill house, with its spacious calm and solid domesticity, was a little too boring. (Or was it Helen who thought that, not Nell? I fear so.) Helen no longer had to "entertain" in the Wexford sense, but interesting people would come around for meals and the kitchen and dining-room were one, so that everyone would sit and drink wine and watch her cook, and she found herself not in the least nervous. Simon would have to go abroad from time to time, and she missed him—well, a little—and that was reassuring. So she lived quietly for a while and told herself that this Muswell Hill housewife was her true self. Well, she was recovering. She had been badly frightened by the world and the people in it. And Nell settled in to her once-every-third-weekend with Clifford well enough, very soon learning that though she could be as boisterous as she wished to be in her mother's house, in her father's she had to move sedately: otherwise something precious might get broken. If she spilled her milk in Primrose Hill it would be on some pristine embroidered tablecloth, and though no one would exactly get cross, there would be a great palaver as the cloth was removed and replaced. In Muswell Hill a sponge would just be produced—or she'd fetch it herself—and the scrubbed wooden table wiped.

And so life continued happily enough. Simon thought it was time Helen had a baby, but Helen somehow kept putting it off. The Pill—in those early days of its use a really heavy daily dose of estrogen—had changed the face of sexual politics almost overnight. Women now controlled their own fertility. Once that had been the man's job: now it was both the woman's responsibility and her right. And every morning Helen, knowing Simon's wishes, and being soft-hearted and kind-natured, stared at her pill and thought perhaps she wouldn't take it after all, but every morning she did. Until one day she woke from a particularly powerful dream about Clifford—reader, she still dreamed about him—that she was in bed with him, and he would be declaring love and she would be amazingly happy. And she felt so guilty about it she put the pill back in its packet, and then threw the whole packet in the wastepaper basket. If she had Simon's baby the dreams might stop. She would settle down. She would forget Clifford. Within the month she was pregnant.

Angie brought news of Helen's pregnancy to Clifford one Sunday morning. The sun streamed in through French windows; the narrow crescent, lately dilapidated, but now newly painted and gentrified, threw back light into the room in the most charming way. It shone upon one of John Lally's paintings, of an apparently dying owl chewing a rather lively mouse, and made even that seem cheerful. Clifford wore a white terrycloth dressing-gown and drank the blackest and best coffee from the most tasteful of earthenware cups. His blond hair was thick and thatched, and Angie thought she had never seen him more handsome.

"Hi," she said, bouncing in, all casualness, arms full of red roses, "someone gave these to me, and I can't stand him, or them, so I thought you might like them. Where's Anita?" (Anita was the Italian au pair.)

"Gone," he said shortly. "Some idiot at the Home Office canceled her visa."

"You know Helen's pregnant," she said, casually, as she arranged the roses in a whole parade of Liberty flower vases. (She had gotten the roses from Harrods' flower department the previous afternoon: six dozen of them, specially ordered.) Well, Angie always got important things wrong. She thought Clifford would realize that Helen had gone from him forever, and would turn to her, Angie. But all he said was:

"Dammit. Now she'll neglect Nell. Angie, would you mind going away? Where did you get the roses? Harrods?"

Angie left weeping, and for once Clifford did not care. Let her telephone her father, let him take as many millions as he liked out of Leonardo's, let him close the entire Old Master Section if he so decided: he, Clifford, had other things to think about.

By the end of the month, Clifford had arranged to set up a branch of Leonardo's in Switzerland. There is a lot of money in Switzerland and those who own it need their taste guided and, fortunately for the likes of Leonardo's, know it. He bought himself a house, by a lake, beneath a mountain. He rented the Primrose Hill house at an absurdly inflated figure—he could, inasmuch as the area had become suddenly and irrationally fashionable. Well, of course it had! It would.

He then contacted, through Johnnie, a Mr. Erich Blotton, who specialized in the kidnapping of children.

"I hope you know what you're doing," said Johnnie, not usually one to admonish.

"I know what I'm doing," said Clifford, and Johnnie Hamilton, alas, believed him and shut up. Well, he had, after all, "lost his judgment," as his department head put it, during a debriefing session in 1944. MI5, thinking itself very clever, had used lysergic acid to prompt its employee's memory of an interrogation he'd suffered at Turkish hands. But he'd only blanked out even more profoundly and, worse, something in his mind seemed, regretfully, to have "blown." But he liked animals and retained many of his former skills, so now he worked happily enough in the Wexford stables, looking after Cynthia's horses and Otto's dogs, a great, shambling, gray-blond man, who once had been the pride of the Allied intelligence services, but who now needed to be told what to do before he could do it, so baffling did the world appear to him. Only Clifford knew just how many of Johnnie's remarkable skills remained, and occasionally put them to use. I won't say "good use"—though I daresay any vocational skill is the better for being employed, even spying for one's country, or the keeping up of seedy criminal contacts. Common sense occasionally flickered through: and if only Johnnie Hamilton had not been so dependent upon Clifford for the excitement in his life, he might have remonstrated further and more persistently. As it was, he set up a meeting between Erich Blotton and Clifford, and went back to his horses.

THE PRELUDE TO DISASTER

Reader, marriage is never over, divorce or not, if love was ever involved, if there is a child of that love. Helen went on dreaming of Clifford. And Clifford, in the language of less discreet and salubrious suburbs than either Muswell or Primrose Hill, went, if you ask me, doo-lally-tap. It was as if, although he had abandoned his rights to Helen's heart, soul and erotic being, he retained a major interest in the womb which had produced Nell. This territory had been invaded by another and his, Clifford's, honor thereby impugned. I can think of no other reason for his behavior. Excuse there can be none.

"I want Nell snatched," Clifford said to Erich Blotton, lawyer-kidnapper. Blotton's name appeared from time to time in the newspapers, as he was censured by his profession or, occasionally, sentenced by judges. His qualifications were at the Argentinian bar, he could be found usually in an English one, he had no proper chambers, and he liked to meet his clients in pubs, when they were open, in drinking clubs when they were not. But Clifford had had him fetched by Johnnie to his office at Leonardo's. What a handsome office it was, too, with its high Georgian ceiling, oak-paneled walls, and immense desk. And the paintings on the walls—well, never mind! But at least a million's worth there—even at sixties prices. Clifford lounged behind the desk, feet up, wearing jeans and a white shirt and sneakers a decade before they were fashionable. He looked casual, but of course when did he ever not?

"Snatched? That's not quite how I like to put it," protested Mr. Blotton, who was a thin, small, apparently withdrawn man, neatly suited and with murderer's eyes. That is to say, they were gentle and icy and interested all at once. "Never snatched. Reclaimed is a better word." He smoked ninety cigarettes a day.

His fingers were yellow-stained, as were his teeth. His clothes were dandruffy and smelled of tobacco.

Clifford tapped his long fingers—the ones that Angie loved and Helen remembered so well—and talked about money, and offered Blotton half what he had hoped. Clifford was not generous, even in matters like these.

"I'm leaving for Switzerland on Friday," said Clifford. "I want the child in my house within the week. Before it clicks with the mother what might be in my mind."

The mother! Not Helen, not Nell's mother, not even my ex-wife, but *the mother*. Oh yes, doo-lally-tap!

And indeed, had Helen read her gossip columns properly, and understood that Clifford was going to live in Switzerland for a whole eighteen months, she would not have left little Nell at her nursery school the following Tuesday with quite so easy a mind. But she no longer read the gossip columns. She didn't want to. Mention of Clifford upset her. And he was always in them, always being spotted here or there, just so long as it was fashionable.

"Neglectful mother, is she?" Blotton asked Clifford. He stubbed out one cigarette and started another. Tobacco was not known at the time to be a killer weed. Doctors still recommended smoking as a mild stimulant and a gentle antiseptic. Research was just beginning to show its dangers but the statistics were volubly and energetically denied by smokers and tobacco companies alike. No one wanted to believe it, so no one did. Well, only a few.

Blotton wished to think badly of Helen. He liked to snatch children with as clean a conscience as possible. We all need justification for our illegal pleasures: we shoplift because the stores make too much profit, we cheat our employers because they underpay us, betray our partners because they don't love us enough. Excuses, excuses! Blotton was no different from anyone else, except that in a world where most things are excusable, how Blotton earned his living was, simply, unequivocally, not.

Nevertheless, he tried. Clifford, to his credit, would not play Blotton's game. He did not deign to reply, simply offered Blotton ten percent less than he'd originally reckoned. He disliked the man quite actively.

"Twenty percent more," he did manage to say, "if she's smiling when she arrives." Thus Clifford planned, quite sensibly, to ensure Nell an easy journey, by air, from her mother's home in Muswell Hill, to his, in Geneva: that Blotton would feed the child, entertain her, reassure her and not lay an improper finger upon her.

Clifford did love Nell, reader, in his own way. He just didn't deserve her. Helen, for all her frailty and her earlier irresponsibility, loved Nell *and* deserved her. Your writer does not mean to imply that women always make better parents than men. In some cases the opposite is true. And sometimes, even, reader, I can see that the snatching of a child from an unloving parent is the only thing that a loving parent can do—it's just so hard to tell, in matters that give rise to such distress, when anger, fear, resentment and thwarted instincts are involved, just what our motives are. Do we act from love, as we think, or from spite? All we can really be sure of is that men like Blotton are toads. And even that is insulting to toads, whom some affect to love.

By air! I said. *By air!* Reader, did not that send a sort of shiver through you? It should have; it did through me. Disaster, one fears, is already waiting in the wings. Most of us can never quite get used to hurtling through the air, rather than crawling more reasonably over the ground; and the more imagination we have, the more we project our scenarios of disaster ahead. And though our fears don't stop us from flying and we talk statistics and tell ourselves we are much safer in the air than crossing the street, even seasoned air-travelers exhale in relief when the aircraft is safely on the ground again. And such visions have been seared into our communal minds! The wretched, wrecked forest site of the great Paris air disaster back in '74—I had a good friend in that one, reader—strewn with a horrible debris: clothing, bits of body—a shoe just lying there in the foreground. I'm sure it was my friend's shoe—long, thin, buckled, never particularly flattering to her foot, but what she liked: now all that was left of her. Or the fireball of the space shuttle, seared into the mind's eye forever, startlingly beautiful yet without symmetry, as if in a split second some new art form had been developed—

Well! What was to be, was to be. Johnnie it was who picked up Nell from nursery school at 11:55 on Tuesday morning. He was driving the Rolls, a reassuring kind of car.

"I didn't know it was her father's day to fetch her," observed Miss Pickford, who didn't approve of divorce. Well, who does? But it was rarer then than now, when it is the way in which one in three marriages ends. But Miss Pickford let Nell go in the Rolls, though she'd been expecting Helen. Why should she not? She knew Johnnie; he collected Nell from time to time. How easily it was done! Money for jam for Mr. Blotton.

Little Nell climbed into the back seat—she loved the soft spaciousness of her father's car. Her stepfather's Volvo was lighter and brighter and she liked that too, but her father's car was more exciting. Nell loved just about everything: it was in her nature to rejoice, rather than to find fault. She took a dislike to Mr. Blotton, though, sitting huddled on the other side of the backseat.

"Who are you?" she asked. She didn't like his eyes: gentle, icy and interested all at once.

"A friend of your father's."

She shook her head at him in disbelief and after that he didn't like her either. He didn't like her bright quick eyes, nor the judgment in them.

"Where are we going?" she asked, as the Rolls took the road to Heathrow.

"To stay with your Daddy. He's got a nice new house with a swimming pool and a pony."

She knew it wasn't right. "Mummy will miss me, and who will feed Tuffin?" Tuffin was her cat.

"Mummy will get used to it," said Erich Blotton.

I think he must have liked the thought of women crying, and of children lying awake and silent in strange beds.

Nell knew she was in danger but not quite what it was. She felt in her pocket for her emerald pendant. Well, her mother's emerald pendant. Just a tiny emerald, heart-shaped, set in gold, on a thin gold chain. It made her feel safe, though guilty. It was very bad of her to have it in her possession at all and she knew it.

"Tomorrow's treasure day," Miss Pickford had said to the children. "Bring in your treasures, so we can all see them and talk about them."

Nell had asked Helen what a treasure was, and Helen had brought out the emerald pendant. Clifford had given it to her the week after their wedding. It had belonged originally to Cynthia's mother Sonia, Nell's great-grandmother. Clifford had lately asked for it back, through his solicitors, pointing out that the pendant was a family heirloom and, since Helen was no longer part of the family, she had no claim to it. But Helen had refused to give it back and, for once, he had not pressed the matter. Perhaps he too remembered the spirit in which it had been given, in which it had been received—that same excellent, loving spirit which had created Nell herself? Anyway, Nell now had the thing in her pocket. She had taken it from her mother's jewel-box to show it at school, knowing she would take good care of it, believing she would put it back and no one ever know. Her best, hers and Helen's greatest treasure, Clifford's gift. When it came to it she hadn't shown the pendant; she was not quite sure why.

"And where's *your* treasure?" Miss Pickford had asked, and Nell had just shaken her head and smiled. "Next time then, dear," said Miss Pickford. "Never mind."

In all her life, it seemed, so far, no one had ever addressed a cruel or unkind word to Nell. Her parents had fought and spat at each other, but never, thank heaven, in her actual presence. This confidence that the world was good was to help Nell survive the years to come.

As Nell and Mr. Blotton approached Heathrow—as Helen wept and begged for help, having arrived at the school gate to collect her daughter and finding her gone—a maintenance supervisor, running behind schedule, neglected to properly check ZOE 05's tail for metal fatigue, telling himself such a check was pointless anyway, since the aircraft was newly in service. And so he failed to report a crack, quite visible to the naked eye and not merely detectable by his equipment, running under one of the tail fins. He signed the okay chit, and ZOE 05 taxied out of its hangar, into position at Gate number 43, Geneva bound. And Nell, not yet four, followed Erich Blotton into the Departure Lounge.

"Can we sit in the front?" asked Nell, as they boarded the plane. "Daddy always sits in the front."

"No, we can't," Mr. Blotton said crossly, pulling her further and further down the aircraft aisle. Now Erich Blotton had insisted that he and Nell fly first class from Heathrow to Geneva, and had asked for cash to this end. Clifford had counted out the money required, though reluctantly. Erich Blotton then, naturally, and as Clifford had known he would, flew economy and kept the change. And because he smoked—as anyone could tell from his yellow fingertips and dusty cough, and because the check-in girl, not liking him one bit, had purposely put him in nonsmoking—he and Nell left their allotted seats and sat in the very back of the aircraft, where the air is thick and stale and the passengers can feel every vibration, every buffeting the unnatural flying machine endures, and suffer it as well. Erich Blotton, being a man without much imagination, could put up with it better than most, and, like all heavy smokers, would in any case rather die (literally) than do without a cigarette.

Nell was quite frightened, but wouldn't show it. Nowadays, of course, a small girl in the sole company of a single man, and as seedy a one as this, would attract not just interest, but suspicion. Would warrant a delay at Passport Control, or at the Boarding Gate—a phone call to parents or police. But those were more innocent days. No questions were asked. Nell had her own passport—to obtain which, at that time, required one signature only: the father's, not the mother's. (You may ask why Clifford did not simply collect Nell from school himself, rather than leaving the matter to Blotton? The answer is, I'm afraid, Clifford rather enjoyed the drama of the snatch—and besides, he was busy, and accustomed to delegating.) And Nell smiled, as was her custom. Had Nell not done so, but whimpered or cried or held back, some authority might have intervened. But the thing was that Nell disliked Mr. Blotton so very much, with his suit which seemed to have been doused in tobacco, that she was determined to be good and not show it.

"Even if you don't like people," Helen had told her, "be good and try not to show it."

Helen's only worry about Nell was that she'd grow up like her father, and display her dislikes all too plainly. Arrogant behavior, just about acceptable in the male, sits badly on the female—or so Helen assumed. These events happened, do remember, in the late sixties, and the new feminist doctrine, that what applied to a man applied to a woman too, and vice versa, was only just beginning to penetrate Muswell Hill, where Simon and Helen and little Nell lived. Or where, as from this particular day, just Simon and Helen were to live.

There was a lot of turbulence that day. The aircraft's tail, as we know, was weakened by metal fatigue; moreover, it had once received a hefty blow, unreported, when taxiing out of the hangar on its maiden flight. During takeoff a whole network of tiny cracks spread from the single savage break overlooked by the maintenance supervisor, and weakened the structure still further. Had the flight over the Channel been calm and placid the aircraft might well have gotten to Geneva safely, and in all probability these faults discovered—they were by now glaringly obvious—and the machine taken out of service. Failing that, of course, the next flight, or the next, of ZOE 05 would have ended in disaster. As it was, as the aircraft approached the French coast, an extra sudden bounce and flick upwards of the tail, followed by a sudden drop of a mere twenty feet, but with a compensating quiver upwards, neatly snapped the roof of the tail section. It hung on for a time, till the floor structure snapped as well. Then the tail section parted company from the rest of the aircraft. These simply silly things do happen; thank God, not often. Meanwhile, the plane dived toward the shoreline below. Sudden decompression caved in the floor of the plane's body, severing its control system. (Aircraft are no longer built in this way, of course. ZOE 05's designers had simply lacked imagination; how can the human race learn, especially when it comes to new technology, other than by its mistakes?) The plane broke up as it dived. Seats, complete with strapped-in occupants, hurtled through the air, sent hither and thither by the force of its disintegration. I hope no one suffered too much. I don't think so. The human mind, presented with such a sudden change of circumstances, goes into instant danger-alert mode, in which no pain is suffered, no fear felt. There was no time, on this occasion, for it to pass into the next, more distressing mode of pain and panic, before death intervened. At least, that's what they say. I hope they are right, I really do.

But what happened to the tail was this. It floated down, quite gracefully, the air billowing through it and sustaining it by some phenomena of aerodynamics, tilting first a little to the right, then a little to the left, as if it were a parachute, and in it were two seats, and sitting side by side were Nell and Mr. Blotton, and the sea air was blowing the cigarette smoke away, and the sun shone, and not far beneath them white waves lapped a soft shore. It was very pretty. It was the most extraordinary ride Nell was ever to take—how could it not be?—and she never forgot it. She was frightened, of course she was, but she clutched the emerald pendant, still in her pocket, and knew she'd be all right. Well, she was not yet four years old.

The tail descended into the shallows below, taking its time. There was no one about. The scattered remnants of the rest of ZOE 05 settled into mud and sand some quarter of a mile upshore. Mr. Blotton and Nell sat shocked, but safe at least from sudden death by air disaster. Presently Mr. Blotton undid his seat belt, and tested the depth of the water, and found it only knee-deep. He carried Nell to shore. Then he put her down. She promptly sat down.

"Come on," he said, "don't idle!" and set her on her feet again, and half carried, half pushed her to the shore-road, and then they started walking to the nearest village.

Erich Blotton was an opportunist, no doubt about it. ZOE 05 had not disappeared for more than fifteen minutes from the radar screens, and the search for her remains was no more than eight minutes old, than he was in the bank in the little seaside town of Lauzerk-sur-Manche, changing Swiss francs into French francs, with little Nell standing beside him. Nell was dazed rather than distressed, having never walked so far so fast on her little legs before. Apart from a limp (due to a couple of nasty blisters from walking in wet shoes) and his still damp trousers, Mr. Blotton looked much like any traveling salesman, and certainly not the survivor of an aircrash which had killed 173 people. And Nell just looked like a little girl who'd been paddling when she shouldn't, and sat down in the water, and been scolded.

A few minutes later sirens were to sound, and all the emergency vehicles that that part of the coast could muster were on their way to the scene of the crash, and newspapermen, film and TV and radio crews too, on their way from Paris, and then from all over the world—and who was to remember one slightly-limping, bad-tempered man, accompanied by a very little girl, changing money in the bank that afternoon?

"Hurry up," Mr. Blotton hissed at the little girl, now dragging her after him to the Paris bus which was standing in the square, about to depart. He had lost his cigarettes.

"I'm trying," she said in her little voice, and it would have wrung anyone's heart but Mr. Blotton's.

The thing was, reader, that before Erich Blotton had boarded ZOE 05 he'd stopped by one of those airport desks—which were everywhere at the time, but since seem to have vanished from the scene, or at any rate are now more discreetly positioned—which sold flight insurance. For five pounds you could insure your life for two million pounds, over and above any claim you (that is to say, your relatives) might make against the airline. Two million pounds! Mr. Blotton had taken out just such insurance, making the amount payable to Ellen, his wife—mailing the receipt to her in the envelope provided just before boarding the plane. He was a nervous traveler and, as we have seen, was right to be so. One cannot, in this life, rely on a million-to-one chance to always turn up trumps. That one should float to earth, and not hurtle headfirst—

Mr. Blotton's mind moved fast. Even as he sat blinking in the tail section of the ruined aircraft, and it sank gently deeper and deeper into the tidal mud, his plan of action had been clear to him. He would be presumed dead. Excellent! Then he would hide out—and that would suit him well enough, a lawsuit or two were turning nasty—until Ellen had claimed the insurance money. Then he would send for her; she would forgive him and come: he would take her to South America, where the eyes of the law get blurry, and live happily ever after, living it up. Not that it was in Mrs. Blotton's nature to do much living-up—she disapproved vigorously of smoking, drinking and foreigners. But perhaps the hot climate and so much money would make her feel more generous? Erich Blotton loved hs wife and wanted her approval of his profession, but it was only grudgingly forthcoming. The Blotton marriage was childless, so at least the wife could understand the husband's motivation; that is to say, "If I can't have my own children, I'll steal yours!" It is the duty of a loving and loyal wife always to see her husband's occupation in the best light, and she did her best.

"What am I to do with you?" Mr. Blotton asked Nell, as the two sped toward Paris on the bus. Here, in the existence of the child, was his only problem, the one obstacle to his plans. Going on four is old enough to blurt out information; but alas too young to bully or bribe into silence. A difficult age, from some points of view.

"I want to go to the bathroom" was all she said, and, only then, after a day in which she had been kidnapped and survived an aircrash, did she begin to cry. Erich Blotton wanted not just to cover her mouth with his hand, but to keep it there, smothering her altogether. Only he could hardly do such a thing in a public bus. But he could see the value of the idea—he could easily enough take the child to some small French hotel under a false passport (Mr. Blotton carried three such), suffocate her in her sleep and then destroy the passport and vanish into the Parisian crowd. The child wouldn't suffer. She'd know nothing about it. What sort of future would she have had, had she lived? Mr. Blotton felt a little toward living children as Dr. Runcorn felt toward those unborn—that sometimes they might simply be better off out of existence altogether. Well, vets feel that about animals, and no one reproaches them. If it suffers—end its life! Let's all have a little peace; let us be spared the misery of other creatures.

"La pauvre petite!" said a smart French lady, leaning forward from the seat behind them, so smart indeed she looked as if she ran a multinational conglomerate and wasn't just a provincial housewife on her way to Paris. But that's the French for you! *"Tu veux faire pipi?"*

Nell stopped crying and smiled and nodded, understanding if not the words at least the tone of voice, so enchanting the French lady with her smile that the latter made the driver pull in at a *lay-by aux toilettes,* and accompanied her while Mr. Blotton sat sulking and seething in his seat. But what could he do?

"My mummy will be missing me," said Nell to the lady. "I want to go home. We went for a ride in an airplane but it fell out of the sky."

But, for all her glamour, the French lady did not speak English, and simply took her back to her seat beside Mr. Blotton, and the coach proceeded, the driver muttering under his breath, and two minutes, five seconds behind schedule, which in France is very bad indeed. But who knew who else had been listening?

"Where are we going?" Nell tugged at Mr. Blotton's sleeve. "Please can we go home?"

"Get lost!" said Mr. Blotton.

"Too dangerous now to kill her," thought Mr. Blotton. "We've been noticed." And besides, where would be the profit in it? A dead body, even a small one, even a child's, is all nuisance, all expense. It has to be disposed of, one way or another, and that costs. (These days, of course, you can sell off bits for illegal spare-part surgery, but remember we're talking about twenty years back, before spare-part surgery was all the rage, and just as well, considering Mr. Blotton's nature.)

As it was, and fortunately for Nell, Erich Blotton hit upon another solution. He would lose little Nell the best and most profitable way he knew how.

Nell slept that night in the dreariest room she had ever encountered; it was in the Algerian quarter of Paris, where Mr. Blotton had friends. Wallpaper peeled from the wall and little blind insects swarmed in and out of every possible crack. There was only a blanket on the bed and no sheets. She slept soundly, nevertheless, her hunger quenched by hot, peppery soup. Mr. Blotton put her to bed but he was gone when she woke. She was glad in one way, but lonely in another. She woke only once and cried for her mother a little, but presently a young dark woman came in and hushed her and spoke in a language Nell didn't understand. But she seemed kind and Nell was not afraid.

Maria—for that was her name—looked through the pockets of Nell's clothes and came across a note from the nursery school about an outing to the theater and crumpled it up.

"Don't do that," said Nell. "Miss Pickford will be cross." But the woman just went on doing it.

Then the dark woman found the emerald pendant. Nell had forgotten all about it.

"You mustn't throw that away," said Nell. "It's my mummy's."

The dark woman sat down and stared at the pendant and then at Nell and tears came into her eyes and rolled down her smooth cheeks. She went away but came back quickly with a child's brooch: a kind of plump tin teddy bear on a big pin. Nell watched as Maria screwed off the teddy bear's head, dropped in the little pendant with its fine gold chain, replaced the head, and pinned it on the lapel of little Nell's coat.

"Ça va," she said. *"Ça va bien."*

With just such a teddy bear had many an unsuspecting child smuggled drugs through customs! The neck join was hard to find, except for those who knew enough to look for it.

"Pauvre," said Maria. *"Pauvre petite,"* and another tear fell. Many a criminal, many a whore, waxes sentimental over the misfortunes of childen. Perhaps they see themselves looking out of the child's eyes? Nevertheless, it must be said that if Maria had taken and sold the pendant, she could have earned her freedom from the brothel—for it was in such a place that Nell now found herself—and lived a decent life. But then again, perhaps in Maria's heart she didn't really want that either, but was quite content to live as she did. At any rate she was good to Nell, of that we can be sure. Nell went back to sleep and slept soundly—which was more than her mother did that night, or any of the relatives of those lost on ZOE 05. Maria didn't sleep either; nighttime, after all, was her working day. She did well that night, and thought perhaps it was God's reward for her kindness to the child.

Mr. Blotton slept soundly, as anyone does who has suffered a severe shock to the system—a black, deep, dreamless sleep. Let us not suppose him to be immune to the effects of drastic events, just because he is a criminal. So stunned was he, indeed, that the truly amazing nature of his drifting journey from heaven to hell scarcely dawned upon him until the following morning. Then, when he rose from his grimy bed, and pulled on yesterday's soiled shirt, and scraped away at his face in the cracked mirror, using the razor Maria used for her legs, he asked her—

"Why was I saved and the others not?" But Maria did not know what he was talking about. How could she? But Mr. Blotton saw God's hand in it, and may have been right, except (in my opinion) it was Nell that God was saving, not Erich Blotton, who just happened to be sitting next to the child. But of course Mr. Blotton could not be expected to see that. He did make two gestures of thanks to God during the day. The first was to resolve to give up smoking; the second was to refrain from selling Nell to a friend (such friends!) who ran a child porno network in Europe. Instead he sold her at a rather cheaper price to an acquaintance who ran a scheme for illegal adoption. He left Nell in Maria's care and went to see him. "Female, white, healthy and pretty," was all Mr. Blotton had to say and

Nell was snapped up at once, sight unseen, for a childless couple who lived in a château outside Cherbourg, and who were not in a position to adopt legally. The acquaintance took ten percent commission and Erich Blotton received one hundred thousand francs—enough to keep him comfortably while he laid low and waited for ZARA Airlines to pay out the insurance money.

"One way or another," Erich Blotton said to Maria, "you could say I'd fallen on my feet," and he laughed uproariously, which I must say was not something he usually did.

And so Nell was out of the brothel and into her new home by nightfall, and put to bed in her own turret bedroom, and what if the branches of great trees rubbed against latticed windows and the walls were of ancient unrendered stone, and little spiders hopped and danced all around on the end of silken threads, at least the hands which put her to bed, man and wife, new father, new mother, were loving and not at war with one another.

Clifford, meanwhile, had gone to the Geneva airport to meet Erich Blotton and his daughter off the plane. He had arrived a little late and was shocked to see, punched upon the arrivals board, in relation to ZOE 05's flight from London, the ominous word OVERDUE. Clifford had intended to send his secretary Fanny to meet Nell—Fanny of the white swan neck, ethereal face and Master's Degree in Art History, always obliging! Clifford hated hanging about anywhere, let alone at airports, doing nothing either particularly useful or pleasurable in the company of just ordinary people. But Fanny had told him, in her gentle, determined voice, that Clifford must go himself, that the sooner Nell saw a familiar face the better.

"It is not often a little girl is stolen by a total stranger from her nursery school," Fanny said primly. "She may well be traumatized."

It will not surprise you to learn that Fanny was Clifford's current mistress; Clifford would, after all, need someone to live in and look after Nell, once stolen. He would be busier than ever setting up Leonardo's Geneva, with all the entertaining and socializing that that entailed: he could see he would not have much time for a child. It was no surprise to Fanny either. She was no fool, for all she looked so soft and gentle.

"But you don't love me, Clifford," said Fanny, when he raised his head from the goose-down pillow, a week or so before Nell was due to fly in, and asked her to live with him. The proposal—if so we can call it—came when Fanny was spending not a night, but part of a night—it was Clifford's custom to send her home by taxi at two in the morning. They were in the bedroom of Clifford's newly built house just outside Geneva. The architect was world-famous, the house all curves, angles, steel and glass. (Leonardo's paid.) It was perched on the edge of a mountain, overlooking the lake, and was armed like a fortress. All mixed up with the switches which remotely controlled the food processors, the air-conditioners, the baths, the vacuum cleaners, spotlights, sliding windows, glass roofs and so forth, were the switches for a host of electronic security devices. Clifford had to have them. His insurers insisted that he did. Clifford, to his credit, would rather have lived simply, but when in the country of the rich it is only polite to keep their customs. Moreover, he had finally brought his ex-father-in-law's paintings out of storage and now at last could hang the major John Lally canvases properly, together with a Peter Blake, a Tilson, an Auerbach, and a couple of fine Rembrandt etchings. All had to be protected. Keeping such company could only improve the value of the Lallys. His wife had proved a dead loss, but his father-in-law would keep him in his old age.

Clifford kept a Lally painting of a dead duck and a mad-eyed hunter above his bed. It reminded him, he told inquirers, of the time his ex-father-in-law had burst in upon him and Helen and discovered them in bed together. Well, many a traumatic occasion later becomes an after-dinner tale. It is a form of therapy in which the talkative often indulge, and I do not exempt myself. Clifford still spoke bitterly about the divorce, although everyone (who was anyone) knew it had been he who instituted proceedings, and that he had not been deflected one whit by Helen's tears and obvious repentance. None so irrational as a man betrayed: the more so if he's accustomed to betraying! Now, beneath the dead duck, Clifford said to Fanny:

"I love you as much as I love anyone, which isn't much. If I had to choose between a Francis Bacon and you I daresay I'd choose the Bacon! But I need someone to run the house for Nell, so I'm asking you. I'm sure we'll get on."

"Nell should stay where she is," said Fanny, briskly, "at home with her mother." She was not afraid of Clifford, and never took too much notice of the unkind things he said: well, she couldn't and still have stayed. "A child of three needs a mother, not a father."

"Her mother is feckless, idle, an alcoholic and a slut," said

Clifford. You could tell he didn't like Helen, but also that he still loved her. Fanny sighed. It was always the subtext of Clifford's words which upset her, not the words themselves.

"A mother is a mother," she said, getting out of bed and starting to dress. She had lovely long slim legs, slimmer and longer than Helen's. If Helen had a bad point, it was her legs, which were distinctly stocky now she was moving into her late twenties. She often wore trousers. Fanny, in those liberated days when women wore anything that took their fancy, only the sillier, the silkier, and the frondier the better, could wear miniskirts and hot-pants to advantage. It was when she turned up at the office in these latter and Clifford remonstrated, saying the good burghers of the canton would not approve, that their affair began. Clifford did not make a habit of sleeping with his secretaries: on the contrary. It was just that she was there, he was in a foreign country, and she had a Master's Degree in Art History and her judgment on paintings was sound, and he could at least have a decent conversation with her, which was more than he could say for the heiresses of the Geneva jet set. She did not, of course, have Clifford's flair for combining art and business, but then who could?

"You've gone doo-lally-tap, Clifford," said Fanny. "Stealing a child is a very wicked thing to do."

"How can you steal something that is yours to begin with?" he demanded. "In the same spirit that I would rescue a rotting Leonardo from a damp church, and not stop to ask permission, I'm rescuing this child from its mother. All you mean is, Fanny, you're jealous and possessive and don't want to share me with Nell!"

Clifford believed, as does many a man, that he was central to the lives of all the women around him, and that those women, although capable of emotional judgment, were not of moral judgment. And I am sorry to say that Fanny, as if bearing him out, gave in, laughed lightly and said, "I expect you're right, Clifford." For Fanny was well aware that her living with Clifford was conditional on Nell's presence in the house. And how much better to live at Numéro Douze Avenue des Pins, with its spectacular view and its stretches of parquet flooring and its heated swimming pool reflecting the icy Alps above, and its servants, than in the small apartment above a delicatessen in downtown Geneva, which was all her salary at Leonardo's enabled her to afford. For although Leonardo's paid its chairman, and its directors, and its investors splendidly, it seemed to think that its ordinary employees—that is to say, the women—should balance the privilege of working at Leonardo's against low wages and be grateful. (But that's the way it is for women out there in the world, especially if they are working in publishing or the arts, or for the public good, teaching or nursing—as I am sure many of you know to your cost.) And Fanny knew well enough that there were many just as beautiful, just as talented girls as she, all too eager to take her job as personal assistant to the great, the famous, the glamorous whiz kid Clifford Wexford, and to do it for even less than she. And that once you are emotionally involved with your boss, you had better do as he asks, because he will no longer behave rationally about the typing, the filing, and so on and may confuse your work with *you,* and you'll be out on your ear.

Fanny, I'm afraid, failed. A for Expediency, C for Integrity. Not a passing mark. No. Fanny agreed to move in with Clifford and forthwith ceased to discourage his plan to send off the dreadful Erich Blotton to kidnap Nell. In her defense I can only say that though she did not admire Clifford's personality, or respect his social and financial dealings with the world, admiration and respect are not required when it comes to love. Fanny loved Clifford and that was that. Clifford, by the way, was a wonderful lover. Affectionate, forceful, not given to doubt. Have I mentioned that to you before? And so good-looking, of course. Anger with Helen had lately given his fair, stern face a kind of cavernous, hungry quality. I tell you, he was terrific in those days, not to mention photogenic. Of course the gossip columnists loved him.

But Fanny did at least insist that Clifford himself should meet Nell at the airport. And Clifford, having absorbed the dreadful word "Overdue," went to have a glass of wine (he seldom drank spirits) in the Executive Lounge (he had useful friends in airports just as he had them everywhere). So he watched the Arrivals Board from a comfortable armchair, but it did not make him more comfortable in his mind. No. If the truth were known, he could scarcely breathe from anxiety, but he did not let it show on his face. Presently "Overdue" changed to "Kindly Contact ZARA Desk." The words took up three lines on the display board and put all the other listings out of kilter. The word "kindly" was of course surplus, and for that reason the more ominous.

Clifford looked at the crowd milling around the ZARA Airlines Desk and knew that the worst had occurred. He did not join the crowd. He went back into the Executive Lounge and phoned Fanny. Fanny came at once.

It was left to Fanny, later, to call Helen, and tell her what had happened.

Now Helen, as you may imagine, was in considerable distress already. She had arrived at Miss Pickford's nursery school at 3:15 to find Nell gone.

"Her father's chauffeur came to collect her," said Miss Pickford, "in a Rolls Royce," as if this latter fact excused and explained everything.

In those more innocent days—we are talking about the late Sixties—child molestation and abuse was a rarer thing than it is today, or at least we were not stunned by example after dreadful example on our TV screens and newspapers, and it did not occur to Helen that what we now know as a "stranger" had taken Nell. She knew at once that this terrible deed was Clifford's doing, that Nell was at least physically safe. She called Simon at the *Sunday Times,* and her lawyer, and reproached Miss Pickford heartily, and only then settled down to weep.

"How can he do it?" she asked friends, her mother, acquaintances, everyone on the phone, that late afternoon. "How can he be so wicked? Poor little Nell! Well, she will grow up to hate him, that is the only comforting thing about this whole horrible affair. I want Nell back at once and I want Clifford put in prison!"

Simon, who had come home at once to look after his distressed wife, said calmly that it would do no good to have Nell's father in prison. Nell certainly wouldn't want that. And Cuthbert Way, the lawyer, came over at once, abandoning his other cases—Helen was stunningly beautiful in this the fourth month of her pregnancy—and said that, since he imagined Clifford had taken Nell to Switzerland, it was going to be difficult to get Nell back at all, let alone Clifford put in prison. That put the cat among the pigeons.

Switzerland! It was the first Helen had heard of Clifford

and Switzerland. She didn't read the gossip columns; she had been too busy putting together the pretty, comfortable house in Muswell Hill and settling Nell in at the nursery, and arguing about access with Clifford's solicitors, and wondering whether or not she was pregnant and buying what in those days was called "junk" and in these days is called Victoriana or even "later antiques"; and one way and another, she told herself and everyone that evening, she'd had no time to look in the gossip columns and discover what everyone else apparently knew—that Clifford Wexford had been put in charge of Leonardo's Geneva, and had a new modern house built at vast expense on the lakeside, no doubt complete with nursery.

The reason Helen didn't read the gossip columns was not the ones she gave. It was, as we know, that it still hurt her to read about Clifford's latest *inammorata.* She wasn't exactly jealous—here she was, after all, happily married to Simon—she just couldn't bear it. It hurt. Simon knew, of course, that Helen still loved Clifford, just as Fanny knew that Clifford still loved Helen, but obviously neither pressed the point. What good would it do but harm to themselves?

Cuthbert Way, the lawyer, said he would of course proceed through the international courts, but it would take time. Helen stopped weeping and protesting her outrage. She became deathly white; she could hardly speak. Shock and outrage were giving way now to piercing maternal anxiety. She knew that something terrible, terrible was happening. (And it was, oddly enough, at just about this time that turbulence hit ZOE 05 and the cracks in her frame widened and deepened and turned into those death-dealing splits.) But of course the misery and anxiety caused, quite reasonably, by Nell's abduction served to mask the other, more instinctive, maternal awareness.

Then came the phone call from Fanny. It reanimated Helen as nothing else seemed able to do.

"Who? Fanny who?" (A hand over the phone) "Clifford's latest, everyone! He's reduced to his secretaries now. How dare she call! What a bitch!"

And then the news. I shan't dwell on this part. It is too

terrible. We know that Nell is still alive. Helen does not. I can't bear to be with her at this moment. But I believe that hereafter Helen went more calmly and kindly through life, and was less given to vituperation. Except of course where Clifford himself, the cause of her grief, was concerned.

LIVING PROPERLY AND WELL

The death of a child is not something to be joked about, or laughed at. It is an event from which a parent does not recover; life is never quite the same again, nor should be, for now it incorporates an unnatural event. We do not expect to outlive our children, nor do we want to. On the other hand, life must go on, if only for the sake of those who are left, and, what is more, it is our duty to learn to enjoy it again. For what do we regret for those untimely dead, but the opportunity to live with enjoyment? If we are to give proper meaning and honor to their death, and our grief, we must enjoy the life we, and not they, are privileged to have, and live thereafter properly and well, without wranglings or rancor.

Alas, of all the people in the world, Clifford and Helen were perhaps the least likely to live their lives properly and well. And though in truth Nell, as we know, was not in fact dead but sleeping soundly in a soft, safe though lumpy, bed not a hundred miles away at the time when Clifford and Helen both arrived at the scene of the aircrash, we could still have wished the apparent tragedy to have united them in mutual grief, not driven them further apart in bitterness and hate.

"I'm sorry," Clifford could have said. "If I hadn't behaved the way I did it would never have happened. Nell would still be alive."

"If only I hadn't been unfaithful," Helen could have said, "we would still be together now, and Nell still with us." But no. They faced each other on those sad sands, she flown in on a mercy flight from London, he chauffeur-driven from Paris, and argued. Both were far too gone in grief to weep; but not, it seems, to quarrel. In the background, rescue teams worked with cranes, diving equipment, tractors, with the useless ambulances standing by. And as the tide retreated inch by inch, it lay bare inch by inch the grisly relics of the crash.

"Not a single survivor," Clifford said to Helen. "If you'd been reasonable she could have come out by boat and train, she would never have been on the plane. I hope you go to hell. I hope you live in hell from now on, knowing that."

"You were stealing her," Helen said, quite calmly. "That is why Nell is dead. And as for hell, you came to me out of it, and dragged me down into it, and now you have destroyed Nell."

She didn't scream or hit; perhaps being pregnant anaesthetized her feelings, just a little. I hope so. Later, Helen was to say that short stretch of time when she believed Nell was dead was the most miserable and despairing of all her days but, even so, she knew that, for the unborn baby's sake, she could not let herself receive the full force of the disaster. She did not see how, otherwise, she could have stayed alive. Grief would, quite simply, have killed her.

"Go back to your mistresses and your money," she said. "It's nothing to you that Nell's dead. Crocodile tears!"

"Go back to your whoring and your dwarf hack journalist," he said. "I pity the baby! I expect you will murder this one too." By "dwarf hack journalist" he meant, of course, Simon, who, though one of the most distinguished political columnists of his day, was certainly not a tall man. Helen, at five-foot-seven, was the same height as her new husband.

And so they parted, Clifford back to his chauffeured Rolls Royce; Helen to sit by herself on the desolate beach and mourn. Clifford had refused to go into the identification hut.

"I am not interested in her remnants," he said. "Nell is dead and that's that."

He did not know why he had come, except that action was better than inaction, in the first stunned days of grief.

Simon had said to Helen, "You are not to go in. Let me," and, while she had sat outside, searched amongst the scraps for traces of the missing child. The authorities like bodies to be assembled, named, accounted for, and disposed of with true religious formality. We must all, past and present, be recorded, logged and numbered, and our story told, lest the wild proliferation of humanity reduce us to despair. And besides, there is the question of insurance.

Arthur Hockney was out of Nigeria via Harvard and New York. He was very tall, very broad and elegantly black. He traveled the world for Trans-Continental Brokers as an insurance investigator. If a ship sunk in the China Seas, he'd turn up to find out why. If a presidential palace was destroyed in Central Africa, there would Arthur Hockney be, assessing villainy or genuine loss. Where he went, crowds parted, and gave up their secrets. So large, strong, shrewd was he, so adept at tracing and outfacing the sharks and vipers of the world, that only the good and the guiltless seemed prepared to argue with him at all. Trans-Continental Brokers paid him well. Very well.

He had had some conversations with Clifford, Helen and Simon. He had seen the tail section swung by crane out of the shallow water a little upshore; noticed the tracery of cracks typical of metal fatigue, rather than the gross fractures of impact; observed the two intact seats, their seat belts unfastened. Perhaps the seats had simply been unoccupied. But why then was the ashtray of one full to overflowing, the torn top of a packet of children's candy under the floor of the other? Careless cleaning by ZARA Airlines, or occupancy during the flight? He would be happier if the body of Mr. E. Blotton—to whom his attention was directed, inasmuch as he alone of the passengers had bought extra flight insurance, and whose character and profession he knew—had been identified. But it had not. However, he would have to await the arrival of the unfortunate Mrs. Blotton to be sure. And where was the body of little Nell Wexford? Out to sea? Possible. Yet the man and the child had been booked into the nonsmoking section; all the neighboring bodies had been found, more or less intact. Again, he would have to wait. The child's father had refused to enter the identification hut. Well, he could understand that, considering the circumstances in which the child was on the plane. And no matter how tactfully it was arranged, how much obliterating plastic sheeting used, the process of identification could only be traumatic. All the same, most parents preferred to see, and know, rather than believe the unbelievable, on hearsay. The child's stepfather was in there now—he had kept his wife away, perhaps rightly, perhaps not. To stand amidst the evidence of mortality, the bits and pieces of human flesh, the scraps of property, the trash left when the soul has departed, soon ceases to be gruesome; rather it becomes evidence of the wonder and value of life. (Or so Arthur Hockney had come to see it. Well, he had to, didn't he. It was that or give up a job which involved him as much with the dead as the living.) Look, strange things happened! Bodies simply went missing. For all Arthur Hockney knew, the child might have been snatched up by a golden eagle and carried away to a Swiss mountaintop, Blotton's body dragged out to sea by a giant squid. Because a thing was improbable didn't mean it hadn't happened. Not for Arthur Hockney the notion that the simplest and most likely explanation was the right one, and it was for this reason that he was Trans-Continental's highest-paid and most successful investigator. That, and because of what he sometimes referred to dismissively as his sixth sense. He just sometimes *knew* what it was unreasonable for him to know. He didn't like it but there it was. There was some pattern to human affairs observable by him and apparently no one else.

Arthur went over to where Helen sat, so quietly and sadly, in that gray place, on that gray day. She turned her face toward him. He thought she was both the loveliest and the saddest woman he had ever seen. He did not let his thoughts go beyond that. She was distressed, pregnant, a married woman: out of bounds. All the same, he knew he would see her again, many times, that she would be part of his life. He tried not to think about this, either.

"They haven't found her yet, have they," she said, surprising him with the lightness in her voice.

"No."

"Well, Mr. Hockney, they won't. Nell isn't dead." The ashen misery seemed to drain away even as he looked. Perhaps she found some strength in him, used his clear eyes momentarily to see through to the truth of things, shared his gift for prescience, just long enough for it to work. She actually smiled. A cold evening wind had sprung up and swirled eddies of drier sand along the damp beach, making the prettiest of pretty, timeless patterns. "I expect you think I'm mad," she said. "Because how could anyone live through that?" And she indicated the mangled wreckage of ZOE 05, still strewn so horribly all about.

Hard to believe that the beach would ever again be a playground for children with buckets and spades—but of course eventually it was. That same spot is today the site of the big campsite "Canvas Beach Safari." I think myself it is a desolate place; somehow tragedy seeps through from other groundsheets and makes even the sunniest day melancholy, and the sea seems to sigh and whisper, and when the wind gets up it's a lament—but there! Northern France shouldn't pretend to be the Mediterranean coast, the climate just isn't right for camping holidays. Perhaps that's all it is!

"People live through amazing things," he said cautiously. "A stewardess once fell twenty thousand feet out of an aircraft, landed in a snow drift, and lived to tell the tale."

"Her father thinks she's dead," said Helen. "But then he would. And so does Simon. So does everyone. So I expect I am mad."

He asked if her daughter had liked Dolly Mixtures.

"Not had liked," said Helen, furiously. "Does she like? No, she doesn't. She has more sense," and then she began to weep and he apologized. It was the kind of detail, he knew, that always wrenched the heart of the bereaved—the little, everyday, apparently unimportant things, the likes and dislikes of the dead which in retrospect add up to the sum of a personality, but which in life went unremarked. But it had to be asked, though the answer made Nell's survival yet more unlikely.

It had been, of course, Mr. Blotton's instinct to pick out, in passing, the very candy Nell most scorned ("*Dolly* mixtures? I am not a dolly!") to keep her quiet on the flight. As if, like some recalcitrant animal, she had needed to be kept quiet in the first place! And then, because she made a face, Mr. Blotton had eaten them all, every one, himself, to get even. What a disagreeable man he was. The more I think of him the more disagreeable he gets.

"I don't know what I think," she said, when she had stopped crying. Her faith was slipping away. He felt he had no right to restore it; what kind of proof was conviction? She shivered, and he placed her coat more securely around her shoulders, and led her back to sit in his hired car, out of the wind, and went back to be amongst the perplexing but unperplexed dead. Mrs. Blotton, he was told, had arrived. He spoke to her. She was a plain, respectable woman in her early forties. She had sandy eyelashes and prominent blue eyes. She did not like black men, he could tell, even a black man such as he, who looked so like Sydney Poitier in *Guess Who's Coming to Dinner*. Sheer good looks, a fine suit, and a persuasive, educated voice could usually overcome the most stubborn racial prejudice. But there were always a few women, he knew, especially of Mrs. Blotton's type, pale, Northern women, inhibited, who could never overcome theirs. Well, they didn't even try: black to them meant a fearful, rampant sexuality. If only they knew just how discreet, how vulnerable, how reticent, how dependent on true love his sexuality was, and how he longed for that rare, releasing emotion—but this was the house of death, not life, and their miserable racism their problem, hardly his.

The sights in the hut seemed to make Mrs. Blotton angry rather than distressed. She limped. She was wearing new shoes. Hard, cheap, discount shoes—not the kind a woman rushes out to buy when she's just illegally contrived two million dollars. Then she would either spend lavishly, unable to control herself, or not at all, for a long time, out of guilt as much as prudence. No. She had no idea, she said, and he believed her, why her husband should have been on a flight to Geneva; she'd known nothing about it until this peculiar Insurance Note had come through the mail slot the day after the crash, with Erich's handwriting on the envelope. No, she hadn't looked at it carefully, only got as far as the flight number. She'd seen the crash on the news, thought anyone who traveled on ZARA Airlines deserved what they got; the flight number had stuck in her mind. And Erich hadn't come home when expected. So she'd phoned Heathrow. And the worst conclusion had been the right one. Her husband had been on ZOE 05. He was dead. Of course, he was dead. Why did she have to go through this grisly formality? And who are you, anyway, asking these questions? Not quite "go back and swing in the jungle" but almost.

"People do survive aircrashes," he said.

"What do you know?" she asked savagely. She pointed at a male hand, poking out of the plastic wrap which discreetly hid the severed flesh. The French did these things properly.

"That's his," she said. "That's Erich's."

Arthur looked at the coding on the identification tag. The hand had already been claimed, but tentatively. Yet it had come from the front section, probably Row 5, where Blotton and the child had been booked.

"You're sure?" he asked.

"Would I say it if I wasn't?" Well, yes, he thought, if two million pounds were at stake—though he didn't think she appreciated the sum involved—or just to get out of the place, or get back home and cry. Even the Ellen Blottons of the world were entitled to cry.

"Tell me," he asked, "is your husband a heavy smoker?"

"Him? Certainly not. I won't have a cigarette in the house."

Her own hands were nicotine-free. She had surprisingly white, small, delicate hands for one so practical, sandy and plain. Again, the detail affected her. She broke down and wept, and was taken out of the hut. The hand was re-tagged as belonging to Erich Blotton. Right age, sex, racial type, without nicotine stains. Why then did he still doubt?

He approached Simon Cornbrook, now leaning against the door, defeated.

"You've done enough," Arthur said. "If you haven't found anything by now, you won't. Come out of here."

"I suppose the body might have been carried out to sea," said Simon, "after all, the body weight—just because the others—"

"Quite," said Arthur. "Well, it will turn up, I expect."

"I wish there had been something," said Simon. "Even a shoe, a ribbon. My wife just won't believe Nell's dead, I know she won't."

He drove the Cornbrooks back to Paris and the airport. He filed a report saying there were no suspicious factors relating to the disaster. A strip of cardboard saying "Dolly Mixture," a full ashtray and two missing bodies, were hardly enough to suggest otherwise. All he had was the conviction he could not quite get rid of, and which Helen had somehow picked out of his head. When he left them in the Departure Lounge, he heard Helen say, "She isn't dead. If she was dead I'd feel it," and Simon reply, "Darling, face facts, for all our sakes," and he felt responsible.

When, a week later, Arthur Hockney found a message from Helen at his hotel—he was attending a Conference on Tax Evasion organized by *Fortune*—asking him to meet her, he was not surprised. He had known it would happen. He dropped a note at a box number, as she suggested, and arranged lunch. He imagined she wished to keep the meeting secret from her husband. He did not let his mind speculate further.

Arthur was already in the restaurant when Helen arrived. He stood up as she approached. People turned to stare. He made the tables, the chairs, seem small and impossibly refined, the strawed bottles of Chianti hanging in clusters for decoration somehow absurd. Helen was dressed in dark blue and trying to be unnoticeable, but of course she was not.

"Arthur," she said, lightly and quickly. She was nervous. "I can call you Arthur, can't I? And you must call me Helen.

Phoning strange men, making assignations, it must seem odd! It's just I don't want to worry Simon. He'd be furious—well, not furious, upset—it's just I *know* Nell is alive, I *know* she's all right, except she's missing me, and I want you to find her. I'll employ you. You're freelance, aren't you? I'll pay anything. It's just we mustn't let my husband know." Ah, the habits of Applecore Cottage, still so strong!

"Helen," he said, and found the word new, strange and wonderful, "I can't do it. It wouldn't be responsible."

"But why not? I don't understand." She had ordered a mushroom crêpe but left it untouched. He devoured a porter-house steak and chips. The Queen Mother, asked for a word of advice to those about to embark on public life, replied, "When you see a toilet, use it." Arthur Hockney, whose work took him into jungles and up mountains and into the more desolate and often hungry places of the world, felt the same about a plateful of food. You never knew when you'd see one again. He took his time replying.

"Because to give you hope would be worse than a charlatan who offers a cancer cure for money, or a psychic who speaks from the grave to a widow, for a fee."

"It wouldn't be like that at all." She was only a child herself. "Please!"

"In the face of common sense, in the face of my report to ZARA Airlines, how can I?"

If you come back to me and tell me she's dead, I'll believe it, I'll accept it."

"But you might not," he said. He should never have given her hope in the first place, talked of stewardesses who survived falls of 20,000 feet. He felt to blame.

"It's just somehow the word dead and the word Nell don't go together," she said, and now there were tears in her eyes. He was relieved to see them. "Perhaps Simon's right, I have gone a bit mad. I need a psychiatrist. But I have to *know*. I have to be convinced. Don't you see? To live with hope is worse than living without it. To watch Simon mourn, and yet be unable to mourn myself—it makes me feel wicked! Perhaps it's just the new baby—my being pregnant? That being so full of life, I can't receive death? Perhaps that's all it is."

"I'll go back and look over the case," he said. "I'll open up inquiries again," and hardly knew why he had consented to say it, except that Helen had asked him, and she was in such turmoil: unable to be unhappy, and that was a rare condition.

NO NEWS BEING GOOD NEWS

As for Nell, she was as safe, well and happy as a child can be who finds herself well treated, loved and looked after, albeit in a strange land, by people who speak a foreign tongue. She missed her mother, her teacher, her stepfather and her father in that order, but presently seemed to forget them, as children will. Others took their place. And if Nell sometimes became pensive, while playing in the château grounds, or eating her supper on the patio in the evening sun, her new parents, the Marquis and Milady de Troite, looked at each other and hoped that soon she would forget altogether and be perfectly happy. Nell was their little jewel, their *petite ange:* they loved her.

They did not begrudge a franc of the money they had spent upon her. The de Troites were not in a position, for various reasons which will soon become clear, to formally and legally adopt a child. And in any case, in this period (in the Western World at least) of rising infertility, the right children were in short supply; certain children valued, above others, as dogs are, if the breed and temperament were right. But anything can be bought on the black market, anything. And Nell—well, what a beauty she was, with her blue eyes, her wide smile, her small, perfect features and thick fair hair, and her capacity to love, to forgive, and make the best of everything! She was cheap at the price.

Nell learned French within a month or so, and, having no one to speak it with, soon forgot English. She remembered some things, as if they came from a dream—that once, in that dream life, she'd had another mother, and that her own name had been Nell, not Brigitte: but the dream faded. Just sometimes a disturbing flicker of memory would surface: where was Tuffin, her cat? Hadn't there once been a Tuffin, little and gray? Where was Clifford, her daddy, with his thick blond hair? Papa Milord had almost no hair at all! (What I must tell you about the de Troites, reader, is that Papa Milord was eighty-two and Mama Milady was seventy-four. *That* was why they had trouble adopting!) But the memories only flickered, and were gone.

"Tout va bien, ma petite?" Milady would ask. Her neck was wrinkled, her lips thick with bright, bright lipstick, but she smiled, and loved.

"Très bien, Maman!" Nell hopped and danced about like the little pet she was. They ate in the kitchen—since the wind whistled through the dining-room ceiling so—on bread baked by Marthe, and vegetable soups, and tomato salads with fresh basil, and *boeuf en daube* aplenty—the de Troites' teeth were not up to anything firm or hard—all of which suited Nell's little body very well. The needs of the very young and the old often overlap. She did not cry or quarrel; there seemed so little to cry about, and no one to quarrel with: no one whose interests, in the household, seemed to be put above her own. An outsider, looking in, might have seen a little girl too quiet, too docile for her own good, but there were no outsiders to look in—they were not welcomed: in case, no doubt, they passed just such a judgment and invited the authorities in to see what they had seen. A child, however overtly happy and healthy, in a totally inappropriate home.

On the shelf in the tower room which was Nell's bedroom and which she loved—with its six windows pacing around the walls, and the trees tumbling about in the wind outside, and the once pretty, now shabby, painted furniture which had been Milady's when she was a child—was a cheap tin teddy bear on a pin. It was her treasure. It was magic. Nell knew it must come undone somehow, but she never tried to find out: on those rare occasions when she was upset or troubled, she would go upstairs and hold the tin bear in her small hand and shake it, and listen to it rattle, and feel better. Milady, seeing she loved it so much, presently gave Nell a silver chain so she could hang it around her neck.

There are certain key objects in this world, reader, mere *things,* which play a part in human lives, and this little jewel was one of them. It had been given to Clifford's mother, as we know, by his grandmother. Generations of Nell's family had looked at it and loved it. It should have been lost, or sold a hundred times, but somehow it had survived. Now Nell, instinctively, took comfort from it and waited for what would happen next.

Nell had a little half-brother, Edward. When he was born he weighed seven pounds, five ounces, and Simon was there at the birth. He was a conscientious and modern father. He held Helen's hand during her contractions, and it was an easy birth, as Nell's had not been. The new baby yelled and shouted for all he was worth, and kicked visibly and lustily, and had a remarkable habit of peeing in a great soaking arch, drenching all his clean clothes whenever he was being changed. It made Helen laugh, and Simon was glad to see it, though Edward's behavior seemed to him more an occasion for scowls than mirth. She had not laughed much lately; so quiet and sad the home had seemed without Nell. And yet, Simon thought, his own grief had been greater than Helen's, his own mourning at her loss more intense—and Nell was not even his own child. It worried him. There was something wrong here; he was afraid his wife still clung to the belief the child had somehow survived the crash. A pity he had not feigned some kind of recognition in the identification hut—it would have been easy enough.

The great benefit of a funeral, complete with body (however incomplete the latter may be), is that it makes the mourners accept the fact of death. A memorial service—such as Nell had had in the local church one Sunday afternoon—was hardly the same. And now Simon came to think of it, Helen had not even attended that service. She had felt faint on the way to church, or said she had, and turned back. He had not attempted to dissuade her—she was heavily pregnant; the service could only be yet another upsetting experience for her. Now he wished he had insisted. He'd supposed she wanted to avoid Clifford, but as it happened he hadn't even turned up. He was abroad, the Wexford grandparents said, with just a hint of apology. But at least they'd come along, as had John Lally and Helen's mother,

Evelyn. What a crew he'd taken on, Simon sometimes thought, when he'd taken on Helen! He came from solid suburban stock himself: his parents kindly and steady, if (he was sorry to say) not very bright. His own struggle out of his background had required not so much the slippery arts of diplomacy as perpetual explanation. If Helen was not frank with him, if she was evasive, if she seemed somehow to be *pretending,* he had only to look to her background to understand why.

Understand it he might, but still it pained him. He wanted all of Helen now, as he hadn't when he married her. He wanted her whole heart, her whole attention. He did not want her clinging to the belief that Nell was alive. Nell belonged to the past, to a dead marriage. Sometimes, when she was playing with the baby, she'd whisper something in his ear, and smile. And the baby would smile in response, and Simon would fancy she murmured, "You have a sister, baby Edward, and one day she's coming home to us." Of course this was sheer paranoia; it must be. But why couldn't she smile like that at him? The fact was, that in keeping Nell alive, Helen kept Clifford alive. She would not let Clifford go any more than she'd let Nell.

Some first marriages are like that, reader. However distressing they are while they last, however unpleasant the divorce that draws them to their untimely end, the marriage seems the true, the only one, and whatever comes after, however well-sanctioned by a marriage ceremony, by the attentions of friends and relatives, still feels fake and second-best, and not just second-best, but second-rate. So it was with the marriage between Helen and Clifford; why it was that Helen so often sighed in her sleep and smiled, and Simon watched her so closely; it was the same reason that Clifford did not remarry, while still blaming Helen in his heart for everything that went wrong, from Nell's death to his own inability to love.

Little Edward knew nothing of all this, of course. He opened his eyes to the world each morning and knew it was good, and bawled and beamed, and made his mark on it the only way he knew—by drenching everything in sight. He found his parents' marriage just fine.

THOUGHTS FROM ABROAD

Reader, in case you're wondering, on the day of Nell's memorial service little Brigitte frightened everyone by complaining of a pain in her tummy and by being so pale they put her to bed and kept her there. Milady burned feathers over her and did incantations involving the blood of a lamb—which she kept by the liter in her new freezer—which seemed to make her better. And on the day of Edward's birth Nell skipped about in her grand, dusty, eccentric house, and gave her nurse (aged eighty-one) an extra-special hug, knowing somehow it was an extra-special day.

"Qu'as tu? Qu'as tu?" asked Marthe, bewildered.

"Sais pas, sais pas," sang Brigitte, but she did. The world was good.

Now if you'd told this to Arthur Hockney he'd have smiled indulgently and said impossible, how could Nell possibly *know.* But he'd be speaking with a forked tongue—he knew well enough that such things happened: that feelings *carry,* just as waves do. That people have auras—that you can tell a villain the moment he enters the room; that some few others come in like a breath of the freshest, most energizing air, and how pleased you always are to see them; that sometimes if you shuffle a pack of cards, you know what your hand will be, almost before it's dealt. That expectations are somehow fulfilled, one way or another. That if you expect good, it happens. But that if you expect the ceiling to fall—it certainly will. And it was for these very reasons—his extra awareness, as it were, that he was so highly thought of in his profession, and why Trans-Continental Brokers went on paying him and didn't nag if from time to time he took time off, as he was doing now, on Helen's behalf. Of course he'd rather be valued for what he did, than for what he *was*. Who wouldn't?

Arthur Hockney stood up to his ankles in water on the beach where the tail section of ZOE 05 had fallen. He had a tide timetable in his hand. He made for the shore road, and Lauzerk-sur-Manche, supposing that he had in his company a three-year-old child. He came to the village, inquired at the bank; there were vague memories of a man with a child who had changed Swiss francs to French francs, but no one was prepared to be exact about the date; possibly days before, possibly days after, the air disaster. The dramatic events of that day—the emergency vehicles, the TV crews, the newsmen—had put ordinary matters out of mind. He took the bus to Paris, but there it was the same thing—no one had any tale to tell of an English man and a little blonde English girl. He made inquiries at cafés and hotels around the bus terminal; and sent messages out through the criminal underworld, but no news came back. The trail, if trail there ever had been, was cold. He thought perhaps it was better for Nell to be dead than alive. He was well aware of the likely fate of stray children in the wrong company. White slavery still exists. All manners of evil exist in this world; they don't go away because the papers forget them for a while. His client made only a distinction between dead and alive: and alive to her meant alive and well. He could not, would not, warn her otherwise.

Back in England, he made further inquiries into Blotton's contacts and professional conduct. Mrs. Blotton shut the door in his face. But that was no indication of her complicity in a fraud, merely of her own sorry nature. The local police agreed to keep an eye on the household. Sooner or later, instinct told him, Erich Blotton would return from the dead to get his hands on his wife's two million pounds. He suggested to ZARA Airlines that they reopen their files and delay, as far as they legally could, the actual transfer of the money. There would be delays in any case. Weren't they busy enough in the courts, handling the ordinary claims of the relatives of the dead, and doing it in reverse alphabetical order, as was their quite understandable custom? It would be a long time before they got to Blotton, even were they trying.

But as to Nell, there seemed nothing more he could do. He met Helen, discreetly, in a coffee shop and told her to accept the advice and help of those around her, those who loved her, and acknowledge that Nell was dead, but somehow she didn't seem to be listening—only to the inner voice that kept repeating "she's alive." He would not accept her check. It was very small, in any case. She had saved it out of her housekeeping money. She had no idea how expensive he was. He didn't tell her.

He wanted to embrace her, if only to protect her. Her future was somehow so threatened by her own nature. Or was the desire to hold her something very different indeed? Well, probably, but what was the point.

She finished her coffee and prepared to go. She placed her white hand on his black cheek for a moment and said, "Thank you. I'm glad there are men like you in the world."

"How do you see me?"

"Brave," she said. "Brave, responsible and kind."

What she meant was, of course, *not like my father, not like Clifford,* and I am sorry to say she hardly counted Simon as a man at all!

CONVERSATIONS

Reader, I shall record some conversations for you. The first one is between Clifford Wexford and Fanny, his secretary/mistress. The scene is Clifford's architect-designed house outside Geneva, all elegant luxury, with its shell-shaped swimming pool reflecting blue sky and snowy mountains, its drawings on the pale paneled walls (the drawings keep changing: today it's a rather fine Frink drawing of a horse, a John Lally sketch of a dead dog, three John Piper landscapes and a very fine Rembrandt etching indeed) and its gently macho pale leather armchairs and glass tables.

"Clifford," says Fanny sharply, "you cannot blame Helen for Nell's death. It was you who had her kidnapped. It was because of you she was on the plane. If anyone's to blame, it's you!"

Fanny is fed up, and well she might be. First Clifford asked her to move in with him simply because Nell was coming to stay. Since the dreadful day of the plane crash, she has stayed to nurse Clifford through his grief and distress, which has been bad enough. She has covered for him at work because his depression has at times been so deep he has drunk too much and been in no position to make decisions. And decisions have to be made. In another five short months Leonardo's must open its new Geneva galleries, devoted to the work of modern masters, and those modern masters, somehow or other, must be on the walls on opening day. Paintings have to be wrested out of artists' studios, or out of the houses they have somehow ended up in—given away when drunk, or sold in defiance of contract—and they carry enormous and problematic insurance premiums. But mostly it is artistic decisions which have to be made: is it to be this painting or that? And it was these decisions Fanny made, in Clifford's name. She had made them very well, and now that he is sober and himself again, he will give her no credit on the catalogue. She is furious. Let him put his arms around her at night as he might, let him sweet-talk her as he would, she is simply not having it.

"You are self-centered, selfish, greedy and conceited!" she yells, she who is usually soft and docile. "You don't love me anymore."

"I never did," he says. "I think we've worn each other out. Hadn't you better pack your bags and go?"

End of conversation: end of affair. She had not quite expected it. She thought he would follow her. He didn't. The very next day a picture appeared in the Geneva morning paper. It was of Clifford Wexford in a nightclub with his arm around Trudi Barefoot, the film star who had just written a best-selling novel. Now that Fanny came to think of it, over the last week Trudi had been putting through a call or two.

Another conversation. Fanny sits at her desk in Clifford's outer office, in Leonardo's cool, new, marble mansion, and wrestles with humiliation and grief. Clifford comes in. She thinks perhaps he will apologize.

"You still here?" he asks. "I thought you said you were going."

So she has lost her job as well as her lover, and what she now perceives to have been love.

Her successor, younger and more conventionally pretty than she, but with a still loftier degree in Art History from the Courtauld itself, and taking an even lower salary than Fanny, arrives just as Fanny is leaving. (She has had to fire herself—hiring and firing is part of the job.) The new girl's name is Carol.

"Are the prospects as good as they say?" asks Carol.

"Let us say they are all-embracing," says Fanny.

"Will I get to make my own artistic decisions?" asks Carol.

"I daresay the occasion will arise," says Fanny, watching four porters steer in a particularly brilliant Jackson Pollock, selected by Fanny in Clifford's name. "But I shouldn't bother."

End of conversation. And Fanny goes back to live with her

parents in Surrey. She had given up her little flat above the delicatessen in Geneva, on Clifford's advice, at the height of their—what? Romance? hardly!—amorous business arrangement. It all hurt, dreadfully. But girls who go into the Art World have a hard time. There's money to spare, and love and excitement too, but only at the top; and it's men who're at the top. Where are they ever not, except possibly in the go-go business?

Another conversation, in another country.

"You don't love me," says Simon Cornbrook to Helen at about the same time as Fanny loses her job. He is pale, and his bright eyes are desperate behind his owl glasses. He is not a tall man, or a particularly handsome one, but he is shrewd, intelligent, kind and, like any ordinary husband, wants his wife's love and attention. Helen looks up at him in surprise. She is nursing Edward. All her attention now goes to the baby and, or so Simon feels, to the memory of Nell, which she cradles to herself as she would another living child, to the almost total exclusion of himself.

"Of course I love you!" she says, surprised. "Simon, of course I do. You're Edward's father!" Now that was not the most tactful thing in the world to say. But it was what she meant.

"And Clifford is Nell's father, I suppose."

Helen sighs. "Clifford is in another country," she says, "and besides, we're divorced. What *is* the matter, Simon?"

We know well enough what the matter is. It is that she has married Simon for the warmth, comfort and safety he could give her, all raggedy and jaggedy as she was, fresh out of her marriage to Clifford, thinking that was all she would ever want from a man again, and Simon knows it; and now it isn't enough. He wants Helen's erotic response, her emotional involvement: he wants her to *care,* and all she cares about is baby Edward, and dead Nell, and lost Clifford. Not Simon at all. Both know it. There is no evading it anymore; he didn't really have to ask. Helen bends further over Edward, and croons gently to him, not wanting to meet her husband's eye. He lifts her head and slaps her. It isn't a hard slap: more as if he is trying to bring her back to life; but of course it doesn't work; it is unforgivable. He has hit a woman, his wife, mother of his new baby, doing nothing at all to offend or provoke him, just sitting there asking him what the matter can be.

Simon mumbles his apologies and goes back to his office, and there finds Janice Best, one of the new breed of brilliant young hacks recently taken on by his paper, and after a session at El Vino's—"Simon, what are *you* doing here? You never come here!"—goes back home with Janice (no, reader, she didn't start life with that name, but it doesn't look half bad as a byline—Janice Best (Jan is best. Geddit?) and whether or not Simon did indeed strike some kind of erotic chord in her, or whether she was just pretending, we will never know, because Janice isn't telling. Either way, she knew Simon would be useful to her. And as for Simon, he knew that in Janice he found a response simply not available in Helen. Janice Best! Janice Best! Your writer feels quite chilly!

But these adult relationships, for all their pain, trouble and complications, are trivial, don't you think, compared to the welfare of a child? If only Helen had been a fraction less foolish and willful, if only Clifford had been a little less intolerant, they would never have parted, and Nell would have grown up in peace, to fill her proper, destined place in the world. As it is, what they have all come to!

Helen wonders what she feels about Simon's affair (making the front page of the scandal sheets) with the ebullient Janice, and finds she feels very little at all. It is as if with Nell's disappearance whole sets of emotions have disappeared too. She is all attention to her little son Edward—but even that love is cautious, as if it too might suddenly be snatched away. Not that he notices.

Clifford telephoned her from Geneva, one evening when she was alone and puttering about quite happily, and drowsing, and reading, and writing to her mother, and wondering a little, but only a little, where Simon was.

"Helen?" Clifford said, and the voice, with its kind of charming, husky, double tone, so familiar yet so long unheard, stirred her at once to alertness, wakefulness, response. And that was good, except that with the waking came that other double tone, the pain and misery. No wonder Helen drowsed through her days!

"You okay, Helen? All this stuff in the papers about the dwarf—"

"Clifford," said Helen, lightly, "they make these things up, as you ought to be the first to know. Simon and I are just fine! How are you and Trudi Barefoot?"

"Why don't you ever speak the truth?" he asked. "Why do

you always lie?" and before they'd even begun, they were having a row. That was the way it was. He offered his concern, she denied it out of pride; she was jealous, he was angry; she was hurt. Around and around it went, the wrong way!

And Clifford was right: these days she did lie. There were truths about herself so great which she declined to face that all the little truths went by the board. If she and Clifford had stayed together, and faced their own natures, and so been in a position to reform them, she would have been less of a liar now, less slippery, less somehow unsatisfactory as a person, less easy for Simon to betray. And Clifford would have been less cruel, less calculating, less vengeful on the female sex: less concerned with his own image. He would have changed partners less frequently, and changed himself instead.

Men are so romantic, don't you think? They look for a perfect partner, when what they should be looking for is perfect love. They find failings in their loved one (of course they do! Who's perfect? *They're* not!) when the failing of course is in themselves: in their own inability to perfectly love. It was still Clifford's habit to make checklists as he searched for the woman who would really, truly, permanently suit him. She must be beautiful, highly educated, intelligent, a little shorter than he, plumply breasted and slim-legged, know many languages, ski, play tennis, be a perfect hostess, an excellent cook, be well-read—and so forth and so on. And yet the woman he had come nearest to perfectly loving was Helen—and she certainly did fairly badly, checked off against the list. Poor Clifford, hoping to find solace in fame and fortune, when there is so little to be found there, as anyone who is anyone knows.

And as for little Nell, now called Brigitte, victim of her parents' failings—consider her plight! She was five; it was time she went to school. Milord and Milady were in a right fix. They had hardly left the château since Nell came into it, for wondering how to explain Nell's presence.

"I shall say she is my daughter," Milady said when Nell first arrived, looking at her aged face in a cracked mirror and seeing a young girl, as was her habit. "What is the problem, *mon ami?*"

Milord was not cruel enough to explain what the problem was—that is to say, his wife's refusal to grow old. It would have been sensible enough to claim Brigitte as a grandchild; few questions would have been asked, she could have gone to school, the matter of papers and documents somehow overlooked. But Milady would not hear of it. Brigitte was to be her child, she was not old enough to be a grandmother—anyone could see that! So all Milord could do was keep Brigitte at home, with an elderly, trusted, discreet servant, and hope the problem would go away. But of course it didn't. Little Brigitte grew older, and longed for friends, and company, and young people, and to learn everything in the world there was to learn. And Milord and Milady, for all their eccentricity, worried on Brigitte's account. They wanted the child to be happy, and normal—as indeed they themselves had once been, long ago, before Time and Senility had started their wicked work. Some grow old peacefully and without woe—Milord and Milady fought every inch of the way; and little Brigitte—sometimes quiet and sad, it was true, for no reason anyone could think of; but more often skipping about her domain, her ancient château, bringing life, laughter and light into every corner of it—was their finest weapon.

Black magic, I am sorry to have to reveal, was the other. Milady dabbled just a little, occasionally, and Milord would help her, when it took his fancy. Rumors of it reached the village, from time to time, and ensured that even fewer people went near the château than otherwise—heaven knew it was a grim and eerie place enough, with its high tower half-hidden by unkempt trees which seemed to toss about even if there was no wind. Nell saw it differently, of course: the château was her home, and we all, especially children, think of home as a safe place. If there was a pentagram or two about, and the occasional drifting smell of heavy incense, what is a five-year-old to make of that? For all she knows it's how everyone lives.

The villagers were indulgent to Milord and Milady. They

were realistic: they didn't believe in magic, black or white, not really. Only the youngsters loved to grow hysterical and claim they were being spooked. Dabble as they might, thought the villagers, the old couple could hardly do themselves or anyone else much harm. Let them get on with it. Had they known there was a child in the château, someone might have intervened. But they didn't know. How could they? And Christmas Day came and went and no one knew it was Nell's birthday. The de Troites, in any case, did not celebrate birthdays. What's more, they did their best to ignore Christmas. They felt that to celebrate the season openly might perhaps be an insult to their master, the devil.

So picture their Christmas breakfast. Milord and Milady tried to make it a day like any other. They tottered downstairs at nine in the morning, as was their custom, carefully avoiding damage to their gnarled hands where the banister was broken, and to their fragile legs where the stair was rotten. They came into the great high kitchen, where mice scuttled happily along roof beams, and black beetles raced along the dusty flag floor—Marthe's eyesight was bad. It wasn't that she didn't sweep; she just couldn't see the floors very well—and found Marthe, as usual, preparing coffee in the tall chipped enamel pot and, unusually, Nell making toast in front of the big fire which burned in the hearth all winter—daily, the four of them dragged and maneuvered branches from the massive pile prepared last autumn by John-Pierre the woodcutter. (John-Pierre's mind had been unhinged in the war, but his muscles were still good. On the days Marthe was sent down to the village to fetch him up, Nell would be kept amused somewhere else in the château. It was not difficult. In its great days the château had housed a family of twenty and a staff of forty, and adding whole wings, not to mention barns, stables, follies, had kept all busily and happily occupied. But these are matters which can't concern us now. We have our own story to get on with.)

"What is the little one doing?" Milady asked Marthe. (I am translating for you, of course.)

"She is making toast," said Marthe.

"What a strange thing to do," said Milord.

Now of course the making of toast is an English not a French habit, if only because the nature of bread is so different in each country. Helen had made it as a child in Applecore Cottage, crouching in front of the fire in the little Register grate, the bread on the end of a long brass toasting-fork, with one bent prong and a lion's head for a handle. And just once, the week before Nell boarded ZOE 05, she'd made it for the little girl, opening the door of the solid fuel Aga in the Muswell Hill kitchen to do so, using the carving fork, to the danger and pinkening of her fingers.

"I am making toast," said Nell, "because it is Christmas Day." She used a long forked stick to hold the chunks of bread.

"How does the little one know it is Christmas Day?" The de Troites seldom spoke to their little Brigitte directly.

"The church bells are ringing and it's winter," said Nell. "So I expect it's Christmas. People do nice things at Christmas, and toast is nice. Isn't it?" she added, uncertainly, for Milord and Milady looked decidedly put out. Rheumy eyes flashed and arthritic fingers tapped.

"I have said nothing," said Marthe. "I expect she has read about it in a book."

"But who has taught the little one to read?"

"She has taught herself," said Marthe. And so indeed Nell had, from the alphabet of rag books left over from the great days of the château, damp and mouse-nibbled but still legible, she'd found in an attic. Moreover, though she knew she was not allowed out of the château grounds, and would not have dreamed of disobeying, she would sometimes sit on the branch of a tree which overhung the lane which wound down to the village, and from which, hidden, she could watch the strange, vigorous, giant people of the outside world coming and going, and had begun to make sense of their lives.

Milord and Milady sighed and tutted but presently ate the toast, charred on the outside and cold and damp inside, and not at all successful—with quantities of butter and Marthe's home-made apricot jam, and all without a word of complaint. And that of course is the best kind of present a child can have—to have her efforts commended, even though at some sacrifice to those who do the commending. Nell hugged them all—Milord, Milady and Marthe—and their dark master kept his distance.

Simon spent that Christmas Day with Helen; they tried, for Edward's sake, to mend matters between them. Simon explained that Helen's coldness had driven him into Janice's arms, and Helen had only to say the word and he would never see her again; Helen said, "What word?" and he was too angry to say "love." So somehow that particular moment for reconciliation passed. Helen wanted to talk about Nell, and how Christmas Day was her birthday, but knew Simon didn't want Nell's name mentioned, and that thought upset her. And though they talked pleasantly and lightly enough over the turkey, beneath the decorations, and went out for drinks with friends later, and all agreed the scandal-sheets were simply venomous and not worth suing in case it gave their lies credibility, nothing was healed. The dull ache of unacknowledged grief and resentment remained in Helen's heart, and the savage pain of discontent in Simon's. There was no question of divorce. What would that solve? There was Edward to think about. For Helen, it was as if her life was on videotape and someone had pressed "pause" and just stuck her on one particular not very pleasant frame. It was a horrible feeling. Edward grew and she did not. She sent a Christmas card to Arthur Hockney though, of a rather nice Xmas tree, outlined in silver, and got one back, of the Empire State Building in the snow, with King Kong wearing a holly wreath. She couldn't put it on the mantelpiece in case Simon saw, and knew she was still in touch with him.

No news, she told herself, was good news. But she did realize that Nell would hardly recognize her, so long had it been since they parted. Or since, more accurately, Nell had been wrenched away. Helen prayed every night that God would look after her daughter, wherever she was, though if you asked Helen if she believed in God, she would only have replied cautiously, "I don't know what you mean by God. If you mean the feeling 'there is more to this than meets the eye,' yes, I suppose I do. But that's as far as I'd go."

Not far enough, some would say, to satisfy a jealous and demanding God. In whose image Simon was clearly made, for all his gentle manner.

But, reader, the fact is that Nell was simply not destined for a quiet life. It was always to be like this. Fate would allow her some small pleasant respite, then whirl her up and set her down on an altogether different and not necessarily pleasant path. Good fortune and bad were always, for Nell, to follow close upon each other's heels, and snapping at hers.

When we are small, things *happen* to us; far more than we make happen. We are in no position to control our fate. Events crowd in upon us. And, reader, as it is for us in the beginning, so it is for us in the end, for all our efforts. We will love and be loved or fail in love; live with extremes of fortune, or a steady flow of predictable income: save all our lives or spend all our lives. (Owe 10p when you're ten, and you'll be owing £100 at twenty, and £1,000 at thirty. Credit will come easily—so will anxiety.) Live plagued by accidents, disasters, or almost wholly free of them. Some of us lightning seeks out—so we'd better not play golf in a storm; others can stride the course with impunity. If we want to know our fate we need only look back to our childhood, for as we get older events seem to string themselves out; the pattern is too wide, almost too familiar to be seen: except for the feeling, as the elastic in our skirt breaks and it falls to our knees—that's the bad news—but fortunately where no one can see—that's the good—that this has happened *before:* how well I know this feeling—oh yes, you are right, it has! You have! It will happen again, what's more, many a time before you die. Mr. Right will stride over the horizon yet again, albeit from the lounge of the old folks' home, and turn out to be Mr. Wrong; Mrs. Wrong will burn your toast, and when you've exchanged her on that account for Mrs. Right, Mrs. Right will do the same. It is your fate to have burned toast set always before you.

We can learn virtues by practicing them, of course we can. We can acquire the habits of courage, even the most timorous of us, by making the effort required to be brave; of good temper, by not succumbing to our irritation; of saving the face of others, by determinedly losing our own; of patience, by learning to bow the head to fate; of shuffling the cards, and not blaming others, and scraping the toast, and biting back pride, and asking Mrs. Wrong to forgive us, and practicing generosity, not meanness, when it comes to her alimony. But the fate, the underlying pattern of fate, the feeling tone (you could almost call it) of our lives, remains the same. So don't struggle too much. Accept your fate, make the most of the cards you are dealt. That's all you can do.

Blame it on the stars, if that's your fancy. Blame it on Nell's Mars being in close conjunction with her natal Sun. Or blame it on her previous life, if that suits you as an explanation. She must have done some very good and some very bad things indeed. Blame it on the clash of internal genes—the uneasy mix of Clifford's and Helen's blood. Or just look at the situation and say: well, landed up with a pair of nutters like the de Troites, something was bound to happen!

And it certainly did. The story went like this:

The Marquise, in her desperate attempt to win back her youth and loveliness—not just out of vanity, but the better to make a feasible mother for little Nell—concocted a Black Mass involving pentagrams, fire, bat's blood (far more difficult than lamb's blood to obtain, as you can imagine) and comfrey root. The Marquis sighed but dressed up as required in black and silver and Marthe groaned "Not again!" and agreed to swing the censor, in which mysterious aromatic herbs burned on glowing charcoal. (The sum of the ages of these three totaled well over two hundred; one cannot, I suppose, *blame* people who explore all possible avenues for regaining their lost youth, though one may certainly accuse them of folly!) The ceremony was to start at the stroke of midnight in the Great Hall of the old château.

Little Nell slept peacefully, and unaware of anything untoward, in her tower room. Outside owls hooted and the wind moaned and black thunderclouds seemed to mass and swirl above the château's towers, though I imagine, and certainly hope, that this was more due to atmospheric conditions than the actual summoning up of the devil.

It was though, and I must say it, a particularly spooky night. Not even a Spielberg team could do justice to it. The midnight trees tossed their heads about wildly as if longing to uproot and be off, anywhere but here, and the château cats hid under whatever ancient, wormy, cobwebby furniture they could find, and their yellow devil's eyes were everywhere.

Nell slept! She always did. That is the great benefit of having a kind heart. Her little head would touch the pillow, her blue eyes close, her breath come evenly and sweetly until morning, when she would stir, sigh, and shoot up wide awake, with that excited, looking-forward animation which only the very young and happy know. And why should she not be happy? There was no one to point out how ugly and peculiar—not to mention ancient—her supposed parents were, no one to frown and raise their eyebrows at the dust and dirt. Nell took Milord and Milady and the château as she found them and, being of a kind and cheerful nature, found them very well indeed.

"Had been" happy, I say, for Nell's stay at the château was to come to an abrupt and terrifying end, that very night.

From the little round room at the top of the West Tower—Nell slept in the East—there flew on stormy nights a kite at the end of a long, supple, metal-bound string. Attached to the end of this contraption was a two-foot-long wax model of the Marquise, lying in a bed of hay. The kite was supposed to draw down lightning—and, with it, life, energy, youth and so forth—into the Marquise. (If it worked no doubt she would have done the same for her husband, and his image in wax would presently have lain there waiting too. She wasn't mean. She loved her husband. Reader, I don't like writing about this kind of thing—it makes me feel, as the children say, quite "spooked" myself.) Let us hurry on, but not before mentioning that Benjamin Franklin, the American philosopher and scientist, flew just such a kite, and did indeed succeed in drawing down electricity, with uncomfortable consequences to himself, being at the end of the metal string; well, he didn't *know,* did he? After that, he did. Some things the human race learns. Just a few.

At half past midnight, when the invocations and chantings and prostrations down below were well underway, lightning streaked down the wire, melted the model of the Marquise right away, and started a fire in the hay. No one noticed. Of course not. Neither the Marquise, the Marquis, or Marthe. They were too absorbed in that fire of youth and passion which the devil was supposed to be creating within those fragile, feeble rib cages—or actually was! I begin to think perhaps the devil *did* brush very near that night, fanned his hideous leathery wings as close as can be to Nell's sleeping cheek. The fire in the West Tower ran like a host of little burning insects which, once they'd eaten the hay, swarmed over the floorboards and down the cracks into the room below, where they ate what they could, grew bigger and stronger, and wanted more! Whoosh! How dry and tindery the château was!

And in another country, a hundred miles away, Nell's mother, Helen, stirred and moaned in her sleep; and Nell's father in another bed, woke, and stretched out his hand for comfort to his partner Elise—he who seldom seemed to need comfort, or reassurance, or help of any kind. I tell you, it was a strange night.

Nell slept in the East Tower. The fire started in the West Tower, crept downward, fanned by the high winds (and the devil's wings, if you asked the local populace, and who's to say they were wrong! If you invoke the devil, something nasty turns up, of that you can be sure, and will do you no good, no matter how strong and wise and able to control you think you are!) and entered the Great Hall, in mid–Black Mass, as a rushing wall of flame. The Marquise, nutty to the last, stepped not away from it but toward it, thinking the pouring waves of flame were some kind of magic fountain of youth: that she would walk through it and emerge immortal and possessed by an unearthly beauty which would bind all men to her forever, and so forth:

and not only that, she'd be able to take Nell down to the village school without remark. She did not, of course, emerge from the flames at all, but was utterly consumed. The Marquis, who loved his wife as she was and did not care one whit about her failure to be eternally young and beautiful, ran after her to drag her back from her insane purpose, but tripped over his wizard gowns and fell: and the little fiery, diabolical insects ran in their hordes over the voluminous folds of dusty fabric and he too died. I do not think either suffered much. I think the strength of their emotions saved them from much physical pain; or even fear of death. She was so convinced of resurrection; he so intent on saving her! They were not, as I say, wicked people; they did not wish to go quietly into the evening of their old age, that was all—and they had their wish, and it consumed them.

Marthe, however, the third party to their diabolic escapade, their disastrous Black Mass, took to her heels at the sight of the fire; she was out the door in a flash. She was a heavy woman in her early eighties, but could move fast enough in an emergency. And this certainly was an emergency like no other. The wooden floor of the circular staircase which led up to Nell's room was smouldering as Marthe pounded up it to rescue the child: from every part of the château roof great flames leaped as if to touch the sky, and the wind roared and howled around.

Nell woke to find herself roughly bundled up and over Marthe's shoulder and down the stairs: bounce, bounce, and wherever she looked there was fire, and Marthe's poor bare feet (the Marquise—God rest her soul—insisted on no shoes when invoking the devil) trod amongst cinders, and as she ran she shrieked *"Le diable! Le diable!"* thus frightening poor Nell more than anything else. No one wants to think the devil is at their heels! Marthe, of course, believed exactly that. It was hardly surprising that she did. She was guilty. Her master and mistress had been punished, killed. She would be next!

Marthe made for the little Deux Chevaux parked in the courtyard and, although—for various reasons which I shan't delay us by going into now—it was at least forty years since she had actually driven a car, she pushed Nell into the back, jumped into the driver's seat, and with a grinding of gears that in other circumstances would have been a source of conversation for days, days, set off out of the inferno. She made for the main road, away from the village, not toward it. She was not looking for rescue; she was trying to put as great a distance as possible between the burning château and herself. But you can't, of course, escape the devil that easily!

Now you remember, reader, that while Nell was living at the château the de Troites had kept her existence secret; she was theirs illegally, a black-market child, and while other secretive adoptive parents can announce themselves boldly as aunts and uncles, or grandparents, or go away for a couple of years and return with an apparently natural child, the de Troites had done nothing so sensible. A few of the villagers had caught a glimpse of a child, but kept it to themselves. So enchanting a small girl, with her delicate fairy limbs and wide haunting eyes, might well be some kind of phantom, and gone before you realized she was there! A pity to drive such a creature away. Besides, you know how rural people are—they keep themselves to themselves, and believe that least said is soonest mended!

The charred bodies of the de Troites were found in the debris of the château. Marthe had vanished without trace, but her bedroom, it was known, had been in the West Tower (where the fire had started) and that had collapsed in upon itself. No one doubted but that her poor old bones were somewhere there; but she had no surviving family and few friends and no one looked. A mention of her, the faithful *serviteuse,* was made on the de Troite "here lies" headstone, and decency thus served. And as for little Nell—no one looked for her remains because no one was certain she had ever been there. She had vanished from the region forever.

It was at about this time, some two years and a few months after ZOE 05 cracked and crashed, when all the insurance money and required compensation had finally been paid out, including an extra two million pounds to Mrs. Blotton, over and above the normal payment of forty thousand pounds for her husband's loss (negligence on the airline's part having been proved), a strange thing happened. ZARA Airlines had a phone call from a lady who kept a fashion house in Paris. She said there was something she felt in duty bound to report. She had been so busy setting up a new business, it had taken her until now to get in touch. Anyway, it was probably nothing. Arthur Hockney, summoned, flew in from New York at once to interview this Madame Ravisseur, and found her to be a most charming and elegant lady in her middle years, if laggardly in this way and that. He stood for a good five minutes at her front door until she got around to answering it. Well, it was in character. Madame Ravisseur, for her part, faced by so distinguished and handsome a black American, was glad of this prompt attention from ZARA Airlines, and spoke freely and volubly in the English she had recently learned. She had, she said, left the seaside town of Lauzerk-sur-Manche forever on the very day that ZOE 05 crashed. She had, after many years, finally gathered her courage together to sell her little *charcuterie,* leave her husband and, rather late in life, set out into the world to make her fortune. Better late than never. It was her motto. She had boarded the Paris bus perhaps an hour and a half after the aircraft came down—they had in fact been delayed along the road by the onrush of emergency vehicles. A very strange pair boarded the bus at the first stop, she said—an ugly, bad-tempered man who smoked too much, and a charming little girl, with curly blonde hair, wide eyes, and rosebud mouth. Now Madame Ravisseur knew her quiet, tiny village very well, and these strangers seemed simply to have dropped from the sky. Where had they come from? The little girl had become distressed on the journey, wanting to *faire pipi;* she, Madame Ravisseur, had stopped the bus and helped the child, and found her shoes sopping wet and chafing, *"la pauvre petite,"* and her socks sandy. The man's trousers, she had then noticed, were wet, and clinging below the knee, as if he had been wading in the sea. Madame had not been able to get out of her head the idea that the man and the child had indeed dropped from the sky, that they were something to do with the aircrash, though what and why she couldn't tell.

"You describe him as a smoker," said Arthur. "Are you sure?"

"Two packets of Gauloises nonstop, and looking around for more! Oh yes, he was a smoker. I did not think he was the father of the little girl—she coughed too much when he came near. His own child would have been accustomed to it. And when he got off the bus—that was in the Rue Victor Hugo, he went straight into a *tabac.* I watched."

"You should have been a detective," observed Arthur Hockney. He liked her strong Gallic looks, the slow surety of her movements. She made him coffee and it took her half an hour to get it together, but when it came it was excellent.

"You've taken some considerable time to come forward with this information," he did remark.

"Time passes so quickly when you're busy," she said, vaguely enough. And indeed, she seemed to have some interior clock which moved at an altogether different pace from that of other people.

He spent a slow, languorous, intensely pleasurable night with Madame Ravisseur, I'm sorry to say. But then, as Simon found, Helen had eyes only for her baby, and unrequited love is long and painful and needs relief; and yes, Arthur Hockney was indeed in love with Helen. Her Christmas card, crossing with his, had made his breath catch and bring him to this realization. In love with a vague, pale, unhappy Englishwoman! It hardly made sense, but there it was. He meant to do nothing about it. Regard it like an illness, or the pain in a broken leg, which presently would pass. Put up with it, and wait till it was gone, withered away for lack of attention. But somehow, in the meantime, it made him more responsive to other women, more readily impressed; more, he feared, alive.

The *tabac* in the Rue Victor Hugo pointed Arthur Hockney's way to a particular café: here money changed hands and what amounted to a guided tour of certain brothels in the Algerian quarter, from which, or so his contacts told him, many deals in human lives were made. It served as an international clearinghouse for the selling of men, women and children into domestic or sexual slavery, and for the new, growing, less dangerous but highly profitable black market in children for adoption. Kidnapped or legitimately orphaned (their phrase) children were smuggled out of the Third World and sold from dealer to dealer, fetching higher prices as they went, until finally reaching the punter. The two markets—for slaves and for children—are kept apart, but sometimes overlap. This, of course, had always been Arthur's fear for little Nell. He was the more relieved when, this time, the trail led him to Maria, the only employee of this house of illest fame to have survived the many staff turnovers (not to mention deaths) since ZOE 05 crashed.

Maria sat and sighed and curled her long dark hair around her finger. She had a childish air, he thought.

"I am a very respectable woman," she said. "I am only doing this for a little, until I can find a proper job."

"Of course," he said.

"And I am doing a kindness to my clients," she said, "and saving their wives from much distress."

"I know," he said gently.

"So long as you understand. I have too kind a heart, that is my trouble. When the little English girl came I took good care of her. I made sure she saw nothing she should not see."

"I thank you, on her parents' behalf."

"Oh, she had parents? Usually the parents are dead. What is to become of these children if no one looks after them?"

"What indeed?"

"The little English girl was fortunate. Sometimes the life is not so nice, especially for a child. She went to new parents in Cherbourg."

"Cherbourg? You are sure?"

"No. The name just came into my head. I have always liked Cherbourg. I went there when I was a child, with my mama."

"Please try and remember. It's important."

"Cherbourg. I am convinced of it."

"The name of her parents?"

"How could I remember a thing like that? You must understand I live a very eventful life. I see so many people."

"Please try."

"I remember thinking, yes, she was very lucky. I know. She went to a Milord and a Milady. If only that had been my fortune! I too was adopted. Everyone laughed."

"Why did they laugh?"

"Perhaps the Milord and the Milady were funny. I am becoming very tired. Perhaps we should go to my room?"

"Not yet."

No, there had been nothing special about the man who brought the child in. No, she couldn't remember if he smoked. Well, it was a long time ago. Many men had passed through her bed since, how could she remember this one? But she remembered the child. She remembered her good turn, in particular. Odd, things had turned out well for her since.

"What good turn was that?" Arthur asked. He had had to buy time with the girl. She had a broad face and strong arms, a lot of body hair and a strong, not unpleasant, smell. She busied herself with tweezers, plucking hair from her legs. She was the sort of woman who liked to make good use of her time. She should have had six children and lived in a farmhouse, Arthur thought. (But that's the kind of thing men do wish for women, without considering just how hard and boring the domestic life can be.)

The little girl had had a jewel on a chain in her possession, Maria said. It was obvious she came from a good home; you could tell, the way you could with kittens; she had been loved and cherished; she was not the scum of the earth which usually turned up, already gray-faced and squinty-eyed from hard times and bad luck. It had made her cry, just to think of it: *la pauvre petite!* So instead of simply purloining the emerald as anyone sensible would have done, she made it safe and handed it back and told her to look after it. Whoever knew, perhaps it would lead the child back one day to her true family? Truth was stranger than fiction.

"Made it safe? In what way?"

Maria told Arthur about the cheap tin teddy bear with the head which unscrewed, in which she'd put the pendant.

"I've heard about those," said Arthur. "But so have all the customs officers in the world. In what way did things turn out well afterwards?"

She'd finished the left leg. She stretched it and admired its smoothness, and moved on to the right. They were good, strong legs. She said her pimp had been murdered the next day, and she was glad; he'd been a violent, nasty man. Now she was with another, who really cared for her. (She sounded, he thought, like an actress talking about her agent.) If Arthur wanted more than talk, she was perfectly willing. He wouldn't have to pay extra. Just talk always felt like cheating to her but it was surprising how many men wanted to do it. Arthur declined the offer, with thanks. He paid her an extra hundred francs, so that her good deed would at least be rewarded in this life. He was not sure how she would fare in the next.

Arthur next went to Geneva and made an appointment to see Clifford. He did not think the interview would be easy. Nor was it. Leonardo's Geneva office overlooked the lake. It had one of the more spectacular views Europe offered, and also one of the highest rents. Clifford, at this busy time, did not like to waste his time on anyone but millionaires; a black insurance-fraud investigator could bring him no profit, only bad memories. ZARA Airlines had recently paid out £40,000 on Nell's life, which had been split between himself and Helen. Helen had given her share of the money to a charity: more fool her. He told himself it was because she felt guilty. If she had not argued so about the access arrangements, he would not have had to fly the child out in secret and she'd be alive today. Helen's fault! Like the divorce, like his unhappiness, like everything! With Helen so much to blame, these days he got on very well with his mother. There had been a time when all his dissatisfactions had been laid at the maternal door, but these were forgotten now, and he was a frequent weekend visitor at Dannemore Court, his parents' place in Sussex. Leonardo's paid for his frequent flights. The check-in girl at Swissair could be relied upon to provide him with the best possible seat. He had had a short affair with one of the senior girls—painful for her, since she fell in love—but sufficiently well-managed by Clifford that she continued to hope, rather than lapse into hate. It is not a good thing to be hated by the check-in girl of an airline on which you frequently travel. They have friends everywhere.

"It's lovely to have you here, darling," said Cynthia. "But isn't it terribly expensive? All this to-ing and fro-ing."

"Leonardo's pays," said Clifford.

"Do they know it pays?" asked Otto.

"It gets swallowed up," said Clifford. Otto sighed. It seemed to him, since Nell's death, that everything good had gotten swallowed up, in a sea of greed, opportunism and self-interest. The superpowers aimed their hideous weapons at one another and beneath this arch of evil the human race gamboled and played. True, the Nazis no longer stalked the capitals of Europe, but the men he had worked for turned out to be traitors, or worse. Now Nell was gone, and with her the future he had once, by sacrifice, hoped to redeem.

"Father seems low," said Clifford to Cynthia.

"He is," said Cynthia. "It's very tiring." She had written a kind letter to Helen, almost a letter of apology, at the time of the ZOE 05 disaster, and had received one back, short but courteous, acknowledging Cynthia's loss along with her own. Had not Nell stayed for some months at Dannemore Court, in the nursery which had once been Clifford's? Did she not too, the paternal grandmother, feel the loss? Should it not be "the death"? Helen had not referred to Nell's death, only to her loss. It had struck Cynthia as a little strange, but she had not mentioned it to Clifford, for fear of seeing his brow darken and his eyes dull, and he too descend once again into depression. Depression, of course, as Cynthia knew, is anger unrecognized and undeclared. Clifford railed against Helen when he should better have railed against Cynthia; Otto railed against Clifford (in private), but both father and son were angry with fate; with the world. Nell's death had triggered a sullen melancholy, which the son was better able to throw off than the father. Cynthia diverted herself with an animating affair with an opera singer from, of all places, Cairo, and waited for things to get better. Things did, in her experience.

But that's by the by. In the meantime Clifford had no wish to be reminded of Nell. ZARA Airlines had paid up, so why was Arthur Hockney persecuting him?

Arthur knew better than to suggest to Clifford that he had reason to believe his daughter was alive. He said merely it had come to ZARA Airlines' attention that perhaps Mr. Blotton, who had accompanied the child, had not been on the aircraft at the time of the crash, but had sent a delegate in his place.

"Unlikely," said Clifford, "since I was going to pay him his second half of the fee when he handed the child over. I would hardly have paid it to anyone but him, now would I? These are stupid questions, Mr. Hockney, on a painful theme, and you have no business raising them."

"Did Mr. Blotton smoke?" Arthur asked. Clifford seemed taken aback.

"How can I remember a detail like that, Mr. Hockney? I'm a busy man. You may very well be able to give me a blow-by-blow account of the events of a day more than two years ago—but I certainly can't. Memories of the past are for those who have no experience in the present. In other words, for those who live dull lives. Good day, Mr. Hockney."

"Did he smoke?" persisted Arthur. "It's important."

"Important to you, perhaps. Not to me. But yes, Blotton smoked. He smelled like an old ashtray. I imagine his death on ZOE 05 saved him from a lingering death by lung cancer."

And Arthur was dismissed. This was the man that Helen loved, who had lain cozily by her side and then, as it were, pushed her out of bed. All the same, he could not wholly dislike Clifford. Like some wounded, flailing animal, he crashed about in the undergrowth to let you know he was coming—he did not pretend to be nice. An un-English trait. Arthur toyed with the idea of spending a couple of hundred thousand dollars on, say, one of Leonardo's newly-purchased Magrittes, just to take Clifford aback, to regain face, but sensibly controlled himself. The painting would have been bought for the wrong motives. It would not bring pleasure, it would hang year in year out in a Manhattan apartment—the only wall-space he owned and which he scarcely ever visited—no, it was absurd. Let his enormous salary, his ten percent commission on money saved for clients, which ran into millions, mount undisturbed in the bank.

Let me explain something to you, reader. Arthur Hockney was an orphan, and felt it. Now you may think: but he's a grown man, strong, effective, wealthy, why should this fact affect him so? Sooner or later most of us will be orphans, people without parents. But because of the circumstances of his parents' death,

Arthur felt he had no business to be alive—which was perhaps why his work was so closely connected with death, in all its most dramatic forms, and he had a bad conscience—though I myself don't think he had cause for one. Harry and Martha Hockney had come North in the twenties, shipped from the South to work in the Chicago stockyards, had become politicized in the union struggles at that terrible time, learned to speak on platforms about class, race and union matters; Arthur, as a child, had lived mostly in a Civil Rights cortège. Until one day, when he was seventeen, his parents' car had been driven off the road—by accident, it was said, but the Civil Rights people knew better—and his parents killed. Arthur had quarreled with his parents that day and refused to go with them. He had a date with a girl, he said. Now that is a hard kind of thing to recover from, and my own view is he never quite did. The Civil Rights people recognized his trauma, consoled him, treated him with every kindness, paid for his college education. I think they saw in Arthur a future leader, the man who would follow in Martin Luther King, Jr.'s footsteps. But Arthur knew he did not have the religious or political convictions his people needed. He did not join them on their marches, on their platforms, and they did not grudge him his freedom or resent his decision. We did all this, they said, for your parents' sake. Think no more of it. But Arthur did, of course, how could he not? Now he saw himself as a man without race, country or roots; orphaned in every sense of the word. He traveled the world in an attempt to elude his conscience, and sometimes, as he stared at the mangled bodies of the dead, and rejoiced in his own strength and health and good fortune, thought he had managed. One day, he thought, when I find a political or human movement I can totally agree with, they shall have all my money. In the meantime, let it stay in the bank and earn interest.

Well now, it was apparent to Arthur that Mrs. Blotton had lied, for reasons of her own. Blotton it was who had fallen out of the sky, and lived. Arthur went back to Helen, in London, to inquire about the emerald pendant. Or shall we rather say, reader, that he went back to Helen in London, *and* inquired about the emerald pendant. Perhaps he should not have done so; not raised Helen's hopes yet again; but gone straight to Cherbourg in search of Nell, because by the time he did so it was too late—but there, that's love.

He visited her at the Muswell Hill house. She asked him over, her voice warm. Simon was away. He was in Helsinki, attending a Summit Conference. She did not add that Janice Best was covering the same Conference. Why should she? She scarcely found it of interest herself. The weather was warm, summer had suddenly dawned out of a chilly spring. He found her sitting in the garden, on a rug, while baby Edward, a fine, stocky, cheerful child, practiced his new walking technique. She was wearing a kind of cream cotton wraparound dress. Her legs were bare, her pretty feet were in sandals, her brown hair tossed and gleamed in the sun. It was cut short and was very curly. But for all her appearance of ease and good nature, he thought she was strained, and thin, and her "Well, well?" too nervous, too quick.

"What news? Is there any news?"

He asked her about the pendant. An emerald, perhaps? Had Nell had such a thing? If not necessarily an emerald, something recognizably precious?

"Nell didn't wear jewels," said Helen, shocked. But something occurred to her and she went upstairs to examine her jewel-box and came down weeping—yes, the pendant was gone. It should have been there in the box. It wasn't. She had never looked at it since before, before—before the aircrash, she meant, but couldn't say it. She hated it really. Clifford had wanted it back, but had given it to her with such love—yes, it was perfectly possible for Nell to have taken it, but why should she have? She'd been told not to touch the box, there were treasures inside—she stopped.

"She said, I remember she said, that last morning, could she take a treasure to school for showing—you know what they do—but I was busy—" and Helen wept and wept again, at the failure of mother-love, to get a child to nursery school properly, on the very day you lose her—or indeed, the greater failure of saving her from harm. And perhaps also because now she was frightened; if Nell was indeed alive, what sort of life was it that she had? Anxiety had to take the place of grief, response of nonresponse. And anxiety is just about the most painful emotion a parent can have about a child, enough, sometimes, to make you wish the child had never been born, than do this to you now, make you feel like this.

Helen wept. Arthur thought she would never stop. Grief for the loss of Nell, for her own childhood, for her marriage to Clifford, for Simon, for the humiliation rendered her by Janice Best, for the wretchedness of everything—all was unlocked and released on that afternoon, as Helen wept and little Edward, without his accustomed audience, fell asleep on the lawn, and was nearly, nearly stung by a wasp on his lip—though no one but you and me, reader, will ever know that!

ALL CHANGE!

And Nell? Where was Nell while her mother wept and her little half-brother slept? I'll tell you. She was sitting mute and puzzled in the interview room of an assessment center for disturbed children on the edge of Hackney marshes, only some twelve miles away. This is how it came about.

Now you might be excused for thinking with Marthe that the devil was after her, having missed his prey the first time. Marthe and the de Troites had certainly done their best, in the course of the black midnight mass, to bring him up from the depths of hell. Or perhaps it was that Marthe was half-mad with shock, guilt and grief, and hadn't driven for a long time, and certainly wasn't used to modern traffic, or how to behave on a Route Nationale—which she now found herself upon.

"Where are we going? What's happening?" little Nell kept asking from the back of the car. She was still in her nightie. Her head was swimming with shock and fright. It was raining. Headlights blurred in front of Marthe's rheumy old eyes, her gnarled hands gripped the wheel, and she steered rather than drove, her foot down hard on the accelerator, not that that made much difference to anything. The Deux Chevaux had seen many, many better days. And if the accelerator hardly worked, neither did the brakes, which evened things up. Marthe's breathing was more like snoring than anything else, but Nell was used to that.

"Please, let's stop!" begged Nell. "I'm so frightened!" But Marthe kept on, and the tires ate up the miles. And still the flames leaped in Marthe's memory, and the sound of the howling which had preceded it echoed in her ears and seemed to be pursuing her. It may, of course, have been merely the sound of the blaring warning horns of other drivers, as they zoomed up to and past the erratically driven, badly lit Deux Chevaux. Who is to say a thing like that?

Presently Marthe stopped the car. She did not draw off the road, or wait for a turnout, she simply stopped. It was now raining hard and the old windshield-wipers could not keep proper pace. Marthe could not see, she could not go on. She sat and wept for her old exhausted aching bones, for the terror in her mind, for her fear of hellfire, for the poor child in the back of the car. Nell got out and stood by the side of the road in the rain. (She wore her tin teddy bear on a chain around her neck. She always slept with it, and the Marquise had always tried gently to dissuade her from so doing, and had always failed.) The child felt she had to go for help, for poor weeping Marthe, somewhere, somehow, but she was only just six and scarcely knew what to do. So Nell stood, and her hand went up to the comfort of her teddy bear, as it always did when she was forlorn and bereft.

The first five cars that passed saw the Deux Chevaux in time, through the rain and spray, and swerved and carried on. The sixth car was not so lucky. In it were English holiday-makers, on the road south from Cherbourg. They were all tired; the father, who drove, had been drinking. He thought brandy would keep him alert. It did not. The Deux Chevaux loomed. Too late! Crash, bang, silence! Wreckage strewed across the road. Into the back of this car went, after the disastrous manner of these things, a massive petrol-tanker, traveling far faster than it should. It overturned, it burst; fire leaped across the roadway, engulfing cars coming in the opposite direction. Showers of burning gasoline poured down over the wreckage, cars, bodies, everything. The conflagration was immense; it made headlines all over the world. Ten people died, including Marthe who, though mercifully unconscious at the time, perished as her master and mistress had, by fire. The devil—if you care to look at it like this—having done his intended work, having pursued and caught his victim, and careless of how many others he took out of this world with her, retreated and lay quiet for a time.

And that's how it happened that little Nell was found wandering, when early morning came, by the side of the road. Shock had rendered her almost speechless. She had a few words of

English, and, so far as they could tell, some kind of retrospective amnesia. The wreckage of five cars in all had to be sorted out—three French and two English. How many people had been in which, and why, seventy miles south of Cherbourg on the holiday route, was hard to ascertain. The man from the British Consulate assumed, naturally enough, that the child was from one of the English cars. She called for her mummy, and wept, poor little thing, but was unable to give any information as to her name, or her address, or where she lived. She spoke like a child of three: they thought for a while perhaps she was mentally retarded. Nor did anyone turn up to claim her.

"I fell out of the sky," she said once, almost proudly, when asked for the umpteenth time where and how she came to be where she was, and that, of course, to her examiners made no sense at all. To you, dear reader, of course it does. She had. But they were right about the retrospective amnesia. Nell, mercifully, had lost all memory of the fire at the château, the accident on the road, Marthe, and Milord and Milady. But now she was amongst English-speaking people and, helped by language, she could go back further in her mind and recall a few details of her earlier life.

"I want to see Tuffin," she said.

"Tuffin?"

"Tuffin's my cat." Well, whatever else, she was certainly British.

So it happened that Nell was shipped home to England by courtesy of the British Consulate and the National Society for the Prevention of Cruelty to Children combined, and put for a time in an assessment home for children run by the Inner-London Education Authority. She had become one of the waifs and strays thrown up all too often by our chaotic and multitudinous society. Many children go missing and are never found, and a great tragedy that is—worse perhaps than any. A few are found that no one seems to have missed. And what becomes of a child with no parents to protect her, no family to guide her, lost as she is in the world of the poor, the helpless and the oppressed? We will see!

A BURNT-OUT TRAIL

"A respectable Milord and Milady from Cherbourg" were the seven words which led Arthur Hockney to be sitting, on a hot October day, in the offices of the Superintendent of Police of that very town, checking the records for just such a pair. Wealthy, titled, and childless until a couple of years back—or perhaps moved suddenly into the area? But none such could the Superintendent bring to mind.

"It could hardly be the *famille* de Troite!" he said, running his finger down the electoral roll, and he laughed.

"Why not?" asked Arthur. "If they're rich, if they're titled, as you say they are—?"

"But they're older than Methuselah—and hardly the adopting kind," said the Superintendent.

"Nevertheless—" Arthur was insistent.

"Besides which," said the Superintendent, "they're dead."

"Dead?"

"The château was consumed by fire only a few weeks back. Not to mention Milord and Milady and an elderly servant too. The people around here say the devil did it, sending a lightning bolt from a clear sky. But it's been a long hot summer as you know. Old people are careless, and these ones drank a lot of good red wine. I am a rational man, Monsieur Hockney, and do not believe that satanic intervention is the most likely explanation for the burning down of an almost derelict château and the death of its elderly occupants!"

Arthur refrained from saying that in his experience when it came to strange events, the most likely explanation was seldom the right one, and made a journey to the site where the château had stood.

He found it a peculiarly gloomy place; it had the odd, sad atmosphere that the scene of a tragedy so often does, but something more as well: a sense of menace, of something nasty left unfinished. He shivered. It was strange. He'd felt this before—in places where terrorist bombs had exploded, or bridges had collapsed, or liners run aground with great loss of life—but it was not usually present at the sites of simple domestic tragedy, on the minor scale. Arthur stayed around a little, poking amongst the dust and ash and rubble, and came across a bright length of yellow ribbon, the kind that would tie a child's hair.

"Well, well!" said Arthur, and stopped to pick it up and, as he did so, a ray of sun pierced through the gloomy trees into the clearing where he stood. It had the effect of a smile; motes danced in the air. A butterfly fluttered past. Arthur's spirits lifted. That was all it took. He was sure of two things. That Nell had indeed been here, and that she was still alive. The sun went in, the gloom and sense of menace returned, and Arthur left.

Further inquiries in Paris and Cherbourg led nowhere. Nell had vanished again. He now doubted she would ever be found. He told ZARA Airlines to close their file; if Blotton did reappear to claim his fortune, it would hardly be worth the trouble of reclaiming what was left of it. And no doubt Blotton would meet his comeuppance presently, if he hadn't already. If lung cancer didn't carry him off, no doubt one or the other of his criminal acquaintances would. He moved in very nasty circles indeed.

SURPRISE! SURPRISE!

Reader, do you hate surprises? I do. I like to know what's coming next. The very thought of a surprise birthday party sends shivers up my spine. I'm bound to be wearing my oldest dress and not have washed my hair for a week. Clifford, on his forty-first birthday, had a surprise telephone call from Angie Wellbrook, and didn't like that one bit. The phone call wasn't a nice surprise for Elise O'Malley, either. She was the pretty young Irish novelist currently keeping Clifford company, and she really thought—rash thing!—she had him nailed. That is to say, Clifford kept talking about how he'd like to have children, and Elise took that to mean he saw her as their mother—which surely must entail marriage. Elise had given up a literary career in Dublin to be with Clifford in Geneva.

Another surprise for Clifford that very day was finding a gray hair in the thick blond thatch which was in those days his trademark—his hair is completely white today, of course, though still thick (and he is, to my mind, no less attractive now than then. But then we all get older, pace by pace, including me). As the decades turned from the sixties to the seventies, Clifford had approached and passed forty and was frightened, and fighting off the inevitability of being no longer young (which was of course why he kept talking about children. Men will have their immortality, one way or another), and the single gray hair, wiry, tough and lifeless as it was, did nothing to help. And then the phone call from Angie.

Clifford and Elise were in bed; Clifford reached out a muscular hand for the receiver. He had a deep reddish-brown suntan and very thick fair hair on his arms. Extraordinary! Just to look at them made Elise shivery with excitement and a sense of sin. The suntan was so jet-setty and civilized: the hair so primitive! Elise was a Catholic; it was ages since she'd been to confession, let alone written a novel. She'd started one recently—about love—and shown it to Clifford, but he'd just laughed and said, "I don't really think so, Elise! Stick to what you know." So she'd put it to one side. Elise insisted on having pure white cotton sheets on their bed. They made her feel less sinful. And besides, her own vivid red hair and bright blue eyes looked well against white; making her, she thought, seem somehow vulnerable and above all *marriageable.* Enough about Elise, reader. You get the picture. The girl's both an innocent and an idiot.

This is what Angie had to say on the phone to Clifford.

"Darling, Daddy's dead. Yes, I am very upset. Though lately he'd been getting quite senile. I am now the majority shareholder in Leonardo's."

"Angie, sweetheart," said Clifford, cautiously, "I don't think that can be quite true."

"It is, darling," said Angie, "because I've bought out old Larry Patt's shares, and Sylvester Steinberg's. You know I've been with Sylvester for the last couple of years?"

"I had heard something of the kind." He had indeed heard about it, and had been both surprised and relieved. Sylvester Steinberg was one of those art critics who, by judicious use of the art journals and learned essays on this painter and that, manipulate the art market. He functioned mostly from New York. Such people work very simply, if discreetly. They buy a canvas by an unknown painter for, say, two hundred pounds, and by the end of the year have created, through their criticism, such an interest in and furor about that particular painter's work that any single example will fetch at least two thousand pounds. And five years later twenty thousand pounds. And so on. Lucky old painter, you might think—except not, in truth. If he (or rarely, she) ended up with twenty-five percent of what his paintings are sold for, first time around, he's lucky. And of course whenever it changes hands after that, he gets nothing. This was one of the reasons Helen's father, John Lally, was in such a state of enduring fury about Clifford Wexford. Moreover, Clifford was not above manipulating the market himself. Eight major Lallys had gone back into Leonardo's London vaults, waiting for the day they'd fetch a fortune. They did no good on Clifford's Geneva walls—the Swiss simply hated them, as did the kind of rich expatriate who turned up in the gallery there. They liked names they knew—from Rembrandt to Picasso, and major stops in between. Not minor, or later.

I must hasten to say in Clifford's defense that at least his own taste is genuine, and not dependent upon monetary value. He *knows* when a painting is good. And even in the Art World, excellence somehow survives, and rises to the surface, above all the murky scum of wheeling and dealing. Nevertheless, John Lally wanted his paintings on *walls,* not in bank vaults. He wanted them looked at. He had long ago given up hope of making money from them! Bitter! If only creativity and money could be separated. But it can't, if only because each artist—be he (she) painter, writer, poet, composer—anyone who makes something where nothing was before, provides occupation and profit for so many others. Just as the criminal supports on his angry shoulders a whole army of policemen, sociologists, magistrates, governors, jailers, prison officials, journalists, commentators, reform societies, Ministers of State and so on—all dependent upon his ability to perform a criminal act—so does each act of artistic creation support publishers, critics, libraries, galleries, theaters, concert halls, actors, printers, framers, musicians, ushers, janitors, academics, arts councils, the organizers of international cultural exchanges, art administrators, Ministers of the Arts and so forth—and the weight can seem excessive, the rewards astonishingly little, and society's expectation that the artist will do it for free (or just enough to keep him alive and still producing) for sheer abstract love of form, beauty, Art, oh Art—while those who are parasitical upon the artist will command high salaries, higher status—oh intolerable, extraordinary! Or so it seemed to John Lally (and so it seems to me, I must confess). But enough of all that art-schmart stuff. Back to Angie's life since last we saw her, and her phone call to Clifford. Now Clifford knew well enough that Angie was a manipulative and dangerous woman, and that a phone call from her meant trouble, but he was bored.

"Are you and Sylvester actually married?" Clifford asked, casually. Elise, in the bed beside him, was tense. Some overheard telephone conversations, you can just tell, are going to change your life and not for the better.

"Darling Clifford," said Angie, "you know I will never marry anyone else but you."

"I'm flattered," said Clifford.

"And you think the same about me," said Angie, "or why aren't you married yourself?"

"I've never met the right woman," he said, working hard at keeping the whole conversation a joke. It wasn't a nice thing for poor Elise to overhear, and worse, looking at Elise lying there, her hair so carefully arranged in its reddish cloud, self-conscious and reproachful both at once, Clifford felt a great surge of irritation with himself and Elise. What was she doing in his bed? Where was Helen? What had happened between him and Helen, those years ago, to have brought him to this? She was the woman who ought to be in the bed, and a proper marital bed at that.

"Clifford," said Angie, "are you still there?"

"Yes."

"I thought you would be," said Angie. "Shall we meet at Claridges on Thursday? Lunch? Or maybe breakfast? I still have the suite there. Remember?"

Clifford did. He also remembered that Angie had always been the bearer of bad news regarding Helen—driving in the wedges which were to split the marriage asunder.

"And how is Helen? Lost to suburbia, I hear. Well, she always was dull."

"I don't know how she is," said Clifford, truthfully. "Why don't you come to Geneva and see me here?"

"Because you're bound to be with some idiot girl who'll get in the way," said Angie. She was wearing a cream silk negligée for the purpose of this phone call. It had cost £799, for reasons known only to the fashion house which contrived it, if not to me. But it did make her feel confident. Wouldn't it you? (It would me.) Perhaps, to a millionairess, the £799 was well spent.

"And besides," said Angie, "now I have all these shares in Leonardo's, I'm awfully busy. It might be sensible to close down the Geneva branch, I think it's seen its day, don't you? You've swamped the market with your boring Old Masters, and Switzerland's awash with them. They're beginning to lose value. And Clifford, all the fun is in contemporary art. You should see what Sylvester gets up to."

"I'd rather not," he said.

Her father was dead. Somehow she felt entitled to have fun, and part of her fun was to make trouble for Clifford. So there he was at Claridges that Thursday, and Elise, weeping, was on her way back to Dublin.

"It's not that I'm tired of you, Elise," Clifford said. "Who could ever be tired of someone so sweet and fresh as you? It's just I think this thing has run its course, don't you?"

CHICKENS HOME TO ROOST!

Those of you who have been paying good attention will have seen how Clifford, in the name of love, deals out misery and disillusion to the women in his life—and though you may feel these women deserve no better, it is certain that Clifford is not happy either. Give him a little of your sympathy! Clifford seems to have gotten caught up in some cosmic game of pass-the-parcel, and the parcel goes around the circle, and at the heart of the parcel is not the little nugget of joy, peace and permanence everyone hopes for, but a vial of very ordinary tears. The music stops, the parcel's yours, there's luscious wrapping-paper everywhere, but somehow nothing, nothing else—and then the music starts again—and Harry whom you love now loves Samantha who loves Peter who loves Harry; you know how it is!—and on the tearful parcel goes.

Clifford was due to see Angie Wellbrook for breakfast on Thursday, at Claridges. That is to say, she proposed a nine-thirty meeting there. It was the fashion in the seventies to have these breakfast-meetings in hotels. It seemed to demonstrate just how busy and *affaire* everyone was—though there was seldom any actual *breakfast,* and the coffee, wrung out of the night staff just as they gave way to Room Service, was usually cold and old. Clifford flew in from Geneva on Wednesday morning and spent Wednesday afternoon at the head office in meetings and on the phone. The situation was much as he feared: Angie was now indubitably powerful as a shareholder, and not prepared to be a sleeping partner but wishing to interfere—actually to question the taste and wisdom of Leonardo's directors. A nuisance! The London gallery had finally achieved a profitable balance between contemporary painters and Old Masters—leaving the mid-period painters—Impressionists, pre-Raphaelites, Surrealists, and so forth—pretty much alone. The wisdom of this policy Angie was thought to be now challenging—not unreasonably, for it was true the mid-period market was increasingly buoyant. But she was also an opponent of Leonardo's practice of mounting enormously prestigious—though not always profitable—public exhibitions. The Board, led by Clifford, felt that any financial loss was more than compensated for in the preservation of Leonardo's image as a semi-public body of irrefutable integrity, and that the exhibitions must stay.

Clifford also had tea with Sir Larry Patt, now living in dusky splendor in the Albany. Yes, Sir Larry Patt had sold his shares to Angie. Why did he ask? Sir Larry had whiskey, not tea, with his cucumber sandwiches. His wife Rowena had left him a year back, for a man half her age.

"I'm sorry," said Clifford.

"I was surprised," said Sir Larry, "as much as sorry. I thought Rowena would look forward to sharing my retirement, but I was wrong. I begin to think I hardly knew her at all. What was your opinion of her?"

"I didn't know her very well," said Clifford.

"That was not what she told me," said Sir Larry Patt. "She was very talkative in the few days before she left!" And that was how Clifford came to understand exactly why Sir Larry Patt had sold his Leonardo's shares to Angie—that is to say to make life as difficult for Clifford as he could, who had spent many a cheerful, youthful afternoon in bed with Lady Rowena.

Clifford finished his cucumber sandwiches and left. Smiles and handshakes were exchanged. A buxom blonde woman in a brilliant red coat with brass buttons came in with a Harrods shopping bag just as Clifford was going, and pecked Sir Larry's cherubic old face. He beamed. She said hello and how are you to Clifford in a voice out of "East Enders," and went to the bedroom. Clifford thought that perhaps Sir Larry had done rather well. Rowena took the blame, Larry ended up with the perks. A familiar enough marital game-play, when divorce is the common objective! Clifford felt used, oddly, and abused, rather than guilty.

Clifford next checked that Sylvester Steinberg was indeed

living with Angie. He checked with Sylvester's ex-boyfriend, Gary, now at Art School.

"Sylvester loves paintings more than he loves any of us," said Gary, sadly and gently. But then he was a sad and gentle person. "The Art World turns him on, not human beings. And Angie's involved in all that, isn't she? If a stag beetle had an Andy Warhol on its walls, Sylvester would love the stag beetle." From which statement Clifford comfirmed what he feared, that though Angie might be living with Sylvester, she was not likely to find emotional or sexual fulfillment in the relationship and so there was not much protection from Angie to be found therein.

Clifford then went home to his little house in Orme Square—an excellent investment, and worth every penny of the live-in couple who had housekept through the years of his absence in Geneva and kept the damp and the robbers out—and wondered what to do with his evening. He would like to take some charming and beautiful woman out to dinner, and impress her with his own charms and beauty, and possibily get to know her better during the course of the night, so that when he met Angie at nine-thirty next morning he would feel even more take-it-or-leave-it than he did already. He knew this was the best stance from which to deal with women, both in emotional or business matters—and the more genuine the feeling the better. They saw through pretense.

Clifford went through his address book, but nothing seemed to satisfy, no one seemed right. Helen's number was in his diary. Every year he copied it out again. He kept up, in the scandal sheets, with the latest details on Simon Cornbrook's affair with hackette Janice Best. He'd told himself that Helen deserved no better. Let her put up with public humiliation—he'd had to, through the divorce. Helen, who through her intransigence had brought about the death of his only child, Nell. Poor little Nell, with her blue eyes full of trust and bright intelligence. Though he could see now that he himself, if only partly, had been in some way responsible. He did not wish to be in the same moral boat as Sir Larry Patt. Helen had loved Nell and not merely wished to own her, to spite him. He could no longer deny it.

He picked up the phone. He dialed. Helen answered, her voice soft and unchanged.

"Hello?"

"It's Clifford. I just wondered if you were free tonight for dinner?"

There was a pause. In that pause Helen turned and consulted Arthur Hockney, but Clifford wasn't to know that.

"I'd love to," said Helen.

IT JUST SO HAPPENED—!

Reader, you know how in real life coincidence happens again and again. Your sister and your son's wife have the same birthday; on the day you meet a long-lost friend, by accident in the street, a letter from that same friend arrives; your boss's wife was born in the house you now live in—that kind of thing! It's against commonly accepted rules for writers to use coincidence in fiction, but I hope you will bear with me, and allow that at the very moment Clifford calls to ask her out to dinner, Helen may very well just happen to be in conversation with Arthur Hockney, whom she so rarely sees, because it's just the kind of thing that would happen, does happen. This story of mine follows real life pretty closely—which is why it may at times seem farfetched. Ask yourself, isn't truth even more unbelievable than fiction? Don't the headlines which greet you every day, in your daily newspaper, speak of the most extraordinary and unlikely events? Don't events cluster in your own life? Doesn't simply nothing happen for ages—and then everything happen all at once, excitingly or terribly, as the case may be? Well, it certainly does in mine, and writers can be no different from readers.

Well, anyway! What an evening for everyone! Picture the scene in Helen's household. It's seven in the evening. Helen has put two-year-old Edward to bed and now finally has time to give Arthur all her attention. He is passing through London. He called Helen from Heathrow; she insisted he come over. Simon is away covering a political convention in Tokyo, and Janice Best is away in Tokyo too. Helen is wearing a cream silk dress, very simple; she settles into a pale green armchair and looks so lovely and so vulnerable that Arthur Hockney all of a sudden feels like one of the criminals it is his life's work to pursue, and understands the temptation to sever someone's brake cables, or poison their drink—that someone being Simon Cornbrook. Anyone, that is, who makes Helen unhappy. What Arthur doesn't understand is that Helen could have Simon back with a snap of her pretty fingers—if Simon goes about with Janice it's in the attempt to regain Helen's loving attention—but she won't, she can't, snap her fingers! Not till Nell is found, until the ghost of the marriage to Clifford is settled. She won't give up. Arthur, for all his intuition, for all his easy way with women, and his kind and cheerful experience of them, is a simple, even innocent man when it comes to matters of the heart, if not of conscience. He sits black and glossy and rather too broad and muscular for the pale green chair he's in (Simon is finely-boned—all heavyweight intellect but lightweight of body—and the whole house reflects it, including the furniture) and listens while Helen says, "I know I shouldn't. I shouldn't even say it, but I still feel Nell is alive. Every Christmas I say to myself, today Nell is four, five, six. I never say 'would have been,' I say 'today she is.' Why is that?"

(The Eastlake Assessment Center in Hackney, by the way, has assigned Nell a birthday. They are six months off in their judgment. Nell is tall for her age, and they have accorded her a birthday on June 1st. They believe she is six years and nine months old. We know her, on this spring evening, to be six years and three months old. A whole half-year wrong. I am sorry to say that all the Center's assessments are pretty much off. They have decided that our Nell, our bright, pretty, lively Nell is E.S.N.—educationally subnormal—but that is not our concern at the moment.)

"Well," says Arthur, imprudently, "I too suspect she isn't dead, but suspicions are not evidence. The important thing for you is to begin to live your life here and now, not as if someday in the future, somehow, when Nell returned, it was going to begin." But Helen just swirls the drink in her hand, and smiles, too politely.

"At least accept that she is lost," he says, "and lost forever, even though she may be alive."

"No!" says Helen, rather in the tone in which Edward says "Won't!" "If you suspect she's alive, you just find her!" And she thought of her father's latest canvases, now worth a sixth of a million each and rising, the ones he kept locked up in his damp woodshed behind the firewood, in case Clifford Wexford or his like got hold of them. Her father would surely part with them, for Nell's sake. "I'll pay anything you like."

"It is nothing to do with money," he says, hurt. "There is just nothing more I can do."

This pale Englishwoman does nothing for the good of the world; he should by rights condemn her. How many thousands of children die each day the world over, either in spite of those who love them, or directly, at the hand of those who don't; or starve because of the state's indifference to their plight? She had nothing to do; why could she not spend her time helping them? But no, all she could do was sit, and be, and consider her own plight, and waste his time, and lie to her husband. By rights he should despise her; he found it painful to discover that in order to love, he did not have to admire. He took it as evidence of his own moral bankruptcy.

"There is nothing more I can do," he repeats.

But she won't have it. She rises and crosses to him and takes his hand and lightly kisses his cheek, and says, "Arthur, please!" using his Christian name, as she so rarely does, and he knows he will do anything for her, even waste his precious time on fruitless pursuits, and that nothing changes, time just passes.

At that moment the phone rings and it's Clifford. Arthur watches Helen, and she does change, as if some new kind of energy now flows with the blood in her veins. It's extraordinary. Her eyes become bright, her cheeks pink, her movements more animated, her voice lighter.

"It's Clifford," she says to Arthur, hand over the phone. "What shall I do? He wants to take me out to dinner." Arthur shakes his head. Her love for Clifford is some kind of fearful drug: the more heady in the short term, the more poisonous in the long.

"Very well," she says to Clifford, taking not the slightest notice of Arthur's disapproval. Of course not. In fact, as she runs through the house, getting ready, she asks him—this dress, that coat, this scent, those shoes, will this suit me? does this look okay?—stopping only from time to time to hug poor Arthur, her thin, white arms actually around him.

"If Clifford and I could be friends, just friends—that's all—"

But of course that isn't what she wants, and both of them know it.

"Arthur," she says, "you will baby-sit, won't you? I've no one else. And I'll be back by eleven at the latest. I promise!"

BEING LOVELY

Reader, Angie Wellbrook had spent that day preparing herself for her next day's breakfast business-meeting with Clifford. She went to Harrods Hair and Beauty Salon and spent a great deal of time and money there. She upset a lot of people, as was her custom. She accused the beautician of not knowing her business, and the girl who waxed her legs of hurting her on purpose. (It is almost impossible to pull hairs by the thousand out of legs without hurting *at all,* and Angie's leg hairs were dark, plentiful and tough.) She upset Eve—who did her nails, and must surely be the best manicurist in London, and never sneers at even the most unkempt hands and the most broken nails and who can keep her cool when faced by the rudest and most demanding of clients—by blaming her for breaking an already cracked nail. Angie had *very* long fingernails, of the blood-red clawed kind, the sort which it is tempting to believe only women without children have, or those who have other women to do their housework. (Though this may be wishful thinking—more likely it's just that they have very, very tough nails and always wear gloves.)

Angie wanted children. That is to say, she wanted Clifford's children. Angie wanted to found a dynasty; and here she was, closer to forty than to thirty, and nothing had happened yet! No wonder she was so cross in Harrods, but the staff there wasn't to know the reason, and mightn't have been all that sympathetic if they had. The fewer little Angies around, they might well have felt, the better. In the hair salon she made Phoebe comb out her hair *four* times, and she still didn't like the result—that is to say, Angie wanted her hair full and frothy (absurd considering her plain, businesslike face) and Philip wanted it simple to the point of severity. But Angie would have her own way and, by the time she had it, Philip's next client had been waiting half an hour. Nor would Angie pay extra—oh no!

Now the client Angie kept waiting was none other than Sir Larry Patt's new blonde young friend Dorothy, the one who was consoling Sir Larry in the months after the sudden, blazing departure of Rowena his wife. Her leaving, as you may remember, was accompanied by startling revelations on her part as to her many and persistent infidelities through the years of marriage. (Reader, never believe in the discretion of your partner. If there is anything to be disclosed, sooner or later it will be disclosed, though it may take years; in the course of passion, or remorse, or rage, or whatever, or even just for dramatic effect, the truth will be spoken. With any luck, of course, it won't be believed. But said it will be!) Larry Patt did believe Rowena when she told him about her affair with Clifford. And the knowledge of it, I may say, relieved him of guilt about Dorothy, whom he'd been seeing on and off for years, long, long before Rowena and Clifford had held eyes across a fashionable dinner-table. Dorothy had been a conductress on London Transport; she was one of those pretty, lively, energetic young things who like to help old-fashioned gentlemen up and down the stairs on the route from Chiswick through Knightsbridge to Piccadilly. Dorothy was pleased enough now to give up work, leave her aged father to her brother to look after, and move into the Albany flat with Sir Larry and spend her days shopping and trying to lose the muscles in the back of her legs. Sir Larry was forty years older than she, but who was counting?

Dorothy was nice as pie to Philip in Harrods Hair and Beauty Salon that day, even though he kept her waiting a full half-hour. Angie of course did not recognize Dorothy as they passed each other—how could she? It was just one of those coincidences you and I know about, reader, in the course of this story, which our protagonists do not. Angie was wearing a white mink coat. Not the same one as before, of course. She'd sold that. (She hadn't given it away, of course, to someone poor and cold. No. The rich stay rich because they're mean.) Dorothy had a really nice hairdo, however, and was in and out of the salon in twenty minutes, and Angie was still wrangling away at the desk—by now refusing to pay anything at all and even threatening to sue Eve for damages to her nails—some time after Dorothy had paid and left. In Angie's defense, she was nervous about the next day's meeting with Clifford. I mention this matter of Angie and Dorothy crossing paths as a demonstration of how all our lives interlink. Angie had slept with Clifford who'd slept with Rowena who'd slept with Sir Larry Patt (just) who was with Dorothy, who if you ask me was the pleasantest-natured of them all, and at least knew what it was to work for a living. Heaven knows just how the girl in the bakery where you buy your doughnuts may be linked to you. Or come to that, the local Master of Foxhounds.

That night Angie dined with Sylvester, her halfhearted, live-in, art-critic lover, and thought what a lugubrious fellow he was, and wondered why he didn't own up and just go off with their handsome young waiter, instead of trying so hard not to be seen looking at him. Angie would certainly not miss Sylvester in her bed. Sometimes he and she discussed marriage—they got on well together, had the same interests and preoccupations; it suited them to share their houses in various parts of the world, since thus they could halve the insurance on their personal art collections, and they liked to have their orange juice and black coffee together in the mornings, and get excited about art prices. He escorted her here, and she escorted him there, thus saving the other's face. They were invited out as a couple twice as often as each would be invited out singly, and both liked outings. And they entertained together—the private patrons and critical *cognoscenti* of the Art World and enjoyed that—but more? No. (Though, reader, would *you* not settle for that? I think I very well might, if I moved in such circles—forget the girl in the bakery, forget the Master of Foxhounds. It's who you have breakfast with that counts.)

"You look wonderful!" said Sylvester to Angie, and so one should hope. She'd paid Harrods £27 in the end, but the proper bill, including the streaking of her hair, electrolysis and a new wonder facial, had come to £147 and £147 can make quite a difference to a woman's appearance, even at today's prices. And we're talking about *then,* fifteen years ago! As of course can real eighteen-carat gold earrings and a rare red-gold necklace worn with expensive black cashmere (rather high-necked, for her skin *was* dull). Make no mistake about it! At least the years have taught Angie how to dress, if not how to behave.

THAT NIGHT FOR THE RICH!

That night Angie and Sylvester spent thirty-four pounds on their dinner for two. (Over a hundred pounds by today's prices.) Angie had a good appetite. They went to a rather grand Italian place in Soho, where the pepper for their pasta came from an antique giant grinder, and the cheese was the very best Parmesan—soft, as fresh Parmesan should be—flown in that day from Italy. The couple also drank rather a lot of gin and tonics before the meal, and very good wine with it, and very, very old port after it which put up the price considerably.

That same night (in London) Simon and Janice Best lunched (in Tokyo) on sushi, and Janice insisted on champagne as well as sake, which emboldened Simon to tell her he thought they should perhaps not see each other again. Gossip, he told her, was distressing Helen. Simon spoke as gently and tactfully as he could, but how can such things be kindly put? Janice threw a glass of warm sake in his face, and though the quantity was small—the Japanese drink a lot, but always little by little, little by little—some of the drink splashed onto a rather rare wall-hanging behind his head.

HACKETTE DOWSES HACK went the headline in *Private Eye,* AS UGANDAN RELATIONS ARE BROKEN OFF. Nowhere's safe! Nowhere's private! Not even, perhaps especially not even, a tucked-away restaurant in downtown Tokyo!

Simon felt obliged to pay the restaurant something toward the cost of cleaning. The bill amounted to almost fifty pounds. He phoned Helen in Muswell Hill at 9 P.M. English time and Helen didn't answer, Arthur Hockney did. Arthur told Simon that he was baby-sitting for Helen. Arthur did not tell Simon, of course, that Helen was meeting Clifford, but somehow Simon knew it. Who else would Helen agree to see, on the spur of the moment, leaving Arthur Hockney of all people as baby-sitter for the precious Edward? Supposing Edward had an attack of croup, to which he was prone? Helen seldom went out, just in case Edward had croup. And now, suddenly, Arthur Hockney baby-sitting? Simon was too aware of Helen's occasional meeting with Arthur; of her continuing refusal to believe that Nell was dead. Simon saw Arther as Helen's co-conspirator and liked him none the better for it. Simon took the first flight home, within the hour. His marriage had to be put on a proper footing, and quickly.

Clifford took Helen to the Festival Hall Restaurant, partly because he thought he'd meet nobody there he knew, and partly because, although not the most modish place in the world, the view is the best in all London. Neither Clifford nor Helen said much at first. Clifford thought she was astonishingly lovely, lovelier than he had remembered. There was something about the gentle, tender, almost submissive way she held her head—and yet he knew how stubborn, how almost vicious (in his terms) she could be. He knew that the air of purity, of steadfastness, was deceptive. She was faithless, sluttish, vapid! Wasn't she? And, as for Helen, she knew that Clifford's courtesy was skin deep; that his charm was a trick, a trap; that he sweet-talked her today only to devastate, hurt, destroy her tomorrow. And the image of Nell stood between them: the child they had loved, but not enough, because the love had been overwhelmed by misery, injured pride and hate. It was their rage, their disappointment with each other which had led to their losing her. How could they talk about any of this? And since they couldn't say what was important, they had to make do with small talk. Even so, through their diffident talk of fashions and events—something else kept emerging: perhaps just the memory of the few stunning, perfect months they'd had together, years ago, which couldn't be kept down. Clifford caught Helen's hand as she reached for a glass and held it, and she let it be kept.

"I want to talk about Nell," he said.

"I can't believe she's dead," said Helen. "I won't talk about her being dead. They never found her body."

"Oh, Helen," he said, distressed for her, "if you want to

believe that, by all means do. If it makes it better for you."

Such unexpected kindness brought tears to her eyes.

"Simon won't let me believe it," she said.

"He's a journalist," said Clifford, wisely not referring to him as the dwarf, "and it's in the nature of journalists to like things cut and dried. You're not happy with him."

"No," said Helen, and was surprised she said it.

"Then why are you still with him?"

"Because of Edward. Because if I leave Simon something terrible will happen to Edward."

It was her superstition, her dread. He understood this, too.

"No it won't," he said. "It was because of me Nell died, not because of you. And Simon will behave better than me. That's in his nature too."

"That's true," she said, and managed a smile. She shook her head as if to free it from a muffling of hearing, a misting of sight.

"Oh Lord," she said, "you make me feel so alive! Life comes pouring in from all directions. What am I to do?"

"Come home with me," he said. And of course she did, forgetting all about Arthur, or if not quite forgetting, certainly not caring.

THAT NIGHT FOR NELL

That evening, as Clifford and Helen's lives came together again with at least a promise of happiness, Nell's world lurched into further disarray. As Helen picked at her salmon mousse, and Clifford at his lamb cutlets, a meeting was being held at the Eastlake Assessment Center to discuss the future of a small group of children, including Nell. Now little Nell had begun to recover from the shock of losing home and family yet once again, and from the terrible sights of death and destruction she had witnessed, and was doing quite nicely, thank you. She was beginning to speak normally, and in English, not French, although she still suffered from patchy amnesia.

She shared a dormitory with five other little girls—Cindy, Karen, Rose, Becky and Joan. They had hard mattresses (healthy, and cheap) and not enough blankets, for what the houseparents saved out of the Center's heating allowance could be diverted into their own pockets. Rose and Becky wet the bed and were smacked every morning and made to wash their sheets. Cindy stumbled over her words and sometimes said good-night when she meant good-morning and was stood in the wastepaper basket to shame her and make her more sensible. Karen and Joan were diagnosed as being out of control, though both only seven, which meant they were very naughty indeed, and would tear up the blankets and kick the doors, and punch you suddenly in the stomach for no reason at all. Nell was very careful to be good, to be quiet and to smile as much as possible. She liked Rose very much and they were good friends. She tried to work out sensible ways of Rose's not wetting the bed; she would take Rose's before-bed orange drink (the yellow, sweet artificial kind, not the concentrated juice, which was expensive) if no one was looking and drink it herself, and it worked. She understood, even at this early age, that no one was being deliberately unkind—they were just stupid, and liked to save money. She had, after all, a profound sense of her own worth; had not her mother and father fought over her, each one wishing to possess her; had not Otto and Cynthia bent over her crib and smiled; had not Milord and Milady de Troite seen her as the source of all happiness, and youth, and hope? These things were vaguely remembered, but assimilated into the depths of her being. Nell saw that she was misunderstood, and therefore devalued—not that she was worth nothing—and therefore survived. She bowed her head but her eyes remained bright and her complexion clear. She knew that she would not be here forever, and in the meantime, as was her custom, determined to make the best of her circumstances. She might cry herself to sleep at night—quietly, in case she was heard and slapped for ingratitude—but she woke in the morning cheerful and smiling, thinking of tables to be learned or spelling mastered, or Karen to be helped, and new games to play with Rose, and ways to avoid the censorious red-rimmed eye of Annabel Lee, houseparent.

Now Annabel Lee, and Horace her husband, were both heavy smokers, and cigarette smoke always made Nell feel quite ill, so that, apart from everything else, she kept as far away from them as she could. We know that this reaction was because of her memories of Erich Blotton, but Nell is in no position to explain this, even if she understood it herself, and Mr. and Mrs. Lee, both gray-faced and coughing from tobacco, did not understand it either. They did not think their behavior deserved quite such a response.

"She still shies away when I come near," said Annabel at the Relocation Meeting. "I don't think foster parents could cope. What we don't want is for Ellen Root to be returned time and time again, when yet another placing fails." Ellen Root! Yes, reader, this was the name by which little Eleanor Wexford is now known. Well, she had to be called something, this child out of nowhere. Remember how she was found, with her few stumbling words of English, standing in a daze on the edge of a Route Nationale, against a background of fire and mayhem? They called her Ellen, because the word she whispered over and over again, when they bent to hear, was "Hélène" and those who listened thought that must be her name. In fact she was remembering and pronouncing her mother's name, dimly remembered, the French way—although the French itself had been driven from her child's brain by shock and fear. So "Ellen" she became, and the "Root" from "Route Nationale." Geddit? Annabel Lee thought she'd been rather clever in choosing the name, and no doubt she had. Annabel was a secret drinker. No one knew it. Not her husband Horace, certainly not the Social Services Authority which employed the couple. How could they? Nevertheless, "Ellen Root" was not the most glamorous of names, and this was perhaps the end Annabel Lee desired. A plain, heavy, hardworking woman herself, she did not much care for spectacularly pretty, charming, light-limbed little girls. Just as well, perhaps, they did not very often turn up at Eastlake.

There was an epidemic of head-lice which plagued the Center, of a particularly stubborn kind, and somehow or other Ellen Root's head was always the one to be shaved, while other children's hair could be satisfactorily combed and shampooed. Mind you, Ellen's hair was so thick and curly—as well as shiny, fair and pretty—Annabel may indeed, just possibly, have had exceptional trouble with it. We must give her the benefit of the doubt. To do so is part of practicing virtues, the better to acquire them.

Someone on the Relocation Panel remarked that the child had been at the Assessment Center for an unusually long time. Nearly a year. Surely it was time she was moved on to somewhere more like a home, even if she was not yet ready for fostering? The Center was a halfway house for children in trouble—either of their own making or the world's—and not intended to be their permanent residence.

"It's fine by me," said Horace. "But where are you going to move Ellen Root *to*? She's E.S.N." (Reader, these initials mean Educationally Subnormal. Backward, that is to say. A right little thicko. Our Nell!) "It's written there large as life on her papers. The only place that will take her is Dunwoody, and that's hardly suitable." Dunwoody was a home for the mentally disabled and disturbed, and Nell, though her I.Q. tests kept showing her up as backward, was at least always quiet and cooperative.

"I don't know so much," said Annabel. "Whenever I try to comb her hair she pulls away." And so Nell did, for fear of having it shaved, but Annabel didn't think of that, or chose not to. "And once our precious little Ellen bit Horace. Remember?" So Ellen had, waking once from sleep, shaken awake by Horace, when a fire alarm had sounded at 2 A.M. and the whole institution had to be evacuated. Memories had come flooding back; she was terrified; she struggled—yes indeed, she had been uncontrollable. She had bitten. Biting! An unforgivable sin in child-care circles. "She was upset," said Horace.

"She's disturbed," said Annabel, grimly. "She bit almost to the bone, like a wild animal." It had been, of course, a false alarm: everyone's peace had been disturbed. (Joan it was who had crept out of bed and broken the glass with the tempting little red hammer, which hung from a hook just at child's eye level.) But fire is a real hazard in such homes—some of the children think nothing of arson—and the threat of it is always taken seriously. Even worse than biting!

Now, reader, you may be wondering why Nell, or Ellen, came off so badly in intelligence tests. It was for a very simple reason. Asked questions such as "Does the sun shine at night?" Ellen would reply "Yes"—thinking of the way the sun rises on the other side of the world even as it sinks on this side—whereas the real answer—as ordinarily given by under-fives—is "No." (And Nell was being given tests for four-year-olds, inasmuch as her linguistic ability was at that level, because of her two-and-a-half years of speaking no English at all.) These things happen. Children in care are assessed wrongly, by accident, stupidity or just occasionally by virtue of adult malice, and end up very much in the wrong place.

And so it was decided that night that Nell should stay a little longer at Eastlake, and not be fostered. "Some evidence of mental disturbance," was entered on her form, adding to the doom of "E.S.N." and another obstacle placed in the path of Ellen's future well-being within our child-care system.

At that same meeting a motion of gratitude was proposed and passed in relation to a certain Mrs. Erich Blotton, who had presented the home with yet another large sum, this time £750. Mrs. Blotton never appeared in person, but was understood to give generously to many children's homes in the area. She was assumed to be some kind of nutter, which didn't make her gifts any the less welcome. It was also voted that a letter be sent inviting Mrs. Blotton to visit Eastlake.

You have heard my views on coincidence, reader. I assure you, this is the kind of thing that happens. Mrs. Blotton, infertile, married Erich Blotton, who wanted children more than anything. If now, having the insurance money from the crash of ZOE 05, she gives it away to children's homes, is that surprising? The world is not an enormous place—no, it is very small: circles within circles, wheels within wheels—look at Angie and Dorothy crossing paths, all unknowing, at Harrods! Just about everyone, so far as I can see, ends up encountering everyone else, the bit-part players in the story of their lives.

TOGETHER AGAIN

It is perhaps just as well that Clifford and Helen knew nothing of this. They are holding hands across a table and looking into each other's eyes. Sometimes it seems that we can have our happiness only at someone else's expense. While we celebrate our emotions here, someone suffers there, from our neglect.

"I have been faithful to you," Clifford observes, which is extraordinary, under the circumstances.

"Trudi Barefoot?" Helen can't help asking. Wouldn't you?

"Who?" He's joking. Trudi has a new film out. Her name is plastered all over the Western world.

"Elise O'Malley?"

"Ah begorah, where's my pills?" He's shocking! Merciless! And Elise so dependent and trusting!

"Serena Bailey, Sonia Manzi, Gertie Lindhoff, Bente Respigi, Candace Snow—" She knows a lot of their names, though not quite all.

"You can't believe what you read in the papers," he says, "at least I hope you can't. Or what about the dwarf and Janice Best?"

There now! He's forgotten and referred to Simon as "the dwarf." Helen takes away her hand.

"I'm sorry," he says quickly. "You know I'm just jealous."

That's better! Helen smiles. Three years now since Nell was lost. She's allowed to smile. And Clifford will allow her to cling to her illusion, if illusion it be, that Nell still lives, and she once again inhabits a world where all things are possible, even happiness.

Reader, after dinner (which cost only some £15, the year being what it is, and Clifford never one to spend extravagantly), Clifford and Helen went back to his house in Orme Square and spent the night together. The cost of that one evening, for the three couples out dining, if it were to include Angie's new gold-leafed shoes, certainly came to over £750, the amount Mrs. Blotton was donating to the Eastlake Assessment Center. Nell's supper of fish fingers and baked beans, followed by jam tart, costing out at 6*d*. If there is any such thing as actual immorality, I think it lies herein, that the haves in this world have so much, and the have-nots so little.

Arthur Hockney, left to baby-sit *all night* without even the courtesy of a phone call, was paid nothing for his pains. Poor Arthur! If you leave out the night his parents were killed and the day he told his mentors he was betraying them, would not after all join the Civil Rights movement, these were the most painful few hours of his life. He didn't need to be psychic to know what was happening. Who would?

Reader, if you are married, do your best to stay married. If you are unmarried, the cynical might say, take care only to fall in love with someone you *dislike,* for you may very well end up divorced, and the worst thing about divorcing, being divorced, is how you have to practice hate, have to learn to loathe and despise the one you used to love and admire, so as to persuade yourself that nothing much has been lost. Wanker! Wally! Him? Her? Good riddance to bad rubbish! The practice of hate is very bad for the character—and terrible for the children! But if you could only start out from a point of dislike, the effort and distress involved would surely be far less. At least you wouldn't have to change your view of the whole universe, and all the people in it. Black could stay black, and white white.

Clifford and Helen, reunited once again that night, in the pretty little Georgian house in Orme Square, laughing, talking and happy, could hardly remember why they had hated each other so much. She could see his infidelities as mere manliness; his meanness as prudence; his absorption in his work as only reasonable; herself as having married too young and not giving Clifford what he needed.

"I was only ever trying to make you jealous!" she said to him, standing lithe and lovely in the marble shower, in a cloud of steam which, like a gauze over a film camera, made her seem to Clifford mistier and more romantic than she had even appeared in his dreams—the good ones, not the bad. And he had, to be frank, dreamed of Helen a good deal, even in the company of Elise, Serena, Sonia, Gertie, Bente, Candace—and whoever.

Clifford for his part could now see Helen's early infidelity as a symptom, not a cause, of the collapse of their marriage. His neglect of her, his selfishness, was to blame.

"I'm sorry," she said, "so sorry! I regretted it so much, at once!"

"You did nothing that I hadn't done," he said, and saw her eyes grow cold with jealousy, but only for a moment.

"I don't want to hear," she said. "I want to forget."

"I behaved atrociously over Nell," he said. "Poor Nell."

"Lovely Nell," she said. And there, they could talk about Nell, easily now, and incorporate her in their mutual pasts. Apologies are important things. World Wars start because they are not made, because no one is prepared to say *you were right, I was wrong.*

So there they were, six years later, hand in hand, so much time and life wasted! And Simon Cornbrook, hand on heart, returning from Japan at five in the morning to repair his marriage, found Helen not in her marital bed, and Arthur the detective asleep on the couch, and little Edward asleep upstairs, coughing away, with a nasty croak in the cough which might at any moment turn into a really nasty attack of croup.

RUNNING AWAY

And what of little Nell, whom this irresponsible pair had tossed to the winds of fate? Oh yes, they were certainly irresponsible—they married each other and should have made at least some effort to put up with each other, once they had Nell. (What married people without children do with their lives is hardly of consequence. They can fly to different ends of the earth for all I care; they only harm each other and themselves and will soon cure.) Well, the night Clifford and Helen were reunited was the night that Nell, or Ellen Root as she now was, ran away from the Eastlake Center, away from stupid Horace and his punitive, drunken wife Annabel. Or at any rate that was how Nell saw them; not, I daresay, how they really were.

Nell, in her short life, though accustomed to sudden, horrible events, had until now been cared for—apart from one day with Erich Blotton—by the most kindly, most sensitive, most responsive of folk, in the prettiest if sometimes rather eccentric surroundings. The Center, with its smell of cabbage, disinfectant and human despair mixed, and its brisk, tough, powerful staff, astonished rather than defeated her. Less traumatic than the aircrash, than when the devil had razed the château to the ground, than the calamity on the Route Nationale, even more amazing. And not pleasant! To stand in the bleakness of the Eastlake medical room, and have her head shaved! To see her pretty curls litter the worn gray linoleum floor! To have no one to embrace, no one to tell her stories, no one to sing to her—well, these she could put up with, for a time. But to be unable to love and be loved—if this went on it would be misfortune indeed—the worst of all the misfortunes, in fact, that could befall a small child, and Nell knew, instinctively, that she must leave, and soon. That anywhere was better than here! That there were good things and kind people in the world and that she must be off to find them.

It was Ellen Root's seventh birthday—according to the Eastlake Center. We know of course that in fact Nell was only six and a half. But seven is the magic age when children are supposed to be legally fit to go to school themselves—to traverse major trunk roads, to avoid the strangers who lie in wait—and Nell listened to Annabel telling her so and thought, if I am old enough to cross roads on my own, I am old enough to leave here, and never, never come back. That day, moreover, she had been sent to school for the first time in her life. So far she had attended the Infants' Class at the Center, for children with Special Needs—that is to say whenever Annabel Lee saw fit to call it together, and could be bothered to organize the Water Play, or find the Sandbox. That she had found boring, but this she hated. A great, wild, clanging, clattering place, full of shrieks and yells and pinches and insults! And there was a tall gray woman there who kept teaching her to read, and wouldn't believe her when she said she already could, and wouldn't even hear her read, so Nell had stayed mute, and the woman had slapped her. No, Nell had to go!

When she came back from the terrible place called school (the others had proper homes to go to, and she had only the Eastlake Center, which they all knew, so they wouldn't talk to her) Nell took a serviceable laundered pillowcase from the laundry room, and wrapped her few possessions in it. Sponge-bag, a thin towel, a pair of shoes already too small, a jersey, a yellow-haired rag doll given to her out of the funds so kindly donated by Mrs. Blotton, and the one item left of all her past—the tin teddy bear on a silver chain—which to retain she had smiled and charmed many a time. She went to bed in the dormitory as usual but kept herself awake—which was almost the most difficult part of the whole enterprise—and when she heard the hall clock strike nine, crept out of her bed, stole down the stairs, unlocked the heavy front door, and was out into the brilliant, starry night, into the big wild busy world, to seek her fortune.

"Run away!" exclaimed Annabel Lee, when told by her husband Horace that little Ellen Root's bed was empty, and the child was nowhere to be found. "The wicked, wicked child!" And she shoved her empty sherry bottle under the bed so her husband wouldn't see it. It was a double marital bed but Horace slept mostly on a camp-bed in the attic, where he had his train set. It was an elaborate and wonderful system, electronically controlled, and the children might have appreciated it, if they had only been allowed up to see it. Which of course they weren't.

Now "running away" is, next to arson, next to biting, the worst thing a child in an institution can do. The child who flees is seen as being monstrously, unthinkably ungrateful. Any institution, to those who run it, is a fine, kind and excellent place. If the child (or the prisoner, or the patient) cannot agree and acts accordingly, it is not only willful and wicked, but puts everyone to terrible and unnecessary trouble. The treatment is to pursue the runaways with great energy, haul them back, and then punish them severely for running, as if this will somehow finally endear the place to the ingrate, so they won't do it again.

"That'll learn you!" cries the grown-up world. Thwack, thwack! "That'll learn you to like it! That'll learn you to love us! That'll learn you to be grateful!"

Annabel Lee set the dogs after little Ellen Root. Yes, really. She had no business doing it; certainly no authority would ever have consented to such an act; but remember Annabel Lee had drunk two-thirds of a bottle of sherry, while waiting for her husband Horace to finish playing trains and, perhaps, come to bed. (Quite a proportion of the money Mrs. Blotton had donated to Eastlake over the years had been spent on the train set, and no one who saw it—though that was almost no one—could deny it was wondrous. So delicate and intricate, with its tunnels and signals and trees and little wayside cottages complete with curtains and electric lights, and some really rare collector's items by way of engines—including the fabulous Santa Fe—and the invoices just said "toys," so who was there to query the expenditure? No one.)

"The dogs! The dogs! Unloose the dogs!" cried Annabel Lee, clambering out of bed, a heavy, incongruous figure in her fine silk nightie (which Horace took no notice of at all, but she never stopped trying). "We can't call the police, there'll only be a scandal! No end of a fuss, and her with nits in her hair, to bring us all into disgrace. What the little miss wants is a proper fright! We'll give it to her, well and truly."

As if, reader, poor little Nell hadn't had a good deal too many frights in her life already.

Annabel Lee kept her two big, black, sleek dogs with their big jaws and sharp white teeth, in kennels, just around the side of the house, outside the dining-room, so the children could see them whenever they came down to a meal. The dogs calmed the children, said Annabel Lee. They certainly subdued them, especially since Kettle and Kim were kept hungry, and on the end of rattling chains just long enough to let the animals press their dripping jaws against the window, squashing their gums, magnifying their teeth.

"If you don't stop doing that" (running in the corridor, forgetting to clean your comb, losing your socks or whatever), "I'll feed you to the dogs!" Discipline at Eastlake was no problem at all.

When visitors or inspectors came, the dogs were moved to a compound at the very end of the long garden, and rabbits put in the kennels instead.

"How nice of the children to have pets!" said the visitor. "As well as so many toys! But where *are* all the toys? Broken, you say? Good Lord! But they're disturbed, aren't they, poor little things. How lucky they are to have you, Mrs. Lee; so warm and friendly and kind. What patience you must have. You put us all to shame!" They said it so often Annabel Lee herself quite believed it.

Most people, of course, believe that they're good. Have you ever, reader, met anyone who thought they were wicked? But someone, somewhere, must be, or the world wouldn't be in the state that it's in, and on the very night that her parents were reunited—though to Arthur Hockney's and Simon Cornbrook's sorrow—our dear Nell wouldn't be running over a warm, summery, moonlit stretch of Hackney Marshes, pursued by a couple of slavering, savage black dogs, and behind them, at the wheel of the Eastlake van, lights blazing, horn blaring, a drunken, equally slavering Annabel Lee.

Reader, I don't want to insult Dobermans. Properly raised and kindly treated, they are the most elegant, responsive, gentle of creatures. It's only when reared by someone like Annabel Lee that they become monsters. And if they had caught up with Nell, I really do believe they would quite probably have torn her to bits, out of the ferocity of their despair. They wanted to be civilized, but had been rendered savage, and hated it.

Annabel's husband Horace, watching the departing trio—the leaping dogs, his shrieking wife—wondered briefly whether to call the police and put paid to Annabel's activities once and for all, but decided against it, and went back up to the attic room to see whether the newly acquired and favorite but rather ancient Santa Fe engine could race the Royal Scot up a one-in-three gradient. I think myself Horace was slightly mad. Perhaps he should be pitied for it, but I can't manage it.

Nell ran: how she ran. She ran across smooth ground and rough; she ran over tussock and stream; she ran toward the roadway, to the noise and the roar and what she thought must be safety. And it is a terrifying thing for any normal person to watch a small child pelt toward such a place, but Annabel Lee was not impressed, any more than she cared if a cockroach (there were many at Eastlake) toppled off the top of the cooker into a pan of boiling potato water—she was like that. If the child was run over it was her own fault; she, Annabel Lee, had done everything to stop her; no one (except Horace who would never tell) would ever understand what had happened. Perhaps Ellen Root should have been killed in that other accident on the Route Nationale; perhaps all she had, after all, was a kind of leftover life: the roads, those ogres of modern life, would claim her for their own and she, Annabel, would do what she could to help. Annabel Lee, reader, was certainly more than a little mad, and very bad, and hated Nell unreasonably and perversely perhaps simply because the child was, unlike herself, sane, and good. She was not at the moment very pretty, of course—Annabel had seen to that. Her head had been shaved a couple of weeks back, and her hair now stood up in a short blonde bristle, in which it seemed to Annabel that nits still sheltered, so obsessive about and antagonistic toward the child was she—and Eastlake was beginning to make her little face pinched and her eyes screw up. She was getting out just in time!

So plain little shaven Nell ran toward the roadway, and death or life, how could she know which? And when she got to the very brink and tripped and tumbled down the embankment and onto the very road itself, Annabel Lee just called her dogs off, and sat in her Land-Rover for a while, and laughed, and then turned the wheel for home.

Now little Nell was lucky, a quality she had inherited from her father. That is to say, apart from the monstrous underlying bad fortune of being a child gone altogether astray in the world, strokes of excellent good luck would come her way—the kind of luck a spider has when it's fallen into a bath and some kind person comes along and, instead of turning on the hot tap and washing it down the drain, politely goes to the trouble of offering it a piece of string, so it can clamber out. Whatever fairy godmother it was who looked after Nell returned to her post (better late than never, I suppose—but really, such negligence!) and offered the poor child a piece of string in the form of a van parked on a police turnout just where she clambered over the embankment and rolled down, down toward the tarmac. The van had a lowered ramp at the back, its headlights were off, the driver Clive and his mate Beano were in the act of switching the license plates by flashlight.

Even as they did so, a second car pulled up, and Clive and Beano helped its driver swiftly and silently shift a massive piece of furniture from its roof rack up the ramp into the van. Then the car backed again onto the dark roadway, and was off.

Nell crouched and watched, regaining her breath. Here obviously lay safety and escape. The minute Clive's and Beano's backs were turned—she ran up the ramp and into the back of the van; the dogs would not follow her there. Clive and Beano finished their task, the ramp was lifted, Nell not noticed, the door slammed shut, and Nell and a fraction of the proceeds of one of the greatest antiques robberies of all time—the pillaging of one of our finest country homes, Montdragon House—were on their way west. And Clive and Beano—a merry pair, though villainous—laughed at the way they'd used the police turnout to beat the officers at their own game, and Nell heard the laughter and felt she was amongst friends again. There had not been much laughter at the Eastlake Assessment Center.

Nell fell asleep and nothing woke her, not rattling, nor bumping, nor voices, nor movement, till suddenly the morning sun streamed in as the van doors were opened, and she was at Faraway Farm, on the edge of deepest, prettiest, greenest Wales, where she was to spend the next six and a half years.

"I'm remarrying Helen," Clifford said to Angie Wellbrook, at breakfast at Claridges, fresh from his night with Helen, feeling clean again, and strong, and that the world was his oyster. "And what is all this nonsense about shares? If Leonardo's closes in Geneva, or stops doing exhibitions, I shall simply resign, and then where would your fun be? Just sit back, Angie, and enjoy the profits. Don't interfere!" And Angie said, weeping from the shock of it, spoiling her expensive makeup, dropping tears upon crêpe de chine that just couldn't stand water and never recovered, "Come to bed just this once, Clifford. Just an hour with me, and I promise to go away and leave you and Leonardo's in peace." And I'm afraid to say that Clifford did, though more out of pity, mixed of course with self-interest (how could it not be?) than anything else, on one of Claridges' old-fashioned bouncy brass beds, *in the morning,* which seems very decadent and disgraceful to me. Then he went around to his lawyers, to see how speedily Helen could divorce the dwarf, that is to say the talented and suffering Simon.

"I'm sorry, Simon," Helen said to her husband, Simon Cornbrook. "But our marriage just hasn't been working at all, has it! And you have Janice Best to go to, after all."

But of course Simon didn't want Janice Best. All he had managed to do, in his attempts to make Helen jealous, was put himself morally and legally in the wrong. Well, it happens all the time. The husband, the wife, confesses to an affair in the hope of making the spouse sit up and take notice; realizes just how much she, he, is in danger of losing if she, he, goes on like this; and all that transpires is that the spouse bounces off with someone altogether else, with a clear conscience and most of the money. Never confess, reader, never be found out, not if you value your marriage. Or you'll end up with nothing—no marriage, no lover (he, she, only fancies you when you were unobtainably someone else's), a guilty conscience and like as not no alimony. You may even lose the children. It happens.

Helen was kind and said of course Simon could continue to see little Edward; really it would make very little difference, would it? Simon was so often away, he might even see the child more, this way. The house in Orme Square was very *towny,* she knew, but there was lots of room for a nanny (Nanny! She who had sworn always to look after Edward herself. How could she!) and Clifford would love Edward for her sake, and would probably be a more attentive father than Simon had ever been, and he'd known when he married her she'd only ever really loved Clifford—Simon mustn't think she regretted any of it, she did hope they would be friends—and he could sell the Muswell Hill house and move in somewhere with Janice Best. They were really suited—Simon and Janice—in the same line of business, after all, and somehow spiritually married: filling column inches together the way others filled marital beds.

"Edward had croup," was all Simon could say. It was somehow the only protest he felt entitled to make. "Edward had croup and you left him alone with a black detective as a babysitter."

"Is that a racist statement?" Her pretty eyebrows went up.

"Don't be so bloody stupid." Simon was almost weeping. "All I mean is a black detective doesn't know how to deal with croup."

"Why not? Because he's black? I'm sure he knows a great deal more about how to deal with a sick child than Janice does." In which she was quite right. But then no one could know less. "In any case, it isn't proper croup, just a nasty chesty cough. This has always been a damp house. The trees needed cutting but you never would."

Janice wanted to marry Simon. It is useful to a woman to be married, especially to someone a little higher up in a profession than she—so long as, that is, it is not what you and I would call a domestic marriage, in which the wife is expected to stay home and keep house. That was certainly not the kind of marriage Janice had in mind. She saw it more as a working partnership. A quick comparison of notes over the breakfast orange juice—the name of a useful contact, advice on the nature of a particular editor—a sharp tool with which to make footholds for advancement up the professional tree. In its own way, I suppose, rather like the Angie/Sylvester relationship, but with mutual legal obligations and bed thrown in. And of course she wouldn't mind Simon's seeing Edward—she had no intention of having children herself; he could hardly want to go through all that boredom again, all that *being tied down*—a journalist had to be free to follow stories to the end of the earth if need be—surely! No, he should certainly sell the Muswell Hill house, and invest the money—giving as little as possible to that boring bitch Helen (Simon, how can it be *your fault* she's gone off with Clifford Wexford? What are you talking about? They deserve each other. For God's sake!)—and then use the income to rent some service apartment in Central London, preferably furnished. They wouldn't be spending much time in it, after all. Yes, Simon, I *do* want us to get married. It is important. It does make a difference. After all that stuff in the paper. All that sake-throwing. Now you're free to marry, don't you see how humiliating it will be for me if you don't?

Oh Miss Best! The new Mrs. Cornbrook. Janice Cornbrook. Yes, with that name you can work pretty well on the quality dailies. As Best—well, you could hardly look higher than the *Mail on Sunday.* Which in its own way is pretty high, of course, in a professional sense—or Simon wouldn't have taken up with her—but Janice was aiming higher still. *The Independent,* or its like.

Poor Simon. His eyesight suddenly deteriorated, so he had to have his glasses changed; he developed a jaw abscess and had to have teeth removed; his hair receded a whole inch—all in that year between his return from Tokyo and his marriage to Janice, by way of the loss of his wife and child. At the registry-office wedding (everyone who was anyone in the Fleet Street

World came, crowding unasked and drunken into a room too small for them, flashing cameras and quite upsetting the registrar) Janice caught a glimpse of Simon under a harsh, unflattering light and realized he was *old* and what would she do if he suddenly lost energy, packed up on her physically, but it was too late then. Serve her right, say I.

Clifford, Helen and Edward lived happily at Orme Square until the divorce came through. "Living together" had replaced "living in sin" by now, and few eyebrows were raised: only Nanny's mother complained. She'd assumed her Norland Nanny daughter (what a training! what an expense!) would end up in a Royal household at best, a banking family at worst—and now look. But Nanny Anne loved Edward and Edward loved Nanny Anne, which was just as well, if you remember what I said about the children of lovers being orphans. Edward looked more and more like Simon as he grew older, which Helen and Clifford tried not to think about—though fortunately Nanny Anne swore he was going to grow up really tall, and she had all that training to back her judgment.

Clifford and Helen lay entwined at night in their premarital bed, intricately, as if fearing some demon might come along and disentangle them, and part them again. But only angels seemed to hover around the bed, dispensing blessings.

An extraordinary thing happened. It went like this: Clifford was passing Roache's, the junk shop in Camden Passage. There was a painting in the window, wedged between a rather nice blue-and-white ewer and an arts-and-crafts pewter candlestick (the things you could get, in those days, for a few pennies! Well, pence; for the currency had changed. Shillings had gone, and with them the silver threepenny bits for the Christmas pudding). The painting was unframed, about twenty-four by eighteen inches and so dirty you could hardly see its subject. Clifford went in, argued with the owner for some time about the candlestick, and bought it for £4, twice what Bill Roache—an old Etonian, who had taken LSD, given up tax accounting, and taken to the antique trade—had hoped to get. Then he casually inquired about the painting. Roache, who knew all the tricks, as only someone from a banking family can, was instantly suspicious.

"I'm not sure I want to sell it," said Roache, extracting it from the window rather brutally, waiting for the sharp intake of breath which would indicate a punter with a more than ordinary interest. None came.

"I'm not sure I want to buy it," said Clifford. "I'm not sure anyone will. Who is it? Anyone?"

Roache rubbed the right-hand corner of the canvas. His fingers were both well-manicured and dirty. A *V* appeared beneath the encrusted grime and then *I,* then *NCE* and then an *NT*.

"Vincent," said Roache.

"Never heard of a Vincent," said Clifford, and since he was a stranger to Roache, how could the latter know his voice was a pitch higher than usual. "Just some amateur, I imagine. What is it, a flower piece? Look at that line there—the curve of the petal—very crude."

Well, if someone tells you firmly a line is crude, you believe them, even if you are an old Etonian.

"I'll look it up," said Roache, getting out his Benozet, the Art Dealer's guide.

"You're wasting your time," said Clifford. "But give it a go by all means. Vincent. That's V. Not many Vs."

Roache looked up the Vs and found no Vincent.

"Well, I don't know," said Clifford. "I'd have to get it framed. I'll give you a couple of quid." Dangerous to put it any higher. Roache was suspicious anyway.

"It's got quite a bit of age to it," said Roache, "and, as I say, I don't want to sell it. I like it."

"A fiver," said Clifford, "and I must be mad."

Money changed hands.

"Where did you find it?" asked Clifford, when the painting was safely in his possession.

"I was clearing an attic in Blackheath for some old lady,"

said Roache. Clifford's heart leaped. Vincent van Gogh used to walk from Ramsgate to Blackheath (and think nothing of it) during his early years in England.

"Any others?" asked Clifford, but this had been the only painting, amongst piles of old clothes and pieces of brass bed. He'd bought the lot for £3.50 and had already taken in £30. This brought it up to £35. Not bad going.

"It isn't anything special?" asked Roache, nervously, as Clifford left. He felt uneasy. Something was wrong. No dealer likes to be made a fool of. Losing face is worse than losing money.

"Only a van Gogh," said Clifford, and Roache thought of suing, but didn't. Not only had he let £35,000 worth of painting slip through his hands, but there was nothing he could do about it. He'd made a colossal profit out of the old lady's ignorance, and Clifford had made a colossal profit out of his. He hadn't slipped the old lady anything extra; he didn't expect Clfford to slip him anything. Clifford didn't. The painting is today, of course, worth a dozen or so million. I ask you!

It made the headlines, of course it did. ART WHIZ KID'S FANTASTIC FIND, GENIUS AMONGST THE JUNK, and many a note in the quality papers. Everyone who was anyone knew all about it! It shook the antique world, too. Every forgotten stack of dirty old paintings in the country (and there were hundreds of them in those days—not anymore) was leafed through and cleaned up—but not another *VINCENT* materialized. Of course not. It took Clifford's luck.

Clifford's luck! That was what so delighted Helen and Clifford—the sheer fluke of it, oh the cleverness of it, the proof of his ability to tell the great from the insignificant: Clifford's fingers so well and truly on the pulse of the great beating vein of art, all mixed up somehow with the power of love, the richness of sex, their finding each other again—oh, there was no end to their triumph. They didn't sell the painting—of course not!—they hung it above the marble fireplace and it glowed, it *glowed*—not sunflowers, of course—but poppies.

John Lally, when he heard about it, said that Clifford was

in league with the devil. But everyone knew that anyway so what was all the fuss about?

Helen said to Evelyn, secretly, for of course she was barred from entering Applecore Cottage again—Mother, if *money's* any help, but Evelyn said no, it wasn't. She was looking tired, Helen thought. Evelyn loved little Edward. She said he looked like John.

Angie called from South Africa to congratulate Clifford on his find. She sounded genuinely happy for him. He'd have to stage an Impressionist Renaissance, she supposed. She gave him ten years to raise the value of Vincent's *Poppies* to a million. Anything less would be a disgrace. She hoped the painting matched Helen's curtains.

Cynthia said to Otto, "I suppose we'll see less of our son now."

"Good," said Otto, adding hastily, "now that he's back with Helen, and happy." But the truth was, he valued the quietness of his weekends these days, undisturbed by Clifford's chatter. He found the excitement and agitation over the van Gogh painting vulgar. Van Gogh had lived and died in penury and obscurity; that successive generations should respond to his work was one thing; that they should profit by it, another.

"Perhaps they'll have children," said Cynthia, hopefully. She felt not as young as once she used to be. She had no lover. Young men were available, still easily charmed and amazed, but these days she felt the indignity of her situation, and theirs. She had liver spots on the backs of her hands. It just would not do, anymore. Except that in the vacuum left by their departing, old age seemed to rush in. She felt that if Clifford and Helen ever gave another baby into her charge, she would this time certainly give it more personal attention. Nell's life had been so short: if only Cynthia had known, how differently she would have behaved; how much less censorious of Helen she would have been. She had failed Clifford as a mother; she had not given him the love and support a child deserved, nor of course had Otto. She wanted another chance, with another child. She gave all her attention, in the meantime, to Otto; but even as she gave up the excitements of the clandestine, so Otto found them again. Strange men would call, bearing news she was not supposed to hear. He wore an abstracted, important look; the phone would ring, then abruptly stop; Otto would leave the house, as many hours after as the number of rings. Well, it kept him young. She did not suppose it was dangerous. And downstairs Johnnie sang and polished the old horse brasses and seemed much less slow of speech and thought than usual.

Helen went back to College and took a course in Fabric Design. Clifford did not object. She was not his child-bride any more. He had learned a lot, inadvertently, from Fanny, Elise, Bente and so forth, especially Fanny. He thought of Fanny quite often. She had fought back, and lost, but he'd listened more than she knew. And her taste had been good. He wondered where she was working. She might be quite useful to Leonardo's, now she'd had more experience.

Clifford wrote a magnificent book on the Impressionists, which sold at £20, an impossible price for a book in those days, even an art book, but it became a best-seller. Harry Blast, the TV art critic, damned it so ferociously—he'd never forgiven Clifford for making a fool of him—for its easy populism that everyone went out and bought it. The only place it's good to have enemies is on the TV screen.

Leonardo's ran smoothly; Angie kept her distance; a Rembrandt Exhibition broke all records for attendance. Then a David Firkin retrospective—and it was a bold step, the first time a contemporary painter had exhibited in the Great Hall—outdid even the Rembrandt in popularity. Leonardo's, like Clifford, could do no wrong. The Queen opened a new annex where experts, as a free public service, priced and gave their verdict on works of art—to the annoyance of antique dealers, who saw their profits whipped away from under their noses, as the public lost its ignorance. Three rather good early Georgian town-houses were demolished to make room for the annex, which was in new brutalist concrete, but that kind of thing was happening all the time, and no one protested, or not much. There just seemed so much of old London around. You could go on pulling it down forever, and not even notice—

As soon as Helen's divorce from Simon came through, Clifford and Helen married, in the Kensington Registry Office. It was a muted affair, for the following reason—that Evelyn died, just a week before the ceremony.

A SACRIFICE

It was with some trepidation, you will understand, that Helen had told her parents that she meant to divorce Simon and remarry Clifford. The Lallys had been occasional, if not frequent, visitors to the Cornbrook household in Muswell Hill. John Lally had not been an easy guest; he would keep lapsing into some diatribe or other about some new villainy perpetrated by the government, or big business, or what he referred to as the Art Industry, all engaged as they were in a conspiracy against the poor, the weak, and the creative artists of this world. Helen was used to it. Simon was not. John Lally would be right in principle but seldom in detail so Simon would see it as his duty to correct the facts, and his father-in-law would then take offense. And no matter how Helen would explain that her husband was in fact sympathetic, and not at all the fascist media-man, on the contrary. And no matter how poor Evelyn (who had begun to look thin and gaunt) would tremble with upset, and beg him to desist, he would not be pacified. And nor would Simon.

And Evelyn had a habit of comparing little Edward's progress with Nell's at the same age, and Simon did not like too much talk of Nell, because it upset Helen, and because anyway Edward did lag rather behind Nell. At two he had barely a few words, while Nell had been talking whole sentences—"Yes, Mum," Helen would say, "but little girls do speak earlier than little boys." And once she explained, "Boys develop their motor skills earlier."

"What funny language they do use these days," was all Evelyn replied. "Motor skills!" Oh, she was sad! "Of course, John and I only had the one child, and that was a girl," she added once, as Helen put a plate of rather good mushroom soup in front of her, as if somehow Helen was nothing to do with her anymore, and why hadn't she been a boy anyway, and that upset Helen even more. She brooded for days. She could not get near her mother, who was locked into some kind of misery-*à-deux* with her father. Helen could not bear to see it, or consider her own part in it and would be glad when her parents went home: relieved of some terrible burden she scarcely understood.

"Why did they only have you?" Simon asked, once.

"I think I cried too much at night when I was a baby," Helen replied, vaguely. "So John couldn't concentrate. Yes, I think that was it."

Oh yes, the artist is as much monster as he's allowed to be. Evelyn had four abortions, put off until the last moment in the hope of John Lally's relenting. He hadn't.

"Have as many babies are you want," he said, "just don't have them anywhere near me," in the same spirit as he would say, if she ventured any kind of complaint, "If you don't like it, leave. I'm not stopping you."

Evelyn hadn't called his bluff. She should have. Evelyn waited, and waited in vain, for the kind word from him to give her the courage she needed. Absurd! She neither stayed, as it were, or left. She just let all that red life-blood go to waste—let out the sons who might have laughed their father to shame—for fear of her husband's temper, her husband's moods. So that Helen, unprotected by the host of chattering, willful, demanding siblings she should have had, withstood alone the full blast of her father's temperament. Moreover, she had learned, on the whole, her mother's way of dealing with it—badly, by meek words and deference, with just the occasional jollying along. And meeting much the same nature in Clifford—attracting him and being attracted as is the fate of such daughters—she dealt with it equally badly.

Of course the marriage to Clifford collapsed: she had in him not quite a father, not quite a husband, more like a husfather. Of course, the weight of that unnaturalness proving too great, she then turned to Simon, a kind of long-lost brother, long-lost out of all existence—and why? Because she'd cried too much as a baby. Helen's fault! All Helen's fault! But how could Simon, husbrother, do her any better? How she flailed about, poor Helen, the victim of her neuroses, wondering why happiness eluded her—and now here she was, trying Clifford again, and just possibly, just possibly this time she'd do better.

And then, of course, leaving Simon and going back to Clifford, she was barred from Applecore Cottage once again. She found it almost a relief. She called her mother from time to time, out of a sense of duty, and sometimes met her, secretly, for lunch at Biba's, and tried not to feel persecuted by her mother's unhappiness, which clouded her own joy.

When the divorce was through and the date for the wedding fixed she spoke to her mother on the phone: "I know John won't come, but will you please, please."

"Darling, it would upset your father so much if I did. You know that. You shouldn't ask. But you'll get on perfectly well without me. And since you've been living with Clifford for nearly a year, and were married to him once before, a ceremony's rather pointless, isn't it? How's little Edward? Is he talking better?"

"She won't come, she won't come," Helen wept into Clifford's shoulder. "It's all your fault!" Oh, she was getting bolder.

"What do you want me to do? Give him his paintings back?"

"Yes."

"So he can cut them up with the garden shears?" He would, too.

"Oh, I don't know. I don't know. Why can't I have parents like yours?"

"Be thankful you don't," he said. "I'll tell you what—go down and beard them in their den. *Make* them come. Both of them. I promise to be nice."

"I'm too frightened."

"No you're not," he said. And, oddly, she wasn't.

So Helen comes down to Applecore Cottage, one Saturday morning, flushed and excited, full of thoughts of Clifford, and determined her parents will be happy for her happiness, pushing open the door, letting sunlight in to the tiny living-room where Evelyn is accustomed to sit and knit or shell peas and wait for

John to appear from studio or garage, in the expectation of either a tirade or a day or so of not-talking, for some fault or act of hers—years old, perhaps—which John has remembered as he stands at his easel; stirring the flake-white or the meridian-blue or the ochre, pondering the nature of color itself, or its appearance in living flesh, rotting flesh, frozen flesh, simmering flesh or whatever that day absorbs him, layering it upon layer, knowing how much better it would be if only he could drum up some intensity of response. But he can't—it has to be poached from somewhere, now that he's no longer young. And paranoia provides a kind of passion and who better (now he so seldom leaves home) to provide the source material for that than Evelyn—and didn't Clifford remark upon it long ago—that Evelyn was part of the gestalt in which John Lally functioned as a painter—

Evelyn knew it. There she sits in the half-dark: the sacrifice. Somehow the room is only dark because she sits there. These days she attracts gloom, the fates move mistily behind her. Helen—coming in with the shaft of sunshine, all things possible again because she is to be with Clifford, and heart, mind and soul are set free, albeit free to tremble and fail as well—sets them moving. The room's haunted, Helen thinks. Why didn't I ever notice? The polished copper pans, hanging from their hooks, sway and tremble as if in a huge wind, but there is no wind.

"Something's happened," says Evelyn. "You're different. What is it?"

"I want you to come to my wedding," says Helen. "And John. Where is he?"

"In the attic, painting. Where else?"

"Is he in a good mood?"

"No. I told him you were coming."

"How did you know? How could you possibly know?"

"I had such a dream last night," is all Evelyn says. She has her hand on her head. "I have a headache. It's a funny kind of headache. I dreamed you were standing hand in hand with Clifford. I dreamed I was dying; I had to die to set you free."

"What do you mean?" Helen is distressed.

"You're too much my daughter, not enough yourself. If you're to be happy with Clifford, you have to be your father's daughter, not mine."

What is she talking about? And Helen hardly through the door, and strange shapes moving in the reflections from the swaying copper pans! Is Evelyn saying that if Helen marries Clifford she will disown her? But Evelyn goes on.

"You have to be with Clifford, I know that, for when Nell comes back."

Helen's mouth drops open.

"In the dream I cast a shadow over you. It was the only shadow there was. So much sunlight everywhere! Nell was walking through green fields. She's nearly seven, you know. So like you when you were a little girl—except her hair, of course. That's like Clifford's."

Helen perceives that her mother is rambling. There is something odd about the way she talks, about the way she slumps in the chair. She calls for her father, up in the attic studio. No one calls up the stairs like that—they're not allowed. He's painting, not to be disturbed. Careful, genius at work! But the note in Helen's voice brings him down, running.

"It's Evelyn—" says Helen.

"Such a headache," says Evelyn. "A funny sort of headache. It's made one bit of my head very clear and the other bit very fuzzy. I'd better just move over, get the shadow out of the way. Don't worry about Nell. She'll be back."

She smiles at her daughter, seems blind to her husband, tries to lift her hand, can't. Tries to move her head, can't; and, looking puzzled, simply dies. Helen can tell, not because the head can't lean any further into the chair than it's leaning already, but that the light in the eyes goes out as if it's switched off. The lids don't even drop. It's John Lally who closes them, although heaven knows he's painted enough dead eyes in his life to be accustomed to such sights.

The doctor says Evelyn probably had two cerebral hemorrhages, possibly three, in the previous twenty-four hours, the last one being fatal.

Helen is left amazingingly at peace. It seems to her that Evelyn, in dying, was simply doing what she'd decided to do. The body had followed the will, obediently. She grieves, but there is a kind of happiness interweaving the grief, which seems Evelyn's gift to her: the sense of life beginning, not ending; a vision of a future which included Nell. Helen rashly told John Lally about Evelyn's dream. He said the balance of his wife's mind was obviously already disturbed, and, incidentally, that if it wasn't a sick joke, and Helen really did want to remarry Clifford, murderer of his grandchild, so far as he was concerned his daughter as well as his wife was dead. Well, he was upset. But you and I know, reader, that Evelyn had not so much a dream as a vision, the kind sometimes given to good people on the point of death, and that she had stayed alive long enough to hand it on to Helen, in recompense for all the many ways in which she had failed her daughter. It is almost impossible, reader, not to fail one's children, one way or another. Inasmuch as our parents failed us.

I wish I could report that John Lally felt remorse for the way in which he had treated his wife during her lifetime, but I can't. He contrived to refer to her—when he remembered her, which wasn't often—as that fool of a woman. Well, there is something to be said for such honesty and consistency. Nothing worse than to hear a newly bereaved spouse talk about how kind and wonderful and good the deceased was, when you have heard them so bitter and reviling just a short while ago. We must try not to speak ill of the living, rather than to speak well of the dead. Time is so short for all of us.

A FUNERAL

How filmmakers love funerals! How often do we not see them on the screen: the open grave, the desolate churchyard, the scattered mourners—everyone looks bleak and chilly and rather cross, as if it was the scene in the film they least liked making. You can almost hear the director's voice: Okay, action. No, Maureen—or Rue, or Henry, or Wendy, or whoever—cut! For God's sake! For the sixth time, you *throw* the earth, you don't just drop it. Shall we do that again, please? Now, the sooner we get this right, the sooner we can all go home. And the wind whips around the legs of the false mourners, reproaching them for the way that this, even this, even death itself is chewed, chumped up, spat out in the interests of plot, profit and fantasy. And even then they seldom get it right—the gritty weariness of it all; the horrid mystery of the coffin; the grisly fate of the mortal remains; the one we knew or loved made nothing, finished, over; the preacher's voice lost in the wind; the sense of futility—oh yes, then at the graveside the tide of our good cheer is at its lowest ebb. How swiftly the generations pass, to no good end, or observable purpose. Why bother with life, the open grave suggests, since death swallows everything up? We even lose our sense of future, the knowledge that as the earth turns, so the water surges up and over and in once more—no, how can the director get all that?

Of course the cameras seldom even *try* to get the spirit of the cremation parlor. What is there here to impress the eye? The more than conventional room, like some suburban dream out of 1950; the plastic flowers; the droning Muzak; the all-purpose preacher; the coffin disappearing on rollers through cinema curtains—not even into the fiery furnace, but simply to be stacked and stored. And whose ashes do you get back, anyway? Yours? Who believes it! Does it matter? Of course not.

The preacher gabbles (twenty services a day), gets his facts wrong, misjudges the deceased, his congregation, yet does his best. It will do. This is the swift, the kindly, the pathetic disposal of the dead. In death we are all ordinary. Let it be.

Evelyn was cremated. John Lally would not attend. Helen, he said, had to choose between having him there, or Clifford. She chose Clifford, since he had never done her mother any harm. On the contrary, Clifford had damp-proofed Evelyn's home, waterproofed her roof, and indirectly provided her with scrag-ends to make many an excellent stew. The villagers of Appleby turned up in number to the funeral. Evelyn had been liked and pitied, and her loyalty to her impossible husband respected. Besides, word had gotten around that Clifford would be there. Clifford Wexford of Leonardo's, whiz kid and publicist, celebrity. He had his own monthy TV program now on BBC, "Finding Your Way Through Art," and though few of them watched it, many of them knew about it. (It wasn't, I am sure, the only reason they came—but the crematorium *was* some way from the village and the numbers *were* remarkable.)

Otto and Cynthia Wexford came, in support of Helen. They would be her parents now, since her mother was dead, and her father, in their eyes, once they heard of his behavior, worse than dead.

Clifford had been surprisingly forgiving.

"As an artist," he says, "he makes little distinction between life and death. That's what his work is all about."

"You mean he's mad," said Otto.

"Half-mad," said Clifford.

"Poor little Helen," said Cynthia. And then, with that kind of sudden intuition which seemed to come out of nowhere and always impressed her family, added, "I expect now her mother's dead, she'll cope with you better."

"I don't need coping with," said Clifford. "I'm the easiest man to get along with in the world—" but he laughed; at least he knew it wasn't true.

"Like God," remarked his mother. She wore fabulous black to the funeral, and a red red rose in her hat. Helen wore the old coat she had worn the night she first met Clifford. She'd never thrown it out. She wasn't sure why, any more than she knew quite why it seemed the right thing to wear to her mother's funeral. It wasn't as if Evelyn had liked it much. But it seemed a token of defiance and love, mixed, which she supposed was apt. She felt she had her mother's blessing.

Anyway, Otto and Cynthia had forgiven her, for whatever it was that had to be forgiven: all the awfulness over the divorce, the arguments about custody of Nell—and she, Helen, must in those days have seemed so very much the villainess. She could see that. But then, after the air disaster, they'd been so shocked and grieved for Nell, so upset by Clifford's part in it—and not just that, but his determination to go on blaming Helen long after the need for it had gone, they'd come to have sympathy for her. John Lally, in their eyes, was now the ogre of the piece. He would do very well to shovel the shit upon, if you will excuse the expression, reader. And I must say, I suffer from the temptation myself. Shit must be shoveled. Helen loves Clifford; I am trying hard to love him too. He loves her; that makes it easier. They are Nell's parents. If we love Nell we must do our best to love her mother and her father both; just as, if we are to love ourselves, we must come to terms with both our parents. Hate one or both, and we hate half or all of ourselves, and it does us no good.

Now Evelyn's vision of little Nell was more or less correct. She romped in the sunlight, in the green fields of Faraway Farm. Farm it was called, but Clive and Polly, its owners, were not so much farmers as criminals, immigrants from London's East End. The place was more of a hideaway for people on the run, and items of value in transit, than for cows, milk, cream and apple trees. It wasn't the cleanest place in the world, either, and Polly's idea of cooking was baked beans on burned toast or, better still, plenty of smoked salmon and champagne, or anything you could eat or drink with no bother at all. All the same, Polly felt herself to be a country girl at heart, and though most of Faraway Farm's twenty acres lay fallow, or were hired out as grazing to neighboring farmers, she would grow the prettiest of creepers over the barns where stolen goods were kept, and where, later, LSD and cocaine were to be manufactured. And, when they were in the money, she'd take a trip to the local garden center, and come home to plant flowers already in bloom. So really, as a thieves' den, it was a prettier place, albeit overgrown, than in the sterner days of its farmhood.

But, reader, I think I go too fast. This is what happened when Nell was discovered at the back of the van on its arrival, in the early hours of the morning, with its loot from the Greatest Antiques Robbery of the century (or so the press called it, though by right they should have said "century so far" for there were still more than twenty-five years to go till its end). Clive and Beano and Polly and Rady heaved out a Chippendale bookcase—carelessly and forever losing a precious chip of inlay, I'm afraid—and then eight very nice little English landscapes (the Rembrandts and van Goghs had been left behind—almost impossible to find a home for stolen major works of art, they're too recognizable) and then a massive pair of Jacobean silver candlesticks—and there crouched at the back was thin little, grubby little, sleepy little, bald-pated Nell.

They helped her out into the sun. *Now* what were they to do? Reader, quite frankly, I hate to think of what might have happened. The most logical thing to do to a witness to a crime, if you are the criminal, is to silence her forever.

But Nell looked around, at the early sun striking the old stone, and the clematis everywhere, and Polly's white cat stretching and sunning itself, and said:

"Isn't it all pretty!" (And I can tell you, reader, compared to the Eastlake Center, it certainly was!) And Clive and Polly, and Beano and Rady, all smiled. Once they had smiled, she was safer.

"What you need is a bath," said Polly, and once Nell had had a bath she was safer still.

Then she shared their breakfast, of Weetabix and cream from the farm next door, and after that what could they do, except keep her for their own?

Nell talked about running away from savage dogs, but they didn't believe anyone could be so wicked as to set savage dogs on a child! She said her name was Ellen Root but Polly and Rady didn't like that. Polly said she'd always liked Nell as a name, so that was what she was called. Polly was a great one for extrasensory preception: she told fortunes from tea-leaves, cast the I Ching, and saw ghosts. Perhaps indeed she had psychic powers. Certainly it was extraordinary that she settled on Nell as a name.

Polly was a wide, laughing, yellow-haired, quick-tempered young woman. Rady was small and thin and brooding and idle. Clive was thin and lithe, and Beano tall and fat. All were under thirty. All believed the next crime would make their fortune, and they could move off to Rio de Janeiro or somewhere exciting and live in luxury together. But somehow they never did; they stayed at Faraway Farm.

Nell's hair grew quickly, and her little face opened out in happiness and contentment. They saw that she was pretty. She picked up a pencil and drew a sketch of Polly's cat, and it was really good and they were proud of her. She was not John Lally's grandchild for nothing. Though fortunately she had inherited only his talent, and not his difficult nature.

"We'd better keep her," said Clive to Polly. "Pretend she's ours, send her to school, join the PTA, that kind of thing. Join in with the locals."

"Me, be a mother!" said Polly in astonishment. The feckless creature had what a psychologist would call "a low self-image." She had never somehow believed she was capable of having a proper marriage, or a proper husband, let alone a proper baby. So here she was at the age of twenty-eight, having achieved exactly what she expected of life. (This is about the age when we discover that our view of ourselves is pretty accurate—or have had years enough to make it so.) But then she said, "Why not? At least I won't have to go through being pregnant, and losing my figure," which was odd, since she had no figure at all to speak of. But young women who have taken a lot of LSD—this was the early seventies, and LSD a real craze—or even a little, do seem to have trouble connecting up with reality. They see the world as they want to see it, not how it is. If they choose to believe there is food in the cupboard, they don't go shopping, whether there is or not. If it's too much trouble for the time to be eight o'clock, and Nell's bedtime, why then the clock reads seven, Polly would stake her life on it! Now there are certain advantages for a child who is brought up this way—a general cheerfulness and let-it-all-hang-out feel to life—but disadvantages too. You do have to learn to fend for yourself and your parents as well, pretty young—to somehow obtain money for food and get to the store yourself, however small you are; to get yourself to bed, no matter how many zonked-out bodies you have to climb over to do so, with psychedelic music in your ears, not bedtime stories. Children like order, security and routine, and if they're not given it, tend to impose it upon themselves. Nell did well enough.

The village school didn't ask too many questions—had the roll fallen by one single pupil, the school was in danger of closing, and at the very sight of Nell, headmasterly eyes beamed with pleasure. The matter of the birth certificate was somehow overlooked, and into Class 2 went little Nell Beachey, Clive and Polly's child. Polly never joined the PTA, of course. There was somehow so little time, such was the flow of stolen goods through the farm, then, in the heyday of the antiques-conscious seventies.

Keep your fingers off the furniture
Your mind on your toys
And keep your pretty eyes to your own little self,
When the grownups have their fun
Whispering with the boys—
That's the time for little children to be deaf and dumb.

—Polly would sing to the tune of "Seven Little Girls, Sitting in the Backseat, A-hugging and A-kissing with Fred," the better to entertain and teach little Nell, as she washed her in the big white bathtub with lion claws, or sang her to sleep in the high iron bed with the soft broken mattress, and the blankets—dusty and thin but plentiful, which were so useful for wrapping furniture, saving it from knocks and hiding its detail from prying eyes. Nell would watch Polly gravely, relearning trust, and new rules. Here food came haphazardly, never on time, but if you were hungry you just took it yourself, from the cupboard or the fridge, and nobody slapped you, or shouted, or frightened you. If you wanted socks for school, you had better find them yourself because nobody else would, and wash them too, if you wanted them clean. Well, that was all right, though going to school in wet socks could be uncomfortable. She could always run away again if anything happened she really didn't like. It had worked once, it could work again.

"Do smile," Polly would entreat her. "Go on, it's a joke!" not knowing that *not* to smile had become for Nell almost a luxury. But soon she didn't have to be persuaded; she smiled at everyone, not out of the need to survive, but because she felt like it, and skipped here and there when she could just as easily have walked—always a good sign—and forgot altogether about running away. This was home. She wondered who her real parents were; she knew better than to ask. No one encouraged questions at Faraway Farm. You just *were*—you just accepted. There were sadnesses in her mind: sometimes she probed them in the same way she wiggled her loose baby-teeth with her tongue, which was both silly, because it hurt, but sensible, because it loosened them and the sooner they were out the better, making eating apples difficult for a time, but the new ones were growing in white, large and strong. There was Rose, who wet the bed; she missed her, and how would Rose manage without her? There was a man and two women, all with wrinkles, in a strange large dark shadowy place; she remembered making toast in front of a fire. She'd make toast for Polly and Clive, and sometimes their friends, if they were still there at breakfast. (She'd collect the empty wine bottles and stack them and say, "Thirteen!" gravely, and "My goodness!" and make everyone laugh.) She didn't like to think too much of the fire: it suddenly got out of control in her mind and was everywhere, a kind of crashing banging wall behind which the three nice old people disappeared. Before that all there was a sort of gentle singing sound, which made her sad and happy at the same time, but she knew was good. That was where she belonged, far away and long ago, and lost forever. Somehow a sea sparkled below, and the sky arched above, and wind blew on her face, and everything was beautiful. Heaven, she supposed.

In the meantime, there was reading, writing, tables, friends, talk and play at school. The rediscovery of a calm yet eventful world. She was shy, quiet and good at first.

"What a bright little girl," said Miss Payne, her teacher, to Polly. "What a credit to you!" and Polly beamed. She became naughtier and livelier as time went on, of course. Never nasty, never ganging up, never one of the tormentors, or the tormented; the peacemaker, whose friend everyone wanted to be. School was fun, and simple, and she could see it was the way forward. She had a little pocket-radio—not cheap, no, fallen off the back of a truck, given to her by one of Clive's friends—and sometimes she'd listen to the talk shows and puzzle over them, and try to work out what was going on in the outside world; not easy at all! When she'd had enough she'd turn to the music program and listen to songs. There was no television at Faraway Farm, not from principle, but because reception was so bad on account of the hills; all you could ever get was a fuzz. So she read, and talked, and skipped, and drew, and presently was happy.

Clive and Polly were excused a good deal on Nell's account. If they could produce so pleasant a child, they couldn't be too bad. And she was talented, too. She did the painting competition on the back of the Weetabix box when she was nine, and came in first in the Under-Tens.

But there, we're running ahead of ourselves. That's something to come, something to look forward to. For the time being, reader, we will leave Nell safely and happily at Faraway Farm, growing nicely, if haphazardly cared for.

BAD NIGHTS

Let's turn our attention back to Arthur Hockney, whom we last saw baby-sitting for Helen, on the night she didn't come home. Arthur Hockney had spent many wretched nights in his life, of course! This is the fate of the insurance investigator. He had all but frozen in the Antarctic on the site of an aircrash, been practically frightened to death by sharks on a minute coral island where a tanker had been scuttled, been tortured almost out of his wits by the gang who'd kidnapped Shergar. But if you asked him what the worse night of his life was (barring the night his parents died) he'd have said, simply, The night I baby-sat for Helen Cornbrook, and she didn't come home.

What unrequited love can do to a man! Did Helen know Arthur loved her? Probably, though he'd never said so. The relationship between them was professional: she employed Arthur to search for Nell. All the same (unless they're your divorce solicitor) it is useful to have your employees in love with you. They charge less and work harder, though they sometimes, it's true, abruptly hand in their notice for no apparent reason.

And of course there was the sheer surprise of it. Helen, during the years when all but she and Arthur believed Nell was dead, had said many a harsh and unkind word about Clifford. If you have lost a man's love, even if by reason of your own faithless nature, it is only natural for you to practice despising and hating him, to make the loss seem not so important. It is the business of saving face, and lessening the grief, I am sure, which makes divorced people so virulent about and spiteful to each other, to the distress and shock of their friends. Helen was no exception, and Arthur, though well-versed in the ways of criminals, in the minds of men who will cheat, lie and kill for their own profit and advancement, knew next to nothing about the heart of a woman. How a woman who hates and insults a man one week can be loving and admiring him the next. Amazing!

The evening Arthur came to visit Helen to report his progress in the search for Nell, and found her second husband Simon away, and the phone rang out of the blue and it was Clifford, asking Helen out to dinner, he did not expect her to say yes. He did not expect her to ask him to baby-sit, let alone to find himself saying "yes."

He did not expect her to stay out all night. He did not expect to be so distressed and angry and jealous as the hours ticked away. He did not expect the pain in his chest, which he thought at first must be illness but presently realized was the effect of a broken heart. He felt not just wretched, but a fool as well. Indeed, it was the worst night of his life. And then, when it became apparent that Helen was going to remarry Clifford, actually remarry the man who had caused her so much distress, he vowed to give up the Nell Wexford case, place it in its special "lost child" file.

And yet. And yet. Forget Helen, forget Clifford, forget his own emotions—here there was still a mystery, and it was in Arthur's nature to solve mysteries. One day, on impulse, he went once more to visit Mrs. Blotton. Three years now since the two million pounds compensation had been paid. Over four years since the accident which had allegedly killed Erich Blotton and little Nell. Time enough, thought Arthur Hockney, for Erich Blotton to believe he could safely return from the dead, if that had been his intention.

Mrs. Blotton was living in the same small, safe house in the same tree-lined suburban road (its numbers ran to 208) as she had before her windfall. She was wearing, Arthur could swear, the same old tweed skirt and thin red jumper as when he'd seen her four years earlier. She was as thin, plain and nervous as ever. He couldn't tell, as ever, whether her nervousness sprang from guilt, or from the fact that he, Arthur, was so black.

"You again!" she said, but she let him into her neat, shabby front room. "What do you want? My husband's dead and gone. And even if he were alive, why should he come back to me?"

"Because of the money," said Arthur.

She laughed a thin little laugh.

"Oh yes," she said, "if money could fetch anyone back from the grave, it would be Erich Blotton. But there isn't much left. I see to that. I give it away. In dribs and drabs to make it last. It's my occupation. It gets me out of the house."

"You have a kind heart," he said.

That pleased her. She made him a cup of tea.

"You blacks!" she said. "Taking over! You're everywhere now. Up and down this very street. Well, you can get used to anything."

"Thank you," he said.

"Nothing personal," she said.

"Never is," he said, though his parents would be ashamed of him, that he should grit his teeth against insult, and do nothing to change or improve the world. The truth was, and he knew it, that he, a brave man in the physical sense, was a moral coward. Put him before a maddened criminal trying to drive an ax into his head and he functioned; put him on a platform and ask him to address a public meeting, and his heart beat hard, his hands trembled, and his tongue was tied. He disgraced himself and the cause he espoused. Faced with Mrs. Blotton's racism, born of stupidity, neuroses, and ignorance, he did nothing to persuade or educate her, and was ashamed of himself.

Mrs. Blotton, in the meantime, volunteered the fact that she gave the money to children's homes. She'd always been upset at what her husband did for a living, but what could she do? A wife's loyalty was to her husband. But all the same—child-snatching! Mostly for fathers, because it was the fathers who had the money, while the mothers had the children. However, that was all over now. She was glad to have a visitor, even one like Arthur. It wasn't often she had the chance to chat. To be frank, she was quite lonely. Just the cat. And not much of a cat either. Scraggy, gutter-thing. She'd have bought a Persian with some of the money, only the neighbors would have stolen it and skinned it and turned it into stew and sold the skin.

"Why don't you leave, go to the South of France, live it up a little? You're a millionaire."

"Hush!" She hated the word; she was terrified of being robbed. And how could she possibly get to the South of France? What would she do when got there? And who with? She didn't make friends easily. No, better just stay quiet and give the money away. Besides, she didn't want to leave the house empty; someone would only break in and mess it up. She lay awake at night, thinking about it, thinking of what her husband had done. Of course he was dead. He's been paid out for smoking. What was smoking but suicide? Well, God had gotten in there first. And for snatching the little Wexford girl. What was her name? Nell? Now there was a real tragedy. She'd like to adopt a little girl, but who would let her? A middle-aged widow! Or even try fostering. She'd like to make amends.

She'd come across a child in one of the Assessment Centers who'd really taken her fancy. Ellen Root. About the same age as the Wexford child. Not much to look at; they kept shaving her head. She'd asked if she could take her home, but they wouldn't let her. The child was backward, so they said. She didn't believe it. She knew French when she heard it. They, being ignorant, just thought the child was babbling.

"French?" asked Arthur. "She was speaking French? Where is she now?"

"She's disappeared," said Mrs. Blotton, and Arthur thought, "That's it! That's her!" inasmuch as a child who disappears once, twice, will disappear thrice. It's a kind of life habit, a tendency, if you like. But Ellen Root? Eleanor Wexford became Ellen Root? It was unthinkable!

"For a black man," said Mrs. Blotton, "you're not so bad. Do you smoke?"

"No," said Arthur.

"Well," said Mrs. Blotton, forgivingly, "that's something. I suppose it takes all sorts to make a world."

"I daresay it does, Mrs. Blotton."

To his surprise, she shook his hand when he left, and smiled, and he saw she had a sort of charm. Perhaps his parents would not think too badly of him, for his way of life. The notion that he should follow in their footsteps, he suddenly saw, had been his, rather than theirs: a product of his guilt, that he should be alive, and they so suddenly and violently dead. He could never bring their murderers to justice, yet his life's work lay in the righting of wrongs. That was surely enough. He left No. 208 with a livelier step and a lighter heart, noticing that even here, down this bleak surburban road, birds sang in the bushes, and roses burgeoned, and cats sat on windowsills and stared, with round judgmental eyes which, for once, seemed to approve and not condemn.

PATTERNS OF GUILT

Arthur Hockney left Mrs. Blotton and went forthwith to see the Eastlake Assessment Center.

He found a low modern building in concrete and glass, the concrete stained with damp and graffiti, and the glass dirty and in places broken. The Center was fairly new, but it had had time to become dilapidated, in that peculiarly sad way that neglected modern buildings have, as if longing to return as quickly as possible to the raw material from which they so ill-judgedly sprang.

Arthur knocked on the peeling door. He heard no sound of children at play, no laughter. He wondered why. Mrs. Blotton had referred to Ellen Root as having her head shaved. Who, in this day and age, shaved the heads of little girls?

The door was eventually opened by a young woman of half Chinese, half (as he was to discover later) Welsh descent. She was, Arthur thought, strikingly pretty. An overweight Doberman walked affectionately at her heels, and from the pocket of her green smock—which did a great deal for her green slanty eyes—she would take the occasional Marrow Bone Snack and casually feed the beast.

"We're closed," said Sarah Dobey, not unappreciative of Arthur's own black good looks, "and not a moment too soon. Which agency are you from? Animal Rights, the Royal Society for the Prevention of Cruelty to Animals, Child Abuse, Fraud Squad, Hornby Electrics? We've had them all." Arthur explained his business over dinner that evening. (Sometimes very pretty, very bright, too clever young girls are without boyfriends. What young man can stand the pace? Takes an older, more worldly man and they're so often married or otherwise unavailable.) The Doberman went too, and curled up good as gold beneath the table, accepting scraps of Sarah's vegetable pie and Arthur's steak. Sarah was a vegetarian.

"Ellen Root?" Sarah exclaimed. "But that was the child who started the whole thing off!"

"Started what off?"

"The scandal! Of course they hushed it up as much as they could. It never got into the papers."

And she told him what had happened. She, Sarah Dobey, had been working as a clerk in the local Welfare Office. (She was overqualified, of course, with her Master's Degree in Philosophy, but who would employ her as a philosopher? Someone who looked like her? Look at her! Annabel Lee, housemother at Eastlake, had reported a child missing, apparently run away. A police search had altogether failed to find her. The Welfare Office, disturbed for some time by reports filtering through from Eastlake, sent Sarah in as a domestic, to see just what was going on.

"You can always tell a white woman's character," said Sarah, "from her behavior toward the cleaning staff, especially if that cleaning staff is what she would call black, brown or yellow and, I tell you, Annabel Lee's character was bad, bad, bad! She covered up well for officials but, being the maid, I soon discovered that she bullied and tormented the children, kept the dogs underfed and locked up, and as for the housefather, although well-versed in child-care-and-development jargon, he was a toy-train enthusiast, and either didn't know or didn't care what was going on, so long as he collected his salary and added to his collection."

She, Sarah Dobey, had made her report, mailed it, and that very night, not knowing much about animals, but upset by their howling, had opened the door of the compound, and they'd leaped out. She hadn't expected it. Annabel Lee had stumbled downstairs, to see what was going on, the dogs had jumped at her, and she had for some reason taken fright and fled across the marshes, pursued by the two animals—("They only wanted to be taken for a walk!" said Sarah. "Poor things!")—onto the roadway, where she had been hit by a passing truck, flung into the fast lane, and killed.

"I wish I could feel sorry," said Sarah, "inasmuch as I daresay it was all my fault. I know I ought to, but somehow I can't. I think it's my Degree in Philosophy. It gives me a kind of perspective. Perhaps I need treatment?"

"I don't think so," he said.

Horace Lee had seemed more upset about having to dismantle his train set—for the Home was closed and the children, to their relief, dispersed—than about the death of Annabel Lee or the loss of his job.

"None so strange as folk," sighed Sarah (who sometimes enjoyed using the vernacular as a relief from her usual measured spoken prose) and Arthur agreed. Oddly, he thought, there was something of Helen in Sarah—the high cheekbones, the limpid look—only in Sarah it was the look of the optimist, not the pessimist; someone who sees the answer in action, not in submission.

Anyway, Sarah had stayed on to supervise the closure and dismantling of Eastlake. She'd found a good home for one of the dogs, Kettle, but not for the other, now under the table, the one named Kim. But she didn't know much about dogs, and couldn't keep the animal for long.

"You might be overfeeding it," said Arthur cautiously, and nudged the animal with his foot, and Kim looked up at him. "On the other hand," added Arthur, "it's just as well to keep this kind of dog happy." He had a feeling the Eastlake dogs had taken justice into their own hands. These things happen. He raised his eyebrows at the dog, and Kim blinked back and laid his head on Arthur's shoe.

"Well," said Arthur, "I'll be Kim's guardian. He'll need retraining and getting back into condition. I have friends who keep kennels on the Welsh border."

And of course Sarah had relatives there and one way and another the connections between them crossed and recrossed and knotted themselves in the most thorough and satisfactory way. Which was, I think, the reward for Arthur's steadfastness and resolution in relation to Nell, and for staying all night babysitting for Helen's Edward, when another man in similar circumstances might simply have walked out. Good deeds get rewards sooner or later, though in unexpected ways.

Ellen Root, Sarah discovered, had disappeared on the night of the great Montdragon antiques robbery. It was known they'd taken the roadway. The whole episode had been peculiar. Ellen Root was a child without a history, an English child picked up wandering on a French roadway and now she was gone, as if she had never been.

"At least," said Sarah, "she had the guts and sense to run! No one else did. And it was because she ran that Eastlake was closed, and not a moment too soon."

"If the police couldn't find her," said Arthur, "I daresay it was because the villains did! Find them, find her." He felt he knew by now the pattern of Nell's fate. He had an instinct for these things and, of course, reader, as you know, he was right. Nell had gone into hiding, along with the stolen Chippendale bookcase.

Kim stretched up and licked his hand, and Arthur felt, suddenly and unexpectedly, that wherever Nell was, she was well and happy, and the dog somehow linked to her fortune, and his, and all he had to do was love Sarah and look after the dog, and one day, one day, fate would bring Nell to him. Life can change so suddenly for the better, reader. If you only forgive yourself, and allow yourself to be happy.

ADMIRING ART

"What on earth is in here?" asked Angie of Clifford, staring into the River Gallery at Leonardo's, a long narrow room, newly opened, overlooking the Thames, its beautifully lit walls lined with what to her looked like a series of ragged scrawls.

"Children's art," said Clifford, shortly. She was on a flying visit. He was about to be the father of twins. Helen drifted around the Orme Square house, happy and languid and secure, barefooted and vast, somehow, gratifyingly, all his own doing. Being pregnant with twins is not usually easy, but Helen was relaxed and content, and only occasionally sighed and groaned. He would be with her in the hospital. Of course he would. If you lose one child, you don't want to miss a moment of the next, even though it comes in the form of a double helping.

"What on earth," asked Angie, "is Leonardo's doing with children's art?"

"Exhibiting it," said Clifford as Angie tucked her arm in his. On her finger was a diamond ring the size of a plum. "Weetabix is sponsoring a children's art exhibition. They asked us if they could use the new gallery. We said yes."

"Good God," she said. "Why? Where's the profit in it?"

"PR," he said. He hadn't told Helen that Angie was over. He didn't want her upset. He wished Angie would just go away. He certainly didn't want to be lured into a Claridges bed with her. She was looking particularly sunbaked and lean.

"Terrible scrawls," said Angie. "The thing about child art is that it isn't quaint, as parents like to think. It's just plain *bad*."

They stopped by one painting, prettily done, which Clifford thought had a kind of ethereal quality. It had won first prize in the Under-Tens. It was the painting of two rather vaguely portrayed people, encased in a kind of conch shell or was it an aircraft tail, or a sort of heavenly descending elevator, being lowered on ropes of doves, at the hands of angels, who leaned out of fluffy clouds and gazed benignly down on a gentle sea.

"How very peculiar," said Angie. "Whoever did that should see someone."

"I think it's enchanting," said Clifford, and looked to see the name of the artist. It was by a certain Nell Beachey (9). He remembered his own Nell and moistened his lips. Grief sometimes still took him unawares, but these days made him sad, not angry. How old would Nell be now?

"Rather Lally-like," he said, "in its way. Except it's not cross, but happy."

"I can't think what you're talking about," said Angie. "I still have this suite at Claridges. Shall we go and share a bottle of champagne and celebrate the twins?"

I am sorry to say that Clifford did, though crossing his fingers in his mind, the better to pretend it hadn't happened. But it had. It did. Angie flew off, victorious. Helen knew nothing about it. Clifford didn't tell. What harm was done? Oh, reader, in the scheme of things, the great balance in which good deeds are weighed against bad, even if no observable harm was done, let us just say it simply didn't help. Now did it!

PEACE AND QUIET

Reader, picture a tranquil valley in the Welsh border country, in the year 1977. Picture gentle hills, rushing streams, the winding A49 and, a mile or so from it, the small village of Ruellyn, about which nothing is unusual except the church with the Saxon tower the occasional tourist comes to see. Envisage Faraway Farm, on Ruellyn's outskirts, secluded, charming and dilapidated, and leaving on the school bus in the morning, and returning in the evening, a neat, pretty, bright, twelve-year-old schoolgirl, in her first year at the Comprehensive. And this of course is none other than Nell Wexford, and I am sure you will be glad to know that she has had at least a few years of peace and quiet, albeit amongst criminals. As indeed have her natural father and mother, Clifford and Helen—though only John Lally and a handful of others would describe the world the latter moved in as "criminal." That is to say, the Art World. Ten years later, now when the past is plundered by the present and the vision of the artist is devalued by the greed of those who know only too well how to exploit it, the word does not perhaps sound quite so inappropriate, so paranoiac, as it did then.

Reader, back to the subject of peace, quiet, and the child. It is my ambition to see the word "punishment" removed forthwith from the English language. I never knew anyone, child or adult, who was "punished" and was better for the experience. Punishment is inflicted by the powerful upon the powerless. It breeds defiance, sulking, fear and hatred, but never remorse, reform or self-understanding. It makes matters worse, not better. It adds to the sum total of human misery; it cannot possibly subtract from it. By all means, slap the child who puts his fingers in the electric socket, or runs across the road without looking—how can you help it? Besides, it is a reaction more than a genuine punishment, and the child forgives it instantly—but if you wish to make a child behave, remember that the frown and groan of a mother who usually smiles is most feared by the child than the wallop and shriek of a mother who always slaps anyway.

I say this because it was to the great credit of those two criminals Clive and Polly that they never punished Nell and were always proud of her and I do believe this is why, in spite of everything, she survived so well in their care. The world reckoned them bad, really bad, but in the scale of human wickedness and cruelty, the receiving, hiding and selling of stolen property isn't to my mind all that frightful. And Clive and Polly were so inefficient at their business that they would leave French-polished tables out in the rain, and stand softwood chairs in damp hay so the legs rotted, and leave tapestries in full sunlight so they faded, and quite often forgot to ask for money, and didn't count it when they did receive it—and once you get a reputation for that, watch out! Nell did what she could. Even as quite a small child she had a natural eye for a "good piece"; she didn't like to see beautiful things going to rack and ruin.

"Clive," she'd say, "shall we just move the table inside? Look, the top's going all bubbly in the sun. I'll help. I'll take this end, you take that."

"Later, darling," he'd say, idly, and probably add, "Whatever did we do without you, Nell?" with total sincerity, but somehow all he did was just take another drag on his herbal cigarette (or that's how he explained the funny smell to Nell) and it never got done, and when Beano and Rady came to collect the table it was all froth, bubble and rot rather than good hard honed salable-if-stolen wood, and there'd be trouble.

I am not forgiving them their criminality, reader, don't misunderstand me. I'm just saying Clive and Polly did well by little Nell in some ways, not others, and will have their reward, as we shall see, on this earth.

"Hippies!" said the villagers of the strange, vague, long-haired folk of Faraway Farm, with their irrational comings and goings, and night visitors, and the sacks full of baked-bean cans and empty wine bottles left out for the weekly dustcart to take away. The refuse team-leader was the uncle of the postmistress, who was the cousin of Miss Barton at the village store, and the people of Ruellyn were not daft, and knew well enough what was going on. But the tenants at Faraway Farm were helpful neighbors and would turn out to look for a lost cow, and let their spare land for grazing, and Polly played the piano at the weekly disco, so they said nothing. And besides, there was Nell. No one wanted to upset Nell by calling the police, or anything drastic like that. They were proud of their Nell, who had won the Under-Tens Weetabix painting competition in 1974 and, though she'd never quite made it to the top again, had had many runner-up and honorable-mentions since.

Miss Barton at the shop held onto the entry forms for Nell, or got them from her librarian sister in Cardiff.

"Nell," she'd say, "how about best essay on the Commonwealth, Under-Fifteens?" or "Young Journalist of the Year is coming up again!" or "What about the Save Our Planet painting competition, Under-Sixteens, Nell?"—hardly seeming to notice that Nell was only twelve, and off Nell would go to do her best. She learned the lesson young that other people's high expectations of you are not only a pleasure, but a burden as well. It is not enough to succeed; you have to go on succeeding. So Nell would stay late at school, with the reference books around, working away; or be up early at Faraway Farm, with a blanket wrapped around her and her hands almost too cold to hold the brush, painting, drawing, sewing. Oil-fired central heating had been installed at the farm before Clive and Polly rented the place, but if they could remember to order the oil they couldn't afford to pay for it, and vice versa, so the winters were very, very cold.

The view of the village was that Nell had really quite a hard time of it. She did after-school and Saturday jobs from the beginning. Even as a seven-year-old she could tell a plant from a weed, and would thin out carrots, with her little dexterous fingers, better and more quickly than many an adult. She would run errands and take parcels to the daily bus and pick gooseberries—a thorny job—without pulling the branches, and in general be sensible and not complain. Later, of course, she baby-sat and child-walked, and the little ones loved her and were good as gold in her care. But it was noticeable that the next day Nell would be up at Miss Barton's spending the money not on crisps and sweets and Sindy Dolls but on things like bread, cheese, eggs, oranges or Ajax, which she'd then lug up the hill to Faraway Farm. Once a month or so Polly would appear in the shop, all long skirts and smiles, with wads and wads of fivers and practically buy up the shelves, but it was little Nell who had to remind her about things like Brillo, furniture polish and dishwashing liquid. The village reckoned it was Nell, and not her mother, who kept Faraway Farm in order, and they were right. Another lesson Nell learned young was that if your environment is not as you'd like it, you'd better not sit about moaning and complaining, but do what you can to improve it.

But as for her not bringing friends home, well, that did remain a problem. Forget that some families are like that: some mothers just can't stand the tramp, noise and mess of other people's children, can they, seeing their own as bad enough? But somehow Polly didn't fit into this category, with her generous bosom and laddered tights. It was odd.

"Can I come over to your house?" Nell's best friend Brenda Kildare would keep asking.

"You wouldn't like it," Nell would say.

"Why wouldn't I like it?"

And Nell would um and ah until one day she found a solution and said, "It's haunted," and that quieted everybody down.

It just might have been true.

Now Nell, at the age of twelve, knew well enough that Clive and Polly were not her true parents. On the other hand, she could see that they loved her, within the limits of their own natures. That is to say, the more Nell was prepared to do in the way of organizing, cleaning, earning, housekeeping, even liaising with their robber friends, the more grateful and dependent they became.

"Nell, you're a wonder," they'd say, as she set some delicate dish of, say, cumin-spiced pork and noodles in front of them.

"Now how about a proper Indian kedgeree for breakfast?" Nell read the cookery columns—perforce the daily cooking-on-a-budget ones, though how she dreamed over the Sunday recipes, all lobster, quails' eggs, cream and brandy! (She had inherited, I fear, her father's taste for luxury.) But she was prudent; she never overspent.

"Only one twenty-five the whole meal," Nell would say proudly. And then, perhaps, casually, "Are Rady and Beano expected down tonight?"

"Maybe." Polly and Clive tried, in a halfhearted way, to keep their criminal enterprises out of Nell's way. To their credit, they wanted her to grow up "straight."

"Because there's a speed trap on the A49 today. They're ever so active at the moment. Perhaps we ought to tell Beano and Rady. They wouldn't want to be stopped for speeding, would they?"

"I'll give them a call later," Clive would say, and take another puff on his "herbal" cigarette and forget all about it, so it would be Nell who'd call up Rady and Beano.

"Go really slowly if you're coming down," she'd say. "Police traps on the A49; you know, that bit where it says forty and everyone goes seventy?"

"Thanks, Nell," they'd say, blessing the day the fugitive six-year-old child had crept into the back of their van and been swept down the roadway to Faraway Farm. Police speed-traps uncover all kinds of things besides motorists with a penchant for speed, so think kindly of them, reader, next time they get you.

WORKING OUT THE PAST

Nell, too, blessed the day she had arrived at Faraway Farm; when, crop-headed, cold and frightened, she had emerged from the back of the furniture van into the beauty of the rural wilderness, and had passed into Polly's haphazard if generous care. She no longer bothered to wonder whose child she really was. At eight she'd decided (as little girls will at that age, even if they have birth certificates to prove otherwise) that she was in all likelihood royalty, or some kind of lost princess. By nine she'd decided that was unlikely. By ten she'd come to the conclusion that whoever her parents were, they were certainly not Clive and Polly. Her real parents, she was convinced, wouldn't live in a smoky cloud of indecision, muddle, unemptied ashtrays, half-empty wine glasses, unfed hens the fox kept getting, unrealized promises and lost opportunities. (Nell, rest assured, very quickly took over the keeping of the poultry, and many an excellent egg breakfast resulted, and sponge cake for tea, made as the best sponges are, with a single giant goose egg, flour, sugar and no fat at all.)

So all Nell had from her past was a memory or two, and the tin teddy bear on a silver chain, which she had long ago unscrewed to discover her mother's emerald pendant. Nell had quietly and silently replaced it, and hidden it in a safe place at the back of her cupboard, where the plaster was holed and crumbly, and where no one was likely to put a casual hand.

For some reason the little green jewel made her want to cry; it brought with it vague memories of silk dresses and a soft voice and smiles, but what was she to make of those? A guilty feeling went along with this particular resonance from the past—a suspicion that she had no business with the emerald in the first place. (Reader, you will remember that Nell, aged three, took it without permission to "show" at her nursery school, on the day that her adventures started, and you will be glad to know that, in spite of her close acquaintance with Clive and Polly, she is still capable of feeling guilt and remorse—that she is, in fact, in no danger of being criminalized!)

When she was twelve, Nell would lie awake at night, watching the branch of the ash tree rub against the window (it ought to have been pruned long ago, of course) in the light of the porch lamp which no one ever remembered to turn off, and listening to the noise of revelry below. Then she would try to make sense of remembered incidents. Now she had a vision of a storm, and a fire, and a terrible wrenching and crashing of metal—and wasn't she nervous about fire and far more cautious than her friends when it came to crossing the A49? And another memory, a kind of very disagreeable close-up, of a dog with a slavering mouth, baring hideous teeth, and she didn't like dogs—and then she'd fall asleep, conscious that all that was in the past, that the present was okay; the sense of being protected, of being enfolded with goodwill, still with her.

But, reader, the law of the land is the law of the land and Faraway Farm cannot continue forever thus, poised between good and evil; and neither can Nell live as if her past did not exist—presently it will rise up and affect the present. Clive and Polly will have to face the consequences of what I suppose we can describe only as moral sloppiness and Nell will have to move on. As we and Arthur Hockney know, it is in her fate, her nature, her destiny.

TWO
INTERCONNECTIONS

Actually, during her stay at Faraway Farm, Nell's past was closer than she dreamed. Once when she was eleven, Clifford's parents Otto and Cynthia had visited Ruellyn Church, and Nell had passed them in the street, and caught Cynthia's attention.

"What a pretty child," said Cynthia to Otto.

"Nell would be about that age," said Otto, and sighed, surprising Cynthia. They seldom spoke now about their lost granddaughter, for Clifford and Helen had the twins, Marcus and Max, Max ten minutes the younger. The present was so full it had somehow unknitted the past. Nell had looked with interest after Cynthia and Otto, as they passed, admiring Cynthia's elderly elegant beauty, Otto's powerful dignity, and determined there and then not to be content with Ruellyn, but to one day go out into the larger, busier world and make her way therein.

And then again, it was because Nell disliked dogs and wanted to overcome the fear that when she was thirteen she took a Saturday job at the Border Kennels, run by her best friend Brenda's parents. You know my views on coincidence, reader, and will not be surprised to hear that it was to the Border Kennels that Arthur Hockney and his live-in girlfriend Sarah had taken the dog Kim for retraining, after its mistreatment at the hands of Annabel Lee; and that this was where they now left the animal whenever they went on holiday. Kim, the very dog which, made savage by hunger, bad treatment and evil commands, had once chased poor little Nell across Hackney Marshes! Now Nell steeled herself and patted him, and he smiled back. Dobermans do smile, when they want to be liked. To make this kind of observation about animals is, I know, to lay oneself open to charges of anthropomorphism—the bad habit of attributing human characteristics to animals—but all I can do is repeat, Dobermans smile when they feel like smiling. I've seen it too often to doubt it.

CAUSE AND EFFECT

One night, when Nell had stayed over at the kennels and was fast asleep in a strange bed, the police raided Faraway Farm. What had happened was this. As the receiving business had expanded, so had the rack and ruin. Rain fell onto antique leather through the barn roof, and ducks laid their eggs in eighteenth-century cedar chests, and moths got into the woolen interfaces of Henry V's (alleged) gold doublet, and of course there were ugly scenes, from increasingly ugly customers. What could they expect? So Clive and Polly switched their interest from receiving stolen goods to the manufacture of LSD in the old pig-shed and eventually brought the full wrath of the police upon them, by way of a dawn raid, and drew to an end the idyll of Faraway Farm.

And, once again, Nell was homeless.

Now of course she was upset. How could she not be?

Everything that was familiar suddenly gone! Clive and Polly vanished from her life: Clive who had walked her to school when she was little; Polly who had sung to her in the bath. Ah it was sad, not to mention sudden. And yet, there was a kind of relief in it too. Nell had been developing more and more of late a kind of resistance—ingratitude, she sometimes felt—to her surrogate parents. She could see that she was exploited, that her hard work supported their idleness. That what was expected of her—no, not quite, because after all she did the *offering*—was all the same unreasonable. That she, in fact, was the child and they the adults, and it hadn't been fair of them to pretend otherwise. When Clive and Polly disappeared into police custody—now you see them, now you don't, like some kind of conjuring trick with which she was all too familiar—the difficult and complicated feelings disappeared with them.

And of course she'd been spending more and more time

with the Kildares, staying the night, watching television (reception was better, just the other side of the hill), helping out in the kennels, sleeping on Brenda's bottom bunk—Brenda always took the top—as if somehow she'd known what would happen at Faraway Farm, and had been preparing a second home, just in case. Well, she needed it now. She cried on Mrs. Kildare's plump, kind shoulder; Mr. Kildare lent her his linen handkerchief—he refused to use tissues, saying they made his nose sore.

"She must live with us," said Mr. Kildare.

"What about the authorities?" asked Mrs. Kildare. "There must be some kind of formality, surely."

"I shouldn't worry about formalities," said Mr. Kildare. "She's way under working age and doing four hours a day so what I say about Authority is, don't stir them up. Let sleeping dogs lie!" And he laughed. Let sleeping dogs lie! It was night. Outside in their kennels they whined and grunted, gruffled and stirred, and snored and jerked in their slumber. And Nell and Brenda, with their Wellington boots and flashlights, made a good-night round just to see that all was well.

"I never liked the thought of Brenda's bottom bunk lying idle," said Mrs. Kildare, who liked things to be orderly.

The washing machine went day and night. Food was on the table at set times. Brenda and Nell sat down with washed hands, and though what there was to eat was mostly Birds Eye chicken pie and peas, or hamburgers and french fries, followed by chocolate delight or angel whip, they'd have done their homework, mixed the dogs' food, cleaned out the kennels, and have an hour's TV to look forward to before the good-night round. For Nell it was a rest from responsibility, and from freedom, which had come to her, perhaps, rather too young.

No one in Ruellyn mentioned Nell to the police. Let the child stay at the kennels, all agreed. They didn't want to lose their Nell, their pride and joy, once winner of a Weetabix painting competition, the one of Under-Tens. The villagers formed around Nell the protective ring of their concern. It was from the milkman they'd first had tidings of the dawn raid on Faraway Farm. Dan had driven his van right into the middle of the police ring; well, how was he to know each bush had a policeman behind it? He'd been moved on, quickly enough, but the noise he managed to make seemed to have given the game away. He reckoned someone in the house had gotten out the back, and that someone was probably the real villain. Certainly it wasn't Polly and Clive—they moved more slowly than even Ruellyn expected, and before they could so much as rub the sleepy-dust out of their eyes they were under arrest, and taking the whole blame for everything.

Dan had taken the news back to Miss Barton at the shop, and a quick phone call from her to the Kildares at the kennels had made sure that Nell stayed where she was.

"A child's room at Faraway Farm? I think they did once have a niece for a month or so," said Miss Barton to the nice Inspector. "But they were kind of sloppy people. I expect they just never got around to dismantling it."

"Kind of sloppy people!" It was Ruellyn's verdict on Clive and Polly, who spent Christmas Day 1978 in separate corrective centers. At Clive's center they were allowed to watch *Bridge on the River Kwai* as a special treat. At Polly's center someone had made a mistake in the ordering and *Mary Poppins* was screened. But everyone quite liked it, especially Polly. She had a nice nature, and I'm glad she only got two years. Clive got eight, for manufacturing and dealing in illegal drugs.

Christmas Day, 1978. What were you doing, reader? Count back, think back. We had turkey, I suppose—but wasn't that the year we had a spectacular roast goose and mashed potato, and everything went right—or was it wrong? Painful, thinking back, if only because the faces around the Christmas table were all so much younger; but pleasant too, because most of our family histories, surely, will include each year a birth, a marriage, a twenty-first birthday, something happy to look back upon? Well, I hope so.

That was the year Nell spent Christmas morning going around the boarding kennels, showing those dogs lucky (or unlucky!) enough to have devoted if absentee owners the Christmas cards those owners had sent them. Brenda went with her.

"There, Pip," they'd say, handing out a special Christmas Good Dog Chocolate Drop, "it's from Mupsy and Pupsy, Happy Christmas, they write, and all our love!" A stroke and a pat, and on they'd go, two of a pair, two pretty bouncy lively girls, full of proper Christmas goodwill mixed up with mirth at the absurdity of their task. Clients are clients the world over, and their will must be done, especially on Christmas morning.

"There, Jax! Take a look! That's a picture of a bone, a b-o-n-e, and that's a Christmas ribbon around it. No, Jax, look at it, don't eat it! Oh, Jax! It was from Mumsy and Dadsy, too!"

Kim the Doberman didn't get a card. Arthur and Sarah, her owners, were too sensible for that. They did phone the kennels, though, so she could hear the sound of their voices. She pricked up her ears and wagged her tail, and Nell was sure she smiled. Kim always seemed especially fond of Nell, but Nell was never quite convinced she trusted Kim.

Clifford and Helen spent Christmas Day with Clifford's parents, Otto and Cynthia. They took with them a nanny and the twins Marcus and Max, Edward, now nine, and also Edward's father Simon Cornbrook. He had nowhere else to go for Christmas Day, and Helen was sorry for him. Janice was off covering a story in Reykjavík, or so she said. Their service flat was bleak and unhomely.

"Helen, this is absurd!" remonstrated Clifford. "Why should my parents have to put up with your ex-husband?"

"He's not really an ex-husband," said Helen. "He hardly ever counted as a husband." Poor Simon, taken so seriously by the world—a lead journalist now, for *The Economist*—and so unseriously by everyone else! "I feel so bad about it all, and Edward would be thrilled—"

And Clifford capitulated but he was not pleased. And, reader, I am sorry to say that Angie Wellbrook, now back art-dealing in Johannesburg, phoned Clifford to wish him a merry Christmas, and if Clifford hadn't been put out at having to sit at a table with a man—however entertaining and civilized—with whom his wife had once shared a bed, he might have answered more abruptly. As it was, he sounded quite friendly, and Angie resolved to fly over to the U.K. very soon. She thought that having twins might well have satiated Clifford with family life—and she was not far wrong.

John Lally, Helen's father the painter, didn't celebrate Christmas at all. That was the way he wanted it. He liked to pretend the day did not exist. Now although unable to report that John Lally regretted the way he had treated his wife during her lifetime, I can at least report with truth that he was lonely without her. Therefore he quickly found her substitute. Within a year of Evelyn's death he was married to Marjorie Field, a very pleasant, competent, rather plain, mature student of Fine Arts, who thought he was wonderful, chivvied him along, and was happy enough to give up Christmas that year, any year, if he suggested it. She was having the kitchen rebuilt. During the afternoon Marjorie was pleased, on John's behalf, to receive a phone call from Johannesburg, from a woman art-dealer, an Angie Wellbrook, who wanted to come over and "discuss John's work."

"Angie Wellbrook?" said John Lally. "Rings a bell . . . no, can't remember! If she wants to waste her money flying over, when I'm already owned by the shysters of Leonardo's, more fool her! Let her come!"

During that Christmas afternoon, Nell and Brenda made a secret excursion to Faraway Farm, and rescued Nell's tin teddy bear from its hiding place. Nell unscrewed the head and took out the emerald pendant and held it in her closed hand.

"Think of me now," she said aloud, "whoever you are, and whatever you are, just as now I think of you." And at just about that time, Otto, in his Scandinavian fashion, raised a toast, and his wife and the guests rose to their feet and lifted their glasses.

"Here's to our lost little Nell," said Otto, Nell's grandfather. "Whether she be in heaven or on earth. And may the memory of Nell remind us how important it is to value those we have, while we still have them."

But of course it was Christmas, a time when it's only natural to think of family lost or far away, so perhaps it was not all that much of a coincidence, after all.

THE RETURN OF ANGIE

We hear a great deal about the biological clock, reader, ticking away the childbearing years—indeed, I think we hear a great deal too much about it—and are thereby made unnecessarily anxious. Doctors shake their heads at us if we're over thirty and contemplating a first child—and if we're over forty seem to regard an ambition to get pregnant as repulsive and unreasonable. But the science that tells us about the risk by the elderly *primagravida* (that could be you and me, reader, pregnant for the first time and over thirty) is, my doctor asks me to remember, the same science that will diagnose and remove a fetus faulty by reason of maternal or paternal age. But then I'm lucky in my doctor—his mother was forty-six when he was born, and he certainly doesn't want himself unborn, and nor do his patients. He told me the other day of a woman doctor in Paris, who, after a little hormonal juggling, gave birth to a perfectly successful baby when she was sixty—so courage, sisters all! Take the time you want deciding *to,* or deciding *not* to. I'm even sorry for Angie in this respect, though in no other, that she wanted Clifford's baby, and here she was, already past forty, and hadn't had it, and felt the desperation common to women who feel time is running out, forget Parisian women doctors, and would rather not have a baby at sixty, thank you very much!

When Helen and Clifford remarried, Angie felt really quite miserable, ditched her pallid escort/lover Sylvester and returned to Johannesburg, there to start a branch of Leonardo's. She had, after all, a major shareholding, and the directors could hardly stop her, though they feared her taste, and what she, a woman, would do to Leonardo's image. She had inherited her father's six gold mines too, as well as the Leonardo's share, and ran them with scant regard for the human rights of her black employees. She was busy, respected, admired, and not loved. She lived in great luxury, and was very bored. Had she been a little nicer and kinder, she would have found fulfillment, perhaps, in bringing major European paintings over and enriching and refining the rather garish White African cultural scene—but Angie was not nice and kind. If the gallery-goers disliked a painting she despised their taste; if they liked it, she despised the painting for being liked by the people she despised. She couldn't win against herself. She had a secret relationship with her black African butler and that was dreadful too; she despised him for fancying her, believed herself to be thoroughly unfanciable. The more she despised him, the more she despised herself, and vice versa. Well, we know all that about Angie already, and it's a common enough predicament.

Angie, one boring Christmas Day, when the conversation around the swimming pool palled, and the mint juleps gave her indigestion and really made her feel her age, and an eighteen-year-old girl had the audacity to flutter her eyelashes at Angie's butler, and she could swear the villain showed his white, white teeth in a responsive smile back—just the kind of day, in fact, that had she been living in Ancient Rome Angie would have had a few slaves beheaded, or in the American antebellum South had them severely beaten and the family broken up—decided it was time to upset a few people.

She would start by confusing her compatriots and buy a few surrealists. She'd go to England and dislodge John Lally from Clifford's sticky fingers and if she had to unravel a few contracts on the way, too bad. Clifford would welcome a fight. She didn't think she'd have much trouble getting him into bed. When had she ever? So long as she wore enough gold, or really precious stones, he capitulated. She imagined Helen, with her sweet simpers, would be beginning to pall. Surely by now! "I hate you, Helen," Angie said aloud. Helen was passive, and faithless, and careless with Clifford's love—yet she had it. And what's more she had Clifford's babies.

"Did you ask for something, ma'am?" inquired Tom the butler, solicitously. He was quite fond of Angie. He felt sorry for her, poor cold unpossessed thing.

"I did not, boy," she said savagely. "I've had enough of you. You're fired!" And so he was. No such thing in Johannesburg as a black accusing a white of unfair dismissal. Think himself lucky, his mother said—he was only twenty-two—not to be up on a rape charge. Such things happened.

And Angie flew into Heathrow.

PROPERTY!

Otto and Cynthia were not as young as they had been. (Well, who is? But you know what I mean.) Dannemore Court was beginning to seem too large for their comfort. The young can stride across large areas of parquet floor and take no notice of them; the old begin to feel that the hundred yards from front door to staircase is too much, and of course Cynthia, when not wearing her outdoor green Wellington boots, never went without high heels. (As I told you, she never quite belonged. She never *slopped,* as the English upper classes will.) Otto had slipped a disk and been told it was inadvisable for him to shoot, or ride, or bell-ring at the local church, which was his delight and the villagers' pain. ("On and on, Sir Otto! You just never seem to tire," from the Vicar's wife) Sir Otto! Foreign names are just not made for English titles, there's the truth of it. But here he was, a knight, who had never looked for it, or so he said. Who is up there who watches our behavior and thus so whimsically rewards us? Otto had headed the Confederation of British Industry at one time, of course, and had generously retired from the chairmanship of The Distillers' (Northern Europe) to make way for a younger man—or was it what no one was saying? His service to this country in the war, and possibly ever since? Probably very lately. Be that as it may, Cynthia was now Lady Cynthia which, as she said, ensured her an appointment at a West End hair salon, but otherwise made no difference that she could see. The title was not hereditary. She turned up her elegant nose a little at that.

The new knight and his lady sat disconsolately after lunch one day, staring at their log fire, he gritting his teeth against the pain in his back, she with the pain in her side, for she had recently fallen while hunting and cracked four ribs. The modern practice is not to strap the rib cage in such cases, else the bones of those enduring the pain knit too tight for the good deep breaths of healthy, active life. When she moved she could feel the ribs grating. The telephone rang. It was Angie Wellbrook, a colleague of Clifford's: did they remember? No, but were too polite to say so. She was in the neighborhood. She asked herself to supper. They sighed, and acquiesced.

"Such a lovely place," Angie enthused. "So very English, so very special. But isn't it rather large, for just the two of you?"

"We live here, we'll die here," said Otto gloomily.

"Please!" begged Cynthia, who hated talk of old age, let alone death. If you ignored it, Cynthia thought, it would go away.

"The heating bills!" mourned Angie, who'd never examined a heating bill closely in her life, and made them agree they were outrageous. Johnnie had made a rather fine French onion soup. It was the servants' day off. Some skills are never forgotten. In the war Otto and he had a for a time run a restaurant in Paris, which doubled as a clearinghouse for RAF crew in transit, who had been shot down over France and rescued by the Resistance—trained men needed back home again. The finest onion soup in Paris made a good cover.

"And what do you keep horses *for,* if neither of you can ride?"

"I can ride," said Cynthia, "and will again the minute my ribs are healed." But her voice fell away. Perhaps she wouldn't. Horses were so big. Somehow the distance between herself and the ground seemed to get greater every year.

"The outdoor life is so bad for the complexion," said Angie, and Cynthia, staring rather unkindly at the younger woman's sun-worn face, had to agree. Didn't she use moisturizers? (If only she knew how Angie tried! Poor Angie. Wicked, wicked Angie!)

"The only time the house is properly filled is at Christmas," said Otto, "when Clifford and Helen and the three children come down. Ridiculous to keep this great place going just for one week a year."

"No it isn't," said Cynthia. "That's what houses are for." *Clifford, Helen and the three children.* It sounded so strong, so permanent. The kind of hollow that had always been in Angie's heart, and made me say "poor Angie," filled up quite suddenly with spite, and resentment, and hate. It should have been Clifford, Angie and the three children. She cursed her mother, her father, her fate. If she couldn't build, she would destroy.

"Anyway, even if we wanted to, which we don't, we can't sell," said Cynthia. "Who to? They'd only turn it into a computer center or a health club and cut down the trees and bulldoze my beautiful garden for a swimming pool."

"I'll buy it," said Angie, brightly. "I need a home over here. I'll keep it exactly as it is. I simply adore it. A part of old England. And you could all still come down for Christmas—you two, Clifford, Helen and the three children."

"You couldn't do that," said Sir Otto, shocked. "We'd have to ask at least a quarter of a million."

"A quarter of a million!" said Angie, in astonishment. "I wouldn't dream of paying less than twice that. It's worth at least half a million on the open market. Believe me, I know."

Cynthia turned to Otto.

"We could buy such a nice place in Knightsbridge," she said. "I need never wear green Wellingtons again."

"But I thought you liked—"

"Only for your sake, darling—"

"But I was doing it for your sake—"

Lies, all lies, but they knew how to keep each other happy. To do exactly what they wanted, while pretending it was only for the other that they did it. Even her affairs had been to reassure him that she was desired by other men, and therefore desirable. Or that was how she liked to see it.

"Half a million might be putting it a little high," said Angie.

"I think half a million sounds exactly right," said Otto.

"Inasmuch as we can keep it a private arrangement, and spare you the cost of real-estate agents—"

And so it was settled, and Angie bought Dannemore Court. That would surprise Clifford, Helen and the three children. They were due some surprises, Angie thought, really quite nasty ones.

DOING BETTER

Angie visited John and Marjorie Lally in their home at Applecore Cottage. The couple was getting along just fine. It was Marjorie's habit to smile, as it had been Evelyn's to weep.

"Don't be absurd, John!" she'd say, when he was unreasonable. "Oh, what a bad temper!" she'd exclaim, apparently unmoved, when he ranted and raved. "John, you *can't* be talking about me. You must be talking about yourself!" she'd say, if he called her names.

He tried in a hundred ways to get the better of her, but couldn't. If he didn't speak to her she seemed not to notice, but fetched the neighbors in for coffee and talked to them instead. She made plans to include him but if he didn't turn up or was late, simply went without him. She spoke about her own feelings, never his. She threw out all Evelyn's shabby old furniture, and brought in properly restored antiques, with no handles missing, no strips of beading put in one of the drawers for safety, presently to be hidden by junk. She got rid of the copper pans and had a window put in, so that bright direct light streamed into the cottage. She had a custom-made kitchen built for a sum which quite shocked the village. She sent her clothes to Oxfam at the end of every season and bought new. She made an inventory of John's work. She understood the predicament he was in artistically, and kept saying so. She did her own embroidery—she exhibited in the Victoria and Albert, and had some small reputation, in a minor field, as she kept stressing—although she worked only when John himself was working. Otherwise she put it by, the better to concentrate her attention on her husband.

Oh, she was a wonderful wife. He didn't deserve her, everyone said. Mind you, she had her own source of income. That made it easier for her. That she did not have to ask him for money.

He was seldom in the pub, these days. He liked his wife's company, her steady smile. She would be in bed first, pretending to sleep. If he woke her, she woke cheerful and willing. If he didn't, she slept on. Perfect! He thought his work suffered. He had started painting pictures of sun over dappled waters, and pumpkins in kitchens. He lost interest in death and decay. He wondered if she was too old to have a baby. She said she wasn't. They tried.

She made John meet Helen in London, at a show at the new Haymarket Gallery. He drew the line at meeting Clifford. Helen came. He could hardly remember what all the trouble had been about. She put her hand in his, and he let it be, feeling some kind of remembered warmth.

"I think I used to be a bit mad," he said. It was an apology. She accepted it. But she had very little to say to Marjorie, who seemed pleasant enough. She ought to have been grateful, but wasn't.

"Be glad he has her," said Clifford. "It takes the weight of daughterhood off you. And wait to see how the paintings change."

He sent Johnnie down to photograph the recent paintings by infrared light, while Applecore Cottage slept, and noted the change not in style but in content. The paintings were not, Clifford thought, as good as they had been, but were actually much more salable. Well, you won some, and lost some, and this might be the break he'd been waiting for. The Tate was teetering on the brink of buying a Lally canvas for £8,000. Not bad. But the deal hadn't come through.

Helen found out that Marjorie was pregnant and wept and wept.

"It's terrible," she said. "Edward and Max and Marcus will be older than their aunt. It's unnatural."

"It might be a boy," said Clifford. "Their uncle."

She hadn't thought of that and cried even more. But it wasn't any of that she really minded. She wept for poor Evelyn, who never got what she wanted, and died thinking the getting of it was impossible. And because what Evelyn couldn't get, Marjorie could so easily.

STIRRING

Anyway, as I say, as soon as Angie had put the purchase of Dannemore Court in motion, she went down one Sunday to visit John and Marjorie at Applecore Cottage. John was polite, civil, sober and shaved, and Marjorie was in a smock. She was pregnant. They talked over roast lamb and red-currant jelly (homemade by Evelyn; the last of the jars) and they talked about Clifford Wexford, although Marjorie tried to put a stop to it.

"Of course," said Angie, "your contract with Leonardo's can't possibly be enforced. It's unnatural restraint of trade. We can take it to the European Court. In effect, this contract confines you to painting only three paintings a year, thus keeping the prices of all existing paintings high, but all and sundry benefiting more than you. The galleries profit; you lose. How much a year is your retainer?"

"Two thousand a year."

Angie laughed. "Miserable!" she said. "Exploitation."

"Of course," said John Lally, "I paint very many more canvases than three a year. I just keep the others off the market."

"He keeps them in the bicycle shed," said Marjorie.

"I'd love to see them," said Angie.

John Lally said some other time: the step was broken; the path was muddy; the light was bad. Angie said she'd been at a party with Clifford Wexford. He'd been telling the story of how the painter had barged in on him and Helen all those years ago. How he'd knocked John Lally down. Clifford was jealous, Angie said, that was all it was. He was the kind of man who longed to be a creative artist and couldn't. She was surprised John Lally hadn't stopped him from marrying his daughter the second time. Once was bad enough.

"No daughter of mine," said John Lally. "She killed my wife."

"Now, John—" said Marjorie, warningly.

"Don't you 'now, John' me," said John Lally, old-style.

"Old-style, John," said Marjorie. He subsided.

After what happened to Nell, said Angie. Of course Helen was my friend then. It was at my place she had to see the child, when Clifford was being so difficult. If it hadn't been for Clifford, said Angie, right out, Nell would still be alive. Clifford got away with too much, and here was John Lally just sitting back and letting him, and for the sake not just of John Lally, but of every living, breathing, suffering, exploited artist in the world, it had to stop. Could she, Angie, see inside John Lally's bicycle shed? She, Angie, took only ten percent as a gallery owner, and arranged initial sales on a royalty basis, so that the artist got twenty percent of all profit on subsequent sales.

John Lally took Angie to the bicycle shed. See me as your friend, she said. We'll drag Leonardo's through the courts. Let the world see what kind of art-lovers they are! So we will, said John Lally, so we will!

Marjorie said to John Lally she rather doubted that Angie was anyone's friend, but for once he wasn't listening.

AND STIR AGAIN!

Angie lunched with Simon Cornbrook at the Dorchester, and mentioned that Clifford was having an on-off affair with a woman colleague at Leonardo's, Fanny by name. It had been going on for years, since Clifford's days in Geneva. Simon Cornbrook refrained from passing on the news to Helen, his ex-wife. He had no reason to like Clifford, but he had no wish to make his ex-wife suffer. There *are* some really nice people in the world, I assure you.

Angie called Clifford and arranged to meet him for breakfast at Claridges.

"Not again!" said Clifford.

"Just once more," said Angie. "It's quite safe. We're beyond that now!"

"You may be," said Clifford. "I'm not."

He turned up at Claridges to find Angie wearing a white silk suit which shimmered and shone, even if Angie herself did not, belted by a very nifty glittering chain which might have been studded with *diamanté* but Clifford had a pretty shrewd idea was diamond and not industrial grade either. Presented with such a belt, and the opportunity of undoing it, it is difficult not to do so, if only to watch it glitter as it falls to the ground. Clifford undid it.

"I don't know how you can have Simon Cornbrook under your roof," said Angie, the whirlwind out of South Africa, safe in the comfy Claridges' brass bed.

"Helen says it's civilized."

"She would, wouldn't she. How come the twins look so much like him?"

And Angie had only just begun.

A TRULY TERRIBLE ROW

Reader, Angie became pregnant by Clifford Wexford. She meant to. She had the timing right. Luck was on her side, as it frequently is of the wicked. The devil does indeed seem to look after his own. Angie was forty-two—no age to get pregnant at the drop of a hat, or the fall of a diamond belt from a white silk suit in Claridges' bridal suite! But pregnant she became, as she had intended. (The nerve of it, reader: booking the bridal suite! Well, you have to hand it to her, I suppose; such chutzpah deserves some success.) Her plan, of course, was not only to have Clifford's baby, which she wanted because she loved him—yes, well and truly loved him; the wicked as well as the good have the capacity to love—but to use her pregnancy as a lever to get him to marry her, once he had divorced Helen.

Now during those momentous hours at Claridges, when Barbara was conceived, Angie put into Clifford's head the notion that Helen's twin sons were not his, but Simon Cornbrook's. Clifford had for four years been coping with boisterous twins, reared in the modern, permissive fashion, in a house in which he also entertained his fastidious and wealthy clients. He'd put up with it because Helen wanted him to, but once the thought had been put in his head, it was hard to get rid of: the twins, not his! Helen had been unfaithful once—she would again. And to get pregnant by her ex-husband Simon, because she was sorry for him and guilty about the way she had treated him, was just the kind of daft, hopeless thing Helen would do. And then foist them on him, Clifford—oh yes, it figured!

Clifford went right home from Claridges. He went, I may say, with a clear conscience. He did not *love* Angie, reader. He did not even like her, though something in him certainly responded to her, and so he did not register himself as having been unfaithful to Helen, no, not at all. He found his wife sitting over a lunchtime glass of wine with her ex-husband, Simon, pleasantly taken on the sunny patio, beneath brilliant hanging flower-baskets.

That did it.

"So," he said to the pair of them, "this is what happens when I'm at work! What a fool I've been! You little slut," (this to Helen) "foisting your bastards upon me!" And so on, including a lot of high-pitched nonsense about how Helen had not only asked Simon to Christmas dinner but how Simon had carved the turkey he, Clifford, had paid for. No use for Simon to point out that Helen had prevailed upon him to come to Christmas for little Edward's sake (her son by Simon, properly, decently and lawfully conceived) and that Clifford had practically bullied him into carving. No! Or that now the purpose of their meeting was merely to discuss Edward's schooling. No! No good for Helen to explain and deny and weep her innocence and love for Clifford. No!

And then Simon said what he had heard earlier from Angie's lips. That Clifford had been having a long-running affair with Fanny so who was he to talk? And so indeed Clifford had been. That is to say, he hadn't exactly registered it as an *affair,* or indeed a *relationship.* Fanny was just someone he made love to when he and she were late at the office, and couldn't decide between a fake and a genuine master. Sex cleared the head. And if poor Fanny was hopelessly and permanently in love with him, Clifford, she certainly knew better these days than to say so. (Though perhaps, reader, she hated him in the kind of close, dependent way some women hate the men they think they love. Certainly Fanny longed to score Clifford's broad fair back with her nails on those occasions, but of course she couldn't. Married men must be left unmarked.)

"If I am," said Clifford, "it is because my wife has driven me to it. Listen to her now—screaming and ranting." And at that, Helen's head cleared. She simply stopped weeping and declaring her innocence.

"It can only be your guilt," she said to Clifford, "which makes you behave like this." She was right, of course. "And what is more, the way you behave is unforgivable. I am going to divorce you for unreasonable behavior, and that is just."

"Get out of my house, then," said Clifford, quite cold all of a sudden, and hating her because now she had done the unforgivable and talked about something which really frightened him. Divorce! *And* in front of a witness too, which made it more real; the more so because that witness was Simon.

And do you know what Helen did? She found her courage, and turned upon Clifford and said—"No, you go!" And such was the force of her righteous anger that, in spite of himself, he did. *He* capitulated, reader. *He* left. How often unhappily married wives get the feeling the house is the husband's, and the only way of parting is for her to leave everything she has—when actually of course it is *theirs.* If anyone has to go, perhaps it should be *him.* And if she says so, loudly and clearly enough, and if he is guilty enough, he will.

Clifford meant, of course, to go for only a week or so, to teach Helen a lesson. So she would realize how much she loved him. So she would beg him to return, apologizing for past misdeeds. So they would be happy once more, their love cleansed, richer, truer. So that he would never have to sleep with Fanny again, or so much as see Angie again—

But, reader, it did not turn out like that! No such luck!

ALONE AGAIN

Clifford moved out of his and Helen's house into the luxurious Mayfair flat provided by Leonardo's for important clients—the kind who could say of a rare Rembrandt unexpectedly come onto the market—"I like that; I'll have it!" But he was accustomed to luxury, and found it no compensation for the loss of his family life. He missed not just his wife but, surprisingly, even the terrible twins. He saw that it did not matter one whit if there were butter smears on his hand-blocked wallpaper or he could not listen to Figaro in peace because of the children's demands; the answer was to have ordinary washable wallpaper and to listen to opera (softly!) after they'd gone to bed, like anyone else. Clifford did not believe, really, seriously, that the twins were Simon's not his. It came to him that he'd chosen to believe it, temporarily, because he was guilty and jealous, and knew it. Moreover, he hadn't meant to upset Helen so much. He saw, all of a sudden, that if he really and truly loved her he would have to abandon his habit of seducing women in order to behave cruelly in his rejecting of them later. For that, he now perceived, to his shame, was what his habit amounted to.

He saw all this because for six miserable weeks he waited for Helen to call and apologize and make it up, and she wouldn't and she didn't; and he was unused to rejection and quite shattered by it. He had time to think. He had kept himself so busy all his adult life he'd had little time for reflection. Even on vacation he'd not just done nothing, he'd made fresh contacts, been seen on the right ski slopes, at the right villa; if all else failed he'd managed the best suntan in town, earlier in the year than anyone else! Oh folly, folly! Vanity of vanities. He saw it all now. He loved Helen, he loved his home, his children. These were all that mattered. (People *can* change, reader, they really can!)

"No," said Helen. "No. I meant it. I want a divorce, Clifford. Enough is enough." She was adamant. She didn't even want to see him. She had had enough, he heard through friends, of being passive, receptive, over-female—masochistic, in fact. And worse, Clifford's parents, Otto and Cynthia, who had unaccountably sold their perfectly pleasant home, and were now trying to fit themselves into a small flat of the kind allegedly suitable for an elderly couple, and had aged ten years in the process, seemed to be on his wife's side.

"You are selfish, self-willed, self-centered and unscrupulous," his mother—his own mother!—said to him. Mind you, she herself was pretty miserable at the time. Take three paces in the flat in Chelsea Cloisters and you came up against a wall. It made her feel quite old. She longed to be back in her own large, gracious home, now sold—what had possessed them!—to Angie. What use was all that money in the bank? Though Sir Otto seemed happy enough, slipping in and out of the Ministry of Defense, taking little trips to the States, with Johnnie at his side, though when she looked in his passport—the only one she knew about—there were no entry-exit stamps to be seen at all.

Meanwhile, Angie was busy turning what was by rights Clifford's family home into an out-of-town auction house, to be called Ottoline's, for rare and fine works of art. The trees had been cut, the garden bulldozed, and the conservatory housed a heated swimming pool. Ottoline's was competition for Leonardo's—which did Leonardo's no good. Sotheby's, Christie's and Leonardo's had controlled the art auction world for decades, settling things happily enough between them—now outsiders were muscling in. What was Angie thinking of? She was, after all, still a director of Leonardo's! She was fouling her own nest. Clifford's nest, too. His family home! How sentimental Clifford was becoming—

Reader, you and I know exactly what Angie was thinking of. She was setting a wall of thorns around Clifford in order to be the one to rescue him. During the course of a single day, when Clifford was at his lowest ebb, she said three things to him. She'd taken him to Oxford; they were punting down the river. He was good at that, still fine, muscular and handsome, and Angie sat with her back to the sun and wore a shady, floppy hat and looked not too bad, for once.

"Of course, John Lally's contract with you doesn't hold water under European law. It is the human right of the artist to paint when and how he sees fit; you are unlawfully restricting him. He's taking you to European Court. Yes, I've advised him to do so. He'll come to me under my Ottoline's hat when he's shaken off Leonardo's." The Lally paintings, reader, were now worth large fractions of millions, not just ten of thousands. (What skillful professional manipulation can do for a painter!) If John Lally now started painting, in any quantity, for Ottoline's, the money earned over the lean years by Leonardo's (or so they saw it) would now in the fat years go to Ottoline's, and Angie. Don't imagine John Lally would see much of it either, in spite of her promises. "Initial purchase," she had said. That would apply only to new paintings, not to anything already completed. But he hadn't thought of that. She hadn't meant him to. He'd drunk quite a lot of Rioja over the lamb and Evelyn's red-currant jelly. She, of course, had drunk almost nothing.

She also said, "Clifford, I'm pregnant. I'm having your baby!" He did not dare suggest an abortion. Even the old Clifford might have demurred, so steely and glittery was Angie's eye. As for the new Clifford, he did not like the thought of life, any life, destroyed. He had become accountably soft, even nice. Reader, if only he hadn't been so greedy; if only gold and money hadn't so appealed; if only Cynthia had loved him better and filled up the bucket of his need—if only! What use are "if only's." Still, they're interesting.

The other thing Angie said was, "Of course, Clifford, if you and I joined our Empires together we'd rule the world." (The Art World, I can only suppose she meant. At least I hope so.)

"How do you mean, Angie? Join our Empires?"

"Marry me, Clifford."

"Angie, I'm married to Helen."

"More fool you," said Angie, and told Clifford about Helen's affair (alleged) with Arthur Hockney, the black New York detective Helen had employed to search for little Nell in the dreadful days after the child's disappearance. You and I know, reader, that though Arthur was for many years hopelessly in love with Helen, there was nothing between them, nothing, and he was now happily with his Sarah, and had even, with her help, lately stood upon a platform and spoken at a Fund-raising for Black Artists in Winnipeg. And Angie knew it, but Angie was never one to let truth stand between her and what she wanted.

"I don't believe you!" said Clifford.

"She told me all about it once," said Angie, "when she was drunk. Some women are like that. Indiscreet when drunk. As Helen is quite frequently. So I expect all London knows. If she'll tell me, she'll tell anyone."

And it was quite true that Helen did sometimes drink too much, and that Clifford hated it when she did, and so Angie's mischief-making was the more effective. Helen was one of those unfortunate (or fortunate, if you like) few people upon whom a teaspoon of wine acts as does a tumblerful of gin on others. And you know what cocktail parties are, and art openings—and trays of glasses being handed around, and what with the noise and the excitement and the pleasure of being all dressed up and ravishingly beautiful—as Helen indubitably still was; each extra child seemed to add glamour, not inches—sometimes her hand strayed to the wine instead of the orange juice—oh you know how it is, reader!

And, reader, one way and another, before three months were out, with Angie's help, Clifford had stifled his grief and turned it into anger and spite, and the divorce was underway.

GREAT EXPECTATIONS

Angie let it be known that she expected Clifford to marry her. He thought he would, inasmuch as now he had lost Helen it scarcely mattered what he did, and Leonardo's was important, and work the only area in which, it now and tragically seemed, he was successful. Even his own mother was against him. (Clifford, in other words, was low, very low.) He might as well marry Angie. Now these are not the terms on which you and I, reader, would consent to be married, but Angie was different. The rich *are* different. They expect to get what they want, and usually do. Pride somehow doesn't enter into it. I won't say they're happier for it—it's just that the rich somehow contrive not to develop too much capacity for unhappiness.

And besides, Angie's baby was on the way, and since he had lost Nell, the apple of his eye, Clifford understood, as too few men do, the blessing a child, any child, bestows upon its parents.

"I'll think about it," said Clifford.

Such a marriage, of course, would present Clifford with many material advantages, as Angie let it be known. The understanding, delicately put, was that when Angie stopped being Wellbrook and became Wexford, Ottoline's would amalgamate with Leonardo's, and Angie would prevail upon John Lally, again, to restrict his output of paintings to maximize the Lally market, to everyone's benefit (except, of course, the artist's). She would also stop stirring things up in the Colonies (as she liked to call them) and keep the Johannesburg gallery bidding in a lively fashion for those Old Masters increasingly unpopular in the sophisticated European markets. In return she could start a similar Australian branch and call it Ottoline's, not Leonardo's—the difference between the two houses now being only in name. And Clifford could visit the twins and they could even come to stay, so long as he didn't see Helen.

"Let Simon visit them," said Clifford. "He's their father," and started counter-divorce proceedings, and won.

Helen wept, and wept, and no one could comfort her, though many tried. This wasn't what she'd meant, no, not at all.

Presently she went home to Applecore Cottage to weep some more; this time she had three children with her.

"I told you so," said John Lally, only once.

"Don't say that to her," said Marjorie, so he didn't. The cottage was crowded with so many in it, and Marjorie was of course pregnant. He retired to the woodshed.

"I'm such a nuisance," said Helen. "I'm sorry."

"You're more than welcome," said Marjorie. "I know I can never take your mother's place; I know you must resent the baby—"

"No, no—" said Helen, and suddenly didn't. It was impossible not to like Marjorie, who made her father happy. He had taken to painting furniture in his spare time. Ordinary kitchen chairs glowed and fluttered with flowers and birds.

"What am I going to do with my life?" asked Helen. "I've made such a mess of it." Another robin—how many bird generations since the first—hopped red-breasted in the garden outside and made her smile. She couldn't indulge her grief; she had the children to think about now.

"That's because you depend upon other people," said Marjorie. "Learn to depend upon yourself."

"I'm too old to change," said Helen, looking no more than eighteen. Marjorie laughed, and Marcus, Max and Edward swarmed into the kitchen, demanding food. They were expensive children. They were used to drinking orange juice, when previous generations had drunk water. You know how it is with today's children.

"I do so hate having to ask Clifford for money," said Helen. "It's like the old days. I can't bear it."

"Then earn it yourself," said Marjorie, briskly. "You have every advantage." And of course, when she came to think of it, Helen had.

MARRIED TO ANGIE

Angie said to Clifford when finally the decree was through and her little baby Barbara already born—"I know, we'll be married on Christmas Day."

"No," said Clifford.

"Why not?"

"Because that was Nell's birthday," he said.

"Who's Nell?" Angie asked, honestly forgetting for the moment, and Clifford as near as dammit didn't marry her, even after all that. Angie had been on her very best behavior lately, of course, but even so in the space of three months had hired and fired as many servants. Clifford could now see that what passed, if you were kind, as sparkiness and forthrightness, was in fact willfulness and rudeness, and that Angie was as bad-tempered as Helen was good—but on the other hand she wasn't likely to betray him with other men, was she? Let alone ask former husbands to Christmas dinner; let alone be vague, forgetful and always late for appointments. No. The Wellbrook/Wexford marriage was highly suitable and six gold mines came with it and a great many very valuable paintings from the Wellbrook Collection—and Clifford soon overcame his doubts.

But at least the wedding wasn't on Christmas Day. It took place on the first Saturday in January, and a very damp, windy day it was too, which blew Angie's hair quite out of curl, and made her large nose red and noticeable, and you and I know, reader, that Angie needs all the help from the Beauty Salon she can get. The weathered look just didn't suit her one bit; or the white dress she insisted on wearing. It was a kind of unkind bluey white, not the yellowy white which flatters, and it was too frilly; brides often lose their dress-sense on their wedding day and Angie was no exception. Some things money doesn't help. Clifford, standing beside her, remembered Helen's fragile, gentle beauty, and almost failed to say "I will." But Angie nudged him. He said it. That was that.

Clifford and Angie lived sometimes in Belgravia (a leasehold house of spectacular grandeur, with overlarge rooms just right for paintings but terrible for human beings) and sometimes in Manhattan (a penthouse overlooking Central Park, so burglar-proof it took ten minutes to get inside). A series of Norland nannies had total charge of little Barbara.

Barbara would stay behind in the Belgravia nursery annex when her parents were in New York. Angie said New York wasn't safe for children, but Clifford knew she just didn't want the child around. The pregnancy had served its purpose: the living child was neither here nor there. Clifford made as much of Barbara as he could—but he was busy; there was never enough time. She was a quiet, docile little girl, who stayed too quiet, too docile. The new Wexford friends were smart, middle-aged and boring. Angie had no time for writers, artists or eccentrics, at least for now, though later she'd stray far further. And so Clifford was bored and wretched, and serve him right. It may have been Clifford's unhappiness, in fact, which led him to sail so close to the law in his dealings with Leonardo's (New York) in the fourth year of his marriage to Angie.

CHILD AND MOTHER

That was the year Nell, settled happily enough with the Kildares at the Border Kennels, took her O levels. Art, History, Geography, English, Math, General Science, Religious Knowledge, Needlework, Rural Studies, French. She was good at everything except Math, and particularly good at French. "You speak it almost like a native!" remarked her teacher. You and I, faithful reader, know the reason for that, even though Nell herself had forgotten. These days she seldom thinks back to the days before her arrival in Ruellyn, being at an age when she liked to live in the present, and let the past and future look after themselves.

She was interested in a boy called Dai Evans, who was too awed by her interest to do much about it. She was altogether too stunning for any ordinary classroom, what with her thick curly blonde hair (that early head-shaving in the Children's Home must have done it a lot of good, or so my hairdresser says), straight nose, full lips, quick bright eyes and slow, lovely, female smile.

And what of her half-brother Edward, and her two full brothers, Max and Marcus? Reader, who was it who said that the children of lovers are orphans? Helen, deprived once again, by fortune and Angie, of Clifford, her one undying, permanent love, turned her attention toward her children and they were the better for it. Edward was twelve by now, and the twins Max and Marcus were eight. Three boys! And she had a half-sister too; Clifford and Angie's daughter, Barbara. On the day of Barbara's birth, Helen had thought she'd actually die from pain, grief and jealousy, so bad the feelings had been. Now no one in the world should hate a baby, let alone so docile a one as Barbara, and Helen knew it, but she did. She couldn't help it. The baby had stolen Clifford from her, and left her and her children desolate. She tried to explain this to Marjorie.

"I blame the baby," said Helen, "for everything that's happened."

"It's hardly reasonable," said Marjorie, the most reasonable of all people. Her baby was called Julian; another boy for the family. Helen's little half-brother, Nell's uncle. Fancy!

"And why should she have a girl?" demanded Helen. "It isn't fair. The devil's on her side."

"But you had a girl," said Marjorie. "You had Nell."

For a moment Helen hated her stepmother for daring to mention her child, but only for a moment.

"The anger inside me is so mixed up," she said presently, "I hardly know where to put it." She'd enrolled again at the Royal College; she was taking a refresher course in fashion and fabric design. It made her feel better on one day, worse on another, as if a whole chunk of life had been wasted. Someone had to be to blame.

That evening she took out the folder in which she kept the yellowy and tattered photographs of Nell's infancy and early childhood, and looked and stared, and the feeling came to her once again, "Nell *isn't* dead. She isn't. She's just as alive as Barbara is." Helen then remembered Arthur Hockney. She wondered what had become of him. She found his work number in an old diary, and called him. They said he'd left. He was some kind of community worker now; he ran a center for underprivileged kids in Harlem. But they gave her his number.

By the way, reader, Nell failed her Math O Level. I think she did it on purpose, for her best friend Brenda's sake. Brenda failed the lot. At any rate, on the day of the exam Nell quite deliberately didn't wear her teddy bear on the silver chain, the old tin thing with the jewel inside, which she always wore for luck.

The fact was, Helen had changed. Remember, she had married young; she'd had very little time to develop her own nature, or discover her likes and dislikes. She'd grown up with a willful and difficult father and a put-upon mother, and had learned early the childish and painful art of conciliation; how to survive as a small buffer state between two large warring ones, forever keeping the peace at her own expense. Then, married to Clifford, her opinions, perforce, had been his; he'd turned her from an artless (more or less) girl into a cool and knowledgeable woman who could read a wine list and tell a real Jacobean chest from a fake without even trying, but had no choice but to like what he liked, despise what he despised. Then when Simon took Clifford's place in the marital bed, she'd adopted her new husband's political views, his kindly, worldly, international cynicism. It is women's capacity thus to learn to keep the domestic peace simply by *agreeing*—but it does them no good in the end of course. They go to sleep confused, and wake up confused, and become depressed.

But now when the three boys asked her questions Helen would be obliged to give answers which were not John Lally's, nor Clifford Wexford's, nor Simon Cornbrook's, but her own, and very interesting she found them to be, too; almost, but never quite, making up for grief, loss and loneliness. Clifford (or was it Angie's doing? Clifford had met his match in Angie!) would now only talk to Helen through solicitors and made her argue and beg for every grudging maintenance check. It was humiliating. But she could see her own fault in it. She'd had talents, and failed to develop them. She'd handed the responsibility for her own well-being over to others, and then complained about it. She'd been a wife, a mistress, a mother, and thought that was enough. But she had not even been a good mother—had she not lost Nell? she had not been a good wife—had she not lost her husband? All she was good at, all she'd been trained for—and she could see it now, deprived as she was of status, invitations and fashionable friends, all now turning out to exist only by courtesy of her marriage to Clifford—was asking for money, and she wasn't even very good at that.

Well, now she was determined to be free of Clifford. She'd taken a refresher course. Now she looked up old acquaintances; she borrowed money on the strength of the one early John Lally she owned, a sketch of a drowned cat given to her on her eighteenth birthday—

"Looks like your mother in from shopping, on a wet day," he'd said, joking (Ha! ha!) on that occasion. Helen had kept the drawing in the back of a drawer ever since, and hated it. But sentiment doesn't pay mortgages, or start businesses. She'd taken out the drawing, gone with it to the bank, left it as security. And here she was, a bright new designer label on the London fashion scene: House of Lally. Her father was furious. She was bringing the family name into disrepute. Helen just laughed. Whenever had her father not been furious? And besides, his fury had somehow lost its bite. He could be seen, any day at Applecore Cottage, actually feeding the new baby Julian with a bottle. Marjorie had trouble breast-feeding—or so she said. It was Helen's belief it was a put-up job, to get John Lally close to his new son. Which he was.

Simon wanted to remarry Helen, of course. She laughed and said, "Enough of that!" Some knots, she could tell, simply needed untying, not further complicating. And, reader, interestingly, the very style of Helen's beauty changed, as did her life. She no longer seemed fragile and just a little mournful—now she gleamed with energy. Clifford, seeing his former wife one day on a television program, was quite put out. What had happened to her? Why was she not pining away for loss of him? Angie said the change was skin-deep, and that underneath the new gloss Helen was the same helpless, hopeless, drifting, stone-around-the-neck, frame-maker's daughter she'd always been, and switched the program off.

It flattered Clifford to agree with Angie, but when the next check he sent Helen (three weeks late, of course) was returned, he did wonder. He almost thought he would visit her, but he could see that to put in an appearance now could only confuse the twins, since he so resolutely denied his paternity. So he did nothing. Only now, once again, Helen entered his dreams, and sometimes little Nell too, as she'd been when he last saw her. Where Angie couldn't follow, there he and his true wife and his lost daughter went.

This was the state of affairs when Helen contacted Arthur Hockney once again. He came visiting with Sarah, now his wife, and the dog Kim, now an elegant, gentle beast who could safely enter the most cluttered and expensive drawing-room in the land. Arthur came reluctantly. He remembered well the pain Helen had inflicted the night he had baby-sat and she had not come home. Why should he revive all that again? But, seeing her, he realized two things: both that she had changed and that he was no longer in love with her. He loved Sarah. Sarah was not second-best at all. It was a wonderful revelation.

"I can't put Nell's ghost to rest," said Helen. "And that's the truth of it. If ghost it be, and not the real, live, living Nell. Arthur, please try!"

"I am no longer an investigator," he pointed out. "I'm here for a conference on race relations." He too had been back to college, he had completed the law course he long ago had walked out of.

But he did try. He called at Mrs. Blotton's little terraced house and found her gone, and in the window a cardboard card announcing the residence of a Mrs. A. Haskins, Clairvoyant. Mrs. Haskins was fifty and fleshy, with loose jowls, a deep voice and large, tired, beautiful eyes. Mrs. Blotton had gone, she said, where Arthur couldn't follow her.

"Where's that?"

"The Other Side of Death," said Mrs. Haskins. "Into the Light of the Hereafter." The poor woman, a nonsmoker herself, had died of lung cancer, the result of passive smoking. "Inhaling the smoke from her husband's cigarettes, year after year."

"I'm sorry," said Arthur.

"Death is a cause for rejoicing, not weeping," said Mrs. Haskins, and offered to tell Arthur's fortune. Arthur accepted. He did not believe, or quite not believe, in clairvoyance. He was aware that sometimes he seemed to know more than could rationally be explained; and if *he* did, why not others? It is always tempting to find out what's going to happen next.

Mrs. Haskins took his black, heavy hands and stared a little, and then pushed them away. "You'd do better telling it for yourself," she said, and he understood her meaning, or half understood it. A tough black lawyer, ex-detective from New York, would rather believe in his own professionalism, any day, than in any convenient capacity for seeing through brick walls! He prepared to take his leave.

"She'll find her own way home," Mrs. Haskins remarked, out of the blue, as she walked flat-footed with him to the door. Her thick pale tights were laddered and the varicose veins showed through like knotted ropes but her eyes were bright.

"Who? What are you talking about?"

"The one you're looking for. The lost child. She's a powerful one, all right. An old soul. One of the greats." And that was all Mary Haskins would say. More than enough, the superstitious amongst us might think!

Arthur went back to Helen and told her Nell's trail was finally cold; that she must live in the present, not the past. He was glad to be rid of the role of detective. The work had been upsetting. It brought him too closely into contact with things which were better brushed past, not lingered with. He too feared for his soul; he wanted to live in the here and now, not forever on the brink of the past, of the present, sensing too much, knowing too little.

"How've you've changed," said Helen. She wasn't quite sure how, or why. But she knew she felt easier in his company. She liked Sarah. She was glad he was happy.

"It's the baby's doing," said Sarah. "He's settled down." And though it's true babies affect their fathers, almost as much as their mothers, with the desire for peace, and a certain future, I think myself it was Arthur's coming to terms with his own conscience, one day in Mrs. Blotton's house, that had made the difference. Mrs. Blotton, in spite of herself, did much good in her lifetime, and deserves to be remembered for it. May she rest in peace.

SUMMER AT THE KENNELS

Mr. and Mrs. Kildare went away for the month of August, the year Nell took her O levels. They went to Greece. They left Nell and Brenda behind, in charge of the kennels. Summer is a busy time in such places. Well, you know how it is, people want to go abroad and can't take their dogs with them; or at any rate, if they do, can't bring them back into the country freely for fear of rabies. Moreover the Kildares had just opened authorized quarantine kennels—here they could take a dozen dogs, and keep them isolated for the required eight months. It meant a great deal of extra work—if also money—as the animals had to be not just exercised and fed, but talked to and cheered up, or else they lapsed into apathy, and either went off their food and grew thin, or became sluggish, fat and mournful—and then there would be uproar from the punters. One way or another Mr. and Mrs. Kildare were glad to get away.

Nell and Brenda were not glad to be left, of course. Brenda had never been abroad in her life, and wanted to very much, and though we know Nell has, she has no memory of it. Never can there have been a kennel maid like Nell, at sixteen! Brenda was good-looking enough—though suffering rather from acne around her chin—but by comparison with Nell she looked positively plain. She was dumpy, that was the trouble; her eyes were small and her cheeks plump. How unfair life is!

"Do you think they can be trusted?" asked Mrs. Kildare.

"Of course they can," said Mr. Kildare, thinking of hot sands and blue skies and no dogs.

The Kildares loved dogs more than people, and often said so, which, for some reason beyond her parents' comprehension, would upset Brenda and bring her out in spots. At the same time, they weren't averse to leaving their charges whenever they could. They'd been away at Easter too, when the girls were studying for exams. This may have been why Brenda managed to fail so many.

"Supposing something goes wrong," said Mrs. Kildare. But Mr. Kildare thought to himself something was more likely to go wrong if they stayed home. He found it difficult not to stare at Nell, he wanted just to touch her, to get her to smile at him in a different way than she smiled at the rest of the world. Perhaps when he came back he'd feel differently. He hoped so. He didn't admire himself. Well, he was forty-five. She was sixteen. A twenty-nine-year gap. Mind you, he had heard of greater. She wasn't a born animal-handler, as his wife was, and Brenda too, but she was good enough. Perhaps he and she could start again together—she was only a waif and stray, when it came to it. She had no background. She would be grateful—"A penny for your thoughts," said Mrs. Kildare, and Mr. Kildare was ashamed of them. But how can a man not think what he thinks.

Something did go wrong, of course. Two sixteen-year-old girls can't look after thirty dogs, and themselves, and the visitors and bookings, and fight off Ned (eighteen) and Rusty (sixteen), brothers from a neighboring farm, who wanted to come in and watch TV, because reception at home was so bad.

"And what else?" asked Nell.

"That's all," they promised. But it wasn't, of course.

After some fumbling and mumbling the girls got them to leave. That was on Wednesday night.

"I hate boys," said Brenda. "I prefer dogs."

"I don't," said Nell. She was worried about her bosom though. She thought it was enormous. It wasn't, of course. But Ned had made a beeline to unbutton it. Why hers, not Brenda's? And she felt she must smell of dog food. She didn't, of course. But she was sixteen. You know how it is.

On Thursday morning two of the dogs refused to eat. On Thursday evening eight had gone on a hunger strike. By Friday evening all thirty of them were off their food. There didn't seem to be much wrong with them. They just sniffed, and lay around, and stared at Nell and Brenda with reproachful eyes and didn't eat. Then the ones who'd stopped eating on Thursday began to sneeze.

On Saturday morning all were sneezing and the girls called in the vet. He diagnosed some kind of food-related viral infection; inspected the scullery where they prepared the food, passed it okay, and gave every single dog an antibiotic jab to be on the safe side. He left a bill for ninety pounds, and said he'd be back on Tuesday. It should be cleared up by then, whatever it was.

He seemed surprised that Brenda and Nell had been left in charge.

"We can cope," they said. "We have before."

"Um," he said, and then, to Nell, "How old are you?"

"Sixteen," she said. He looked her up and down. She wasn't used to it. "You look older than that to me," he said.

Nell resolved to go on a diet. She didn't eat for three days, not a morsel. Nor, when it came to it, did the dogs.

"It's the food," said Nell on Monday evening. The dogs were no longer reproachful, but full of protest, howling and moaning and restless. "It must be. They're just acting like hungry dogs."

"It can't be the food," said Brenda. "It's the same sack we were using a week ago; and they were eating it then." (The dogs were fed on kind a of canine muesli, which was mixed into a slop with hot water. It had a pungent smell.)

"I just know it's the food," said Nell, and mixed some to try herself.

"You can't!" cried Brenda.

"I'll spit it out," said Nell. Oh, she was brave. She brought the spoon of slop to her lips; she grimaced: she sneezed. At that very moment Ned appeared in the scullery door, with a tearful Rusty more or less under his arm.

"You know what he's done?" said Ned. "He's put sneezing powder from the joke shop in your animal food. I brought him up to say he's sorry."

"Sorry," said Rusty. "Except I'm not. Who do you think you are anyway—" and he tucked a heel under his brother's calf, and was free, and off. Brenda helped Ned up and Nell opened a new sack of food and mixed it up for the dogs. They ate with gratitude. The vet came on Tuesday and gave them another bill—a £25 house-call fee, and made no apology at all. The Kildares were furious on their return. Calling the vet out is what no one who keeps animals for profit likes to do. And I'm sorry to say Mr. Kildare's feelings for Nell hadn't altered one bit.

"You've gotten thin," he said, looking her up and down.

"Not thin enough," was Nell's silent reply, "in that case," and after that Mrs. Kildare had quite a lot of trouble tempting her to eat at all. You know what girls of that age are. The only good thing that came out of the whole episode was that Brenda and Ned got it together; and though that left Nell rather on her own (Rusty was a dead loss, obviously) she was glad, for Brenda's sake. She did some really good dog drawings, which the Kildares used on their brochures, and had printed up as Christmas cards, and sold. They didn't pay Nell anything, of course. They fed her and housed her and clothed her, didn't they. And they'd see her through her O levels. They felt they were generosity itself.

TALK OF THE DEVIL

Reader, I wish I could tell you that Angie was happy, now she had what she wanted—that is to say, Clifford. But you know how it is—traveling is better than arriving. Angie wasn't in the least happy. She was bored and restless, and had too much money, and too much spare time, and though I don't think she noticed particularly about Clifford not loving her, it must surely in some way have affected her. It would me, and probably you. She was bothered and irritated by her little girl Barbara, if and when she saw her, as mothers sometimes can be when they don't have the day-to-day handling of their children. And so she filled the emptiness of her life as best she could. That is to say she got mixed up with a chalk-faced, black-leathery pop group named Satan's Enterprise who, though in truth rather gentle and nervous lads, dabbled in black magic and cocaine for the sake of PR. Some say Marco the lead singer was her lover, though I don't think that was necessarily true, and nor, once he'd met him, did Clifford.

But if you weave nasty spells, and pretend to raise demons by horrid incantations in deserted chapels, even for fun, profit and the benefit of cameras, you might very well bite off more than you can chew, or stir up more than you can handle. Disagreeable things happen; scandals ensue.

This is how this one went.

Clifford and Angie were due at the first night of *The Exorcist.* Clifford turned up on his own, without Angie on his arm. The press sensed trouble. It was their habit to follow Clifford around, in the hope of snapping him with the wrong person in the right place, or vice versa, sometimes succeeding. Then they would besiege Angie, hoping to catch her unawares, in distress, which of course they never did. She'd be rude, shut the door in their faces. Once she even poured a kettleful of boiling water over some photographers from the window of Barbara's nursery.

"It isn't sensible to upset the press, Angie," Clifford said. "They'll get their revenge."

"It should have been boiling oil," she replied. "Water loses heat too quickly. And don't you upset me, and then I won't upset them."

It wasn't like Angie to miss a First Night: she'd been looking forward to seeing *The Exorcist.* She'd heard about green vomit and necks which swiveled all the way around. Earlier in the day she'd appeared on a live TV show in an afternoon program about "How I Look After My Face" and she'd said so. She also said all she did was wash her face with soap and water and slap on a little face cream. Lies! Worse than Helen in the early days. Helen never lied, these days. It was beneath her dignity. My own view is that married women lie far more than the single or the divorced. Ask a wife how much a joint of meat cost and she'll take a third off. Ask a single woman and she'll tell you straight. But that's another story. Cynthia, by the way, watched Angie on TV, and said to Otto, "There, I knew she never used moisturizers. What a fool the woman is." They saw as little of Angie as they possibly could, being upset about the fate of Dannemore Court, though all Otto said was, "Well, she paid twice what she should for the place. And it had served its purpose. How was I to know she'd join the family?"

Anyway, Angie's nonappearance caused a stir; the empty seat (so expensive!) beside Clifford spoke of domestic emergency. Clifford seemed to be white with anger, and actually, instead of "No comment," said, "What my wife does is her business."

Word got around that Angie had left the TV studios in the company of Marco, of Satan's Enterprise. A group of reporters dispatched themselves to the mews house in Kensington where the group dwelt, arriving in time to see an ambulance outside, and Angie, naked and overdosed, carried out. Neighbors spoke of drugs and orgies.

Angie was revived in St. George's Hospital and her stomach was, rather unkindly, pumped. All Clifford would say, emerging from the screening of *The Exorcist,* was that he hated the film, and no, he would not be visiting his wife in the hospital. Nor did he.

Well, the press loved all that, didn't they, not liking Angie. Clifford had been right. They got their revenge. They went for the jugular. Barbara's best friend was a small princess, with whom she shared a coat-peg at nursery school. Barbara would go to a royal household for lunch; the princess would come to Barbara's for tea—and Angie would be hovering then, you bet, all maternal smiles out on the step for the press on those occasions, as the two met and embraced. Now it was—

DRUG TOT IN PALACE NURSERY SCANDAL.

DRUG EVIL BRUSHES PALACE TINY.

ROYAL CHILD VISITS DRUG DEN.

And so forth. And somehow, though the fuss in the papers died down, the palace tot no longer came to tea, or shared photographers, or dancing class, and no more royal invitations came for Barbara.

Clifford laughed, and said, "You brought it on yourself," and Angie stamped and said, "You drove me to it." Barbara grieved and was more silent than ever. She'd lost a friend.

And somehow, after that, the fun just went out of everything for Angie. There seemed nowhere to go. Clifford was depressed (of course he was depressed, his talent and spirit so overshadowed by the enormity of Angie's wealth). He seemed to have no spirit left. He wasn't the catch she'd thought. She said so, rashly, and for once wished it was bitten back the moment it was out.

In retaliation, he kept out of her bed. Even if she'd put the biggest diamond in the world in her navel, he wouldn't have cared. Angie went away for a month to a beauty farm in California and had a facelift and a skin peel in an attempt to improve her complexion—thinking perhaps that was the trouble—and something went wrong. Her skin erupted into bumps and crevices and was worse than ever.

"Serves you right," said Clifford, when she came back. No amount of Max Factor Erace (cheapest but still the best) helped.

She wore enormous dark glasses and collars up to her ears and Barbara screamed when she saw her.

"She's forgotten who you are," said Clifford. "Lucky little thing." No man likes his wife taking off for a month, even if he doesn't like the wife.

Poor Angie—yes, really, poor—Angie, thought she deserved pity and help and all she had was Clifford looking at her with a kind of hard look, as if she was a failure in the world. She pondered briefly whether she mightn't be happier if she gave all her money away, but only briefly, remembering her father saying, "The trouble with you, Angie, is that you were just born unlovable." In which case, obviously, the richer she was the better.

She called Marco, not having spoken to him since all the silly fuss about the overdose. Nor had he called her, but she was used to that. There had been four of them, three men and her. She didn't usually do that sort of thing. Drummer, bass guitar, Marco the vocalist, and she was the angel. The Black Angel. They'd black-boot-polished her all over. There'd been black all over the hospital sheets. The nurses had thought it so unfunny she'd had to laugh. In California they'd said something about the residual chemicals from the polish upsetting the skin peel, but that was their way of not being sued. Fat chance they had.

"Hi," said Marco.

"Hi," said Angie. "You know the chapel we hired for the video?"

Marco did. They'd recorded a song called "Satan's Tits." It had risen to Number 24 on the strength of the video, a mini-spectacular staged in a disused, but not unconsecrated chapel, on the grounds of a crumbling English country house. The owner, called by phone in Monte Carlo for permission to use the chapel, had said drunkenly, "Do what you like. It's haunted, anyway." And a certain Father McCrombie, who lived alone in the one uncrumbled wing of the house, had opened it up for them. He was the caretaker. They'd filmed his thick old hands on virgin flesh. Opportunists!

"What about it?" asked Marco.

"I'm going to buy it," said Angie. "I'm going into films."

"Oh yes," said Marco. "And what will you do for an encore?"

"Just shut up," said Angie, "and tell me the name of the priest who was hanging around. I've forgotten."

"You take too much stuff," said Marco. "It plays hell with the memory. And while we're on the subject, Angie, we could have done without all that nursery palace shit. Our street credibility is shot to hell, thanks to you. It's why we only got to twenty-four. His name is Father McCrombie, and he's an ex-priest, not a priest, and there's been nothing but trouble since we made the farting video. So watch it. And in the meantime, don't call us, we'll call you."

Who wants you anyway? thought Angie, putting the receiver down. Little boys with acne. Took three of them to make one of Clifford. And where was Clifford?

In the meantime, Father McCrombie sniffed the damp air around the chapel and scented something exciting in the air, something on its way. He had a nose for these things. He rubbed his fat, thick, trembling hands together, and waited. Father McCrombie had once been a good man, and a good man gone to the bad is rottener to the core than an ordinary man merely touched by sin and bruised.

Let me tell you about Father McCrombie. He started life as a bright schoolboy with a pious nature from a good Scottish Protestant home. His father was a builder. He joined the RAF; he was a Battle of Britain pilot; he won the Distinguished Flying Cross; he helped save his country. Alone in the great silent sky, waiting for the bang and crash of battle, he would talk to God. He talked also to young Lord Sebastian Lamptonborough (the country, in its *extremis,* had become quite democratic in its habits: there was much interclass chatting) who, though brave, was not good. When demobilized, Michael McCrombie took holy orders. He looked for a wife (a clergyman must have a wife) but found he was by nature celibate, and presently was taken into the Catholic Church, and given a parish in Northern Ireland. In those days he did not drink or smoke. He worshipped God sincerely and kept the Pope's laws and encouraged his flock to do the same. He was sober and he was loved. But Father McCrombie had one flaw. He was, to put it frankly, a snob. He liked a title; admired wealth; was flattered by the company of the famous, assumed it would be easier for a cultured man to reach the Kingdom of Heaven than a yobbo. This was not Jesus's view. Now you may see snobbery as a small failing in a man (or woman). I see it as one of the Deadly Sins. It is envy. It works away from within, destroying goodness. It certainly ruined Father McCrombie. When Lord Sebastian Lamptonborough, scion of one of those wealthy High Catholic families who have had the ear of cardinals for centuries and who could get their indissoluble marriages dissolved at the drop of a papal hat, wrote to him and asked him to come and minister to the Lamptonboroughs, hear their confessions, mediate between them and their God, he accepted at once. He left his flock mid-crisis-of-faith, mid-pregnancy, mid-catechism and was off to England, fine claret, a charming chapel, beautiful ladies and drunken lords with drastic habits.

Christabel Lamptonborough, a pale and lovely eighteen, would kneel before him in the confessional and tell him her heart's and her body's desires. Father McCrombie wrestled with her soul. He never heard her giggles as she left, or if he did, he shut his ears to them. He lit tall white candles in the chapel and prayed for her immortal soul, and thought once he saw our Lord, standing in the light which slanted through gothic windows, elongated, his thin robed body reaching up to heaven—or was that something Christabel had dropped into the sacramental wine? Christabel thought Michael McCrombie was handsome and forbidden. She thought she'd have him. She did. She fell soon after from her horse and broke her back. Her soul was on his conscience: not to mention his own. But at least he worried. Sebastian was taking LSD. He liked to have Father McCrombie as the good friend who would accompany him on his trip to heaven (or hell) and see him safely back into the world of ordinary perception. But of course Father McCrombie was no longer good. Now LSD is funny stuff: mostly it just stuns and dazes and blanks out numerous brain cells, but it can turn people into their opposites, while keeping them somehow within their accustomed framework. I have known it to turn critics into writers, civil servants into claimants, income-tax inspectors into tax accountants, policemen into criminals, bank managers into debtors, and vice versa. This one bad trip turned Sebastian from a man who cared about the past, and his inheritance, into a man who despised it. Thereafter, if a tile blew off the roof of Lamptonborough House he took no notice. A tile fell into the conservatory and he ignored it. Stairs rotted and gates fell off hinges.

"Tear it all down," he'd say. "Put up a housing estate!"

Christabel died while Sebastian was on trip number seventeen. Father McCrombie—who would have been defrocked and excommunicated by now, had the inquiring Cardinal not suffered a heart attack on his way back to report and the matter gotten lost in the Archbishop's files—overwhelmed by grief and guilt and the knowledge that his prayers could hardly help her out of purgatory, took acid himself. After that Sebastian claimed the house was haunted; he thought, of course, by Christabel, but I think by Father McCrombie's good self. Now Sebastian lived in Monte Carlo, and gambled away what was left of his inheritance, and the house crumbled and Father McCrombie drank, and lit black candles in the chapel where once he had lit white. And when a pop group turned up to make a video called *Satan's Tits,* he was not in the least surprised.

He'd just wait to see what happened next.

And where, in the meantime, was Clifford?

A NEW WORLD

Reader, while Father McCrombie glowers and rots, and waits in his haunted wood, and Angie plots, let us look at our cast of characters and see how the new world of the eighties is treating them. The glittery kaleidoscope that is the Art World had ground on a turn or two (you know that rough, difficult sound of scraping glass?) and stuck, shimmering and deceptive, at a point where for once John Lally was at an advantage. Already fairly well established (thanks to Clifford) and a familiar name in the art journals, his vast paintings (Clifford was right: alter the gestalt and you alter the paintings; marriage to Marjorie had released something, shifted his sense of scale) were now in great demand. Their tenor suited the times, which I'm afraid is no particular compliment. Half abstract, half surrealist, they suited the wealthy, uninformed buyer. Looking—to be crude—both arty and plotty, the paintings cast cultural credit on their purchaser and gave him something to talk about at dinner. And the wealthy, uninformed buyer was everywhere these days, begging to be relieved of money which would otherwise go into taxes, and desperate to find someone reliable to inform him.

Clifford managed to be art consultant to a whole handful of the new spectacular private galleries which in Europe and the States were springing up under private patronage, at the behest of big business; not to mention a vast clutch of art-buying multi-millionaires. All were competing for reputable canvases to cover their architect-designed walls. Reputable canvases, that is, which would not lose value. Clifford it was who decided on the "reputable," juggling his duties to himself, his clients, and Leonardo's. In the current climate, Leonardo's—as well as national galleries throughout Europe—was having a bad time. Getty, to name but one, could outbuy anyone, even governments.

And governments everywhere seemed more interested in funding Defense than Art.

But John Lally, for once, was happy enough. He could command such high prices for each canvas he currently covered with paint that he scarcely cared about the fate of his early works. Indeed, he looked at them and despised them. So much *angst,* doom and gloom—where had it all come from? He no longer had to brood about the unfairness of the sell-on-at-a-profit system for works of art, which so ignored the rights and involvement of the artist. Now that the original price was so high it was easy enough to see it as a once-and-for-all buy-out. If Ottoline's and Leonardo's turned out to be the same organization, what did it matter? His paintings were now so large he could hardly do more than two a year anyway, let alone three. He had wanted money not because he was greedy, but to be free of financial anxiety; so he could buy as much flake-white as he wanted, and more. Now he could paint when and what he wanted—for wasn't he financially secure? Rich, even?

If John Lally scarcely knew anymore what it was he wanted to paint, he hid the knowledge from himself. He painted what would sell—well, perhaps that was coincidental, or perhaps that was what he'd always wanted. Who was to say? What money, comfort, a happy marriage and a young son can do for a man.

He had a large studio custom-built at the end of the garden at Applecore Cottage, disregarding the pleas of neighbors. It was his pleasure, and their punishment. It was a very tall building; it had to be, to house the new canvases. City-planning permission had been a problem at first, but he'd simply given a painting—an early one—to the Town Hall and the difficulties had melted away.

And Helen? I wish I could report that she at least was happy and content. She should have been. She deserved to be. She was, after all, free of a philandering husband; she was independent, and successful. She had recovered, or so she thought as the years passed and Clifford and Angie were long married, from the shock and pain of the divorce. And did not everyone agree this time around that Clifford was most definitely the guilty party, whatever the law said, and herself blameless? And weren't the twins the image of their father, no matter what Clifford had to say about that? Did she not have three children to keep her busy (as if she weren't busy enough already) and fill her house with gentle, sleeping, nourishing breath at night? Did she not have friends and admirers aplenty? Had not the world changed around her, so that a woman alone was not pitied, but (by some, anyway) envied?

And as for House of Lally—well! What a runaway success!

Young Royalty, not to mention anyone who was anyone, simply adored her designs. Clothes by Lally had a color, a richness, a softness and quality of fabric which made them sensuous rather than flashy, honorable rather than vulgar, as sometimes the most expensive clothes can be. The fashion story of the century, according to the press! As soon as the Lally label appeared on a rack—no matter how expensive, how exclusive—it was snapped up within minutes. Even John Lally had to grudgingly admit the fabrics were okay, the designs passable, whilst disapproving of the kind of person who bought them. He still had no time for the idle rich, which was sensible enough, when you consider Angie. Though, mind you, Angie's trouble, or ours with her, may have been that she was not idle enough. If only she'd just lain back and enjoyed her wealth and her butler, and not been forever poking and prying and stirring things up—

But no one could accuse Helen, these days, or Clifford, of being idle. Leonardo's troubles kept Clifford busy, at any rate in such times as he had free from his other clients to devote to them.

STIRRINGS

As for Nell—well, guess who comes to visit Nell one day, but Polly! Polly's lost a stone or two. Polly looks ever so smart in a navy two-piece suit. Her face is made-up, her hair bobbed. She looks, and is, a successful businesswoman. While in Holloway she had the benefit of a psychotherapist who has changed her life (Polly says). Clive will be out soon and Polly won't be waiting for him. Polly is off drugs and now runs a Health and Beauty clinic outside London.

"You can't stay here!" says Polly, looking around the gloomy bungalow which is the Kildare's household, the wire compounds outside, the overhanging Welsh hills; the whimper and howl and barks of dogs forever in the ears; the smell of disinfectant and animal mixed.

"I rather like it," says Nell. "They've been ever so good to me."

"Hmm," says Polly, setting up a seed of doubt in Nell's mind, which was to grow and grow.

"What about boys?" asks Polly. Well, that's the important question.

"There's someone called Dai Evans," says Nell, blushing. Now Dai Evans, as we know, keeps well clear of Nell; he's a nice lad and knows when he's out of his class, which is more than Nell does. If you live in the Welsh hills, doing A levels, helping out in the kennels, teenage culture passes you by and you have very little sense of your own capacity to attract. But sometimes he meets her for coffee in the little café behind the Ruellyn fish and chip shop and that makes Nell's week.

"That's nice," says Polly, and so, if you ask me, it is.

Nell is in love, turning the emotion over in her mind, freely, testing it out—it is, for Nell, almost a theoretical matter. Pain and joy are mixed; sex has not yet entered into the equation. She fights off other boys, instinctively.

"Still drawing?" asks Polly.

"I'm into fabrics more," says Nell. And so she is, to her Art Teacher's despair. Art A level is a funny subject—you don't pass it by doing your own thing or developing your own taste. "You know there's a special kind of tree lichen with ever so pretty fluted edges which makes such a lovely yellowy dye you can't imagine?" Nell's teacher did not want to hear it.

"I hope you're having no trouble with him?" asks Polly, meaning Mr. Kildare, whom she's never liked.

"Trouble? What do you mean?" asks Nell, and indeed, Mr. Kildare, to his credit, has managed to keep his feelings about Nell under control. Or perhap he's just waiting until the kennel profits have topped the £100,000 mark, when he can afford to buy a piece of land he's got his eye on, where he could abandon dogs and go into horses. There's more money in horses. He has this idea of starting life all over again, with someone more suited to him than his wife. They've really stayed together because of Brenda—or so he sees it—though he's never said as much to Mrs. Kildare. But all that's another story, and a rather gloomy one, reader.

"Nothing," says Polly, glad of the response. "I often think of you, Nell," she says. She has a kind and sentimental heart. Nell asks to hear the story, once again, of how she arrived at Faraway Farm, and listens carefully. Perhaps somewhere here is a clue to her origins—but there's nothing.

"Polly," says Nell, "can you do me a favor?"

"What's that?" says Polly.

"I don't have a birth certificate or Health Card or anything," says Nell. "I need a passport. Just in case I ever want to go anywhere. Not that I do, of course"—how could she ever leave Dai Evans, not see that curly head, those young brown eyes again? "But just in case—"

"Easiest thing in the world," says Polly, and they go off together to the Ruellyn Post Office where there's a photo machine and take two pictures of Nell, which the postmistress signs on the back and six weeks later a passport comes in the mail for Nell. What it is to have friends in certain, if not high, places.

Look, reader, I think it's just as well that Dai Evans didn't respond to our Nell, the way she hoped. (He liked her very much as a person—who wouldn't?—but in fact was to grow up to be far more interested in his own sex than in Nell's.) So many girls—and usually the best and liveliest—fall in love too young, marry too young, and thereafter have a decade or so's trouble getting themselves back onto the right path—and there are children to think about, aren't there, and divorce is horrid, and they're not trained or equipped as they ought to be. Whole lives get wasted. And hard luck on the boys, too, come to that.

ILL-WISHED

Angie, as we know, was bored and cross. Angie became particularly cross one day. It was with Harry Blast, who had lured her onto his "Art Today" program on BBC and then portrayed her as the kind of rich dilettante who dabbled in art to the detriment of artists, and what is more, lit her so badly that every flaw in her complexion showed.

"Dabble! I'll give him dabble!" she said, as one who liked to do exactly that with the Black Arts. She got Father McCrombie, who was now in her employ and caretaking for the Satan Chapel, to light a black candle or two and invoke a curse upon Harry Blast's now-balding media head.

Angie ran a company called Lolly Locations, which hired out sets and properties to film and television people. The Satan Chapel was much in demand. It had a fine, quiet location in a particularly spooky wood, not far from Elstree Studios, and was permanently wired inside and out so there were few of the normal problems with lights. Angie knew how to do things. Father McCrombie kept caged bats, which could be released—behind fine, almost invisible netting—and retrieved at will. He kept a couple of falcons which could pass as eagles. A man of many parts. He himself was in demand as an extra—he had a broad, lined, decadent face, which if lit properly looked positively devilish, and red contact lenses, which (for a fee) he was prepared to slip in to enhance the effect. Angie allowed him to live in the little toll-house, adjacent to the chapel, and paid him enough to keep him in drinks, young boys and the long clerical gowns he loved. He was grateful, but like her, got bored. And his drinking made him not perhaps as specific as she would have liked when lighting his candles and invoking his powers.

No trouble, anyway, fell upon Harry Blast's head. The Dilettante program was hugely successful and "Art Today" rescheduled for prime time. But trouble seemed somehow to spill over in other directions—there where Angie's real, profounder griefs and resentments lay.

But how can one be sure? Was it one of Father McCrombie's spells which tipped Clifford's dealings over from sharpish practice into sheer dishonesty and lies? Or was it just pressure of circumstances, the unsure responses of an unhappy man; something that was bound to happen sooner or later? The unhappy do lose their judgment.

What happened was that when Homer McLinsky, the young press tycoon, made an inquiry about a rather indifferent Seurat passing through Leonardo's hands, Clifford said he'd already had an offer of $250,000, when in fact that offer had been $25,000. "What's a zero?" thought Clifford. That was in the New York offices, where "What's a zero?" is easily thought. McLinsky looked at Clifford a little oddly and gave Clifford an opportunity to retract, but Clifford didn't. The old Clifford would have noticed the look and done something about it. The new Clifford, what with Father McCrombie's black burning vengeful candles glittering away in the Satan's Chapel, simply didn't notice.

Now Angie had never told Father McCrombie what went on inside her secret soul, but somehow he got in there and knew more about it than she did herself. Poor Angie! No one nice had ever tried to get inside her soul, so now it was left to horrible red-faced, red-bearded, pop-eyed, occasionally red-eyed evil Father McCrombie, and she knew no better than to let him. The world had failed Angie, as much as she had failed it. It was a two-way system.

Father McCrombie lit black candles for Helen. He named her on the slip of paper wound around the wax, fixed with a drop of McCrombie's spittle. This, or something, gave Helen a nasty patch of sleeping badly and suffering from really horrid, murderous, obsessive thoughts. Around and around they went in her head. There were anxious, worrying, busy thoughts—such as—if she could only find Nell, then Clifford would come back to her. There were bleak, lowering, fateful thoughts—for example, that losing Clifford was her punishment for losing Nell. ("Losing Clifford" seemed once again a real concept.) And then there were the terrible thoughts, the murderous rage and hate, focused against little Barbara. At the very thought of the child of her rival (Her rival? What sort of thinking was this?) bile and spite would rise in her throat. She would wake in the morning with a sour taste in her mouth. And around and around the half-sleeping thoughts went through her waking day. If only Barbara would die, then Clifford would return to her. Yes, that was the way! So she planned the child's death in her mind: by fire, road accident, wild dogs—horrible! She knew it was disgusting but she couldn't stop it. Remarkable, is it not? This propensity we all have to deflect our hate and anger from its proper source to someone standing innocently on the sidelines. As if somehow this will safeguard us, stop our curses deflecting back on us, as curses have such a habit of doing!

CURE

Helen spent a weekend with the children at Applecore Cottage. It was no longer in her father's nature to ban her on this account or that. And now that she had his affection and approval (well, more or less) she could not understand why the lack of them had not afflicted her in the past. There was a guest annex now; the apple tree in the garden had been cut down to make room for it. The bough was gone on which the robin had once sat and twittered its easy comfort. Was this what it had foreseen? Worldly comfort, worldly success? (You can see how sad she was!)

Well, the annex was comfortable, and centrally heated. The children had their own TV. (Once John Lally had banned it altogether from the house.) The beds were new and softly firm, and the pillows were, she thought, plumping with an experienced hand, goose-down. What Evelyn, whose body in life and sleep lay on a broken mattress, her head upon a lumpy pillow, would not have done for such luxuries! How easily Marjorie extracted good things from her husband, how she had changed him and chained him! Helen marveled at it, and these days without resentment or jealousy. Little Julian, Marjorie's son and her own half-brother, had a somehow stolid, ordinary look, as befitted the child of not so extraordinary parents after all. Her own boys, beside him, were animated, vulnerable and alert. But they played cricket together, happily enough, on the lawn which was once Evelyn's vegetable patch. Marjorie had had it turfed over.

"Father's looking well," said Helen to Marjorie. She had a headache. They were in the new, custom-built kitchen. The walls between outhouse and pantry, pantry and kitchen had been taken down. Nothing strange moved now in the half-dark. All was bright and light and sensible.

"I stopped him drinking homemade wine," said Marjorie. "I put a lot of his former troubles down to that."

"But how did you stop him?"

"I poured the lot away."

Poor Evelyn! Season after season, in the interests of economy and ecology, with nettles, rosehips, parsnips: plucking, picking, digging, stripping, sieving, pounding, boiling, brewing, funneling, filtering, lifting, storing. Poured the lot away! Helen felt a dart of hatred toward Marjorie. It was quite uncalled for, but she couldn't stop it. It made her headache worse. She put her head in her hands.

"Whatever's the matter? Something's wrong, isn't it? You're so white and pale." Her stepmother (she had never thought of Marjorie in such terms before) was kind and concerned. Helen wept.

"Thoughts in my head," she said presently, "which oughtn't to be there."

Marjorie had an answer. She always did. She assumed that if there was a problem it could be solved. She recommended a Dr. Myling, whom she'd seen herself. He was a psychiatrist, but of the holistic school.

"The what?" asked Helen.

"It doesn't really matter what it's called," said Marjorie. "If you ask me, all these new healers are just priests under another name."

"But I'm not religious," said Helen. "Or not particularly." She remembered there'd been a time when she'd prayed to God, quite instinctively, though of course as a child she'd never gone to church. Then she'd thought the universe was benign, and needed, and wanted, simply to *worship*. But something had happened, long ago, to put an end to it. What was it? Why of course, the death of Nell. Now there, she'd said it. She accepted it, at least. And the shadow above her, instead of lightening, as everyone had predicted, simply darkened. The dark was beginning to press upon her, almost physically; as if it wanted to squelch her into mud, make her part of it.

"I can see," she said, with an effort, "that if you believed, faith-healing of the mind could work, just as it does with the body, but I don't really believe. I wish I did."

The wish made things a little better, enough to write down Dr. Myling's address, and let Marjorie make an appointment. Though, as Marjorie said, it's usually better to make the appointment yourself. To go of your own volition, not be pushed, feeling the urge toward health and sanity not as the mere desire to please someone else.

"Just sometimes," said Marjorie, "the cure is not in yourself, you need another human being to take you by the hand. In the same way that people who go on acid trips need to take a friend with them," she said.

Odd that she'd made that analogy. It was a subject (in case you're wondering) she knew little about. It was on one such trip, remember, that Father McCrombie had escorted Lord Sebastian, and lost his former self in transit, the way some people lose baggage between Singapore and Paris.

Dr. Myling had an address in Wimpole Street, and shared an ugly, quiet, grand waiting-room with a group of other doctors, who were mostly orthopedic specialists, judging from the creaking backs and cracking joints of the waiting patients. Quiet, quiet—creak, crack—Helen wanted to laugh. She felt she hadn't laughed for a long time, but surely this was not the time to do it? Even her own mirth oppressed her. Dr. Myling was a young man. He was barely thirty. He had the strong jaw and quiet good looks so loved by those who let people into medical schools. She thought, when she had explained her symptoms—unnecessary, nasty, murderous thoughts, laughter at what wasn't funny—that he'd ask about her childhood or give her pills, or suggest she was having an early menopause and suggest Hormone Replacement Therapy.

"Do you have murderous thoughts?" is one of the questions asked when a lack of estrogen in a woman's hormonal balance is suspected. Instead he asked if someone was ill-wishing her.

"I can't think who," she said in astonishment, "and if there was, what could I do about it?"

He considered, asked a few brisk questions about the past

and Applecore Cottage, and then suggested she pray to her mother. Helen laughed again, in her surprise, and said she didn't think her mother, dead or alive, could stop anything. It wasn't in her nature.

"You'd be surprised," he said. "People change." (What could he mean?) "Come back in two weeks, and if it hasn't worked, then we will try pills. But only then."

So Helen tried praying and, reader, whether it was Evelyn's spirit blowing out Father McCrombie's cheap and nastily labeled candles, or just Helen's naturally kind and healthy mind asserting itself, but the night horrors simply went, Helen slept soundly again, paid Dr. Myling's bill for £45, and left it at that.

Clifford had no one to pray to, no one to intercede for him, and would probably have been too proud and rational to approach such a person anyway, whether living or dead, and so his troubles got worse, not better.

Our Nell, in trouble! Unthinkable. But even the most charmed amongst us, in their growing up, seem to go through a couple of bad years, when they scowl and jeer, are unhealthy, dirty and generally ungrateful, and seem to enjoy making a nuisance of themselves. Then all their elders and betters can do is grit their teeth and sit it out, and wait for a benign and kindly spirit to once again inhabit their child. Nell's bad years came between seventeen and nineteen.

Perhaps now at last she could take the risk of misbehaving? When her future seemed set Fair? In her early years she had been torn this way and that, as if both bad and good fairy godmothers had bent over her cradle, each claiming Nell for her own. Clifford had raged and Helen wept, the skies themselves had spat her out, Milord and Milady had invoked devils. There had been the trauma of the roadway inferno; the abrupt end to the criminal idyll of Faraway Farm—and though each disaster had been balanced by some good event, these traumas and distresses were there in her mind and must in the end take their toll. This was it, the fine exacted by the past upon the present.

On her sixteenth birthday all was still well. She was a nice, bright, lively, loving girl who passed exams, helped her quasi-family the Kildares (she worked in fact as a kennel maid, unpaid, and never complained) and tried to catch Dai Evans' eye. Then Polly visited. By seventeen she had shorn her thick curly hair almost to the scalp and dyed it black, she was anorexic, she was so offended by her art teacher's view of what was good and bad in painting that she gave up A Level Art altogether. She caught her history teacher out on a matter of fact and refused to attend another lesson thereafter. So that was History A Level out, which left French and she was deciding to take moral exception to

Racine, so presumably French didn't have long to go. And Dai Evans had gone into the Navy so what was the point of going to school at all: a point which occurred to Mrs. Kildare, the day when Nell should have been at school and simply, somehow, wasn't.

"Heaven knows what's the point of you going to school at all," said Mrs. Kildare, listening to Nell's account of the general folly and wrong-headedness of her teachers. She was overworked. The quarantine section had been expanded and business was good, but wages were (by custom and practice) low, and the kennels miles from anywhere, so staff was always hard to find. Mrs. Kildare was in the kitchen boiling up meat for the dogs: the hot-plates in the scullery were no longer enough. A horrible smell but they were all used to it.

"Neither do I," said Nell, for once not arguing.

"In that case," said Mrs. Kildare, "you'd better leave school at the end of term and earn your keep properly, for once." Mrs. Kildare, as we know, was going through a hard time, otherwise she wouldn't have added "for once." A pity she did.

Nell left school that very day, to the great distress and protest of teachers and friends, to work full-time at the kennels.

What had happened, reader, as you and I but no one else should know, was that Mr. Kildare, aged forty-five, worrying about being fifty, looking foward to a future in which nothing happened except changes in the quarantine laws at best, and growing older at worst, had stopped simply lusting after Nell and fallen in love with her. These things happen. Poor Mrs. Kildare! Lust can be disguised; love can't. Hands tremble, faces pale, voices quiver. Mrs. Kildare had her suspicions. It didn't improve her temper, or make her more patient with Nell. And poor Nell too! There was no one in whom she could confide. How could she talk to Mrs. Kildare about what was going on? Or Brenda, or any of her school friends in case it got back to Brenda? If she cut off her hair it was to make herself unattractive. It didn't work. If she stopped going to school it was to make herself stupid. That didn't work, either. All that happened was that everyone disapproved except Mr. Kildare. He would come up to her at feeding-time—and her hands smelled horrid from the mix, but not even that put him off—staring with his great brown eyes, and beg her to run off with him.

"Why are you so unkind?" he'd ask.

"I don't mean to be unkind, Mr. Kildare."

"Call me Bob! Don't be so formal. Aren't you grateful for all I've done for you?"

"I'm grateful to Mrs. Kildare too."

"If we explain properly, she'll understand."

"Explain what, Mr. Kildare?"

"Our love, Nell, I've never loved my wife. We've just made do. Stayed together because of Brenda. And now you've come along. I think God sent you—"

"Not *our* love, Mr. Kildare. Yours. And please, please, don't tell me about it; it isn't fair."

But he would, he did: his hands came nearer and were less easy to push away. And Brenda began to look at her oddly. Oh, it was intolerable! Nell packed her things one night, put her lucky tin teddy bear around her neck, took her savings (£63.70) out of the bank and caught the train to London. It would upset Mrs. Kildare but what else could she do?

The smoke of Father McCrombie's black candles drifted over the Kildare household, twining in and out of the trees, puffing around the kennels, making the dogs whine and grow restless. Or something did.

"What's the matter with them lately?" Mrs. Kildare asked. "I expect they miss Nell," said Mr. Kildare. Now Nell was gone the smoke was getting out of his mind; it was clearing again; he could hardly remember his own behavior, his own straying, pinching hand. Of course he loved his wife. He always had.

"It happened before she left," said Mrs. Kildare. "If anything, they're better now. It's just me who's not," and she cried a little. She missed Nell and not just because now she had to work twice as hard—up at five and in bed by twelve, when the last upset, homesick, howling hound had been soothed and quietened (and even later sometimes when the moon was full and bright), but she'd loved her almost as much as Brenda, for all that she'd been such a problem of late.

Only Brenda said nothing about Nell. She didn't know what to say, Nell was her best friend, and she'd seen how her father looked at Nell, and now Nell was gone, and she didn't know whether to be glad or sorry. She became rather stolid and spotty and dull-eyed, as girls who look after animals seem to do in their late adolescence. Evil never clears completely away; it leaves a residue, a kind of greasy film over hope and good cheer. "I like animals best," she'd say, as she'd heard her parents say before her. "They're much nicer than humans." But she agreed to get engaged to Ned. She'd rather be a farmer's wife than the daughter of kennels, for now Nell had gone it was as if the sunlight had gone with her. She could see the place for what it was—muddy, noisy, dismal, sad. And, like Nell, she wanted to be out of it.

Of course Angie had no idea that Nell was alive. Had she known it, I have no doubt she would have instructed Father McCrombie to light a black candle for her, too. As it was, the dark father just had to direct ill-will in a general direction, which is why it got to Mr. Kildare's heart, but not to Nell's. In fact, things turned out very well for Nell as a result. Or was that Evelyn's doing again—Evelyn, looking down from heaven, puffing out the candles as fast as Father McCrombie lit them?

Look, we could speculate on this forever. Middle-aged men fall for young women without the dark powers having to be involved, God knows, so let's just say Mr. Kildare was a dirty old man. But I don't know—say that of Brenda's father? It seems unkind.

MEETING UP!

Be that as it may, at about the time that Helen recovered from her night horrors, and the dangerous Homer McLinsky looked oddly at Clifford (who had no protector: why should Evelyn even *think* of the man who caused her daughter so much trouble), Nell turned up at the House of Lally workshops behind Broadcasting House in London's West End. She was a black-haired, punkish, too-thin, scraggy Welsh girl with rough hands and no A levels, let alone an Art School training.

"I want a job," she said to Hector McLaren, Helen's business manager. He was a broad, fair man with boxer's shoulders, and thick stubby fingers which moved surely and delicately amongst fabrics, seeing profit or loss in every swatch. Which was just as well, since Helen could be carried away by beauty and cease to be practical.

"You're not the only one," he said. He was busy. A dozen girls a week turned up, on spec, in just the same way. They'd read about the House of Lally, or seen the clothes on a young Royal back, at some Royal spectacular, and wanted to be involved. They were turned away, automatically if kindly. The House of Lally took on ten apprentices a year, and trained them well. Two thousand applied, ten were chosen.

"I'm not like the others," she said, as if it was obvious, and smiled, and he realized she was both beautiful and bright, and doing him the favor, not he her.

"Let's have a look at your portfolio then," he said, not quite sure why, and someone else answered the telephone. A call from Rio.

He knew before he opened the portfolio, stretching and releasing the neat, white confining bands, that it was going to be exciting. He'd opened thousands. You got to know; the pleasure of discovery couldn't restrain itself, got to you a moment too soon. He was right. What a portfolio it was! Swatches of natural fabrics, lichen dyed, but finely finished. Now how had she contrived those? Wild, brilliant squares of embroidery, intricately worked. She liked color—if anything it was too strong, too bold—but what he usually saw in such portfolios was so tentative, so well-behaved. And then sheet after sheet of dress designs—untrained and amateurish, but done with such a surety of line—almost a kind of blind conviction. A handful were even usable—a couple more than usable.

"Um," he said cautiously. "When did you do all these?"

"I just sat in class and drew," she said. "School gets so boring, doesn't it?" (Late nights and hard times at the kennels, reader. Mostly she was just short of sleep.)

She was very young. He asked a few personal questions. He thought he was getting lies in return, so he changed tack.

"Why House of Lally?" he asked. "Not Yves St. Laurent? Not Muir?"

"I like the clothes," she said, simply. "I like the colors." She was wearing jeans and a white shirt. That was sensible. If you can't afford clothes, don't try. Wear what you look good in. He hired her.

"It's hard work and low pay," he warned her. "You'll be sweeping floors."

"I'm used to that," she said, and didn't say what came into her head next, that at least this kind didn't get any harder and longer when the moon was full. It occurred to her that perhaps she'd had, for her age, quite an experience of the world. The thought both pleased her and saddened her, and she longed for someone to talk to; but of course there was no one, and then the kind of whirling pleasure and triumph came: "After all that, I've done it, I've got a job, I've actually got the right job, I'm exactly where I want to be," and there was no one to tell about that, either. So she just smiled again at Hector McLaren, and he thought, now where have I seen that smile before, half happy, half tragic, but he did not make the connection. Afterwards he wondered, now what *have* I done? Why did I do that? We're overstaffed as it is. Helen had the same effect on him, sometimes:

overriding his better judgment in the most extraordinary way. He decided he was just susceptible to women. (Which of course he wasn't, reader, or only to Lally women.)

And that's how Nell came to work for her mother. Well, since like calls to like, it was not surprising. Something of John Lally's talent ran in both their veins, mother and daughter alike.

Nell left home on Wednesday and was taken on by Hector McLaren on Thursday, and started her job on the following Monday. She lodged in a small hotel in Maida Vale—her room free in return for two hours' cleaning between 6 A.M. and 8 A.M., six days a week. She walked to work. There she swept floors, and was allowed to hand-sew a seam or so, and watched the cutters carefully. In the evenings she went out to discos and fell into bad company. Well, not very bad, just rather brightly-haired and with the odd safety-pin through earlobe and nose; amiable, passive and, for Nell, safe. Her new friends made no demands on her, intellectual or emotional. They drooped about and jigged around, and smoked dope. So did Nell, having noted how it had soothed and cheered Clive and Polly, forgetting how their general idleness had led to their downfall. She got to work tired, but she was used to being tired.

One Friday afternoon Helen Lally herself came into the workshop. Heads turned. She wore a cream suit and her hair was piled on top of her head. She went into the office and spoke for a little while to Hector McLaren, behind the glass. Then she came out and crossed straight over to where Nell sat, and picked up the coat she was working on, and inspected it, and seemed to approve of what she saw, though Nell knew the seam wasn't perfectly straight. She'd fallen asleep over it, at one point, and hadn't bothered to go back.

"So your name's Nell," she said. "Mr. McLaren speaks very well of you. Nell's such a pretty name. I've always liked it."

"Thank you," said Nell, pleased and blushing. She did her best to look tough and cross, but it wasn't much use. Helen thought the girl was too young, too thin, and probably living away from home and shouldn't be. Later she spoke to Hector about her, looking through the glass to where Nell's dark cropped head bent over the cloth.

"She's too young," she said. "It's a responsibility. Not like you to take her on, Hector, and her seams do wander, rather. We're overstaffed."

"Not if the Brazilian order comes through," he said. "We'll be really pressed if it does." At which point the phone rang with confirmation of the order from Rio. It was the kind of thing the House of Lally seldom undertook—an entire wardrobe for an impossibly rich and fanciful young woman, newly married, who had a penchant for red roses—or else her husband had—and such a flower had to be either discreetly or effusively, at House of Lally's discretion, delicately embroidered on, or flamboyantly fixed upon, every single garment, from suspender belt to greatcoat.

"Why ever did we say we'd do it?" mourned Helen. "It's so *vulgar*."

"We're doing it because of the money," said Hector, briskly. "And whether or not it's vulgar depends on how it's done."

"But I'll have to stand over someone *all* the time"—and then, cheering up, "Well, I suppose a red rose is what you make it."

And so indeed it is! Hector thought of Nell's portfolio and Nell was extracted from the ranks and embroidered a specimen rose or two, from scarlet buds to crimson extravaganza, which woke her up no end—and within the week was sitting in the attic studio of Helen's St. John's Wood house, sewing roses for all she was worth, upon fabric of every shade, weight and texture, adjusting color and thread with a sure instinct.

"Good heavens," said Helen, "what did I ever do without you!" and to Hector she said, "I hardly have to tell her a thing. She seems to know how my mind works. And it's really nice to have a girl in the house—I've gotten so used to boys."

"So long," said Hector, "as you don't start seeing her as a daughter! She's an employee. Don't spoil her."

It was Hector's opinion that Helen spoiled the boys; indulging them, allowing them their own way, spending too much money on them. And he may have been right—but they were a happy household, and there is no point at all in "beginning as you mean to go on." Why? Why not just have good times while you can, is the way many a mother feels when the children's father is gone.

"Nell," said Helen one day, when Nell was a week into the rose spectacular. "Where are you living?"

"In a squat," said Nell, and then, sensing concern and offering reassurance, as was her habit, "It's okay. There's water and mains services. I was paying my way as a chambermaid but the squat works out cheaper."

And she smiled, and Helen thought, where have I seen that smile before? (On Clifford, of course, but she tried not to think about Clifford.) If I had a daughter, Helen thought, I would love her to be like this. Direct, kind, open to the world. I would like her to be living somewhere other than in a squat, of course. I would like her to be less waif-like, not so thin, properly looked after. Bother Hector, thought Helen, and pursued the conversation.

"Most of our girls live at home," she said.

"They have to," observed Nell, "because you pay them so little." And she smiled to take the sting out of the words. "But I don't have a home. Not a proper home. I never have."

Perhaps if Helen had been listening she would have pursued Nell's history further, and made necessary connections, but she was still brooding about what seemed to her an accusation. Did she really underpay the workshop girls? She paid the going rate: was it enough? She brooded, of course, because she knew in her heart it was far from enough. House of Lally traded on its reputation in this respect also—if people line up for the privilege of working for you, you need pay them very little. This, reader, is what I see as natural justice. If Helen hadn't been guilty she would not have been riled, and brooded, and would have regained her daughter earlier. As it was, she had to wait.

She would bring up the matter with Hector.

"Do you have a boyfriend?" she asked Nell, and Nell blushed.

"I do in a way," said Nell, thinking of Dai, who had written to her once, "and I don't in a way," because when she came to think of it, or rather him, she no longer felt what she had. Distance had somehow dispersed obsession—which no doubt is why parents are forever taking girls on long trips abroad (or used to) in the hope they'll forget an unsuitable love. At the same time, Nell could see, loving Dai, at least in theory, kept her out of all kinds of trouble.

"No thank you," she could say to importuning boys. "Nothing personal. It's just that I've got this one true love—" and they would defer, regretfully, to this mysterious passion and leave her alone. And if they didn't, it was remarkable what a swift upper (or lower) cut not necessarily to the jaw our Nell had developed at Ruellyn Comprehensive School. Smiling her glorious smile the while. Quite a girl. Helen, who knew only a fraction of all this, looked at her daughter, whom she did not recognize as daughter, puzzled and impressed.

"Nell," said Helen, "if I found proper lodgings, would you move into them?"

"How would I pay for them?"

"The House of Lally would pay. I'd see to it."

"I couldn't do that," said Nell. "The other girls wouldn't like it. Why should I have something the others don't?" Which was why Helen, after much argument, prevailed upon Hector to raise the workshop girls' wages by a full twenty-five percent—which meant the garment prices had to rise by five percent. And the market stood it without apparently noticing. So they notched them up a further five percent. And Nell consented to move out of her squat—she was heartily glad to go, as it happened. Her friends were wearing thin—quite literally, a couple were on heroin by now. The trouble with drugs, as Nell now remembered from the old Faraway Farm days, is that they're a dead stopper on conversation. If you want to talk, tell your life story to your doper friends—forget it! Nell lodged with Hector and his wife. The food was good, the hot water plentiful, the attic room was warm and she saved up and bought an easel and even got a little painting done on weekends. She woke in the mornings to the agreeable feeling, which the young have when all's going well for them, of life opening up, and the right choices being made, that the world was her oyster.

"Tell you what," said Helen, one momentous day, as Nell moved on to the eightieth rose, and scarcely two had been the same—she was now using as many as twenty different reds to a single rose, and experimenting with a kind of 3-D effect, so that the tiny lush petals seemed to burst from their center—"if you promise not to let it go to your head, we'll try you out as a model."

"Okay," said Nell, trying not to look pleased.

"When will you be eighteen?"

"In June," said Nell.

"I had a daughter called Nell," said Helen.

"I didn't know that," said Nell.

"She kind of got lost along the way," said Helen.

"I'm sorry," said Nell. What else can one say? Helen didn't go into the manner of her loss, and Nell didn't ask.

"She would have been eighteen next Christmas. On Christmas Day."

"I'm always sorry for people who're born on Christmas Day," said Nell. "Only one set of presents! I'm a midsummer baby myself. Do you really want me to be a model?"

"You have the face and figure for it."

"It's just that models are two a penny," said Nell. "Anyone can be pretty. There's no possible merit in it." And Helen wondered, now who do I know who says that kind of thing? Her father, of course, but how was she to make the connection?

"I'd rather be a dress designer," said Nell. "That takes real talent."

"And time," said Helen, "and experience, and training."

Nell seemed to get the point. She smiled.

"I'll be a model, if I can keep my hair like this," said Nell. It was short, black, spiky and brushed straight up.

"It's hardly House of Lally image," said Helen. But she could see it might be easier to change the House of Lally image than Nell's mind, and Nell won. Then the boys came in—Edward, Max and Marcus—and were introduced, but Nell was only one of the staff so they didn't take much notice of her. They wanted their mother to come down to the kitchen and make supper, and, being her mother's daughter, she went with them to do just that. Nell felt oddly lonely when they were all gone, as if an overhead light had been switched off and left her in the dark. She finished the rose, and later that evening phoned Mrs. Kildare, just to say she was well and working, and Mrs. Kildare wasn't to worry, and love to Brenda, and, oh, yes, regards to Mr. Kildare. Then she went and signed up for A level evening classes in Art, History and French. She was back on course again.

Now, reader, shall we get back to Angie's complexion? Remember how she had what the cosmetic surgeons call a facial peel and it went wrong? How the crevices and bumps were worse than before? She didn't really want to sue the clinic: the publicity would be agony. But when in the course of their correspondence with her they suggested the trouble was unrelated to the peel and psychosomatic in origin, but that they would pay for a psychiatrist's fees, she accepted. She went to Dr. Myling, of the new holistic school. She'd heard he was young and good-looking. He was.

"What do *you* think the matter is?" he asked.

"I'm unhappy," she heard herself saying. She was amazed at herself.

"Why?" He had bright blue eyes. He could see into her soul just as Father McCrombie did, but he was kind.

"My husband doesn't love me."

"Why not?"

"Because I'm unlovable." The words shocked her, but they were her own words.

"Go away and try to be lovable," he said. "If your skin's still bad in two weeks, we'll try pills. But only then."

Angie went away and tried to be lovable. She did this by calling Father McCrombie and saying she was selling the chapel and no longer needed his services. She was beginning to feel spooked at the whole thing. Sometimes, in the night, when Clifford was away—which was usually—she'd hear her father laughing.

"Selling the chapel might not be wise," said Father McCrombie, lighting another black candle. "Begorah and it might not at all." Father McCrombie was Edinburgh-born, as we know, but people liked the Irish brogue, and he'd cultivated it. Sometimes, he played not the devil's disciple, but the lovable rogue; sometimes he even thought his good self had returned, and his soul was his own again.

"You can't frighten me," said Angie, though he did. So instead of having her social secretary simply call the real-estate agents and say "Sell!" Angie went around in person to their offices. She wanted to do it herself; she wanted to be courageous; she was not used to feeling fear. She wanted to get the better of it, to taste it properly before spitting it out. I think she was very brave. (You know my policy on speaking well of the living—never mind the dead.)

It was a wet day. You could hardly see for the rain. Angie stood at the junction of Primrose Hill Road and Regents Park Road, just about where Aleister Crowley, the Beast of 666 fame, used to live, and wondered which way to turn. Horns blared and lights blazed toward her. She could not make sense of them—noise and light seemed to leap together into the air—there was a second's soaring silence, and then a thwack from above, which crushed light, life and soul out of her. Perhaps the lesson is that the bad should not attempt to be good. The effort will kill them.

FREAK ACCIDENT KILLS DRUG-CASE MILLIONAIRESS said one paper, trying to hide its mirth. A gasoline truck, careening out of control down Primrose Hill, had struck the curb, overturned, sailed through the air and landed flat on Angie. POOR LITTLE RICH GIRL CRUSHED AS ART-CASE HUSBAND STANDS TRIAL IN NEW YORK said another.

"The world's well rid of her," said John Lally, in spite of the way that Ottoline's had served him, and I am sorry to say there were few to disagree. Only little Barbara wept.

Angie, dear Angie, I don't know what went wrong, what made you so cross and sad, able to bring pleasure to so few. Should we blame your mother, inasmuch as she never loved you? Well, Clifford's mother, Cynthia, didn't love him either, and granted, it didn't do him much good, but it didn't make him unlovable. (Well, look at Helen. Look at your author, who keeps excusing him. He at least has some insight into himself; and a kind of honesty in his selfishness, not to mention a capacity for change—perhaps the most important quality of all.) It is too easy to blame mothers for all the ills of the world. Everything would be okay, we tell ourselves, if only *mothers* did what they should—loved wholly, totally and completely, to the exclusion of all others. But mothers are people too. All they can do in the way of love is the best they can, and the child's report of them always goes "could do better if tried." Should one blame fathers? Angie's father, we know, found her unlovable. Did that *make* her unlovable? I don't think so. Helen's father John Lally was pretty impossible, but Helen was never *nasty*. Feckless and irresponsible in youth, no doubt, but the opposite in her maturity.

Angie, I search for good things to say about you, and can find very little. Yet, wait. If it were not for Angie, Nell would not be alive. She would have been lost to the horrid snip, snip of Dr. Runcorn's metal instruments. Angie's motives were not good—but to do good for the wrong reason is better than not to do good at all. And now we have searched her past and found at least this one good thing, let us mark her memory RIP, Rest in Peace, and set about picking up the wreckage Angie strewed around her in her life, and piecing it together again as best we can.

We all live by myth, reader: if only by the myth of happiness around the corner. Well, why not? But how good we are at holding the myths of our society in one corner of our minds—say, that most people live in proper family units—father out to work, mother at home minding the children—while the evidence of our own eyes, our own lives, shows us how far this if from the truth. And how bad we are at facing truth. But we are stronger than we think. The myth might hurt, but the world won't come to an end. The sun won't go out. We are all one flesh, one family. We are the same person with a million million faces. We include in us Angie, and Mr. Blotton and even Father

McCrombie. We must learn to incorporate them, include them in our vision of ourselves. We must not hiss the villain, but welcome him in. That way we make ourselves whole. Angie, friend, rest in peace.

A TURN OF FORTUNE

You know how it is, when nothing seems to happen for ages and then everything all at once? With Angie's death it was as if a whole tangle of threads was suddenly pulled tight. Everything shifted, changed, interlocked. There was certainly no stopping the process, though how it was to go, of course, depended on the way the threads had been placed, with good intent or bad, over the past decade.

Now Father McCrombie, the ex-priest, in return for a bed to sleep on (a foam mattress in the toll-house), a bottle of brandy (or two) a night, a very small fee (Angie was as mean as only the born-rich can be—you know my views on that), had been in the habit not just of lighting black candles whenever he thought of it, but of conducting a rather formal weekly Black Mass in the Satan's Enterprise Chapel (which Angie didn't know about. She'd only have laughed, mind you, half believing, half not-believing, in all such nonsense). Father McCrombie, if the truth be known, these days only half-believed as well, but took good money from those who did turn up and took it seriously. Nevertheless, ill wishes do no one any good, for when Angie phoned out of the blue to say she was selling the chapel and thus depriving him of his income, and Father McCrombie had lit his own big black candle and called down the wrath of the Devil, had not Angie on that instant been squashed flat, like a swatted mosquito? It was enough to frighten a saint, let alone a villainous ex-priest, defrocked and excommunicated, his mind blasted by psychedelic drugs.

Father McCrombie decided enough was enough, blew out his candles, said a quick and partly sincere Hail Mary, bade adieu forever to the ghost of Christabel, closed the chapel, and lumbered out into the world to make his fortune some other way.

Father McCrombie's friends being who they were, and his connections with Angie what they were, it was not surprising that in his search for semi-honest employment he presently met up with Erich Blotton, who now went by the innocent name of Peter Piper of Piper Art Security Limited, a firm which supervised the transport from place to place of national art treasures, protecting and insuring them against theft, flood, fire, ransom, switching and general deception.

Remember Erich Blotton? The chain-smoking, child-snatching lawyer who had escaped with Nell when ZOE 05 crashed? Erich Blotton, on the strength of one short interview with Clifford, years back in the days of his child-snatching, had decided to go into Art. There, obviously, money, power and prestige lay—not to mention rich pickings.

Piper Art Security worked out of rather small, smoky offices in the Burlington Arcade, above a knitwear boutique. The boutique's owner complained that the stench of cigarette smoke got into her stock, but what could she do? Peter Piper would certainly not stop smoking. It was, he told her, and with some truth, the only pleasure he had in life.

Erich Blotton was not a happy man. He missed his wife, who had given two million pounds away to children's charities, and died the week before he'd judged it safe to slip back into the country and bring her out with him.

"You'd better come back soon, Erich," she'd once told him on the phone. "Because until you do, I'm going to spend, spend, spend!" Men had come around looking for him, she said. Big, dangerous, black men. Such men could only be, he supposed, hit men, out to get him. Too many people altogether had been looking for him. Bereft and angry parents, he'd come to realize, make bad enemies—more dangerous than police, or criminal associates. So he missed his wife's funeral, changed his name, his profession, and his way of life. He thought he was safe. But it was all such hard graft; he lamented the past.

Father McCrombie went to see Peter Piper and said, "Begorah, how would it look if a man like me came in with a man like you? I have my talents, you have yours."

Peter Piper was never a big man. He smoked a hundred cigarettes a day and coughed, wheezed and trembled as a result. He had bad circulation in his right leg. Canvases are large and heavy. So was Father McCrombie, and frightening too, with his red hair, red beard and strange rolling red eyes. A good man to have around. Or so it seemed to Peter Piper. Perhaps Father McCrombie had hypnotic eyes?

"Why not?" said Peter Piper.

They talked briefly of Angie Wellbrook's death. Much of Piper Art Security's business was with Ottoline's.

"Tragic!" said Peter Piper. "Poor woman!"

"Poor woman," said Father McCrombie, and crossed himself.

May God have mercy on her soul.

No thunderbolts descended, but should have.

"Of course," said Peter Piper, "her death is a great misfortune to Piper Art Security," and Father McCrombie felt it was his bounden duty to help the new firm out in whatever way he could. And there, for the time being, we leave the two of them, plotting away, but at least without the help, for once, of disagreeable cosmic forces, though Father McCrombie sniffed the air, and felt expectation in it—the expectation of excitement and evil. Something of the atmosphere of the Satan Chapel seemed to travel with him; there was not much he could do about it.

Peter Piper said, "Can you smell something?" and sniffed as well, but he smoked so much it was hard for him to differentiate between one smell and another, hamburger onion from the spoor of the Devil, so he lit another cigarette and gave up, and downstairs Pat Christie of the Knitwear Boutique picked up the phone and made arrangements to break the lease. Somehow the girl didn't like the place anymore.

BLOWING THE GAFF

Clifford was in the dock of a criminal court in New York at the very moment that Father McCrombie blew out his final candle. McLinsky had taken the unusual step of going to the police with an account of his dealings with Leonardo's (New York). Now perhaps the general feeling was that the English were muscling in too hard and too fast on the Big Apple's art scene, and had to be taught a lesson or two—perhaps McLinsky's outrage was genuine and his Puritan stock simply showing—but there Clifford was, actually indicted, and a charge of deception and fraud to be faced.

A hundred pressmen and cameras were there as well, of course. This was the stuff of world headlines. Leonardo's, that august institution, thus insulted and impugned; Clifford, his face familiar to TV viewers the world over. Nor were things going well. The Leonardo's battery of lawyers was gray-faced. The Court was frowning. You just cannot throw zeroes around with impunity, even in conversation, in circles where conversations equal deals and those conversations were *taped.* Taped?—the faces of Leonardo's lawyers turned from gray to white.

Poof! Poof! Poof! Out went the candles in the Satan Chapel. Clifford's head lightened—or was it just coincidence? Enough is enough. He was no criminal. He stood up.

"Look here," he said. "If I could just address the Court—" How polished and perfect his English was. The Court decided to go for it, not resist it.

"If that's the way you want it," said Judge Tooley. And Clifford spoke. He spoke for an hour, and no one's attention wandered. He borrowed from John Lally's indignation, now past, but well-remembered by Clifford. He presented it without its cloak of paranoia; and how convincing it was. The truth is.

He told those serious people there assembled about the disgraceful State of the Art. Of the involvement of big, barely honest, money; of the enormous fortunes made and lost on the backs of a few struggling artists. Well, it had always been so. Hadn't van Gogh died alone and in poverty, Rembrandt likewise? But another element had entered in—mega-money, and all that went with it. He spoke of the strange social hierarchies of the Art World, the dubious structures of the auction houses, the rings which controlled prices; the outrageous commission taken, the breaches of contract, the ignorance of experts; the ranks of unscrupulous middlemen who stood between the artist and those who simply wished to enjoy his work, of the buying and selling of critics, of reputations wrongly made and others cruelly ruined, all in the name of profit.

"An extra zero?" he asked. "You need a *tape* to tell you if I added an extra zero? Of course I did. This is the atmosphere in which I work, and the noble McLinsky knows it very well, or he's a fool. Which I'm sure he doesn't wish to appear to be." Out went the candles and Clifford was back in form, no longer cringing, but outrageous, passionate, charming and, in his way, sincere.

The Court and the jury cheered and clapped, cameras flashed, and Clifford left a free man and a hero and, that evening, took to bed a tough, bright, frizzy-haired young woman called Honesty and, as usual, longed for Helen's softness. Or was she soft, these days? Perhaps success had toughened her? How could he know?

The phone rang. Angie? She had a knack of disturbing him at such moments. "Don't answer it," said Honesty, but Clifford did. He stretched out his blond, hairy arm and heard the news of Angie's death. He took the first flight back to England and to Barbara and, I'm sorry to say—if we are one whit sorry for Angie and I am, just a bit—to Helen. He did not even wait until after the funeral.

HELEN AND CLIFFORD

"Clifford," said Helen, "you're being absurd!" She sat in her pleasant front room, all pale-green watered silk and blond furniture, the white telephone in her hand. She wore a soft cream-colored dress, embroidered over the bosom with tiny yellowy flowers, and her brown curly hair fell over her face. At the sound of Clifford's voice she had turned pale, but she allowed no tremor into her own. Nell watched from a corner of the room, no longer sewing roses—that order had long ago been completed—but just somehow still part of the household. How could she not be? She shouted at the boys to wash up, clean their rooms, answer the telephone for their mother, and they just laughed and groaned and did as she said, accepting her. It made Helen laugh, too, to watch her. She's my daughter, she thought, the daughter I never had. As for Nell, watching Helen on the phone to Clifford that night, she thought she'd never seen a woman so beautiful, so clearly destined to affect the hearts and lives of men. "If only I could be like that," Nell thought. "If only she was my mother." And then thought, "No, I never can be like that, I am too spiky and blunt, and glad of it. I don't want to live my life through men. Beside them, of course, but not because of them."

Nell herself, now that she had Helen to take care of her, to insist on her eating and sleeping properly, to give point and purpose to her life, was beautiful enough, but scarcely knew it, as girls without fathers tend not to. Her hair, still short, black, spiky and absurd, now that she was House of Lally's leading model, had become her trademark; it added a kind of permitted frivolity to the rich but slightly serious Lally tag. The danger always had been, and Helen knew it, that the clothes, following money rather than taste, would drift in popularity up the age groups and become just rather stodgy. Nell kept the Lally image young. She thought her success was some kind of fluke. She could hardly take herself seriously. That too is the fate of girls without fathers.

"Clifford," said Helen lightly, "we have been married twice already. Three times would be two times too many. And the twins wouldn't like it."

"If you say the twins are mine, I'll accept it," said Clifford, which was as near to an apology as he could get, but still not quite enough for Helen. "Who cares anyway?"

"They do," she said.

"We'll go into that later," he said. "You're free to marry, aren't you?"

His voice was loud and firm. Nell had no difficulty in overhearing it.

"I am," said Helen, "and I like it. I want to stay that way."

"I must speak to you seriously," said Clifford. "I'm coming over."

"You're not," said Helen. "Clifford, for years I've waited for this call but now it's come too late. I've just met someone else."

And she put down the phone.

"You haven't, have you?" asked Nell, in alarm. And then, "I'm sorry, that was private. I shouldn't have been listening."

"How could you help it?" said Helen. "Anyway, you're part of the family." (Nell's heart leaped.) "Of course there's no one else. I just don't want to be hurt again," she said, and wept. Nell didn't like that one bit. She was accustomed to seeing Helen calm, cheerful and in charge, which was how she tried, very properly, to present herself to the children.

"At least if you hurt you know you're alive," said Nell, and felt silly, but it was all she could think of to say.

"Then I'm alive," said Helen. "Very much alive."

"Phone him back," said Nell. "I would."

But Helen didn't.

The next few dresses Helen designed just didn't somehow work (I'm afraid love does this to some women. It undermines their creativity. With other women, of course, it works the other way. They blossom and flourish in it, workwise) and Nell, given the sketches to finish, had to redo them almost in their entirety. Helen hardly noticed. The designs were *things.* Nell's eyes gleamed. This was her real ambition. Anyone could model—put on clothes, stand in front of cameras, this way, that way, but this! Ah, here was real achievement!

Clifford called Helen daily, and daily she refused the calls.

"What *shall* I do?" Helen asked Nell, all aquiver.

"He does seem to love you," said Nell, cautiously.

"Until the next one comes along," said Helen, nose in the air.

"He's ever so rich," said Nell, always practical.

"*Her* millions," said Helen. (Poor dead Angie, ungrieved for!) "Really, he's despicable. And I would never look after the child. I know he'd expect me to. In fact he probably only wants me because she needs a mother, and he thinks I'll do. I can't even remember her name."

"Her name is Barbara," said Nell, firmly. Helen must surely know what it was. The rest of the world did. She'd always been news, since banned from the Royal nursery. The ban was now rescinded. Barbara visited the Palace. PALACE PITIES MOTHERLESS TOT, observed the papers. WEEKENDS OK, PALACE DECREES. (That could only include Clifford, now rehabilitated in polite society. An indictment, these days, when men in high social places had themselves up for murder and worse, is nothing to speak of. Besides it was in another country.)

"I just *couldn't,*" said Helen. "I'd only do something terrible to the child, I know I would."

"But why?"

"I don't know." Helen felt hopeless, and helpless, and that it was all too late. A little wall of Father McCrombie's black candle smoke still hung in the air. Such stuff is hard to get rid of.

"But you do love him?" inquired Nell.

"Oh, you're so simple," Helen complained. "Of course I *love* him."

"Then marry him," said Nell. It was what she wanted to happen, though she was not sure why. On the face of it, remarrying Clifford—whom Nell knew only as a face in the papers, and a strong insistent voice on the telephone—was the last thing Helen should do. But Nell said it, and poof, out the window went not quite the last of the smoke, but most of it.

"I'll think about it," said Helen.

Clifford, of course, had no intention of being put off. Helen, whatever she had said to Nell, still refused to see him, so he found ways of seeing Helen.

REFORMATION

And that was how it came about, reader, that Leonardo's (New York) mounted an exhibition of Designer as Artist; and that the English House of Lally was to feature prominently therein. That was why it came about that Clifford made his peace with John Lally, going so far as to finally return the canvases which had lingered so long in Leonardo's vaults; surprising John Lally and Marjorie in their neat garden—or what was left of it—saying, "I have five of your canvases in the back of my car. Take them. They're yours"—thus making John Lally a millionaire, and not just a hundred-thousander, for the early paintings were enjoying a surge in popularity—that is to say price. (They were still not the easiest paintings to hang on the walls and enjoy.) No matter that Clifford could easily afford such gestures—all Angie's wealth was now his; no matter that he did it in part to win favor in Helen's eyes; I think he also did it because he felt he ought to. Clifford could see that natural justice required just such an act. Perhaps in his speech to the New York court he had actually converted himself? I hope so.

John and Marjorie unloaded the car and carried the canvases into the studio. Clifford helped.

"Gloomy old paintings," said Marjorie. "You must have been in a state to paint them, John. I bet Evelyn was glad to get them out of the way!" (Those who live happy lives have simply no idea what it is to be unhappy.)

Neither John nor Clifford replied.

"A pity you and Helen can't get together," said John Lally to Clifford. It was his way of apologizing. "Those boys of yours are a handful."

"I'm not much of a father," said Clifford. Though he was trying, and trying hard, with Barbara, who took the news of her mother's death with surprising equanimity. She just clung to her nurse a little tighter and said now perhaps Nanny could stay and she wouldn't have to have a new one for Christmas.

"We can all change," said John Lally, and picked up a cricket ball and threw it for young Julian, who was playing about rather forlornly with stumps and bat. Julian looked both astounded and gratified.

"It certainly seems so," observed Clifford.

Helen, hearing the amazing news from her father, called Clifford. He'd known she would.

"Clifford," she said, "thank you for that. But what are we going to do about me? I can't sleep, and I can't relax, and I can't work. I want to be with you, but I can't do that either."

"It's Barbara who's stopping you, isn't it?" he said, with that surprising acuity of feeling which characterized his new self. "And it's quite true that if you take me on, you have to take her on as well. She has only me in all the world. But at least come and meet her."

Helen did and, seeing Barbara in the flesh for the first time, pale and sad, dressed in the stiff, old-fashioned, unbecoming way that elderly, highly trained nannies, however nice, even these days seem to insist upon, felt such a rush of pity for the child that it drove out anger and hate once and for all. She could see that Barbara was her own person, main player in her own drama, and not a relic of Angie at all. Nor was she Clifford's substitute for the daughter lost so long ago. Which of course was what she had feared: that in accepting Barbara she would finally deny Nell.

Reader, to the happy all things come. Happiness can even bring the dead back to life. It is our resentments, our dreariness, our hate and envy, unrecognized by us, which keep us miserable. Yet these things are in our heads, not out of our hands. We own them; we can throw them out if we choose. Helen forgave Barbara and in so doing forgave herself.

"Yes, Clifford," said Helen, "for good or bad, of course I'll marry you."

"Poor Angie," Clifford was to say presently. "A lot of it was my fault. One way and another I've done a lot to be ashamed of." He could say it because he was happy, and was happy because he could say it and mean it. The two went together.

And so presently, that Christmas Eve, a private plane stood on the tarmac at Heathrow while the pilot waited for clearance and a runway to be pronounced free from drifting snow. Clifford and Helen sat together and held hands. Barbara sat across the aisle and stretched out her arm to hold Helen's other hand. She had found a mother; she could keep her nurse. Her grave face was already lighter and brighter. Young Nell Kildare sat behind, House of Lally's leading model, her cropped black hair sticking defiantly upwards. They were on their way to Christmas in Manhattan, and the opening of "Designer as Artist" in the big new modern gallery overlooking Central Park. Nell hated flying. She wore her teddy bear around her neck, for luck.

Edward, Max and Marcus had been sent ahead, in the care of a couple of stoical nannies, for a whole week at Disneyland before joining Helen and Clifford in New York. That had been Nell's idea. Helen was accustomed enough to their noise and energy, and deserved some peace. Clifford, Nell could see, was not so accustomed. He would have to be broken in gently to the boys. He reminded her of someone, but she couldn't think who. She was shy of him; it was not a feeling she was accustomed to. It surprised her. She kept out of his way. She kept reminding herself she was just an employee, not one of the family. She must not let herself become too fond of them all. It was her experience, remember, reader, that the people you love suddenly vanish; that the good times suddenly stop. More, that it was her fault. That as you loved, you destroyed, by fire and mayhem. Ah, she was cautious!

Barbara had been asked if she wanted to go ahead with the boys.

"No, no," she'd cried, butting her head into Nell's tummy.

"They're so rough! Won't!" She was beginning to look after herself, and doing it very well.

John Lally was there too, with his wife Marjorie. He was Leonardo's leading painter, after all, and these days an artist has to keep a high profile. (No more hiding in fields painting sunflowers in obscurity.) Marjorie wore a patchwork shawl over her dress: she had worked it herself. Some of the squares were made from the remnants of the old, ribbed blue dress worn so very often by Helen's mother Evelyn—waste not, want not! You and I know this, reader. No one else noticed, not even Helen. Little Julian was being looked after by Cynthia. They'd moved out of the grand flat and now had a small home with a garden in Hampstead, where a small child was always welcome. Oh, Cynthia had changed too! She'd been so proud of Clifford, that peculiar jet-lagged day in New York. Her family had turned up in droves; she could no longer hold that far-off past against them. How wrong time had proved them—Otto, once the humble builder from the wrong side of the Copenhagen tracks, still mysterious in his dignity, and now wealthy, respected, honored by the community, more than their equal. It's good to look back on your life and know you've been right.

Helen, by the way, wore a dress of a new heavy silk fabric that John Lally had consented to design. It was patterned with very small golden lions and tinier white lambs were not being devoured by the lions, but simply lying down with them. The dress itself was of a pattern much influenced by the hand of Nell—done at the time Helen was in such a state over Clifford. In the aircraft hold were eight Lally canvases, destined for exhibition at Leonardo's (New York): four of the old, savage and despairing paintings, four of the new, more charitable kind. On the whole the early works now ended up in galleries, the latter on private walls.

Clifford had smiled at Nell in an ordinary, friendly, not at all lecherous fashion, when she boarded the plane. He knew how fond Helen was of her. He would go along with it easily enough. She was a pretty, bright, cheerful girl, who fitted in well. Though he wasn't sure about her hair.

Sometimes, you know, I wonder if I'm right to be so forgiving about Angie. Perhaps she was even wickeder than I thought. Perhaps it was in the flight from Angie that Clifford fell into so many arms, bruising and harming as he fell? And yet that still means only that Angie was an aspect of Clifford, for who do we ever flee from but ourselves? All the same, it does seem that only once she was dead was Clifford free to be himself; and that that self was far, far nicer than anyone had dreamed. Some curse had been lifted.

And who else but Arthur Hockney and Sarah and the baby Angela—an olive-skinned, sloe-eyed little beauty—sat further back in the plane. They were hitching a free ride to the States, to spend Christmas with Arthur's family, and show off the new baby. There was space on the aircraft. Clifford, on Helen's request, had been happy enough to offer it. If these people were friends of Helen's, they were friends of his. There was some faintly disagreeable memory of an encounter with Arthur some time in the past, Clifford thought; but he did not trouble to recall it. Kim was being looked after at the Border Kennels, now, alas, under new management. Brenda had married her Ned; and her spots, by the way, had quite disappeared. It looked as if her mother was coming to live with them, though, until she was back on her feet.

And further back on the aircraft—indeed in the very back row, always Peter Piper's favorite—were two representatives of Piper Art Security Limited: Peter Piper himself and Father McCrombie. Both of them were made uneasy by Arthur Hockney's presence on the plane.

"I hadn't reckoned on him," said Peter Piper. "Six foot four if he's an inch." He lit another cigarette, with fingers which trembled more than ever. Not surprising; a lot depended on the events of this day.

And then, reader, the following events happened. Once the aircraft had passed the point of no return, Father McCrombie walked casually through into the cockpit, and no one thought to stop him or wonder why, and when he came out he was herding the pilot before him at gunpoint. It took time for the passengers to absorb what was happening; it all seemed so unlikely. Only Barbara moved quickly, diving for Helen's lap and hiding her head. And now here was Peter Piper standing at the back of the aircraft, and he was pointing a gun as well, a nasty black deadly-looking Luger.

"Sit down," he said to Arthur, who was on his feet. Arthur sat.

"No one's driving the plane," complained Marjorie.

"It's on automatic," said Arthur. "It's okay for a bit. Just keep calm."

"You just shut up," said Peter Piper, and Arthur shrugged and did. It never does to take villains too seriously. On the other hand it's best not to provoke them, because they're nervous, and nasty things happen. They're also usually stupid; to predict what they're going to do is therefore difficult. You have to think about it, not just assume.

Now the pilot was sat forcibly down in the seat vacated by Barbara. He hadn't simply been shot, so obviously these villains were not of the deepest dye. They could be negotiated with. Arthur patted Sarah's knee. "Don't worry," he said, but of course she did. Peter Piper took over passenger control and Father McCrombie returned to the cockpit and changed course for a small coastal town north of New York, where he had friends and helpful acquaintances. The whole affair had a dreamlike quality. No one screamed (not even Marjorie), no one shouted (not even John Lally). It was as if they had passed from real life into a film without even knowing it. Arthur held his peace, and waited. Peter Piper spoke.

It wasn't a kidnap, he said, or even a ransom. It was merely armed robbery; he wanted the Lally paintings and meant to have them.

Clifford laughed. "All I can say is," he said, "that I hope you have some new market in mind, and are not relying on the existing network. Buyers of stolen paintings only want Old Masters, the French School and occasionally a Pre-Raphaelite.

Anything post-Surrealist, forget it. Contemporary British? You're joking! Even those involved in art theft are obliged to know something about art! What did you say your name was?"

Arthur hoped Clifford had not gone too far. Peter Piper's pallor deepened. It is never nice to be shown up publicly for ignorance, and especially humiliating when the person who does the showing up is meant to be your victim, and should be terrified.

His language was terrible. I shan't repeat it, reader. He called Clifford every name under the hellish moon, and the aircraft bucketed and rocked as it went through turbulence and even when it didn't. Piper's gun seemed suddenly the least of everyone's worries. It was some time since Father McCrombie had flown, and he'd had to drink a lot of brandy to steady his nerves. He remembered how in his youth, when he was a Battle of Britain pilot, he had spoken to God, and God had answered him. Now, drunkenly, he addressed his Maker once more, and fought the plane, which swerved and bucketed, as if the Devil had gotten into the air currents through which it flew. Peter Piper took no notice; he went on to accuse Clifford of conspiracy, theft, seduction, illegitimacy and child-snatching, using the most vivid and shocking words.

"Erich Blotton!" interrupted Clifford. "You're Erich Blotton!" He was staring now at Piper's trembling, nicotine-stained fingers. How could he ever forget them?

At which both Helen and Arthur wanted to cry out, but if you're Erich Blotton, and you're alive, where's our Nell? But they couldn't, because Erich was strutting and fuming and his finger was once again on the trigger, and John Lally had reverted to some earlier self, and was beginning to shout and rave about his paintings not even being worth stealing, and Marjorie was trying to hush him, as if she were Evelyn, and Erich was ripping the necklace from Helen's neck and throwing it away outraged because it was only plastic (*Fun* jewelry? This is *fun?*) and demanding that everyone hand over their wallets (he had to get *something* or he'd look very foolish indeed) and found nothing much in those either, only credit cards, and the plane was bucketing, and Blotton bashed the pilot on the head with the butt of his revolver and he fell back unconscious—or was he feigning?—for prophesying disaster if he wasn't allowed to get back to the controls at once; and baby Angela was crying and Helen and Clifford were trying to comfort Barbara, and Arthur Hockney was still biding his time (or was he paralyzed—had he forgotten everything he ever knew, lost his courage along with his guilt?); and Sarah was airsick all over Erich Blotton's shoes—it would all have been funny if it hadn't been so frightening. And Nell? Nell had seen criminals enough during her time at Faraway Farm. She knew bluster when she saw it, and that the pilot was pretending and that the worst danger was accident, not malice.

"Now look," she said calmly to Erich Blotton. "Calm down. At least I've got something valuable you can have." She pulled out her teddy bear from beneath her jumper and took her time unscrewing the head; her movements were precise and confident; everyone fell silent and watched. Nell took out the little jewel and handed it to Erich. It grieved her to do it but she knew necessity when she saw it.

"It's a real emerald," she said, "and a good-luck token besides, but you can have it. It seems to me you need it." Helen looked at the jewel in Nell's hand and then at Nell and Clifford did the same, and Arthur too, and realization dawned on all three of them at the same time.

"It's mine," said Helen. "Clifford gave it to me. You're Nell. Our Nell. Clifford's and my Nell! Of course you are! How could you not be?" At which moment, when the pilot caught his eye and nodded, Arthur made his lunge for Erich Blotton, who was a hopeless kind of criminal, as most of them are, and found him easy enough to disarm and bundle into a seat. Then, with the pilot, Arthur went forward into the cockpit and heaved the wretched McCrombie out of it. McCrombie was not unhappy to be replaced at the controls; the more he'd spoken to God the more silent God had remained, and the worse the aircraft behaved, which you and I, reader, will not wonder at.

"Oh begorah," he said, suddenly, "I'd be better off dead,"

which I for one don't think was true, considering. And so it happened that by the time the aircraft landed safely and only a few minutes late at Kennedy Airport, to hand Blotton and McCrombie over to the waiting police, Clifford and Helen had found their little Nell, and she had found her parents, and none of them were disappointed in the other.

"Our sister, is she?" said Edward, Max and Marcus, full of tales of Disneyland, but seeming not in the least surprised. "What's for dinner?"

"Our granddaughter," exclaimed Otto. "She'll have to do something about her hair!" But you could tell he was pleased. And Cynthia skipped about, and seemed to have lost twenty years. She nearly made an assignation with a friend's husband, but stopped herself in time.

"Why doesn't she stop messing around with clothes," said John Lally, noisily, "and do some paper painting instead," which was his way of accepting her.

And Nell could see that loving people was not perhaps quite as dangerous for them as she'd thought. She allowed herself to fall in love with an impossible young art student who rode around on a motorbike, and believed everyone should wear uniform clothes in blue Chinese cotton. It wouldn't last, and wasn't meant to, but it was a start. Just holding hands made her feel less tough and brisk, more soft and vulnerable, like her mother.

And what stories Nell had to tell her parents—of the château and the de Troites, and Eastlake (and the horrible Annabel) and the clouded paradise of Faraway Farm and the puzzling events at Border Kennels. Clifford and Helen were more guarded in what they had to say, as you, reader, will understand. They did not want to hurt each other, or Nell. Besides, the older we grow, the less admirable our pasts must seem.

But how lucky they were, to be given this second chance—and how little, you might think, they deserved it. Our children are to be loved and guarded, not used as pawns in some sad mating-game. And as to whether Helen *should* have taken Clifford back, well, you will have your own opinion. I'm not so sure myself. Not, of course, that Helen would listen to advice. She loved him, as always, and that was that. The best we can do is wish that they all live happily ever after, and I think they have as good a chance as any of actually getting away with it.